Enjoy ♡

RaeAnne
Thayne

THE CLIFF HOUSE

RaeAnne Thayne

THE CLIFF HOUSE

HQN™

ISBN-13: 978-1-335-00490-1 (original hardcover edition)
ISBN-13: 978-1-335-00788-9 (Barnes & Noble Exclusive edition)
ISBN-13: 978-1-335-00789-6 (Target Exclusive edition)
ISBN-13: 978-1-335-14527-7 (International Trade Paperback edition)

The Cliff House

www.HQNBooks.com

Printed in U.S.A.

As always, I have legions of people to thank for helping to bring this story to life. I am deeply indebted to my editor, the wonderful Gail Chasan, and her assistant, Megan Broderick; to my indomitable agent, Karen Solem; to Sarah Burningham and her hardworking team at Little Bird Publicity for tirelessly helping spread the word about my books; to my assistants, Judie Bouldry and Carrie Stevenson, for keeping me on track; and to everyone at Harlequin—from the art department for their stunning covers to the marketing team to the copy editors, sales team, production crew and everyone else I may have failed to mention.

I must also thank my hero of a husband and our three children, who somehow manage to love me even in the midst of deadline chaos. You are my heart.

Finally, this particular book would not have been possible without three brilliant friends: Susan Mallery, Christine Rimmer and Jill Shalvis. I can't thank you enough for all your help!

THE CLIFF HOUSE

1

DAISY

A man was staring at her in the oral care aisle.

A gorgeous, make-your-ovaries-shiver man.

Though it taxed her considerable powers of restraint, Daisy Davenport McClure did not stare back. She wouldn't give the stranger the courtesy of knowing he had rattled her.

She couldn't help feeling discombobulated, though. Dark, wavy-haired, green-eyed strangers did *not* stare at plain, boring her in the grocery store. Or on the street. Or in a car or on a boat or a train or anywhere else Dr. Seuss could have come up with. She simply wasn't the sort of woman who drew that kind of male attention—and that was exactly the way she liked it.

Why was he staring? She was almost positive she had checked her reflection in the rearview mirror when she picked up her sister outside their aunt's house twenty minutes earlier. She didn't remember seeing anything weird. No stray leaves from the yard work she'd been doing earlier, no smudges on her cheek, no splotched paint, no lettuce in her teeth.

There was no reason she could think of why this man might be looking at her as if she were his salvation.

She almost turned around to head down another aisle but despite her certainty that she didn't have any leafy vegetable residue in her teeth, she still really needed toothpaste, which was why she was here. She drew in a breath.

"Excuse me," she murmured, reaching around him for her favorite brand, the one that promised to whiten, give her fresh breath and vanquish any hint of tartar or gingivitis.

"Sorry," he said, easing back a little. The man looked pale beneath his tan and she thought she saw white lines around his mouth.

Probably hungover. Maybe he was a tourist who had started his vacation here on the beautifully rugged Northern California coast by doing his own Cape Sanctuary happy hour pub crawl and now was paying the price.

He didn't really *look* like a tourist, but one never knew.

She grabbed her toothpaste, tossed it into her basket and stepped away, careful not to make eye contact.

"Sorry. Have we met?" he asked. His voice was an appealing tenor with a slight accent she couldn't quite place. Australian, maybe? New Zealand? It was as gorgeous as the rest of him. Naturally.

"I'm sure we haven't," she answered curtly. While she considered herself eminently forgettable, she certainly would have remembered him.

"Sorry. It's odd. I feel as if I should know you, somehow."

"You don't," she assured him, then grabbed a box of dental floss she didn't really need and hurried out of the aisle.

It was the kind of interaction strangers had all the time—banal, meaningless—but somehow the encounter left her rattled. *He* left her rattled. When was the last time she had noticed how long a man's eyelashes were or the strong angle of his jaw or the little indentation that hinted at a dimple?

Longer than she could remember. That she had focused on those features of a stranger who was probably wasted did not say much for her taste or her wisdom, two things she usually took great pride in.

Edgy and unsettled, she tried to put the guy out of her head and went instead to find her sister so they could finish their shopping and make it back to their aunt's in time.

As Daisy might have expected, she found Beatriz in the magazine aisle, leafing through a tabloid. Her sister might be a twenty-eight-year-old divorced mother, but she was sometimes a teenage girl at heart.

Now, *Bea* was a woman that someone like the tipsy stranger in the toothpaste aisle would notice, with her dramatic dark curls, the little pierced diamond in her nose, her perfect makeup—though she wore it a little heavy to Daisy's taste. Everything about Bea drew attention, from her clothes to her hair to her wide, generous smile.

Bea had been boho before boho was a thing, with her own unique style and the voluptuous body and serenely classic features to pull off whatever look she wanted.

Daisy was only a little envious of her sister's style. They were half sisters and didn't look much alike, except for the hazel eyes they had inherited from their mother. Daisy's stick-straight hair was lighter, a boring chestnut color, and she wore it in a shoulder-length classic bob, using hairbands or pulling it up into an updo to keep it out of her face while she worked.

She looked down at her own respectable three-year-old summer dress and matching sandals. She dressed for comfort and ease, not fashion, fully aware that she often looked like somebody's boring aunt—which she supposed she was, since Bea's daughter, Mari, was her niece.

So why had the man with the delectable accent even noticed her, let alone stared at her like he was…hungry?

It didn't matter. She would likely never see him again. The tourist season on the Northern California coast never really ended but August was particularly crowded. Tourists rarely stayed long. He would probably be gone by Monday.

She didn't miss the fact that her sister's arms were empty and there was no cart in sight. "You were supposed to be picking up the birthday cake and the candles!"

She had a sinking suspicion they were going to be late.

"Sorry. I got a little distracted by this."

She flipped up the magazine so Daisy could see the cover. There, in vivid color, was a picture of one of the most famous men in the country, looking tortured and sexy. Lean, tattooed, dangerous.

Above his photograph read the headline in huge type:

Cruz in seclusion after attack by crazed fan.

In smaller type that ran across his legs, in the tight leather leggings his fans loved, another headline read:

Whereabouts of rocker unknown.

"They've done a two-page spread on it." Bea flipped the magazine around so Daisy could see a scattering of several other pictures, one that looked like a grainy picture of Cruz on an ambulance stretcher and another of a man whose face she couldn't see, slumped against a gray wall and holding his hands against his abdomen, a red stain spreading out across his shirt.

She couldn't read the caption from where she stood. Was that the assailant or the mysterious man who had rushed to the rescue?

The attack on hometown boy Cruz Romero had been the talk of Cape Sanctuary since it happened a week earlier. People were talking about it everywhere she went in town. Every single client who came into Daisy's accounting and financial planning office that week had brought it up to her, asking if she knew anything about where Cruz might be, how badly he had been injured, if it was true that he had been attacked by a jealous husband.

She imagined Bea had it much, much worse.

Cruz was her ex-husband, after all.

"Still no word?"

Bea shook her head. "Not since he called the night of the attack to make sure Marisol heard it from him first, before the rumors started flying at school, to assure her he only had a scratch. He was rattled and didn't make much sense."

"That's understandable."

"I guess. After only a couple of minutes he said he had to go, that he was heading to the hospital for a few stitches and to check on the guy who saved his life. He promised he'd call, but it's been radio silence since then."

"From Cruz, maybe, but you've heard from his people."

"Yeah, his manager calls every day. Cruz is in seclusion but Lenny assures me he's fine and he'll call as soon as he has the chance."

That was strange enough to Daisy, since Cruz loved connecting with his fans on social media. She had never had a close brush with death, though, so it wasn't for her to judge.

"Buy it, if you want. Buy all of them, but I would suggest you don't let Mari see them yet. She's still upset about her dad."

"She's probably read the online edition on all their websites already, along with everything else she can find," Bea muttered.

Daisy didn't doubt it. Her niece was not only tech-savvy and headstrong, but she also adored her father and would want to read as much as possible about the accident that had nearly claimed his life.

"You buy your tabloids, I'll pick up the candles and the cake. We still have to stop by Melenzana's for the gnocchi she wanted."

"Right. Sorry. I'll take care of the candles and grab a bottle of wine."

Bea snatched several other magazines with Cruz's face on them from the racks and tucked them into Daisy's basket.

Daisy hurried to the bakery. Though located in the grocery store, where one might not expect to find gourmet fare, they still made the best cakes in town.

For months, Stella had been insisting she didn't want a grand party to mark her fortieth birthday. She said she only wanted their family—the three of them and Bea's daughter, Mari—together for dinner, in the garden of Three Oaks, Stella's two-story Craftsman.

Her aunt deserved a party attended by everyone in town. She deserved a freaking ticker-tape parade, as far as Daisy was concerned. She knew all the other lost souls Stella had rescued over the years would certainly agree with her.

She couldn't go against Stella's wishes, though. She loved her aunt too much. If Stella only wanted her immediate family to celebrate her milestone birthday with her—and the money they would spend donated to her charity instead—Daisy would make sure that was exactly what happened.

She picked up the cake they had ordered weeks ago, threw in some crusty Italian bread and some of the high-quality olive oil the store stocked, then headed for the checkout.

The cashier in her line had worked at the grocery store as long as Daisy had lived in Cape Sanctuary, while the bagger was another of her aunt's rescues.

"Hey, Daisy," he said, not quite making eye contact. Tommy Mathews was on the autism spectrum. When he had come to Stella, he had been considered unmanageable and difficult, close to being institutionalized after his mother died. He had lived with Stella for two years, from seventeen to nineteen, and had thrived with her loving care before moving into his own apartment with two other young adults who had special needs.

Now twenty, Tommy had a steady job at the supermarket

and was taking classes to earn an associate's degree at the community college in the next town over.

He had come so far because of her aunt, whose circle of influence was legendary.

"Hi, Tommy." She adored him and all the other young people who had come in and out of their lives since Stella began opening her home up to other foster children in the years since she and Bea had moved out.

They were the first, she and Bea. Stella's nieces. Her aunt's influence started there and rippled out like concentric waves from a tiny pebble thrown into a pond.

The tears suddenly burning behind her eyes took her completely by surprise. She usually kept much better control over her emotions.

"Is that cake for Stella?" Tommy asked. "It's her birthday tomorrow."

"I know. It's a big day, isn't it?"

"She said she didn't want presents but I have one for her anyway. I'm going to take it to her tomorrow."

"Oh. That's so sweet of you."

"It's a plant, the kind she likes with pink flowers. I can get it for a discount from the floral department here. It was only sixteen dollars and twenty-three cents with tax, but don't tell her, okay?"

"I won't say a word, Tommy. I know she'll love it."

"Yeah. She will," he said with a confidence that made her smile.

Stella had fostered about twenty other children, some with special needs like Tommy and others just in need of a temporary home for a while, like Cruz Romero.

So many lives, changed for the better because Stella was a generous, kind soul who loved to help people.

Unlike Daisy, who hid away in her house on the cliff, afraid to even smile at men she didn't know who talked to her in the toothpaste aisle.

The checker had rung up the last item when Bea hurried up, candles and a wine bottle in hand. "Sorry. Took me a while to find them. Hi, Janet. Hi, Tommy! Daisy, put this on your check and we'll split the total."

The cashier gave a rather sour smile as she ran the candles and the wine through and added them to Daisy's total. Her sister would pay her, Daisy knew, minus the cost of the toothpaste. These days Bea was much more careful with her money, though it had taken Daisy several years to convince her the healthy alimony and child support she received from Cruz wasn't exactly a blank check.

Tommy looked happy to see her sister. "Hi, Bea," he said. "Tomorrow is Stella's birthday. She's going to be forty."

"Isn't that great?"

"I bought her a present from here, a plant with pink flowers. I get an employee discount."

"Oh, she'll love that. Nice job, Tom."

He beamed, as charmed by Bea as everyone else in the world.

"See you later," Daisy said, used to being invisible around her more vivacious younger sister.

He gave an almost-smile as he handed her the cake. Bea reached in and grabbed the wine and the bag with the rest of the groceries.

"Bye, Tom," Bea said. She stopped to give him a quick hug, which seemed to please him, though he didn't hug her back.

As they walked out of the store, they had to pass a late-model luxury SUV limousine that was idling in the fire lane, one of Daisy's pet peeves. It wasn't just because of environmental reasons and the pollutants their idling vehicles were sending into the atmosphere. She hated the sense of entitlement, when people thought they were so important, they shouldn't have to walk fifteen more feet to a parking space like the rest of the peons.

A man was climbing into the back seat as they passed. He looked up, and for just an instant, their gazes met. She should have known. It was the gorgeous man with the sexy accent.

He gave her a rueful sort of smile and a wave, which she pointedly ignored as she marched behind the vehicle toward her own fifteen-year-old BMW.

"Who was *that*?" Bea stared after the limo.

"No idea," Daisy mumbled.

"He looked like he knew you."

"He doesn't."

"Are you sure? He waved at you and everything. He looks familiar. Is he some kind of celebrity?"

Maybe. Daisy didn't watch much television and her knowledge of pop culture was nonexistent. She couldn't even tell which Kardashian was which and had no idea why she should care.

"You're the one who reads all the tabloids. You tell me. I don't know who he is. I only know I've never met him before in my life."

Before she bumped into him ten minutes earlier, anyway.

"It doesn't matter," she said. "We've got to go or we'll be late."

"Trust me, Stella won't notice. Mari's over there already and the two of them are probably in the middle of a hot game of slapjack."

She had to admit Bea was probably right. Stella hadn't wanted them to make a fuss over her birthday anyway and wouldn't care if they were a few moments late. "Here. You hold the cake. I don't want to set it on the seat and risk it falling off."

Bea made a face but held out her arms for the cake. After a quick stop at the Italian restaurant their aunt loved so they could grab the preordered meal, Daisy drove to Three Oaks, the sturdy, graceful Craftsman house Stella had purchased for a song when she brought the girls here to Cape Sanctuary all those years ago.

It had been a mess when they first moved in, she remembered, with only one tiny working bathroom and two inhabitable bedrooms. She and Bea hadn't minded sharing, so grateful to be together again and with their beloved aunt.

The three of them had worked together to make this a home: learning to put up drywall, painting, sanding floors, refinishing woodwork. Daisy had loved painting most of all, which was kind of ironic now, when she thought of it.

It had taken them the better part of three years but the result was a lovely home, filled with laughter and joy.

When they walked in, they found Stella in the kitchen wearing a ruffled apron splotched with huge yellow sunflowers. She was taking a tray of something out of the oven—her famous Oreo cookie mini cheesecakes, by the looks of it.

Her face lit up when she spotted them. "Girls! You're both here at last!"

She set down the muffin tin on the stovetop, took off her oven mitts and rushed to kiss first Bea as soon as she'd set down the cake, then Daisy.

Daisy hugged her back, so very grateful to this woman who had rescued two lost girls.

"You're not supposed to be doing anything," Bea scolded. "We brought dinner for you. That's what you said you wanted for your birthday gift."

"You know me. I'm not good at sitting around. These are so easy, though. Mari helped."

"Where is my child?"

"In here," Mari called from the room off the kitchen that Stella had always called the library, which functioned as an office, homework station and computer center.

"We were watching a YouTube video one of her friends posted on the computer when my timer went off," Stella explained as she set the cheesecake bites onto a rack to cool.

Daisy watched her aunt with the same unease she'd been feeling for several weeks now.

Though forty, Stella looked years younger. The three of them could have been sisters, really, as her and Bea's mother, Jewel, had been ten years older than her only surviving sibling. Stella was only ten years older than Daisy.

Stella had elfin features, high cheekbones and wide green eyes. She was petite, just over five feet two inches tall. Many of her middle school students topped her in height, something they all seemed to find hilarious.

While Stella's features were familiar and beloved, when Daisy looked deeper, she saw that her aunt still had the guarded, closed, almost *furtive* look that Daisy had first noticed several weeks ago. Something was up. She didn't know what it was; she only knew Stella was keeping secrets.

Her aunt was usually an open book, free and spontaneous. She had even been known to tell her life story to strangers she met at the diner in town.

Since about Easter, that had begun to change. She would take phone calls in another room and would often beg off arranged meetings for mysterious reasons.

Was it a new man in her life? About time, if it was. Stella deserved nothing but unicorns and rainbows. She deserved the very best man around. As far as Daisy was concerned, no one would ever be good enough for Stella.

She had often wondered why Stella had never married. She had dated here and there but nothing ever very serious, usually breaking things off right around five or six weeks.

"Do you want us to set the food up here or out in the garden?"

"Oh, it's a lovely evening. Let's eat outside." Stella looked around. "Is Shane meeting you here?"

Bea looked surprised. "You said only family."

"What do you call Shane? He grew up next door and was in

and out of here more than his own house. He lives with you, for heaven's sake. You should have invited him, poor man."

"I think he has plans, anyway," Bea said. If Daisy wasn't mistaken, her sister looked slightly put out by that, making her wonder what the man's plans were and why they bothered Bea.

"Shane has plans a lot lately." Marisol, followed as usual by their little dog, Jojo, came in and swiped one of the cheesecake bites off the cooling rack. "We hung out with him more before he moved into the guesthouse. Hi, Aunt Daisy."

"Hello, darling niece." Daisy hugged the girl she adored with all her heart.

"Shane is busy right now," Beatriz explained. "Sometimes we don't see him for days. You know how it is. It's the beginning of the football season. We won't see him again until January."

After playing college football and spending several years in the pros, Shane Landry, Bea's best friend since they moved here to Cape Sanctuary, was in his second year of teaching biology at the high school and coaching the state championship high school football team.

One of these days Bea would get smart and figure out the man was crazy in love with her.

"Do you know of any celebrities staying in the area?" Bea asked their aunt. "We saw this gorgeous guy outside the grocery store tonight in a big SUV limo. He looked familiar but I couldn't quite place him. He only had eyes for Daisy."

"Do tell!" Stella's own eyes widened.

Daisy felt herself flush. "He thought he knew me. I told him he was mistaken."

"You didn't tell me you talked to him!" Bea exclaimed.

"Apparently, I missed the family rule where I had to tell you everything going on in my life in a twenty-four-hour period."

"Not everything, just the juicy parts about gorgeous strangers who show up in Cape Sanctuary and act like they know you."

"Well, that rule is stupid since that has only happened the one time."

"You're stupid if you think I wouldn't want to know you talked to him!" Bea said.

Stella laughed. "We all do. Tell us everything."

"Nothing to tell. I bumped into him in the toothpaste aisle. Like I said, he thought he knew me. I said he didn't. We went our separate ways. End of story."

Bea, she knew, wouldn't have let that be the end of the story. Bea would have flirted with the man, would have tucked one of those long, luxurious curls behind her ear as she turned her head just so. At the end of sixty seconds of conversation, Beatriz would have had him hanging on her every word.

But Daisy wasn't her younger sister, she thought as she carried the meal outside to the garden of Three Oaks, with its long pine table and mason jars hanging in the trees, filled with solar-powered candles already beginning to spark to life in the gathering dusk.

She wasn't her sister by a long shot.

2

BEATRIZ

"Do you really think Dad is okay?"

Bea tried not to think about those tabloid photos or the man with the blood seeping out of his gut.

"Yes, honey. I do," she assured her daughter. "He said so himself when he called that first night, and his manager swears he only needed a few days to process what happened before he returns to his regular activities."

"Where do you think he might be?" In the rearview mirror, she caught Mari's frown in the back seat of her SUV.

That one was harder to answer. "I'm not sure. Maybe with his extended relatives down in Mexico or at the island he likes off Panama. He'll be in touch."

"He should be answering his phone. It's irresponsible of him not to. He has to know I'll worry about him."

Sometimes she thought Mari was born sounding about Stella's age.

"You know he'll be in touch as soon as he can, honey."

She was annoyed all over again at Cruz for not considering the impact on his daughter of the highly publicized attack against him. How hard would it be for him to make a freaking phone call to assure their child he was okay?

Then again, he had never been particularly good at checking in with *her* when they were married and he was touring. Why should he change his habits for their child?

When they returned to the house she had moved into along the coast road after her divorce, the lights were on out by the pool.

"Looks like Shane is swimming!" Mari said. "Can I go out and swim, too?"

She might have guessed he would be there, probably with his sweet yellow Labrador retriever, Sally, either playing in the water with him or lounging on the side.

Her elaborate pool with its secret grotto, waterfalls and high-tech hot tub had become his favorite part of living in the guesthouse. Just a few nights earlier, he told her the pool would be the thing he missed most when the renovations to his own house were finished.

She still wasn't sure why that had stung so much.

"He might not be there much longer. We don't know how long he's already been in the pool. But I don't mind if he doesn't. Go ahead and change into your suit."

"I'll hurry. I can go fast. Come on, Jojo," she said, already racing for the door with their little dog scampering along behind her.

Mari, like everyone else in town, adored Shane. Bea had gone with him to enough restaurants or community events to see how people in town respected Shane. Everybody wanted to talk to him, to tell him about their son or nephew or grandson who was on his team, to shake his hand and tell him thanks for all he had done for the town and to wish him well on bringing home the state championship again.

After the shoulder injuries that ended his glowing NFL career, Shane could have thrown a serious pity party. Instead, he had moved home to be with his father during Bill Landry's final two years and spent six months of that time finishing his teaching certificate to go with the biology degree he earned playing college ball.

He could have taken a position on a major university football staff and possibly worked his way up to a Division One head coach. She knew he'd had offers. Good ones. Instead, he was choosing to make his home here in this little town on the Northern California coast, teaching freshman and sophomore biology and coaching a ragtag group of kids.

Feeling restless for reasons she couldn't identify, Bea headed to the vast master suite, which she slept in alone, to change into her swimming suit.

Since Shane had moved into the guesthouse two months earlier, something had changed between them and she wasn't sure what it was or how to fix it.

They used to be best friends. She used to be able to talk to him about anything going on in her life: her latest art show, the problems Mari was having with a friend, how Daisy had frustrated her that day. All her hopes, dreams, worries.

He had been there when her marriage broke up and she tried to find her way as a single mom.

She, in turn, had helped him navigate the end of his NFL career and had provided emotional support during the final difficult months of his father's life as heart disease and diabetes eventually claimed Bill Landry.

Bea had been the unofficial football team mom to his high schoolers the previous year. She took refreshments to practice; she hosted game-viewing parties in her home theater; she knew all their names and cheered on every single game, home or away.

Things had been fine until Shane decided to renovate his father's home next door to Stella's. The place hadn't been updated since the sixties when it was built and needed extensive work. It had been Bea's bright idea to offer Shane the guesthouse here while the inside of his place was gutted and redone with new electricity and plumbing.

She wished she had never opened her big, stupid mouth.

She hated this edginess that had tormented her around him over the summer. She wanted things to go back to the way they'd been before.

Life rolled on. That was one of Cruz's songs that she had helped him write, back in the glory days of their relationship. Life rolled on. You either rolled with it or let it flatten you as it rolled by.

She changed quickly and found her daughter throwing on her flip-flops near the patio doors.

Shane was swimming laps and didn't notice them at first, giving Bea a chance to admire the picture he made in the moonlight: muscles rippling across his wide shoulders, tapering down to slim hips in red board shorts.

She used to tease him that if he grew his sun-streaked hair out to his shoulders, he could pass for Thor before the buzz cut of the more recent movies.

She sighed. She hadn't teased him in a long time. When she tried, her words tangled and she ended up sounding stupid and awkward.

Marisol didn't wait for him to notice them. She jumped headlong into the deep end, just feet in front of him.

Shane paused in midstroke and lifted his head out of the water. His hair was wet, droplets clinging to his face, and Bea curled her fingers at her side against the urge to wipe them away.

Cut it out, she snapped at herself. He didn't see her that way. To Shane, she was like a kid sister, one he'd had to bail out of one too many scrapes.

He smiled as Marisol swam toward him like the little fish she was. "Hey, Sunshine."

Mari grinned at the nickname he always called her, a play on the *sol* part of Marisol, which meant "sun."

"Hey, Shane. Guess what? We went to Aunt Stella's birthday party tonight. She turned forty. Can you believe she's that old?"

He sent an amused look toward Bea that made butterflies explode to life inside her. "Forty is far from old, kiddo. And anyway, your aunt Stella is the youngest forty-year-old I know."

"I guess. Race you to the other side. I'm gonna win this time."

"Says who?" He took off after her and the race was on.

Bea contented herself with swimming laps while the two of them were being silly, taking turns on the diving board with the most elaborate dive, then playing a hot game of one-on-one basketball with the freestanding hoop Shane had bought the previous summer.

Bea swam into the grotto and watched them play through the waterfall. Jojo and Sally, the best of friends, had climbed out some time ago and were curled up together on the outdoor carpet that marked one of the seating areas around the pool.

They loved the pool as much as their humans.

Keeping it heated year-round was sheer indulgence, but Bea didn't care. Fortunately, Cape Sanctuary had a fairly temperate climate and the thermometer rarely dipped below freezing.

As she might have predicted, Mari started to tire after about an hour in the pool, especially as she'd already had a long day with friends earlier, then the excitement of Stella's party.

After winning the basketball game by one layup, her daughter climbed out of the pool and started drying off, which seemed to signal to Shane it was time to do the same. After a moment Bea dived through the waterfall so she could exit, embracing the cold drops on her back.

She had left her towel on the chaise next to his and she tried not to stare at his broad, muscled chest as they both dried off, or the network of ugly scars on his shoulder that had ended up changing his life. What would he do if she pressed her lips just there, to the biggest and ugliest of the scars?

"How's Stella doing with her big birthday?" Shane asked, obviously oblivious to her turmoil.

She swallowed, appalled at herself. "I don't know," she admitted. "She has been acting really strange lately. Daisy thinks she's hiding something from us."

"It's not every day a person turns forty. Could be she's taking it harder than you might have expected."

"Maybe."

She suspected there was more to it than simply another cycle around the sun, but Stella could sometimes be an enigma.

"She was mad at me for not taking you along to her party. Apparently, you're as much a part of her tribe as me or Mari or Daisy."

His mouth twisted into a smile as he pulled on a T-shirt from his NFL team and she tried not to be too disappointed as he hid all those glorious muscles.

"How was your day?" she asked abruptly.

"Good. The bedrooms are all framed and the drywall subcontractors are finally coming tomorrow."

"That's terrific! That will make a big difference. The place is coming along."

"Yeah. It's too bad we had so many delays with the plumbers' and the electricians' schedules. I would have liked to be out of your hair before the football season started, but we should be back on track now. Probably another month and I'll be gone."

She wanted to tell him he wasn't *in* her hair, nor was she in a big hurry to send him on his way. She couldn't figure out how to say either of those things without sounding weird.

"You know you're welcome to stay as long as you like," she finally said.

"I know. And I appreciate that. But friends try to be careful not to overstay their welcome."

"I'm just saying. If you want to wait until the season is over and you have more time to move back, it's fine."

"Thanks."

He held her gaze long enough that she felt flustered and reached down to put on her flip-flop. Somehow she stepped on an uneven paving stone on the pool decking and started to lose her balance.

Shane, with the reflexes he'd always had as a wide receiver, reached in to catch her like she had been thrown by Tom Brady himself.

The heat and strength of him enveloped her and she froze, his face inches from hers. His shirt was damp from where he'd thrown it over his wet muscles, and she wanted to stay right here forever.

Her gaze drifted to his mouth, firm and well shaped and beautifully familiar. She wanted to kiss him. Right now, even with Mari playing with the dogs on the stretch of grass outside the pool area.

"Shane," she began, not at all sure what she wanted to say after that one word. Whatever she intended was lost by the dogs' sudden barks and her daughter's exclamation.

"Daddy!" Mari cried.

If Shane hadn't been holding Bea already, she would have toppled to the ground in shock.

Cruz. Here? She whirled around and found the man, the legend, the last person on earth she wanted to see right now walking toward them.

Out of all the moments out of any day, Cruz would naturally pick this particular one to make an entrance.

"Hey, Mari Mia!"

Shane's arms tightened around her for just a moment before he helped steady her so she could stand on her own.

"*Hola*, Beatriz, my lovely wife."

Ex-wife, she wanted to tell him. Don't forget those all-important two letters.

He didn't look any happier to see Shane than vice versa. His long-lashed dark eyes seemed to go flat, his lean features to tighten.

"And Landry. Hey. Fancy seeing you here."

"Shane lives here now," Mari piped up, so very helpfully.

Cruz greeted that information with a scowl. She probably should have mentioned that fact to him before now, she suddenly realized, especially where she was so very diligent about vetting everyone staying with Cruz when he had visitations with Mari.

"Temporarily," she said, then wished she hadn't when Shane's mouth firmed.

She was suddenly annoyed with both of them for this dance they always did, circling around each other like bighorn sheep, ready to bang horns at any moment.

"He's renovating his father's house next door to Stella's and it was faster to move out so he could gut it and start over, rather than working room by room, living in a construction zone. The guesthouse has been sitting there empty, so I offered it to Shane while the work is being done."

She didn't owe him any explanations. It wasn't like anything was going on with her and Shane. Even if it were, she and Cruz had been divorced for years and she didn't doubt her ex-husband had slept with plenty of women in that time. Tabloids like the one she had picked up earlier were always posting pictures of him with some young beauty or other.

Shane was her oldest and dearest friend. If she wanted him to move into the guesthouse here at Felicidad permanently, Cruz had no right to object.

"Are you okay, Daddy?" Mari asked, oblivious to the tension between the two men. "We've been so worried about you, ever since we heard you were attacked."

"I'm fine, *mija*. Just fine."

"The tabloids said you got stabbed. My friend Jamie said you almost died."

"That's an exaggeration. I've told you not to pay attention to what you read online or in magazines. I just had a scratch. A couple of stitches, that's it."

He sank down onto the comfortable glider next to their loungers and Mari sat down beside him, still holding his hand. "I'm not saying it wasn't scary," Cruz went on. "If it hadn't been for a friend of mine who pushed me out of the way, things could have been much worse."

Like many celebrities, Cruz had plenty of acolytes and hangers-on, but she couldn't imagine any of them risking their lives for him.

"We tried to call you and left like a hundred messages." Mari didn't bother to hide her frustration with her father. A frustration Bea certainly shared.

"I'm sorry, *mija*. Things have been crazy with all the press calling for comments, so I ended up turning off my phone and going silent. Lenny said he called you regularly with updates."

"He did," Bea said. But hearing from a third party wasn't enough when a girl was worried about her dad.

She was familiar with that from firsthand experience and it made her heart ache that she and her daughter both knew what it was to suffer from parental neglect. Bea's own father had been a piece of work. Unlike Daisy, Bea at least knew who her father was, but their relationship had been minimal.

Her stepmother had disliked her intensely and made sure Steve Hidalgo devoted his time and energy to the children they shared and had as little to do with his love child as possible.

That was the main reason she did all she could to keep Cruz in their lives. Girls needed their fathers, if at all possible. Without their influence, the scars from that neglect could lead them to do crazy things, like get pregnant when they were seventeen and marry their rocker boyfriends.

Not that she knew anything about that.

"Next time you're stabbed, do a better job of updating those who are worried about you, okay?" Bea said.

"Sorry," he said again. "I'm here now, right?"

"I guess." Mari hugged him, always quick to forgive.

"The good news is, I'll be around for a while. I'm taking an extended break here at Casa Del Mar."

As usual, her desire for her daughter to have as healthy a relationship as possible with her father warred with Bea's desire to live outside the shadow of Cruz's notoriety.

"How long are you staying?" She had to ask. Forewarned was forearmed, right?

He beamed at her and at Mari. "At least a month. Maybe longer. Won't that be great?"

Bea did her best not to gulp. "That long? Aren't you in the middle of a concert tour?"

"We have two weeks left for the new album. I postponed them and will make up the dates in the fall. My fans understand. After what happened in Dallas, I need a few weeks to recover."

Why did he have to recover *here*?

She knew she hadn't spoken aloud but he answered as if he read her mind. "I couldn't imagine anywhere better to recharge my batteries than here in Cape Sanctuary, with my two favorite girls."

Shane made a sound that could have been a scoff or a laugh, she couldn't quite tell. He wrapped the towel around his neck and reached a hand out to Cruz.

"It's good to see you, but I should go," Shane said. "We're working on some new plays for the season. I'm glad you weren't seriously hurt."

"Any knife wound is serious. That's what the doc says. The risk of infection is huge."

"Right. Well, let's hope that doesn't happen. Thanks for the game of hoops, Sunshine. You get better every time we play."

Mari beamed at him. "Night, Shane. I won't rub it in your face that you lost, I promise."

"Thanks for sparing my feelings," he said with a grin. He kissed the top of her head then leaned over to give Bea their usual hug.

She could smell him, chlorine and shampoo and delicious male. To her surprise, he didn't stop with a hug but kissed her cheek, and she fought a powerful urge to lift her mouth to his.

Where on earth were all these strange impulses coming from?

"Good night," she murmured.

"Night. Come on, Sal."

He waved to them all, then headed to the guesthouse on the edge of her property with his yellow Lab following after him.

The place wasn't huge, a one-bedroom with a separate combined kitchen and living room and a decent-size bathroom, but it was plenty big enough for one man and a dog, especially for only a few months.

It had seemed a great idea a few months ago, the perfect solution when he needed somewhere to live during the renovation. In retrospect, she wished she'd never invited him to stay here at Felicidad. She wanted their friendship back.

"I wish you'd told me he was living here," Cruz said when Shane went inside the guesthouse and they, in turn, headed inside the main house.

She sighed. "He's not living with me. He's living in the guesthouse, as you can clearly see. Farther away than when he lived next door to Three Oaks."

Even if Shane were living inside the main house, in one of the six bedrooms, she had more than enough room.

It was too much house for only her and Mari. She knew that and some part of her wished she'd chosen differently when she was shopping for properties. But Daisy had advised her this was a good investment and she did love her studio that overlooked the ocean and had all the natural light she could ever want.

As usual, though, she had been weak and let other people determine her destiny.

"I'm going to change out of my swimming suit. I'll be right back," Mari said, hurrying off to her bedroom at the end of the hall, the one with the loft bed Shane had helped Bea build.

"I bet Landry jumped at the chance to move here," Cruz said when she was gone.

She frowned. "What is that supposed to mean?"

"You know what it means. Shane has always had a thing for you."

What did Cruz see that she didn't? Those strange butterflies seemed to flutter around again.

"You're crazy. He has not. We're friends. Best friends. We have been since fifth grade."

Cruz scoffed. "Shane Landry wants more than friendship from you. You're the only one who doesn't see it."

He was wrong. He had to be. She'd been divorced for *years*. If Shane was interested in her, why didn't he do anything about it? Sure, he had been busy with his NFL career then the injury that had ended it, then caring for his ailing father the past few years. But he had dated other women in that time. He certainly hadn't shown the slightest inclination that he wanted to kick their relationship to another level.

Cruz didn't know what he was talking about. She wasn't in the mood to argue with him, though.

"Are you really planning to spend an entire month here in Cape Sanctuary? Mari will love it, but you can't be away from your career that long, can you?"

"My team understands that I need this. I want to spend more time with my family. My baby girl. I almost died, babe. That crazy bastard wanted me gone. When I close my eyes, I can still see him coming at me."

She couldn't even imagine. "It must have been terrifying."

"That kind of thing messes with your head. I've had nightmares every night since it happened. I wanted to fly back here that night after they stitched me up to be with you and Mari but I didn't feel right about leaving Gabe. That's the guy who saved my life."

"Was he seriously hurt?"

Cruz nodded, looking uncharacteristically grim. "It was touch and go for a while. He ended up losing part of his liver."

"Oh, no!" She'd had no idea things had been that grave for the man who had stepped in front of a knife for Cruz.

"For a while there, the docs said he might need a transplant. I was going to offer, but we both know mine's probably not in the best of shape."

He grinned but she didn't find the comment at all amusing. His drinking and his recreational drug use were partly responsible for the breakup of their marriage, helped along by his chronic infidelity. Cruz, known as one of rock's sexiest bad boys, had a tough time resisting his legion of groupies.

He didn't look particularly bad now, sprawled out on one of her kitchen chairs. "Turns out, they just removed the damaged part."

"Is he okay now?" Bea asked.

"He's out of the woods. That's another reason I'm back. After he was released from the hospital, he needed a place to recover. I told him there was no better place on earth to recuperate than here in Cape Sanctuary. He's back at the house."

Along with probably a dozen groupies and other hangers-on. The king of rock had to travel with his court.

"I'd love you to meet him," Cruz continued. "Both you and Mari."

"Before I can let her stay, you know I'll need to have Peter run a background check on this Gabe person and everyone else who is here with you at Casa Del Mar."

"Yeah, I know."

She had made it a requirement of their custody agreement,

that she needed to vet all the people who surrounded her famous ex-husband before exposing her daughter to any of them. Her attorney who handled that for her was on speed dial and she would call him in the morning.

"I'll get you the names," Cruz said. They had been through this routine so many times that he only sounded a little annoyed. He understood by now that she was only concerned for their daughter's safety.

The circumstances of the past few weeks reinforced that her husband lived in a precarious, larger-than-life world where strangers could attack with hunting knives and change a person's life forever.

"Are you really okay?" Bea asked. She had loved Cruz once, as deeply and passionately as a teenage girl could. Even in her early twenties she had cared for him, until his success had changed him from the earnest, loving boy with the golden voice and poet's soul to a man addicted to his fans and his fame.

"I'm fine physically. Like I said, just a scratch." He paused. "Emotionally and mentally, that's another story. Coming this close to death, knowing I could check out at a moment's notice...that has made me reevaluate everything."

"And what startling conclusions have you come up with?"

"That I never should have agreed to our divorce," he said bluntly.

The words came out of nowhere and just about knocked her over. If they had still been standing by the pool, she might have toppled in.

"Of course you should have. It was your idea in the first place! We were miserable together."

"I don't remember being miserable. I remember being madly in love. You've always been the only one who gets me, babe."

She *so* did not want to have this conversation. Not when Mari could come back into the room at any moment.

Once, this man had been everything to her. When she found

out she was pregnant, she had been over the moon, couldn't wait to run away with him to Los Angeles so they could get married and he could become the big star they both seemed to know was his fate.

She had sacrificed everything for his music career. Even while pregnant and in the months after having Mari, she had worked three jobs, checking in a supermarket in the mornings, delivering pizzas in the afternoon and waiting tables at night.

When his momentum started to build and he found representation that believed in their vision of him, too, they thought all their dreams had come true.

She and Cruz might have made it work. There were certainly couples that could handle juggling a family and standing in the limelight, too, when one of them had a high-powered, very public career. Beatriz and Cruz Romero hadn't been one of those couples.

They started to fight about his drinking and drug use, about his friends, about the other women he couldn't seem to resist.

They had loved each other passionately, but little by little that love had dried up, until there had been nothing left but the empty husks of what they had once been to each other.

Now, apparently, Cruz wanted to see if they could resurrect those seeds.

"I want you and Mari in my life again," he said with the same earnestness he brought to his ballads that made teenage girls everywhere go weak-kneed. "Every day. The three of us against the world. I want the chance to prove to you I've changed. I'm a different man than the one who let you go."

"Because a crazed fan came at you with a knife."

"Because I've grown up. I've come to realize nothing else matters but you and Mari."

He reached for her hand, wrapping both of his around it. "You were the best thing I ever had going for me, babe. I've always known that. I would never have come this far without you."

She couldn't deny there was some truth to that. She had helped shape his early career, cowriting some of his early songs and laying the groundwork for the awards, sold-out tours and multiplatinum record sales that would follow.

She had walked away from that world, had devoted the past five years here in Cape Sanctuary to giving their child a normal life and rebuilding the jagged pieces of her heart.

How could he simply stroll into her home, utter a few words and think she would be willing to jump right back into the mess?

She slipped her hand from his and moved to put a chair between them.

Cruz noted her movement with a frown. "You have that look on your face."

"What look?"

"The Cruz-is-loco look."

"Of course I think you're crazy! I'm sorry, but you can't just walk in here after we've been happily divorced all these years and drop a bombshell like this on me without any warning!"

"I'm laying my cards out on the table from the very start. I want another chance with you. You don't have to make any decisions right now. I knew it wouldn't be that easy. I betrayed your trust."

"Again and again and again," she pointed out.

He stuck his lower lip out, looking remarkably like Mari used to as a toddler when she wanted a toy in the store. "I know there's a price for my bad behavior but I think I've been paying that all these years."

"Have you?"

"I've been without you and my little girl. Isn't that enough of a price? I don't want to spend the rest of my life alone. I still care about you and want to see if we could rebuild something on the ashes of what we burned down."

"Let me guess. That's a new song you're working on."

"It should be, right?" He grinned, teeth gleaming, and she

could feel herself weaken. She was as susceptible to that famous Cruz Romero smile as the rest of the female population of the world, she couldn't deny.

Fortunately, she was saved from having to answer and from her own weaknesses by the appearance of their daughter, who hurried into the room and right back to her father's side.

"Can I stay at Casa Del Mar tonight, Daddy?"

A few years ago he probably would have said yes, leaving Bea to explain to her child that there were certain steps that had to be taken first. This time, after a quick glance in her direction, he shook his head. "Not tonight. I'm sorry. But soon, I promise."

Marisol huffed a little but accepted his words. She couldn't seem to stop hugging her father, clearly delighted to have him in town.

Bea suspected that if it was up to their child, she and Cruz would have reunited years ago. Marisol would love nothing more than for the two of them to get back together. Whenever Cruz left after one of his infrequent visits to town or whenever she returned from staying with him somewhere on the road or at his house in Southern California, she would mope around for days.

Bea knew too well how that felt, to pine for something she couldn't have.

Shane Landry wants more than friendship from you, Cruz had said. *You're the only one who doesn't see it.*

It wasn't true. It couldn't be. She would have picked up on the signs earlier.

Still, the very idea that Shane might want to deepen their friendship left her ridiculously breathless. She would rather think about that than try to figure out what she was going to do about Cruz and his sudden, nonsensical desire to reunite.

3

STELLA

This was one amazing fortieth birthday present.

Stella Davenport looked at the array of tests laid out on her bathroom counter, a half dozen of them, all giving her the same message.

She had done it. She was pregnant.

She couldn't deny the truth when it was staring at her from six different pregnancy tests. Positive signs in every direction confirmed everything she had been suspecting for the past two weeks but had been too afraid to verify at the doctor's office.

Preggers. Expecting. Knocked up. A bun in the oven.

She still couldn't seem to believe it.

For months she had been waiting for this day. She had hoped, prayed, yearned. She had charted her cycle religiously, had pored over sperm donor files to find the perfect one, had dipped into her savings account for a healthy chunk to cover the four times she had been artificially inseminated.

She had suffered the indignity of feet in the stirrups, the catheter, the waiting half an hour with her hips raised, then hoping and praying and yearning for results.

If this one hadn't worked, she wasn't sure what she would have done.

Nothing, she told herself. She would have been fine. She would have called the state foster care agency to see if there was any chance they would reconsider and let her foster an adoptable infant this time, as a single working mother.

Other teachers had babies and there were certainly foster care babies who needed homes.

If that didn't work, she would go on as she always had, providing a stable, loving, comfortable home for older children and teenagers in need.

She loved her work as a foster parent. It had been both necessary and rewarding, helping young people who had few options left to them. At last count there were twenty of them who had stayed with her in the ten years since Beatriz ran off with Cruz Romero, sometimes with her only a few months, sometimes a few years. Each had left an indelible imprint on her heart.

It had all started with Bea and Daisy, of course. She had loved being a mother figure to them, struggling to form a family and build a home together when she was barely twenty-one and they were nine and eleven. She could still picture them, two lost and damaged girls who had suffered so very much because of their irresponsible, selfish, fickle mother.

The girls were the daughters of her heart and she would always consider them such.

Because of them, she had started Open Hearts, in an effort to do what she could to make sure all children who had to be in the foster care system received loving and supportive placements.

She was proud of all she had accomplished, but she wanted something else now. She wanted her own child, and according to the pregnancy tests assembled around her, she would have her wish in about eight and a half months.

Pregnant.

Joy burst through her, incandescent and perfect, and she pressed her hands over her abdomen and the tiny life growing inside her.

This was it. Everything she had dreamed about for the past year.

She was having a baby!

Dear God. She was forty years old and she was having a baby!

She was crazy! What had she been thinking? She was going to become a mother at an age many women were starting to think about becoming empty nesters.

Panic started to chew at her jubilation. She pushed it away. No. She wouldn't let it take over. For this moment she wanted to simply savor the miracle of life.

She had to tell someone. The news was too big inside her, like a dancing, whirling wind looking for an escape.

Fortunately, her best friend, Cleo, had texted an hour ago that she would stop by with a birthday present, despite Stella's insistence that she wanted nothing from her friends.

She had the best gift of all.

She touched her abdomen again. "Hello, little baby," she whispered. "I love you so much already."

Her child would never spend a moment of his or her existence wondering what it felt like to be loved.

The doorbell rang while she was whispering softly to her child and she jumped up. Cleo. She was the perfect person to tell, had been supportive from the moment Stella told her this was something she wanted. She was the only one who knew about the past months of fertility treatments. How perfect, that she was the only one who would know about the baby for now.

She scooped up the closest pregnancy test and rushed to the front door then yanked it open.

"Look. Just look! I did it! I'm pregnant!"

As soon as she said the last word, a long, drawn-out affair that seemed to take about a dozen extra syllables, shock drenched her like a January rain.

The person at her door wasn't her best friend, the woman she considered the closest thing she had to a sister.

The person at her door was a man, lean and distinguished and gorgeous.

A man she hadn't seen in nearly twenty years—and had tried her best to forget.

All the blood seemed to leave her head to pool somewhere in the vicinity of her favorite pair of Birkenstocks and she had to grip the door frame with her free hand to keep from toppling over.

"Ed!" she exclaimed.

"Um, congratulations," he said at the same moment, looking as bemused as any man would under the circumstances.

She was still holding the pregnancy test, she realized on some appalled level. But she couldn't think about that now. Not when Ed Clayton, the love of her life, had suddenly appeared out of the freaking blue.

"Ed!" she said again. She couldn't seem to make her brain connect to her voice to say anything else.

"Hello, Stella."

This couldn't be real. Maybe this was all some kind of bizarre dream, brought on by the Italian food she and the girls had the night before. No. The pregnancy tests were certainly real.

She couldn't seem to catch hold of her wildly scrambling thoughts. Was this the pregnancy brain she'd read about, where cheerful, perky bloggers nearly half her age warned that her synapses would turn into a jumbled mess?

Or was this simply a normal reaction to the bizarre confluence of events, suddenly discovering the only man she had ever loved on her doorstep the very moment she learned she was going to be a single mother in approximately eight months and change?

"May I...come in?" He sounded real enough, with a wary hesitance in his voice. She couldn't really blame him for that. The last time she had spoken to the man, she had made it more than clear she had no use for him and never wanted to see him again.

The blatant lie of her words couldn't be more obvious as she all but drank in the sight of him.

He had aged, of course, with lines at the corners of his eyes and a little sprinkling of gray in his brown hair. She found it totally unfair that those things only added to his appeal.

"Ed. Wh-what are you doing here?"

He gestured to the pregnancy stick in her hand. "I don't think I'm quite the person you were expecting."

"How could I possibly have been expecting you when I haven't seen or heard from you in years?"

"I've obviously come at a bad time. I can come back later. You probably need to call someone else besides me to tell them the news. Your...husband? Boyfriend? Significant other?"

She obviously didn't have any of those things, which was why she had to be artificially inseminated.

"I don't need to call anyone," she said. "This is my baby. Mine alone."

He arched an eyebrow. "You do remember I was a medical student with plans to become an OB-GYN when you walked away. I've been in practice for more than a decade now. I think I have a pretty firm grasp on the basics of what's required for a successful pregnancy."

He had been twenty-three when they met, already finishing his second year of med school, earnest and compassionate and eager to make a difference in the world.

While she could never claim to have any gift for telling the future, she had known without a doubt that he would be a brilliant doctor someday.

How many times over the years had she wondered about him?

43

She could admit to herself it had taken all her self-restraint not to google him or find him on social media.

Somehow she had known that making contact with him would be a mistake, would stir up all the emotions she had struggled bitterly to overcome.

"This is obviously not a good time." He scratched his neck, looking rueful. "I think it would be better if I came back later."

Yes, she wanted to tell him. Go away.

Stella needed at least a few moments for the joy to sink in, to savor the idea of being pregnant. She wanted to imagine burying her face in her baby's neck to inhale the intoxicating scent, to think about how wonderful it finally would be to cradle that sweet, warm weight against her after all these months of dreaming.

She had no desire to traipse down memory lane with a man she had done her best to forget.

She should invite him in but she didn't want to. She wanted him to walk back out the way he had come, to go on and live his life without her, as she had forced him to do.

Good manners wouldn't let her go quite that far. "You're here. You obviously have a reason for that. You might as well come in."

She held the door open, and after an awkward moment, he moved past her. She had a wild urge to pinch him to make sure he was truly there and not some strange pregnancy-induced apparition. Somehow she was able to refrain.

"I take it from what you said that you're not married. Does that mean you're planning to raise the baby by yourself?"

She refused to let herself panic about how very daunting that task suddenly seemed.

"Yes. I'm certainly not the only woman in the world who has ever done that."

"True enough. And you raised the girls yourself, so you had plenty of practice, right?"

With preteens and teenagers. Not with an infant. That panic flared again and she stuffed it down. She was forty years old, far more experienced than she'd been when she took custody of the girls. She could do it.

"What are you doing here, Ed?" If she asked enough times, he would have to answer her, right?

He again looked uncomfortable, his gaze shifting away from her. "It's a long story. The short answer is that I wanted to give you fair warning that I'm moving to Cape Sanctuary with my daughter."

Moving. Here. Of all the places in this vast and beautiful country, he was moving *here*? She had spent twenty years trying to forget him. How on earth was she supposed to do that if he was living in Cape Sanctuary, a town of only ten thousand people?

She couldn't wrap her head around that. Instead, she focused on what was probably the least earthshaking part of his sentence. "You have a daughter."

The somewhat harsh planes of his face softened with a tenderness that made her throat feel tight and achy.

"Yes. Rowan. She's almost twelve. Smart, funny, curious. Amazing."

As a middle school teacher, she couldn't help being touched by his words. She knew too many parents who came to parent-teacher conferences armed with only criticism and frustration toward their child for not measuring up to expectations.

"How lovely. And her mother?"

His smile slipped. "She…died two years ago," he said curtly.

Oh. Poor Ed and poor Rowan. Compassion nudged its way past the shock. She knew what it was to lose her own mother at a young age and how hard it had been on Bea and Daisy, too.

She had so hoped that by leaving him after she took custody of the girls, by allowing him the freedom to pursue his dreams unencumbered by all her baggage, she was providing him the chance to find the happy-ever-after she had been incapable of providing him.

After his own rough youth, largely putting his own life on hold from the age of twelve to help his single mother raise his own brother and sisters after his father walked out, she couldn't ask Ed to do the same thing all over again with two orphaned, needy girls.

It hurt more than she might have expected to know her hopes for him to have a beautiful, happy life hadn't been realized. He had walked his own tough road. He had loved again, lost again and was now a widower.

"I'm so sorry."

"Thank you. That's why I'm here, actually. Not here in your living room but here in Cape Sanctuary. My daughter and I were in need of a fresh start and a good friend from medical school told me her partner was retiring and asked if I wanted to go into practice with her. You might know her. Joanne Chen."

Her stomach suddenly twisted with the vague nausea of the past few weeks that had been hinting at the truth she had been afraid to verify.

"I do know her," she said. "Quite well, actually. She's my doctor."

He made a face. "When I saw you standing there with the pregnancy test, I feared as much. That's one of the reasons I looked you up and decided to stop by, so that neither one of us had any sudden shocks when we run into each other at the clinic or on the street somewhere."

"You mean like the kind of shock I might have had when I opened my front door to find you on the other side, after all these years?"

He gave her a rueful look. "Yeah. Exactly like that one. I'm sorry. I should have thought things through a little more and phoned you first. In retrospect, I probably should have reached out to discuss it with you when Rowan and I were first considering the idea of moving here."

"You can move wherever you want, Ed. I'm not queen and supreme ruler of Cape Sanctuary. Though I have to ask, of all the places you could have gone, why here?"

"My previous practice was in Pasadena and I wanted more of a small-town atmosphere. And Rowan wanted somewhere with a beach. She is learning to surf and wants to be a marine biologist. I bumped into Jo at a conference several months ago and she mentioned what a lovely town it was. It seemed the perfect place for us. Not tiny but small enough to feel like we're part of the community."

"You remembered that I lived here?"

"I remembered that this is where you took the girls when you left. I remember you talking about how much you loved it here, how your time in foster care in Cape Sanctuary was the happiest of your life, when you felt the most safe."

Had she said that? Probably. After their mother died when she was eight and her only sister, Jewel, ten years older, took off with the first of a long string of boyfriends, Stella spent five difficult years being bounced from foster home to foster home throughout Northern California. At thirteen, she finally landed in Cape Sanctuary with a wonderful, loving couple that showed her by example how a family should function. With mutual respect, with kindness, with compassion.

Cape Sanctuary had become home. Naturally, this was also where she had been compelled to bring Daisy and Beatriz when she obtained custody of them after Jewel's lifestyle caught up with her.

"I guess, maybe I was looking for some kind of peace for me and for Rowan. She's struggling a great deal over losing her mom. Holly's death was...difficult. The idea of finding a sanctuary somewhere held a great deal of appeal. To be honest, I figured you probably weren't here anymore. I just assumed you would have married and moved away and had the half-dozen children you always talked about wanting."

She hadn't. Just the girls and this tiny life growing inside her, though she wanted to think she had been a mother figure to all the foster children who had found temporary refuge here at Three Oaks.

"I'm still here," she said, stating the obvious. "Thank you for warning me. Now I guess I'll have no excuse to freak out if I see you in the street."

He was quiet, those handsome features she had loved so much looking tense and uncomfortable. "I want this move to work for my daughter, but not at the expense of you and your comfort here in town."

"It's fine. It doesn't bother me at all," she lied. "You can move wherever you want, Ed. I hope that after all this time, we can be friends."

"I would like that," he said softly. "I've learned that true friends in this life are as rare as they are precious."

He gave her a careful look. "Now that we've cleared the air and gotten the initial shock of seeing each other again out of the way, tell me about this pregnancy. How far along do you think you might be?"

She knew exactly how far along she was, five weeks to the day since her last rendezvous with the doctor's turkey baster. She wasn't about to tell him that, though.

"About a month," she said.

"Jo is an excellent doctor. You're in good hands."

"Yes. She's been my OB-GYN for years."

"Then you know her skills well." He cleared his throat. "Thank you for being understanding. It's really great to see you, Stella. And congratulations again."

"Thank you."

"I guess I'll see you around."

Not if I see you first, she wanted to say, but that would probably sound juvenile coming from a forty-year-old schoolteacher who was about to become a mother.

"Right."

To her astonished dismay, he leaned in and kissed her cheek, then turned around and walked through her door, leaving behind a little swirl of his distinctive scent that took her right back to those intense college days when she had been young and completely in love.

Those heady months they had been together had seemed full of amazing possibilities. She had been close to graduating, in the middle of her last semester of coursework before doing her student teaching.

It had been an important time for her scholastically but she had barely been able to keep her mind on her schoolwork that final semester because she'd been in love for the first and only time.

Stella sank into her favorite chair, the one she had saved and saved to buy, with its whimsical forest scene created by her favorite artist, the anonymously infamous Marguerite.

The chair usually centered her. It was the one she meditated in, read in, sat in to write in her diary. This time she couldn't seem to find anything resembling peace as the memories crowded in.

She had been so in love with the gorgeous medical student she'd met at the UCLA student health clinic when she had sprained her ankle playing beach volleyball with friends over the holiday break.

Sparks had flared between them instantly and she had slipped him her phone number, something she had never done before or since. He called her the next day, ostensibly to check up on her ankle, and the two of them ended up talking for hours. Ed had dropped by the next night with a pizza and a bouquet of flowers and she had fallen hard. From that instant on, they spent every available moment together. They studied together, met up for meals on campus, spent all their free time hiking, riding bikes, or just taking a drive and talking.

He had proposed after two months. It was entirely too early in their relationship and they were both too young. Plus, he had years of med school, residency and internship ahead of him.

Both of them knew getting married had been a crazy idea but things seemed so right and real and perfect. Ed had been old-fashioned, hadn't wanted to move in together without marrying her, and by that point neither of them could imagine being apart.

She had known she wanted to build a life with him, so she had said yes. He was warm and loving, honorable and kind and amazing.

She wasn't sure what he saw in her, a former foster child with an alcoholic mother and a deadbeat father who had disappeared long ago, but she didn't care. She had been lost in the wonder and magic of knowing he would be hers and they would build the family she had always wanted.

And then she had found out purely by accident that her sister, Jewel, had died months earlier of a drug overdose, and Jewel's daughters, her nieces, had been put in separate foster homes.

And that was that. In that single moment her entire future had changed and she had known exactly what she had to do.

The girls needed her.

She had broken things off with Ed. What choice did she have? She could never ask him to help her raise two troubled girls, not when he needed all his energy and focus to become the brilliant doctor she saw inside him.

He would have done it. He would have put all his dreams on hold to help her obtain custody of the girls and would probably have quit med school to help support them all.

She couldn't let him. So she had just…walked away. Eventually, she had told him she wasn't in love with him, that she was too young to be married. That part was probably truth. She told him she had an offer to do her student teaching in Cape Sanctuary, at the other end of the state and a world away, and she was taking it.

She had cried herself to sleep the first three months she was away from him and had tortured herself by keeping a picture of them on the beach in the drawer of her bedside table until she had finally forced herself to put it away.

And now he was here.

What kind of weird wind had carried him back into her life now? And what was she going to do?

She wiped at the tears she hadn't realized she still had inside her for Ed Clayton and a love that seemed as real and strong now as it had then.

It didn't matter. She touched her abdomen, to the tiny life growing there. She couldn't *let* it matter. She had more important things to worry about now, like how in the world she was going to raise this child by herself.

4

DAISY

She was late, and if there is one thing she hated more than last-minute tax filers, it was being late.

Daisy pressed the buzzer at the wrought iron gates leading into her ex-brother-in-law's estate along the cliffs overlooking the Pacific. Casa Del Mar was beautiful. It was by far the most luxurious and expensive house along this area of coastline. Built in the Spanish Colonial style, it was massive, around seven thousand square feet, with a recording studio, huge swimming pool, tennis courts and even a two-lane bowling alley. Its biggest draw was the view, though, spectacular from just about every window.

She lived in a house on the cliffs above the ocean, as well, just a half mile down the road, and had a stellar view herself, but the entirety of Pear Tree Cottage would probably fit inside Cruz's master suite.

He could afford it. As one of his team of financial advisers, she had a full picture of just how successful Cape Sanctuary's hometown boy had become. The commission she earned handling his interests went a long way to helping her afford the property taxes for that house on the cliffs she loved.

"Yes?" A disembodied voice spoke out of the tastefully hidden speaker. She didn't recognize the greeter, which wasn't a big surprise. Cruz's staff rotated with dizzying frequency.

"Daisy McClure. I have an appointment with Cruz."

The voice went silent for a moment then returned to the intercom. "Mr. Romero is busy right now. He's about to have a massage."

She glanced at the clock on the dashboard of her BMW and frowned. She was five minutes late, granted, but she had a feeling the massage wasn't some not-so-subtle dig at her punctuality. She was fairly certain that Cruz had completely forgotten about their appointment. He had a bad habit of doing exactly that.

"Tell Mr. Romero he's the one who called me to meet him at this time. He said it was important. This is the only time I'm free in several days. I'm here now. He can have his massage when we're done. If you'd like, I can tell him that myself."

She spoke firmly, not worried about offending Cruz. She had known him since he was a kid living with his grandmother. She used to help him with his math homework after his grandmother had to go into assisted living and he came to live with Stella. He knew she wouldn't take his crap—which might be why he entrusted a substantial share of his wealth to her keeping.

"One moment."

An instant later the door glided open silently and she drove up the long, winding driveway lined with cypress and pine. Here and there, she caught glimpses of blue as the ocean peeped through.

When she pulled up to the house, she saw several luxury SUVs there, indicating he had guests. From here she saw two people playing tennis and was positive that if she walked around the house, she would find more in the pool.

Where was Cruz, however? That was the question du jour.

She rang the doorbell and waited three or four moments, then finally pushed her way inside.

As she might have expected, no one was there to meet her in the huge entryway, with its soaring ceilings and the colorful tile-work staircase and wrought iron banister focal point.

"Hello?" she called out.

Silence echoed through the entryway in response. She frowned, annoyed all over again. Give a guy a few *Rolling Stone* covers and include him as one of *People* magazine's sexiest men of the year, and he thought the world revolved around him.

She had a couple of options. She could wander around the vast house playing Find the Pop Star. Or she could handle things a different way.

She pulled out her phone and texted him.

I'll be in the sitting room off the great hall. I can wait for ten minutes, then I'll go and we can reschedule. My time is valuable, too.

He texted her back immediately.

Sorry, babe. Forgot you were coming. Be there in a sec.

She sighed. Cruz might be selfish and narcissistic, and her sister might have divorced him for completely understandable reasons, but he was still family and she loved him.

She headed for her favorite spot in the house, a small, comfortable room near the sprawling kitchen, with a beautiful view of the Pacific. The windows opened here and she could usually find a lovely breeze, sweet with the sea and the scent of the climbing roses that grew outside.

It also had three original Marguerites, an intricately painted table and two matching chairs.

She knew to the penny how much Cruz had paid for them, a staggering amount that still made her blink.

Cruz liked to think he had discovered the mysterious furniture artist. In a way, she supposed he had. It was a spread of this house in *Architectural Digest* where he gushed about her work that had put Marguerite on the wish list of every designer in California.

If she had hoped she might have a few moments to herself to enjoy the functional art while she waited for Cruz, she was sadly disappointed.

Someone was already there.

A man who was asleep, his feet on the coffee table and a drink on the extremely expensive Marguerite side table—without a coaster.

She knew this man, she suddenly realized. She had last seen him climbing into a luxury SUV outside the supermarket the night of Stella's birthday party.

He wasn't staring at her now. He was out, probably sleeping off a night of partying with Cruz into the wee hours.

She was aware of the sting of disappointment at discovering the man she had thought about several times since their brief encounter was only another one of her ex-brother-in-law's sycophants and freeloaders.

A gorgeous one, yes, but that didn't make up for being a slob.

She grabbed a walnut-and-leather coaster off the little tray—they were right there, for heaven's sake—and bent over to slide it under his drink.

"Well. That's a lovely thing to wake up to."

She jerked her gaze down at the deep voice and that slight, hard-to-place accent and found his stunning green eyes open and fixed somewhere south of her neck. Only now did she realize the position she was in, bending almost over him so that her unfortunately abundant girls were just at his eye level.

Making matters worse, the top button had come loose on

her tidy dress shirt, she realized, revealing plenty of cleavage as well as a hint of the decadent lace from the minimizer bras she favored.

"Oh." She straightened quickly, blushing as she worked to button her shirt.

He sat up, wincing a little. "Sorry. That was the drugs talking. I'm usually not such a pig, I promise."

She couldn't help her inelegant snort of disbelief. A slob, a pig and a junkie. Typical of Cruz's guests.

It was completely unfair that he could still manage to look rumpled and sexy, hair messed and the perfect degree of dark stubble.

She stepped away from him and glowered.

"I have an appointment in this room momentarily with Cruz. We're going to talk about big important, boring things, like taxes and annuities and investment properties. I suggest you find somewhere else for your nap. I'm sure there are all kinds of bikini-clad women out by the pool for you to ogle."

He blinked a little but she refused to feel guilty for the attack.

"Wow. Thanks for looking out for me and my ogling." He glanced at the coaster. "And my water glass, apparently."

"As Mr. Romero's financial adviser, I am compelled to protect his assets. Have you any idea how much an original Marguerite goes for these days?"

"Entirely too much, if you ask me, for hand-painted folk art."

She did her best not to hiss and tried to rein in her temper. "I didn't. Ask you, I mean."

Yes, she sounded bitchy, but she was fairly protective of the artist in question.

The insufferable man gave her a closer look. "You must be a fan."

Daisy had no idea how to answer that. "I admire the woman for building an artistic empire while keeping her anonymity."

"If Marguerite is a woman. From what I understand, no–

body knows. Could be a ninety-year-old hillbilly with a pot gut and gout who woke up one morning in the nursing home and decided to pick up a paintbrush and go to town on some old furniture."

She gripped the strap of her briefcase to keep from walloping him on the side of the head with it. "Isn't it funny how everyone has a theory, but nobody seems to have any proof?"

"He makes sure of that, doesn't he? And that only adds to the mystique, which I'm sure is quite deliberate. I wonder if everyone would still show the same kind of frenzied interest if they found out Marguerite is some middle-aged housewife with too much time on her hands."

"Make up your mind. Is Marguerite a bored housewife or a ninety-year-old man trying to pass the time in a nursing home?"

"Does it matter? The taste arbiters don't care. They only want what everybody else wants."

Who was this man? He seemed older than Cruz's usual assemblage of unfortunates, the name she had given the acolytes or aspiring rockers or groupies who were drawn to her ex-brother-in-law's fame.

There was an intelligence in his eyes that seemed to glimmer through the bleariness of sleep and the haze of whatever drugs he was on.

Who was he, and what was he doing here at Casa Del Mar?

"Do you see something wrong with that?"

"No. I always find it fascinating when something takes hold of the public consciousness. You have to wonder why, right? What makes a musician like Cruz hit big? Talent is part of it, certainly. He is unquestionably talented. A brilliant songwriter with a decent voice and a strong stage presence. But so are hundreds, maybe thousands, of others trying to make it big. There's something else, some hidden cultural zeitgeist."

"Cultural zeitgeist."

"Do you know that humans are among only a very few species

in the animal kingdom who excel at passing on certain behaviors through imitation, not DNA? Some songbirds do and great apes to a small extent, but that's about it in the animal kingdom."

"What do songbirds and great apes have to do with Cruz Romero? Or Marguerite, for that matter?"

"Look at the things we call fads. We want what someone else says we should want. Do you know that nobody cared about Vermeer until about two hundred years after his death, when somebody decided he was a genius and the rest of the world jumped on board?"

"I guess it's lucky Marguerite and Cruz didn't have to wait that long, then, isn't it?" she answered tartly.

"Lucky for them, anyway," he answered. "I'm not so sure about the rest of us."

Fortunately, her ex-brother-in-law wandered in before she could deck his guest.

Cruz wore his stardom well, dressed in loose linen slacks and a T-shirt from his latest tour.

"Daisy, my darling sister-in-law. Bring it in."

She sighed and hugged him. "Ex-sister-in-law."

"For now," he said with an enigmatic look. "Divorce or not, you'll always be my baby girl's aunt, which means we're connected forever."

"Not to mention the fact that I handle a significant portion of your assets."

He laughed and turned to the other man in the room. "I see you've met Gabriel."

How inappropriately named. He wasn't at all angelic. "He was just leaving, I believe. And taking his booze with him."

"Just water, babe," Cruz said. "The man is boring enough to be a preacher. His body is a temple, apparently."

She hated having to agree with Cruz on that point.

"It's worked out well for me so far," the unworthily named

Gabriel said with a smile. As he rose, his smile turned into a wince that had Cruz taking a step forward.

"You okay, man?"

Daisy raised an eyebrow at the genuine concern in Cruz's voice.

"Fine. Just a little stiff. I'm going to take a walk."

Now her ex-brother-in-law looked anxious. "Be careful. You know you're not supposed to go far."

"I'll be fine. Don't worry. I'll just walk around the pool and back. You know you don't have to babysit me every moment, right?"

"I promised the doctors I would make sure you take it easy," Cruz said, confirming Daisy's growing suspicions. "That's the only way they let you out of the hospital."

"In case it's escaped your attention, I'm not hooked up to monitors anymore. Nobody has to know that I dared walk a hundred yards."

"I know. Now Daisy does, too. You're a miserable patient, Ellison."

Gabriel Ellison. She knew that name. She frowned, trying and failing to place exactly how. He wasn't a celebrity, she was sure of it.

She was also sure that she owed this man an apology for her attitude toward him. Gabriel was the person she had seen in the grainy, out-of-focus picture in that tabloid, the one who had been slumped against a wall holding his hands to a knife wound.

This was the man who had saved Cruz's life. And she had been treating him with contempt and disdain, as if he was some druggie parasite.

Shame twisted through her. When would she ever learn not to jump to conclusions?

"I'm a miserable patient and you're a mother hen. You're not responsible for me."

"I beg to differ. You lost half of your liver saving my sorry ass, which means I'm responsible for making sure you listen to the doctors."

Gabriel Ellison made a face. "Exaggerate much? It was a small section of my liver. Barely even a few centimeters. I'll be perfectly fine once it heals. Now, if you'll excuse me, I'm going to take a walk and find another comfortable and quiet spot to read my book."

He picked up the glass and the book she hadn't noticed before and moved past her. She had to say something, before things became even more awkward between them.

Daisy cleared her throat. "I...I feel like I owe you an apology, Mr. Ellison."

Why was that name so familiar?

"For what? Having a difference of opinion? I enjoyed the conversation. It was a pleasure meeting you, Daisy."

He moved past her a little unsteadily. She frowned after him.

"Will he be okay on his own?"

"Give me a minute and I'll make sure my security people keep an eye on him."

He called a number, spoke a few murmured words, then hung up. "Now. Tell me again how much money you've made for me while I've been gone."

With a sigh, she turned her attention from the mystery of Gabriel Ellison to business, something she knew and understood.

5

GABE

Somehow, by the grace of a God he assumed had forsaken him a long time ago, Gabe managed to walk out of the cozy, warm little sitting room he had found the day before without making a complete ass of himself.

It was a close thing. He felt as weak as a damn day-old Bengal tiger cub. He wasn't sure if it was from his lacerated liver, from the infection he was still fighting off or from the painkiller he had finally taken in desperation somewhere close to dawn after a mostly sleepless night.

Whoever would have guessed he would come to this point?

As an adventure documentary filmmaker, he might have expected to meet his fate on some bitterly cold mountain somewhere, in the midst of giant ocean swells, or while trudging across a vast, sun-parched desert.

He never would have guessed the injury that would take him lower than he'd ever been and make him wonder if he would actually survive would happen in the tunnel of a football stadium prior to a concert for a pop star whose music he didn't even particularly enjoy.

It had all been a fluke, mere chance. He wasn't supposed to be there in the first place but had been in Dallas meeting with some producers when he met Cruz Romero at a party. Cruz was apparently a fan of his work and had been a fan of Gabe's father, which shouldn't have surprised him but somehow did.

Cruz had expressed interest in investing in Gabe's next project, showing the extensive efforts under way to protect tiny indigenous tribes along the Amazon, and had invited him backstage for his show later that night to discuss it.

He should have turned him down. But he hadn't had plans that night and as a lifelong learner had been interested in what went on behind the scenes at a major concert venue, so he'd agreed.

He shouldn't have been there. Yet he was. He had been standing next to Cruz just after he came off stage when a huge linebacker of a man lunged at the performer with a wild look in his eyes and a massive, wicked-looking hunting knife in his hand.

Gabe could have slipped away. It wasn't his fight, after all, and the crazy dude wasn't after him but the man he apparently blamed for the breakup of his marriage—Cruz.

He hadn't. Instead, his instincts kicked in, the instincts he had honed from a lifetime of living in dangerous situations.

He had deflected the guy's aim slightly, though not completely, but what would have been a gouge straight to Cruz's heart had glanced off his arm instead.

Unfortunately, this had only enraged the guy more and he turned his attention to Gabe, thrusting the knife into his gut hard before bodyguards had finally come to the rescue and taken him down.

Turned out, the man's wife had been a groupie who had actually slept with Cruz two years earlier after a previous concert in Dallas. She had been so certain he wrote one of his love songs for her that she'd left her husband and two kids to follow the pop star around the country.

He couldn't really blame the guy for wanting a little revenge. He just would have preferred he boycotted the concert, maybe walked outside holding a placard or something, instead of trying to even the score with a ten-inch hunting knife.

In the days since the attack, Gabe had learned some interesting facts about knife wounds.

He had learned livers were one of the most common organs injured by knife and gunshot wounds, largely because of their size and vulnerable position in the abdomen.

He had learned that a damaged liver could heal on its own, one of the rare organs that could regenerate new cells instead of scar tissue.

He'd also learned that any abdominal injury was prone to infection—and that recovering from one was a hell of a lot harder than he expected.

He hadn't died from blood loss, as he now knew the ER doctors had fully expected would happen. He had made it through the first twenty-four hours and then the week after and was well on the road to recovery now.

He hadn't wanted to come here to Cruz's estate to recover, but with his only fixed address a third-floor walk-up in Manhattan Beach that he used as a home base, he hadn't had many choices.

Gabe still wasn't sure he liked the guy's music but had to admit Romero had stepped up to show his gratitude, insisting on staying with Gabe through those early days in the hospital and then arranging for him to fly here upon release.

Cruz hadn't listened to a single argument.

There were far worse places to rest and recuperate.

Gabe sank into a bench overlooking the ocean, enjoying the waves crashing against the rugged cliffs below.

He would rest here for a minute, he told himself. Just long

enough to avoid the prickly Daisy, whose last name he still didn't know.

She was lovely. He couldn't deny that. At first glance she seemed almost forgettable but then a man looked closer and saw those stunning hazel eyes, full mouth, lush curves.

He hadn't been able to look away when he'd seen her in the grocery store the other day. He was rather embarrassed to remember that he might have stared. She had seemed familiar to him and now he knew why. In the hallway outside his room was a picture of Cruz and a little girl he assumed was his daughter. Also in the picture was a woman who looked a lot like the little girl, which he now figured was Cruz's ex-wife, an older woman with short hair and glasses and the voluptuous Daisy.

Those hazel eyes had gazed out of the picture, hypnotizing him.

He would love to photograph those eyes. Maybe he would pose her on that Marguerite table she loved so much, wearing nothing but scarves, with only her vibrant eyes visible above the filmy material...

The image came out of nowhere, unsettling him...and arousing him, he realized, as his body stirred to life.

That was a relief. The business downstairs had been listless and uncooperative since the stabbing.

Good to know things appeared to be in working order, though apparently nearly dying had the odd and unexpected side effect of making him develop a sudden fierce attraction for prickly businesswomen with sharp tongues and questionable taste in art.

6

STELLA

"It is one hundred percent official. You are pregnant, my dear."

Stella gazed at her friend and longtime OB-GYN, still reeling from the shock of it. "You're sure?"

"The numbers don't lie, honey. Congratulations."

She smiled at Jo, who had held her hand through the entire process of fertility treatments. "I feel like you did half of the work. Shouldn't you be passing out cigars right about now?"

"I'm afraid it doesn't quite work that way. You get to do all the work from here on out, until the last bit."

She wasn't going to stress about that part until she had to. "I don't know how to thank you. Seriously. You've been amazing."

"Everything looks good so far. I would say, considering the date of your last insemination, that puts you at approximately six weeks along—assuming you haven't been finding a little action on the side, anyway."

"No action here, except you and your turkey baster, which I'm sure doesn't surprise you. It's all you, Jo."

"Well, I couldn't be more thrilled."

"I don't know how to thank you. It's amazing."

"Don't thank me yet. We have a few weeks to go."

Six weeks down, approximately thirty-four to go. She couldn't quite believe this was happening. She would be holding her own baby in just a little over eight months.

"Do you have any questions or concerns for me?"

"That depends. How much time do you have?"

Jo laughed. "I can give you another fifteen minutes. If you have more than that, we'll have to meet for lunch next week."

"Fifteen minutes will at least get us started."

The truth was, Stella had been dreaming of this day for so long, visualizing what it would be like to be right here, finding out positive news from her doctor, that she had already researched everything she might have wanted to know. She had just about memorized the stages of fetal development, what symptoms she might be experiencing at each stage of the pregnancy and any concerns she should be watching for.

All that and much, much more was available with the click of a keyboard. Seriously, how had women survived all the questions of pregnancy before the internet?

She knew the answer. They had a village. Mothers, sisters, grandmothers, friends. She had that, too, and was deeply grateful.

They talked about a few of her symptoms—the breast tenderness, the sleepiness, the hints of nausea she'd been feeling throughout the day.

"That might get worse before it gets better," Jo warned. "Make sure you let me know if it becomes more than you can handle."

She knew as a woman past forty—barely!—she would face additional challenges and was completely confident in Jo, grateful she would have a friend and solid partner in this whole baby business.

"If that's it for now," her doctor said, "I'd like to see you again in my office in two weeks. Be warned, I'm going to be following you more frequently than most first-time moms. Because of your age, this is considered a high-risk pregnancy, which means we'll become even better friends before we're done here."

"Sounds great to me."

"Go ahead and get dressed and the nurse will be in with the bundle of information we give to all first-time expectant mothers."

She was an expectant mother. It still didn't seem real.

"Thank you."

"I'm so thrilled for you, Stella. You're going to be an amazing mother."

She wasn't at all convinced of that. She was fairly certain self-doubt would be more of an issue throughout the pregnancy than anything else. She was in it now, though. Like every other mother, she imagined, she would have to figure things out as she went along.

The nurse, Katie Frye, had been Stella's student years ago. She knocked just as Stella finished dressing. "Come in," she called.

Katie marched through the door carrying a large cotton tote with flowers on it. "Here you go. This is the swag bag we give to all new prenatal patients. There are samples, coupons, leaflets and a nice pregnancy journal, as well as a book we give expectant moms. You might find it answers your most common questions. Read through it when you can. And congrats, Mama."

Her stomach, which hadn't felt the most stable all day, seemed to twist at the words.

"Remember, you can call us any day or night," Katie went on. "Now, make sure you stop at the reception desk to set up your next appointment."

"I will. Thank you."

When she walked out to the luxuriously appointed reception area, she saw a couple of women she knew, including one who was a notorious gossip. She waved, grateful the swag bag was somewhat discreet and didn't scream Baby Mama on it. She wasn't ready for the whole world to know yet. She didn't even know when she wanted to tell Daisy and Bea.

After making the appointment with the receptionist—another of her old students—she was entering the info into her phone's calendar when the door behind her opened. She couldn't see who it was, but she felt a collective burst of energy ripple through the room as if every woman had suddenly put her hormones on notice.

With a growing sense of dread, she turned around and, as she feared, discovered Dr. Ed Clayton walking through the front door, accompanied by a gamine young girl with brown hair and a sprinkle of freckles across her nose.

His face lit up when he spotted her. "Stella! Hi. I didn't expect to see you again so soon."

Of all the OB-GYN offices in all the cities along the coast, he had to walk into hers.

"I told you Jo was my doctor." She held up the bag of swag. "First appointment."

How was it possible that Ed Clayton was the only other person besides Jo and Katie who knew about her pregnancy? That was just as unreal as the pregnancy itself.

"I hope all went well."

"So far so good," she answered.

"Glad to hear it. Actually, I'm happy we bumped into you. I wanted you to meet my daughter. Rowan, this is Stella Davenport. She's an old friend and also teaches at the middle school."

"Hi." The girl looked at her curiously, but without any hint that she knew her father and Stella once had a relationship.

"Hi, Rowan. It's so nice to meet you. Are you in sixth grade or seventh?"

"Starting sixth." A hint of worry showed in the girl's eyes

that were remarkably like her father's. "We just drove past the school and it's huge."

"Her previous school was a small, private elementary not far from our house," Ed explained.

"This is my first time in public school. I really hope I don't get lost."

"It's not bad once you walk around a little. If you'd like, I can meet you there ahead of time and show you around. When you get your schedule, I can give you the tour and come up with a map to your classes."

"That would be great. Thank you."

Stella felt a pang of sympathy for the girl. She remembered that terrifying feeling of showing up to a new place when you didn't have friends, didn't know the routine, had no idea of the customs or cliques.

How many times had she endured that through her childhood?

Her past experience meant she had a special place in her heart for new students. She figured school was hard enough at this age without throwing in a complete change.

"It can be daunting to start at a new school but I think you'll find plenty of friends. I actually have a great-niece going into sixth grade and all her friends are very nice girls."

"That's good."

She could almost guess what the girl was thinking. *How lucky for your great-niece. How is that going to help me?*

"You know, I'm sure Mari would love to meet you before school starts. Would you be interested, if I could arrange for the two of you to hang out? Maybe she could invite some of her other friends to a little pool party at her house, just to make sure you have a few familiar faces on the first day."

This stirred Rowan's interest. She gave Stella a look that seemed both wary and eager. "That would be really nice. Thanks."

"I'll call her. I'm sure she would love to meet you. And if you have any questions about Cape Sanctuary or the things young people your age like to do around here, I would be happy to answer them or direct you to someone else who can."

"Thanks, Stella," Ed said. He glanced at the reception desk. "I'm here to drop off some forms they need before I start working next week, but if you're free, would you be interested in going to lunch with us to maybe give us some of those pointers?"

She gazed at him, clutching her baby swag bag. "Lunch."

He smiled. "Yes. You've heard of it, I'm sure. The meal between breakfast and dinner."

She wanted to say no. A few days ago she thought she had put Ed Clayton firmly in her past. It may have taken years of effort but she had almost managed to forget him.

She could do nothing about his decision to move here to Cape Sanctuary but that didn't mean she had to willingly sign up to entangle their lives together again.

She was about to refuse but then she saw the eager expression on Rowan's face and couldn't do it.

For his daughter's sake, she could handle a little thing like lunch. "Did you have somewhere in mind?"

"You tell us. We don't know restaurants in the area. That's one of the areas where I could use help."

"I like The Ocean Club. It's on Seaview Drive, near the Pine intersection, just a block from here."

"Do you want to walk?"

She needed to stay active during her pregnancy, for the baby's health and her own. "Sure."

"Give me a few minutes to take care of the reason I came here."

He handed the receptionist some signed forms. "Here you go. I think that's everything you needed from me but let me know if I left anything off."

The receptionist apparently was not immune to the gorgeousness that was Ed Clayton. She tucked a strand of hair behind her ear and smiled at him. "Thank you so much, Dr. Clayton. We can't wait for you to start."

Stella had a feeling that as soon as word trickled out about the sexy new doctor, the women of Cape Sanctuary would be lining up for appointments.

Stella felt extremely conspicuous as she walked into The Ocean Club with Ed and his daughter. She had taught all three of the owner's children and also knew several of the patrons eating at the comfortable café. The place was frequented by both locals and tourists alike, known for its excellent and extensive menu and spectacular view of Sea Glass Beach.

She waved to Elena, the owner, who raised her eyebrows in Ed's direction, all but wiggling them, Groucho Marx style. She frowned at her friend, hoping Ed didn't notice.

"Elena Jimenez, this is Ed Clayton and his daughter, Rowan. They've just moved to town. Ed is a doctor, joining Jo Chen's practice."

"Nice to meet you, Ed. Hi, Rowan." Elena gave them both a friendly smile. "Welcome to Cape Sanctuary."

"Thanks."

"Do you want to sit outside on the patio? It's a beautiful day."

"That sounds great. Thanks."

"Go ahead and sit where you want," Elena said. "I'll send Leilani out in a minute to take your order."

Stella was nervous as she led them to a lovely spot near the patio edge, with a striking view of the curving beach below and the dramatic rock formations offshore.

"This is nice," Rowan said.

She smiled at the girl. "The food is good, too. And reasonably priced."

They spent a moment going over the menu, then gave their order to Elena's sweet daughter, who helped her mother out at the restaurant.

"So do you have a place to live yet?" she asked after the server left.

"We opted for a short-term lease our first few months, to give us time to figure out what neighborhood we want to settle in for the long haul," Ed answered. "For now, we're in the Surfside condos."

Surfside was a lovely development not far from Three Oaks. "You'll like it there. It's a nice area. Plus, they have that great pool complex."

"It's got a good view of the ocean. That was my only requirement."

"You're not far from the middle school there, only a few blocks," she said to Rowan. "You should be able to walk or ride a bike."

"Or my longboard," Rowan said.

"That would work, too." She knew many students rode longboards to school and stored them in their lockers. "You know, we have a really great skate park north of Dragonfly Park. That's about three blocks from your condo."

She knew all about the skate park since she had been on the committee that persuaded the city council to build it. Several of her foster children had been into skateboarding, and the park provided a safe place to do it where they didn't annoy business owners.

"I hear from those who've used it that it's pretty boss."

"That could be cool." The girl sipped at the soda Leilani brought her. "What about surfing around here? Is it always too cold? I was just starting up back home and was hoping I could take more lessons here, but we went down to the beach the other day and it was *freezing*. I only waded in and I thought my toes were going to fall off from frostbite."

"You have to wear a full-body wet suit but there are plenty of folks around here who do. There's a nice surf break up a little north of town at Hidden Beach. I'm not an expert, I'm afraid.

Surfing's not my thing but you can talk to the couple that runs the surf and bike rental shop down the street and they can give you all the info you need."

"I will. Thanks."

"So," Ed said when the conversation lagged. "Tell me what you've been doing the past twenty years."

Missing you.

She cleared her throat. "Teaching. Raising the girls."

"You have daughters?" Rowan asked. "How old are they?"

"Nieces, actually. And they're grown now. Daisy's turned thirty this year and Bea is twenty-eight."

"Do they live around here?"

"Yes. Daisy is an accountant and financial planner in town and Bea is an artist. As a matter of fact, she has some lovely pieces in the gallery next door."

"We'll have to check it out," Ed said.

"It's her daughter who is around your age," she told Rowan. "Marisol is a very funny, creative, kind girl. I think you'll like her."

"Maybe."

Stella didn't miss the hint of wariness in the girl's voice, as if she was afraid to get her hopes up. It made her even more determined to help her connect with Mari. "I'll talk to her mother and see what we can arrange before school starts."

That might mean she had to spend more time with Ed, but for the girl's sake, she was willing to make a sacrifice.

"What other sorts of things besides longboarding and surfing did you like to do back in Pasadena?"

Rowan fiddled with her silverware. "I don't know. Just stuff. Ride my scooter. Watch movies. Listen to music."

She wondered if Rowan liked Cruz Romero's music but decided not to blow her mind by telling her the pop icon was her niece's father.

"Sounds like the same stuff Mari likes. I'll call her mom as soon as we finish lunch."

Leilani brought their food a moment later, and while they ate, they spoke of Rowan's previous school and Ed's practice, their dog, Boomer, and a trip the two of them were planning over Christmas break to Hawaii.

She would be done with the first trimester by then, she thought, and into the second, with a nice baby bump.

The meal was much more pleasant than she might have expected. She was aware of the currents simmering between them, all the unanswered questions about why she had walked away and their difficult last meeting so long ago. But Ed seemed willing to put that aside. Wouldn't it be lovely if they could build a friendship, after all these years?

He insisted on paying for lunch as recompense for all her advice about the community. By the time she finished eating, she was exhausted and wanted to find a nice corner of the restaurant to curl up in and take a nap. She had a feeling that getting through the school day while fighting this fatigue was going to be one of the hardest parts of the pregnancy.

"Thank you," she said after they rose to leave the restaurant. "This was a great place. I appreciate you directing us to it."

It would probably be tough to have a friendship with him when his smile still made her insides shiver.

"You're welcome. If you want, I can give you a list of some of my favorite restaurants in town. Or you can just explore. Trial and error is good for finding your own favorites."

"I would appreciate a starting point. Thanks."

She forced a smile as they walked out of the restaurant. Since both of their vehicles were still parked back at the women's clinic, they started in that direction when the door to the art gallery next door opened and she spotted a familiar person coming out. Bea looked lovely in a flowery, flowing sundress and a floppy hat.

"Hey, Aunt Stella!"

Oh, dear. She didn't want either of the girls to see her with Ed and get the wrong idea about them. It was too late to worry about that now. The damage was done.

"Bea. Darling. We were just speaking about you."

"Were you?"

"About Mari, actually. I suppose I should introduce you. Bea, this is Ed Clayton and his daughter, Rowan. They've just moved to Cape Sanctuary. Dr. Clayton is going into partnership with Jo Chen."

"Oh. Welcome, both of you." Bea gave them a wide smile, making Stella grateful for her kind nature. Though she had been a bit of a wild, rebellious girl once upon a time, motherhood had settled Bea a great deal.

"Thank you," Ed replied. Was Stella the only one who found the way he smiled with his eyes enormously sexy?

"I was telling Rowan here how amazing my great-niece, Mari, is and how I'm sure they would love each other if they met. They're both a little too old for playdates at this age, so I was thinking we could set something else up. Maybe a swim party or something with some of Mari's other friends, just so Rowan can meet some other girls her age before school starts in a few weeks."

"What a great idea! Mari would love that. I'll talk to her and see what we can figure out."

"Thank you, dear."

Bea's gaze was fixed on Ed, a slight frown furrowing her forehead. "Ed, you seem familiar somehow. I'm sorry. Have we met?"

Stella froze. She could only think of one reason Bea might recognize Ed. The girl had once stumbled onto a picture of the two of them together, one Stella couldn't bear to throw away.

"Ed and I are old friends, tracing all the way back to our university days at UCLA," she said quickly. "He's moving up from Southern California."

She still had the picture. She kept it in a little carved box of papers and receipts and the few photographs she had of her and Jewel when they were young. Once in a while, she stumbled onto it. Seeing Ed's face always seemed to knock the wind out of her.

"I'm actually glad I bumped into you." Bea changed the subject, much to Stella's relief.

"Oh?"

"I wanted to give you a heads-up, if you haven't already heard. Cruz is in town, staying at Casa Del Mar. So far, the paparazzi haven't found him but that could change at any moment. You might want to avoid that section of Seaview Drive until he's gone again."

The curving, tight road could be dangerous under the best of circumstances. Sometimes when Cruz was in the middle of some scandal or other and came back to town, the paparazzi's vehicles could block the entire road.

"Thank you for letting me know. I'll be careful. How is he?"

Though she could never quite forgive him for getting Bea pregnant when she was barely seventeen and taking her away from them before she could graduate from high school, she would always have a soft spot in her heart for Cruz. He had been her student first, with a poet's soul she had recognized early, then had lived with her after the grandmother who had been raising him had to go into a nursing home.

"He seems to be okay," Bea said. If Stella wasn't mistaken, her niece still seemed troubled, despite her words.

"I'm so glad. Did he tell you or Mari how long he plans to stay?"

Bea's mouth tightened, confirming Stella's suspicions that she wasn't particularly happy with her ex-husband right now. "A month. That's what he said, anyway."

"That means he'll be here for the Arts and Hearts on the Cape Festival."

"Probably."

The huge festival in September had become the signature fund-raiser for Open Hearts. "Maybe he would agree to attend one of the events. Imagine how the attendance might soar if people knew Cruz Romero was attending!"

"Cruz Romero? You know Cruz Romero?" Rowan's eyes were huge.

"You could say that," Bea muttered.

"Cruz and my niece here were married once. He is Mari's father."

"Really?"

"He has a house here in Cape Sanctuary. You might have seen it, a really big, sprawling Spanish Colonial just on the edge of town, overlooking the water."

"Remember that big house we saw the other night? The one you said looked like a hotel?" Ed said.

"That's the one," Bea said grimly. "Go ahead and ask him about the festival. You know he can never say no to you. Meanwhile, I'll talk to Mari about the pool party and let you know."

"Thanks, honey." Stella kissed her niece on the cheek and Bea waved and headed on the way, but not until she gave Ed another searching look as if still trying to place him.

"Thank you again for having lunch with us," Ed said as they neared the clinic.

"I enjoyed it," she answered, and was surprised to find it was true. "What are your plans for the rest of the day?"

"I thought we would walk around downtown a little more, just to get the feel of things."

She was reluctant to leave them, suddenly. Her fatigue seemed to have disappeared as quickly as it appeared.

"Have you been to the library yet? In my opinion, you don't

truly belong to a community until you have a library card. We have an excellent library here in Cape Sanctuary."

"We have not made that stop yet."

"It's right across the street on the corner. And across the next street from that is the local historical museum, where I am a do-cent a few times a month. I can show you that, too. It will give you a nice overview of Cape Sanctuary."

"That would be great," Rowan said, obviously still dazed at discovering Cruz Romero lived close by.

As Stella led the way, she told herself she was only being friendly to two people moving to the town she loved. Her offer to show them around had nothing to do with any desire on her part to spend more time with the man whose memory she had cherished for nearly two decades.

7

BEATRIZ

After Bea left her aunt outside The Ocean Club, she crossed the road and, on impulse, went inside the building and climbed the stairs to Daisy's second-floor office.

From the landing outside Daisy's office, she had a clear view down the street and could see her aunt walking with Ed Clayton and his daughter.

As she watched, she saw her aunt lightly touch the man's arm and point to something in the window of the bookstore where Stella attended her monthly book club meeting.

He looked down at her, just so, and bells started clanging in her memory. Suddenly, she knew exactly where she'd seen Ed Clayton before.

She shoved open Daisy's office door and waved to her receptionist and friend, Donna Cook.

"Is she free?" she asked urgently.

"For a few moments," Donna said, looking concerned as Bea

rushed to Daisy's door, knocked and pushed it open without waiting for an answer.

Daisy was working on something at her desk—Bea had no idea exactly what her sister did, other than it involved numbers and money, two things that intimidated the hell out of her. She looked up at Bea's entrance.

"Come here. Quick," Bea ordered as she raced to the window, which afforded the same view she had seen from the landing.

"Nice to see you, too," Daisy said. "Why no, I'm not in the middle of anything important. Why would I be? I'm happy to drop everything to go look out the window and snoop on some unsuspecting soul."

Bea didn't have time for Daisy's sarcasm. "Hurry, before they're gone."

Daisy sighed as if she were a hundred years old and rose from her computer, moving to the window with all the speed of a turtle on crutches.

"What do you see?" Bea demanded, fighting the urge to shake her sister and remind her she was only thirty freaking years old and didn't need to be so measured all the time, like some senior citizen whose bones could barely hold her up.

"Um, a few clouds. The ocean. A slow, beautiful August afternoon. What am I supposed to be looking at?"

She ground her back teeth. "Down there! Can't you see Stella? She's walking with a guy and his daughter."

Daisy's gaze followed her pointing finger but she appeared singularly unimpressed with the sight. "Okay. And?"

"It's him! It's the guy in the picture!"

"What picture?"

Ugh. Daisy didn't have a romantic bone in her body. She never had. She'd married a dying man twenty-five years her senior, for heaven's sake. If that didn't tell a person all they needed to know about the stick she had up her butt, nothing else would.

"You remember. Come on. Think. She used to keep it in a

drawer by her bed. I know I showed it to you once. It was a picture of a young version of Aunt Stella, looking up at a guy with so much emotion on her face, it made my heart hurt. He was looking right down at her the same way."

She could still remember how sad the picture made her, and how curious. What had happened to that man? Why hadn't they ended up together? She had never found the courage to ask her aunt.

"Once, she found me looking through her drawer and got so mad at me."

"She was probably worried you'd find her vibrator."

"Ew." Okay, their aunt was still young, too, only ten years older than Daisy, but Bea really didn't want to think about *Stella* and *vibrator* in the same sentence.

"No. It was the picture. I'm sure of it. She snatched it away from me and put it away somewhere and I never saw it there again."

"Exactly how often did you go snooping through the drawers of Stella's bedside table?"

"Not often."

Never after that, she remembered. She had been so struck by the pain in Stella's eyes, she hadn't dared. "That picture meant something to her. *He* meant something to her or she wouldn't have kept it and wouldn't have been so upset at me for looking at it. The man in the picture is Ed Clayton and he's just moved to Cape Sanctuary with his daughter."

"How can you be sure?"

"I just am. I think they loved each other passionately. I can remember how it dripped from the photograph. They must have loved each other once and something must have gone horribly wrong."

"You don't know that."

How hard must it be to exist inside her sister's skin, always closed off to the joy and magic of life? Bea didn't even like imagining it. "I think this Ed Clayton is the reason she never married."

Daisy frowned. "*We* were the reason she never married. She was too busy rescuing us."

Were they the reason Stella and Ed Clayton hadn't made a go of things?

They owed Stella so much. Everything, really. She had rescued them from a future of foster care and group homes. Bea might not always understand her sister but she loved her. That year they had been separated after their mother died had been the worst she could remember of her childhood.

She suspected things had been harder for Daisy. Her sister had always been the more serious of the two of them, probably because Jewel relied on her for everything. She had taken care of everything, from babysitting Beatriz to fixing meals while their mother went out with men or painted or sat at an arts festival stall somewhere, selling her wares.

She had always been more serious than Bea, but Daisy had come out of foster care…different. Not cold, exactly, just controlled.

Bea had always idolized and adored her older sister but their relationship had never quite mended from that year they spent apart.

"I hope it's not true, that she didn't ever marry because she was busy taking care of us. But if it is, we have to do something to help her get back together with the man she used to love."

"Slow down," Daisy began.

She didn't let her finish. "I won't slow down. For once, will you listen to me? She has done so much for us! We need to give her this chance to finally be happy!"

"You think she can't be happy unless she has a man? Are you saying she's been miserable all these years, when she's been helping us and the other foster children she cared for over the years? That teaching English for twenty years couldn't possibly fulfill her, nor did founding a charity that has benefited hundreds, if not thousands, of other children in foster care?"

"I'm saying you should have seen her face when she introduced me to this Ed person. I've never seen her so flustered and nervous."

"Oh, well, then. We definitely need to make sure she has more of that."

She sighed at Daisy's tart tone. Bea loved her but really wished sometimes she had an ounce of whimsy in her, instead of always coming across as a stuffy, prickly old lady.

"Don't you want her to be happy? Don't you want her to find what she gave up all those years ago when she took us in?"

"You don't know that she gave up anything. We don't even know this man. For all we know, he could be nothing but trouble. What if he's married?"

She didn't think so. Stella had said that Ed and his daughter were moving to Cape Sanctuary. She hadn't said anything about a wife.

"What if he's the love of her life?" she countered. "We have to make sure she doesn't lose the chance to be with him again."

Daisy sighed. "As usual, your heart is in the right place. But this time maybe you need to let your head do the thinking. You would be best to mind your own business and let Stella figure things out on her own. She won't appreciate you meddling in her life."

That might very well be true, knowing Stella, but Bea didn't care. Every time she thought about that picture of Stella and this Ed Clayton, her heart ached.

Maybe Bea hadn't made the best choices in the romance department, with a teenage pregnancy and subsequent divorce behind her. That didn't mean she couldn't wish for a happy-ever-after for a woman who deserved that and more.

"Does that mean you won't help me play matchmaker?"

"That means I'm going to stay out of it and I suggest you do the same."

"Fine. You can be that way. But I love Stella enough that I want her to be happy and I think this Ed Clayton and his daughter are just what she needs to shake her out of the weird mood she's been in the past few months."

She was going to do anything she could to push them together, no matter what her sober, starchy, fuddy-duddy sister had to say about it.

8

GABE

He would say this much for the coastline here in Northern California. The sunsets were nothing short of spectacular.

Gabe stood at an overlook along Seaview Drive, watching the sun hovering on the horizon, huge and orange, beautiful, its dying rays turning the sea various shades of coral and amber and lavender.

Since he had been staying at Casa Del Mar, he couldn't seem to get enough of these nightly color shows. In a lifetime spent traveling around the world, he had seen plenty of sunsets before but couldn't remember ever feeling this resonance inside him as he viewed them, this bone-deep wonder.

It might have something to do with his brush with death. Maybe the subtle realization that he had come close to never seeing another sunset made each subsequent one feel like a gift.

He shot a few more pictures with his still camera, enjoying

the cool breeze against his skin and the way the clouds dramatically absorbed the different colors along the light spectrum.

When the sun was almost down, the night took on the pale light of twilight. Normally, if he was shooting pictures or taking video, he would wait until after sunset as that was sometimes when the best color appeared in the sky. This time, he figured he should probably be heading back down the road before Cruz sent the bloodhounds looking for him.

He probably wasn't supposed to be this far away from Casa Del Mar, but once he started walking, his steps had led him here, to watch the sunset from this high vantage point along the cliffs above the water.

The truth was, he was weaker than he wanted to admit, even two weeks out from his injury. He knew his strength would eventually return but he found it so damn frustrating that he could barely walk for five minutes without having to rest.

He put the cap on his camera lens and started walking back toward Cruz's house when a sound, out of place and unexpected, caught his attention above the wind. A whimper from below him, like some kind of wounded creature.

He frowned. What was it? He strained his ears, trying to isolate out the endless cry of the gulls and the waves down below to focus on the discordant sound.

There. He heard it again. A plaintive, distressed cry, coming from somewhere between his position on the cliff top and the water far below.

He peered down the steep slope. "Hello? Anybody there?"

Another little whimper followed his call, then a hoarse-sounding bark. A dog, then. Somewhere below him, about twenty feet or so.

He took the cap off his zoom lens and tried to focus on the area below him, until he spotted a little slate-gray dog that almost blended into the coastal scrub. The dog seemed to be perched on a flat spot about ten feet long by about three feet wide.

How had he gotten down there? There was a narrow gap in

the vegetation, almost a path, but it ended about three feet before the dog's perch. He must have wandered down and then fallen the rest of the way.

The dog was truly stuck, unable to climb back up and with nowhere to go below as the cliff abruptly dropped about four hundred feet down to the ocean.

Poor little guy.

The dog's tail wagged when he spotted Gabe or smelled him and he barked again, a hoarse rasp that made Gabe wonder how long the dog had been there without food or water.

He couldn't just leave him there. The dog would either starve to death or fall down that cliff into the water.

Gabe had a sudden memory of a trip to Patagonia with his father when they had been overnighting and ended up making camp late one night, past dark. They hadn't realized until morning that their tent was maybe three feet from the edge of a cliff like this one, with a steep, terrifying drop on the other side.

His father had thought it hilarious when he woke the next day to discover what they'd done. Gabe hadn't been nearly as sanguine. He remembered sobbing for a good ten minutes when he realized how one misstep in the night could have ended in disaster, before Chet Ellison snapped at him to pull it together and be a man.

He had probably been seven or eight at the time.

He pushed the memory away, focusing instead on his dilemma.

The light was fading fast. He estimated he had maybe twenty minutes left of visibility to pull off any sort of rescue.

He found the idea of making his way down that steep trail with nothing on the other side but air every bit as terrifying as waking up on the edge of a cliff had been to his seven-year-old self. He would have to switchback his way down to the narrow cut in the shrubs, then figure out how to get the dog up the remaining five or six feet.

He was in no shape for a technical descent, especially not with the stitches still holding his gut together.

A smart man would find somebody to help him. But who? Someone back at Cruz Romero's house? There wasn't time to walk to Casa Del Mar, round up help and be back here before dark. Anyway, he had a strong suspicion none of the indolent cabal around the pop star would be willing to risk their lives for a little gray mutt.

It was insane. His doctors would kill him for even considering it.

He was going to do it anyway. He couldn't leave the creature here alone overnight.

Gabe set his camera body on a rock and pulled everything out of his backpack except for his flashlight. At least if he went over the side, somebody might see his gear and know where to look for his broken body.

He didn't really find that amusing, especially not under the circumstances, when he had cheated death just days earlier.

Once upon a time, he had no fear. Like many young men, he had believed himself immortal and would have treated this situation like a big joke. He didn't find it funny now. He hadn't been so nonchalant about the gift of life in a long time.

He huffed out a few breaths, shook his hands out, then started making his way down the foot-wide path in the scrub, grabbing hold of whatever sturdy branch or rock he could on his way down. He imagined the trail was probably made by erosion rather than any living creature stupid enough to go this way on purpose.

The little dog seemed to know Gabe was on his way. He barked that hoarse, raspy sound again, like a sick sea lion, which made Gabe wonder again how long he had been stranded.

"Hang on, buddy. I'm coming," he said.

By necessity, his progress was slow and painstaking, and by

the time he reached the area just above the drop-off to the ledge, sweat was dripping off him and his knees felt weak.

Now, how the hell was he going to pick the dog up from here? Again, he wished for a rope. Since he didn't have that, he made his slow way to the edge of the cut that sloped upward, narrowing the drop to about four feet. With effort, Gabe grabbed hold of a sturdy chaparral branch and slid down until his feet hit the ledge.

The little dog—he could see now it wasn't a mutt but a far more regal French bulldog—whimpered and barked, wriggling in excitement. He was on the small side, weighing only about ten or twelve pounds.

"Easy now, or you'll knock us both over," Gabe warned. "Sit."

The dog obeyed instantly, though he was matted and dirty. He had big ears, blue eyes, slate-gray fur and a distinctive white streak from his chin all the way between his legs and across his stomach.

"What are you doing out here? Huh, buddy? You're lucky a hawk didn't decide you would make a good afternoon snack."

He petted the dog, who licked him eagerly. He obviously needed water but that would have to wait until they made their way back up to the road.

"I hate to do this to you but we're going to have to climb out of here before the sun goes down the rest of the way or we'll both be stuck."

The dog gave him a trusting look and didn't make a sound when Gabe scooped him up and shoved him into the backpack. He had a collar on but no tag, Gabe noted, even as his abdominal muscles cried out at the movement. He wasn't supposed to lift anything heavier than a paperback book. Certainly not a wriggling dog, however small.

"I'm going to need you to hold really still back there while we make our way out. If you can do that, I'll have water for you up top and we can see about finding where you live."

The dog barked hoarsely and licked Gabe's ear as if he understood completely.

The return journey was just as grueling. The hardest part was climbing off the ledge. It took all his strength and then some to make it back to the narrow path.

By the time he reached the road, all his muscles were trembling, much to his dismay. At the top he pulled off the backpack, unzipped it and pulled out the little dog. He didn't have a bowl but poured some of the water into a low indentation on the rock where his camera had been, and the dog licked eagerly at it again and again until the bottle was empty.

He also gave the Frenchie a power bar he had in his bag, hoping it wasn't bad for dogs. It was peanut butter, which he knew dogs liked.

He'd never had a dog, though he'd adopted a few strays here and there in his travels for the week or so he was in their territory, until he had to move on again.

"There you go. Drink the last of the water. Then we really do need to find your home."

He felt a ridiculous sense of accomplishment at saving the dog.

Technically, this was the second time in a month he had saved a life. Somehow rescuing the dog seemed much more of an accomplishment than jumping in front of a knife to rescue Cruz Romero.

The dog wasn't a stray. The collar was proof of that. Did he belong to one of the houses here along the cliff? Probably. Where else?

Gabe looked up and down at the handful of residences perched along the road, high above the water. Most of them were fancyschmancy places like Cruz's sprawling Spanish Colonial.

He sat for a moment, still catching his breath, settling his adrenaline and trying to figure out what to do.

He didn't want to take the little dog back to Casa Del Mar.

It would be best to reunite him with people who were probably looking for him.

"Come on, bud. Let's try to find your people," he said, and headed for the nearest house.

9

DAISY

That was an evening well spent.

She loved these rare moments when she was all caught up and didn't have any impending tasks hanging over her head.

Daisy finished cleaning up her workspace with the satisfaction of knowing she had worked hard for hours to tick off several items on her to-do list. Now she had several pieces ready to ship off to eager buyers.

She stretched her muscles, tight from several hours in front of her computer at the office in town then several more out here in her secret, private haven.

Whenever she spent time here, she felt a deep, aching pang, missing James and his quiet support and friendship more than she ever imagined.

She owed her late husband so very much, especially for this haven that had become so precious to her.

The pang of grief in her chest was as much a part of her by

now as the pale freckles she did her best to hide, though it had begun to fade after two years. She would always miss him and was so very grateful for his support and encouragement.

She knew he would have been happy with the way she was using this old storage building.

A song came on the radio, one of Cruz's that she had always particularly liked, "In Your Arms." It had a slow, sexy beat, one she could never resist. She turned it up to maximum volume and began salsa dancing around the room, holding her arms up for an imaginary partner.

Before the illness began to take away everything he loved, James had adored dancing. He had dragged her to a place the next town over that held salsa dancing evenings every week.

When she danced like this, she could remember how kind he had always been to her and how their marriage, though unconventional, had been a joy and solace for both of them.

She whirled to the music, eyes closed, and was lost in it until nearly the end of the song.

"Hello? Anybody there?"

She jumped and squealed at the male voice calling over Cruz's mellow tones.

"Who's there?" She looked around frantically for some kind of weapon. The only thing she could find in a rush was a paint scraper and a heavy paperweight. She had pepper spray somewhere but couldn't remember where she'd put it after she bought it.

She swiveled around, weapons at the ready, to find Gabe Ellison, her ex-brother-in-law's savior and guest, opening the door. He looked muddy and bedraggled and was holding a furry gray bundle in his arms.

"Sorry. I didn't mean to startle you. I called out a few times and nobody answered."

She dropped the paperweight and the scraper, feeling stupid. "So instead of taking that as a sign, you decided to barge in anyway. Maybe that should have told you something, that I wasn't in the mood for company, Mr. Ellison."

"Please. Gabe. Is this your place? I didn't realize you lived so close to Cruz."

Under her initial surprise, another deeper panic began to flicker. She had to get him out of here.

"I helped him find Casa Del Mar when it went on the market," she said. She didn't add that Cruz had been rootless, unsettled, for several years after the divorce. She had been worried about him, especially because of the usual riffraff that hung out with him. As his financial adviser, she had suggested real estate was always a good idea, and having a permanent place to stay when he came to visit Mari could only make visitations easier on both of them.

In retrospect, she wasn't sure that had been the best decision. She knew he drove Bea crazy with his unannounced visits. And right now she was questioning anything that brought Gabe Ellison into her particular orbit.

Gabe looked around at this part of her converted storage building and she wondered what he saw. At least most of Marguerite's things were safely tucked away out of sight in the workroom.

The smell of paint and sealer permeated everything in the building, though. Nothing she could do about that.

As she feared, he picked up on the signs. "You're an artist," he exclaimed.

She'd heard people refer to their blood running cold but had never really understood the saying until right this moment. She felt as if an iced slushy drink was suddenly seeping through her veins.

"I'm an accountant. I do taxes and financial planning," she corrected, hoping her voice didn't tremble.

"And you're an artist. I can see the paint under your nails."

She looked down and saw at once that he was right. Damn

him for being so observant and damn her for not washing her hands as carefully as usual.

"Residual, only. I was cleaning up some old paint cans in the back of the shed here. I'm afraid I spilled some."

He gazed around at the space and she knew immediately when he picked up on the large boxes, ready for delivery and adorned with the distinctive floral label.

He walked over to them and stared. "Marguerite. These have a return address for Marguerite. The very same Marguerite we were discussing the other day."

He shifted his stare to her. "You... Are you Marguerite?"

The ice spread out to her fingertips. She forced a laugh. "Me? Marguerite? If my sister heard you say that, she would bust a gut laughing. I'm the most unartistic person in the world. Ask Cruz. Ask Bea. Ask anyone."

"Then why do you have a stack of boxes with Marguerite's label on them?"

Why, oh why hadn't she locked the outside door? She always did. It was her protection from the world.

Of all the people who might have stumbled onto an open door of her workshop, why did it have to be him?

Gabe Ellison.

After that encounter at Cruz's she had googled him. Now she knew exactly who he was, why his name had seemed so very familiar.

Gabriel Ellison was no ordinary backstage lingerer who had somehow been in the right place at the right time to save Cruz's life. He was an award-winning documentary filmmaker. According to the information she had found, he had started young, filming the exploits of his own adventuring father as Chet Ellison climbed mountains, surfed remote waves, trekked through deep jungles.

After his father's death, Gabriel had become renowned in

his own right and had been nominated twice for an Academy Award.

And he was here, asking questions about Marguerite.

She had a contingency plan, the one she had practiced for this very possibility.

She sighed. "I really wish you had knocked, Mr. Ellison."

"Gabe. And I didn't. Cat's out of the bag now, Marguerite."

She forced a laugh. "You guessed part of the truth. I am connected to Marguerite, in a way. I represent her. It's a very closely guarded secret but I'm her agent with the outside world. I handle deliveries for her, receipts, contact with galleries. She prefers to remain anonymous but somebody has to handle the business side of things. We have a…complicated arrangement. In order to maintain the secrecy she needs for her creative muse, she needs someone to connect with the outside. In exchange, I take twenty percent of her considerable profits. It's a win–win for everyone."

By his narrowed gaze, she couldn't tell whether he believed her or not.

"Her business manager."

"Yes."

He didn't look convinced. "So is she someone in this area?"

"I can't tell you that. In fact, it would be better if we stopped talking about this altogether. You would only hound me and hound me until I divulged more than either Marguerite or I feel comfortable telling you. I help her keep her secrets. That's all you need to know. Now, what can I do for you, Mr. Ellison?"

As if on cue, the little furball in his arms began to stir. He lifted his head and looked around and Daisy discovered Gabe was holding an adorable dog, gray with big ears, a flattish face and blue eyes.

"Oh. Who's this?"

He made a rueful face. "I was hoping you could tell me that. I found him out on the cliffside near the bend, about two hundred yards up the road. I was hoping he belongs to this house or maybe one of your neighbors."

Daisy did a quick mental inventory of those who lived close to her. Several houses were vacant, used only by wealthy vacationers from the Bay Area who wanted a house on the coast. A few others were empty, for sale. She didn't know anyone who had a little French bulldog.

She shook her head. "I haven't exactly gone door to door in the neighborhood taking a dog census, but I don't think I've ever seen this guy before. I can ask around, though."

"Any chance you have an old bowl you wouldn't mind him drinking out of? I gave him my water bottle but I'm sure he's still thirsty. I get the feeling he was stranded on the cliffside at least overnight."

Cliffside. She keyed in on that word. If the dog hadn't been able to climb up on his own, how difficult must it have been for Gabe to climb down and rescue him, especially with his own injuries?

She huffed out a breath. Great. It wasn't enough that he saved her ex-brother-in-law's life. Now he had to go and do something completely admirable like rescue a cute stranded dog.

How on earth was she supposed to resist *that*?

Easy, she reminded herself. She only had to remember that he was entirely too perceptive and, with a little digging, could ruin everything.

She shifted her attention to the dog, who did look thirsty and bedraggled. He cocked his head, big ears out, completely stealing her heart.

"Oh, you poor little thing. Did you have a rough night, hmm? I'm so sorry."

She almost cooed but caught herself just in time, especially with Gabe watching her.

She did not want the man inside Pear Tree Cottage—her personal sanctuary—but having him here in the workshop was infinitely more dangerous, especially if he tried harder to suss out Marguerite's secrets.

"I don't have bowls here," she said. "We'll have to go over to the house."

She did, but they were old paint bowls that she wouldn't want anybody trying to use for drinking water.

"That's fine. Lead the way."

He held the dog as he followed after her, waiting while she firmly locked the door this time.

His steps were slow, measured, reminding her he had suffered a major abdominal injury just days earlier.

"Are you supposed to be out of bed?" she asked as they walked the short distance on the pressed gravel pathway between the workshop and her house.

He was silent for a moment, his breathing unnaturally even. "I am cleared to go walking," he said tersely.

"But not maneuvering your way down a cliff," she guessed.

"That might have been a mistake," he admitted.

In the glow from her outdoor lights, she could see his features were tight.

"Are you okay?"

"Fine," he answered with a smile that didn't convince her. She had the feeling he was the exact opposite of fine though she was equally confident he would never admit it.

Her house was locked and it took a minute of fumbling with the keys for her to open the door. She sighed. She remembered to lock her house but not the storage building. Naturally. If she had taken care of that little detail, they wouldn't be having this conversation. She would be safe inside, dancing in secret to soft, sexy Latin music.

"This is nice," he said as she led him up the back porch steps into the house. "You must have one hell of a view in daylight."

"There aren't very many houses along this stretch of road that *don't* have a stellar view. In the springtime we get the gray whale migration and you can sit here for hours with the telescope or binoculars and look for spouts."

Not that she had time to sit anywhere for hours, but she loved the idea that she *could*.

She did love watching storms roll in and the waves pound the cliffs far below. It soothed her spirit on days she was tired of crunching numbers and trying to meet unrealistic expectations of her clients, who wanted her to give them astronomical return on their investments with zero risk.

"There's a powder room right there, off the mudroom, if you would like to clean up. I can get this little guy some water."

She couldn't very well pour a bowl of water to the dog on the porch then send the two of them on their way. Giving him the chance to clean up was the polite thing to do and he *had* saved the life of someone she cared about.

Cruz had his problems and weaknesses and she wasn't sure she could ever forgive him for breaking her sister's heart, but he would always be her niece's father. She cared about him and would have grieved if he had been killed by that jealous fan.

"Thanks," Gabe said. "I appreciate that. I have a feeling I've busted through a couple of stitches in the midst of my daring rescue."

Though he said the words as a joke, she suspected it was true. She knew how steep those cliffs were. She wanted to think she would find the courage to rescue a stranded dog but she wasn't entirely certain of it.

He held out the dog for her and she took a step forward. Only now did she realize there was no way to take the creature from him without touching Gabe Ellison. Butterflies started salsa dancing in her stomach.

As she stepped closer, heat radiated from him. He smelled delicious, a unique combination of sea and sun, fresh dirt and coast brush and man. She fought the urge to stand there and inhale.

She would *not* do something stupid like let herself be attracted to the man. It was impossible. He was entirely too dangerous. Like the heat of his skin, he radiated raw masculinity. Exactly the kind of man she always tried to avoid.

She quickly scooped up the dog and backed away. He was about ten pounds, heftier than the kind of purse pooch some of the country-club set favored, and she wanted to kiss that grumpy little face all over.

She hadn't had a dog in years. Her last one had been a mutt she had found hanging around the middle school when she was about fourteen. She had loved that dog wholeheartedly from the moment she took him home, but somehow he had gravitated toward Bea.

Big surprise there. Everyone favored Bea, with good reason. Her younger sister was everything Daisy could never be—funny, exuberant, warm, beautiful.

She sighed, pushing away the ugly voices.

"I'll just be a minute," Gabe said. "Thanks."

"I have first-aid supplies in the medicine cabinet, if you need them. Bandages, cleansing wipes, that kind of thing."

"Got it."

"If you really did break through your stitches, you're going to need professional help to sew you up. Don't ask me. I faint at the sight of blood."

She didn't. In fact, she was usually the calm, levelheaded one in a crisis, but she wasn't sure she trusted herself to get anywhere close to Gabe and his injuries.

"Good to know," he answered, then headed toward her guest bathroom.

When she heard the door close, she lifted up the little dog and planted a quick kiss on the top of his head that smelled like sun and fear.

"I'm sorry you've been through a rough time, buddy. That must have been so scary for you. You're safe now. We'll get you sorted and find your owners."

In response, the little bulldog wagged his stump of a tail and tried to lick her and she fell completely in love.

"Let's get you some water, bud."

She quickly pulled a bowl from the cabinet and filled it with cool water, setting the water and the dog on the ground. He lapped it eagerly until the bowl was empty, so she filled it again for him then went to the refrigerator to see if she had anything that might be dog suitable.

She unearthed some chicken and a hard-boiled egg and gave him both, to tide him over.

She was running a bath in the sink to wash off some of that mud when Gabe returned.

"Looks like you have things under control here."

Pain lines branched out around his mouth and she had to fight the urge to take care of him, as well.

"He just needed a little food and water. I figured a quick bath wouldn't hurt."

"Good idea."

She sighed. "Sit down, Mr. Ellison. You look pale, like you're going to fall over."

"Gabe," he insisted, but to her relief, he pulled out one of her kitchen chairs and lowered himself into it. She didn't know what she would do if he passed out.

"Did you break through your stitches?"

"Not the stitches on the outside, anyway," he answered.

She poured a glass of ice water for him, too, and he drank thirstily, making her feel guilty for not doing that earlier.

"Thank you. Here's a little word of advice. Never take a hunting knife to the liver, if you can help it."

"I'll do my best," she answered. "Can I get you anything? I have more chicken. I could make a sandwich or salad."

"The water is great. Thank you."

He sipped at it again and she had to fight not to stare at him as she tried to remember when she last had a man in the kitchen.

"He's a cute little guy, isn't he?"

Adorable. "Yes. How do you think he ended up on the cliff-side?"

"Good question. There was a little trail through the brush. I wonder if he just wandered down and then couldn't figure out how to get back up."

"Lucky you found him." She paused. "What's your plan with him? Are you going to call a shelter or take him back to Cruz's house while you look for his owners?"

"I don't really like either of those options. I'm a guest at Casa Del Mar and don't think I can suddenly show up at Cruz's mansion lugging a stray that might or might not be house-trained, especially not with those big Dobermans he has."

Cruz's guard dogs were well trained, she knew, and would probably leave this little guy alone, but their presence might scare him.

"I also don't want to take him to a shelter. While they do good work, I think he would be better in a home. I've always felt that dogs, like children, deserve to be in a place where they can be loved."

Despite her best efforts to resist him, Daisy could feel warmth seeping through her at his words. Considering her own experience she didn't like to think about, she would completely agree.

Stella would love him for that sentiment, if she was here. It was the entire reason she had taken in foster children for years.

"Do you know if there's any kind of foster dog organization in town, somewhere he can stay until we can find his owner?"

No, she told herself. *Absolutely not. Forget it. You have too much going on. The last thing you need is the complication of a foster dog.*

The Frenchie toddled over to her and rubbed his head against her leg, more like a cat than a dog, and she was lost.

"I guess he could stay here," she said, ignoring the voice of reason.

Gabe looked startled, as if he never would have expected her to offer. She felt vaguely insulted by his surprise.

"Are you sure? That's a big commitment."

The urge to blurt out that she had changed her mind, that she had spoken without thinking, was almost overwhelming. Even suggesting it was crazy. She had so much on her plate right now, between her day job, Open Hearts, the festival coming up in a few short weeks and everything else. The last thing she needed was the stress and obligation of caring for a dog.

But she looked into that adorably ugly little face and knew she had made the right call.

"It should only be for a day or two, right? I imagine his owners are looking for him. He's got a collar, which means he has a home."

"From what I understand, French bulldogs are quite highly prized and don't come cheaply."

"He might even have an ID chip. I can take him to the vet tomorrow to check," she said.

"Good idea. I would offer to come with you, but unfortunately, I'm not cleared to drive yet."

She heard the frustration in his voice and could only imagine how difficult that must be to a man who had spent most of his life traveling the world.

"I can take care of it."

She would have to take the dog to the office with her during the day. That wouldn't be a problem. Her assistant would love the chance to help her care for him.

Gabe crouched down so he could scoop up the dog. She didn't miss his wince when he stood up. Again, she had the urge to take care of him and quashed it. He was a grown man. He didn't need her help.

He petted the Frenchie's big ears. "I will have to insist on visitation privileges. I saved his life, which means we're bonded now."

"Does the same hold true for Cruz?"

He laughed roughly, a low, sexy sound that sent a shiver rippling down her spine. "Not if I can help it."

She did her best to ignore her reaction. "I'll have to run to the grocery store to pick up something for him to eat. I can drop you off at Cruz's place while I'm out."

"I'll pay for any supplies."

She opened her mouth to argue but closed it again at his firm look.

"My rescue. My responsibility. I can't physically take care of him unless I go check into a hotel somewhere, but I insist on paying for his supplies."

"We can split the cost."

He shook his head. "You're a stubborn woman, Daisy McClure."

"I'm not the one who climbed down a cliff to rescue a strange dog when I am still recovering from a knife to the liver."

"Good point." He smiled at her and Daisy felt everything inside her sigh. The man was entirely too gorgeous for her peace of mind but somehow she would have to find a way to resist him.

1 0

GABE

"You really didn't have to come along. I would have been happy to drop you off at Cruz's place and simply bill you for your half of the dog's supplies," Daisy said yet again as they drove along the cliffs and down toward town.

He hurt like a mother trucker but there was something infinitely soothing about sitting in the passenger seat of Daisy McClure's comfortable old BMW with a dog in his lap as she drove with the same brisk competence he had a feeling she brought to everything else.

He couldn't find any rational reason for it, especially considering she had mostly been prickly and difficult, but he felt a kind of peace in Daisy's presence. There was something calming about her, maybe because he knew instinctively she was someone he could trust in his corner. He only knew he liked being with her and wasn't in a hurry to return to his guest room at Casa Del Mar.

He would rather hurt with her than be more comfortable at home.

"So, Daisy. Tell me about yourself."

She shifted her gaze from the road only for an instant, then turned back to focus on driving. "Not much to tell. I'm an accountant and financial planner. I guess you already know that, considering I had an appointment the other day with Cruz to talk about his investments."

"How long have you lived in Cape Sanctuary?"

She looked for a moment as if she didn't want to answer him but she finally spoke. "My sister, Beatriz, Cruz's ex-wife, and I moved here with our aunt Stella when I was eleven and Bea was nine. I've been here ever since."

There had to be more to that particular story. "What happened to your parents?"

She glared at him. "I agreed to watch your dog, not tell you my life story."

"You have to admit, it was the logical next question."

It was his job as a documentary filmmaker to dig into people's lives. To probe and observe until he reached the heart of them.

People and their stories fascinated him. It was one of the reasons he had agreed to come to Casa Del Mar to recover. Cruz interested him. Not the man himself, necessarily, but the almost cultlike obsession of his fans.

Now he found his interests shifting to Daisy McClure, who seemed to have layers of secrets.

"Our mother was a bit of a free spirit, I guess you could say," she finally answered, just when he thought she would ignore his question. "She was an artist, like Bea, and traveled around the country to art shows and different art colonies."

"And your dad?"

Her mouth tightened, giving him the impression this was an

old wound that ached when pressed. "I never knew him, and Jewel, my mother, didn't talk about him. He was someone she knew once. That's all she would say. Bea and I have different fathers. She knew hers, but he wasn't really in her life. It's a long story but most of our childhood, he was married to a woman who didn't want the burden of a wild stepdaughter. He chose his wife over his child and didn't have much to do with Bea. The random trip to the beach or to Disneyland. That was about it."

Gabe could certainly relate to that. His own mother had done the same, chosen to leave him and his father for a man who could provide her with the comforts she thought she deserved. Most of the time he didn't think about her. As far as Gabe was concerned, she had lost the right to be called his mother when she handed a five-year-old boy over to his wild, irresponsible father.

"That must have been tough on her."

Which was harder? Never knowing your father, like Daisy, or having one who wouldn't fight for you? He wasn't sure he could answer that.

"Jewel died when we were girls and eventually Stella was able to get custody and bring us all here."

He knew there had to be more than that to the story but she didn't seem inclined to discuss her childhood. He couldn't really blame her, as he didn't like thinking about his own.

"After you stopped by Casa Del Mar the other day, Cruz told me you were married and your husband died a couple of years ago. I'm sorry."

For just an instant, he saw raw pain flash across her features before she once again composed herself.

"Thank you. Pear Tree Cottage was his."

The dog shifted in his lap and Gabe tried not to wince. "It's a lovely home," he said.

"Thank you."

"So how did you come to be representing the infamous Marguerite?"

He didn't miss the way her hands gripped the steering wheel. Even in the darkened interior of the vehicle, he could see the muscles of her face tighten.

"I told you, I can't talk about it."

He didn't completely believe her protestations that she wasn't the artist but it was still tough to fathom that the stiff, prickly woman he had met could have created nuanced, whimsical work in secret.

"Enough about me," she said abruptly. "What about you? What would possibly lead an Oscar-nominated documentary filmmaker to step in front of a crazed fan to protect my niece's father?"

How had she known he had been nominated for a couple of Academy Awards? It wasn't like he wore a sign proclaiming it to the world, though sometimes he wanted to.

Had she googled him? If so, what else had she read?

"Would you believe me if I told you it was all a weird, cosmic, random accident?"

"So much of life is," she murmured.

"I wasn't supposed to be at the show that night but I was in Dallas on business and met Cruz at a party. Apparently, he was a fan of the work I did with my father as well as some of my more recent films and invited me to his show."

"Cruz loves movies of all kinds. That doesn't surprise me."

"I should have said no but I didn't have anything else going on that night and was at loose ends so figured why not. Now, of course, I'm wishing I had given a different answer."

"I'm sorry you were hurt but very glad you saved Cruz's life," she said. "Mari would have been shattered if he'd died."

Suddenly, for the first time, he was glad, too.

They arrived at the grocery store before he could answer.

"You're looking pale," Daisy said when she pulled into a parking space. "Why don't you wait in the car with our new friend here? I'll run in and out in just a few minutes."

He didn't want to sit here like some old man but he was feeling embarrassingly weak and didn't want to fall over in front of her.

"Yes. Okay."

He shifted the dog in his lap. "You know we're going to have to come up with something else to call him until we can find his owners."

"You work on that while I'm in the store."

After she exited the car, he decided instead to look up everything he could find on the elusive Marguerite.

He found a wealth of information about the highly valued artist, including the shocking information that a similar side table to the one he'd left his drink on the other day was going for more money than a luxury sports car.

He did an image search and found many of her works exhibited in private homes and even in a few museums. As he scanned through the work as a whole, he began to better appreciate the appeal. They were dense, intricate pieces with a rich, evocative beauty.

He also couldn't believe they could be painted by Daisy. She seemed much too...prosaic to have created the artwork.

What about her sister, Bea? Cruz had told him she was an artist. What if she had another secret identity as the mysterious Marguerite? Or this aunt Stella that Daisy had talked about. She could be the one.

He was so busy looking at the images online that he didn't realize she had returned until the dog on his lap lifted his head at the same moment the rear door opened and she deposited a bag of dog food and another bag that looked like it held dog accessories.

He fumbled with his phone, embarrassed that she'd caught him digging deeper into the mystery.

"Looking at porn?" she asked when she slid behind the wheel, surprising a laugh out of him.

"I'm not quite desperate enough to wank off in a supermarket parking lot, thanks."

On a hunch, he decided to tell her the truth. "I was doing a web search on the famous Marguerite."

She visibly tensed, then seemed to force herself to relax. "You won't let it go, will you?"

"It's you, isn't it? You don't have to lie to me, Daisy. Why keep it such a big secret? Is the anonymity simply to increase the mystique about your work?"

"You don't know what you're talking about," she snapped. "Please drop this subject right now."

He should respect her wishes. She obviously didn't want to discuss it. But somehow, he couldn't let it go. "Tell me," he said softly.

She glared at him. "Let it go," she repeated. "Why would I tell you anything? I don't even know you."

"That rhetorical question seems to suggest you have something you'd like to tell me."

She shook her head with an exasperated look. "You're crazy. The reason I don't want to tell you anything is simply because there is nothing to tell. Now drop it, unless you want to find your own ride back to Casa Del Mar."

She had a stubborn set to her jaw that convinced him she wasn't going to bend. "Fine. Keep your secrets. You know I won't stop digging, right?"

Unease flashed across her gaze, making him a little sorry for his words but more convinced than ever that she wasn't being truthful with him.

In response, she chose to start the car and change the subject. "You were supposed to come up with a name for the dog. Did you have any luck?"

He had been too busy looking at painted furniture. "No. Nothing. What about you?"

She looked at the dog in his lap, then back at the road. "Well,

THE CLIFF HOUSE

he's a French bulldog. What about Pierre or Gaston or Jean Michel?"

"He doesn't look like any of those. How about Archie? Or Otis?"

He went through a few more names as she drove through the night back to Casa Del Mar.

"What about Louie?" Gabe suggested after about a hundred other ideas. "That's French, sort of. King Louis the Fourteenth was kind of a big deal over there."

The dog's ears perked up and he gave a low bark as if in agreement.

Daisy made a face. "He doesn't exactly look like a Sun King or anyone else who should be hanging out at Versailles, for that matter, but that seems to be a winner. All right, Louie it is."

A few moments later she pulled up to the gates of Casa Del Mar and Gabe used the remote Cruz had given him to slide them open. "You don't have to drive all the way in," he said. "You can let me off here."

She ignored him and drove through the gates, for which he was secretly grateful. Much to his chagrin, he was hurting more than he wanted to admit.

She pulled up in front of the main house and he climbed out of the car and set Louie on the seat, trying not to wince like a big crybaby as pain clutched at his gut. Gabe rubbed the dog's head to distract himself and the dog whined a little, obviously sensing he was leaving.

"You'll be okay. Daisy here will take great care of you," he assured him. He couldn't have said how he knew that but he didn't have a doubt.

He was surprised at how sad he felt at leaving the dog behind. He had always thought he wasn't a pet person, mostly because the wandering lifestyle he and his father had shared hadn't been very conducive to taking along a dog or a cat.

"Thank you for watching over him," he said again to Daisy

after he had pulled his backpack and camera gear out of the back seat.

"You're welcome," she said, with a hint of hesitancy in her voice that made him suspect she was regretting her offer to take the dog.

"I'd like to stop by tomorrow to walk Louie here. Is there a time you'll be home?"

"I'll be there in the afternoon. But you don't have to walk him. I'm planning to take him into work with me. Between my assistant and me, I am sure we can find plenty of exercise for him."

"Humor me. I need to walk and also want to feel like I'm doing my part to care for him. I told you I wanted visitation rights."

She paused, clearly torn. Was it because she didn't want to see him again? If so, he only had himself to blame for pushing her so hard about Marguerite. He should have kept his mouth shut.

He wanted to promise he wouldn't ask her about the artist again but he was afraid that wasn't a vow he would be able to keep.

To his relief, she finally nodded. "That's fine. I'll be home after four. You can walk him then, assuming the vet doesn't find a chip and he's not home with his owners by then."

He wanted the dog to be reunited with his family but was also happy he now had a good excuse to see the dog again. Not to mention the intriguing Daisy McClure.

11

BEATRIZ

"Please, Mom? Can we go? Please?"

Bea gazed at Cruz and their child, frustration simmering through her like an old, forgotten song she now couldn't shake.

"You don't have other plans, do you?" Cruz asked. "I don't want to step on toes if you did. We could eat here just as easily."

Meaning, she could cook for him. She sighed.

"I have been in the studio all day and haven't thought that far ahead," she said.

Cruz beamed. "Great. Then this is the perfect night to celebrate Marisol's birthday."

Except it was three months late. Cruz had been touring during the actual birthday. He had sent a large box of presents but hadn't been able to make it here for the day in question.

She didn't want to go out to dinner with them tonight. She

was tired and her back hurt from being hunched over a sculpture commissioned by one of her favorite clients.

But she didn't know how to say no to either of them.

"Fine. We can go."

"Yay!" Cruz stepped forward and kissed her cheek. He looked as excited at the idea of a simple dinner as Mari did when her favorite YouTube star came out with a new video.

He smiled at her, that old, familiar smile that used to make her feel safe and warm and loved. "This is going to be great. We'll be all together as a family again, just like old times."

"I just need to fix my hair again. Then I'll be ready."

"Your hair looks beautiful, as always," Cruz said, that warm light in his eyes that used to make her glow for days. It had taken four years of marriage for her to figure out he used it on everyone.

"Five minutes," she promised.

In her room she quickly pulled her hair into her favorite classic yet comfortable bun and reapplied the makeup she had put on earlier that day.

She changed into one of her favorite loose dresses and went looking for the coral-colored sweater she liked to wear with it, especially when going to restaurants that liked to keep their air-conditioning set permanently to arctic tundra.

Her cardigan was out by the pool, she remembered. She'd worn it earlier in the day when she'd been sitting out there, trying to sketch out some designs while the light was good.

Her master bedroom had its own private exit to the pool, so she hurried out that door, intending to grab the sweater and circle back inside to the living room, where Cruz and Mari were waiting.

She found it right where she left it, on the table next to her favorite chaise. Just as she picked it up and shrugged into it, the door to the guesthouse opened and Shane walked out.

He wore a dark blue dress shirt and gray slacks and looked completely luscious.

"Oh. Hello." She felt completely flustered, which annoyed the heck out of her.

This was Shane. Her best friend. She had no reason to feel awkward around him, simply because she had started seeing him in an entirely new light.

She forced herself to step forward and give him a casual hug. He smelled delicious, too, with just a hint of some sporty, sexy aftershave she had only known him to wear a few times.

"You look nice," he said when she stepped away.

"Thanks. I was going to say the same thing to you. Are you heading to a football thing?"

The high school team he coached hadn't opened its season yet but she knew Shane often got together socially with his staff.

He shifted. "No, actually. I've, uh, got a date."

A date.

The news seemed to wallop her from out of nowhere, as if he'd picked up one of Mari's boogie boards from the pool storage and whacked her over the head with it.

He dated. She knew he did. She had even tried to set him up with friends of hers, with little success. Since he'd moved into the guesthouse, though, she hadn't been aware of him going out. She should have expected it, though.

She did her best to try for a casual tone. "Oh. With whom?"

"The new French teacher at the high school. Mademoiselle Martin."

"That sounds nice," she lied. They were friends. She should be happy for him, not feeling suddenly sick at the images suddenly flashing through her head of him sharing croissants with an elegantly dressed, perfectly made-up woman.

The woman taught French. She wasn't necessarily French herself. The reminder didn't help.

"What about you? Where are you off to?"

She didn't want to tell him, suddenly. He and her ex-husband weren't exactly the best of buddies—probably her fault, since she had cried on Shane's shoulder as her marriage was imploding.

"Cruz is taking us to dinner to celebrate Mari's birthday."

He raised an eyebrow. "You mean the birthday she had months ago?"

"He was on tour in Europe at the time and couldn't arrange to make it back in time."

Cruz could easily have flown Mari to Italy to meet him but he hadn't suggested it and she hadn't, either. She'd been selfishly glad. She liked having her daughter to herself on Mari's birthday.

"So a makeup birthday dinner."

"Yes."

"Sounds like fun. Have a good evening," he said.

"Same to you. Say *bonjour* to the new French teacher."

His mouth worked into what might have been a smile as he turned away, but she couldn't quite tell.

She waved him off, then let her hand flop back to her side when he was out of sight.

Well. That answered that. He couldn't have made it more plain that he didn't care about her spending time with Cruz. She had obviously imagined this new dynamic to their relationship, the awareness simmering between them. And Cruz had obviously been imagining things when he hinted Shane was interested in being more than friends.

He was dating other women and hadn't blinked when she told him she was spending time with her ex-husband. She needed to accept that she and Shane were friends. It was unfair of her to suddenly change the rules and want more.

When she walked into the kitchen, she found Mari and Cruz watching a video featuring people lip-synching one of his songs. They were laughing uproariously at some of the garbled lyrics. She had to admit, it was pretty funny how people could get the words so wrong.

Who was she to laugh at anyone else when she was getting everything wrong in her life right about now?

"Okay. I'm ready," she said as soon as the clip ended, before Mari could find another one. "Sorry to keep you waiting."

Cruz flicked the remote to turn off the small wall-mounted TV. "You were worth the wait, babe. You look great."

She had been working all day and felt frumpy and disheveled, but she would be lying if she said she didn't feel a burst of warmth at the appreciation in his eyes.

She was a woman. She liked to feel attractive to *someone*, even if it wasn't necessarily the person she wanted noticing her.

"Thanks," she answered.

When they walked outside to the circular driveway, she found one of Cruz's shiny black luxury Cadillac SUVs. He probably had a half dozen of them.

He held the passenger door open for her—props to him for that—and helped Mari into the back seat.

"No driver tonight?" Cruz usually didn't go anywhere without Diego, who was both bodyguard and chauffeur.

"No need. I'm with my family in Cape Sanctuary. Nothing will happen here."

She doubted he had expected anything to happen to him that night in Dallas, either, she wanted to point out. In the interest of getting along, she held her tongue.

"Dad," Mari said as soon as Cruz pulled out of the driveway, "did I tell you about the new friend I made? Aunt Stella introduced me to her the other day. She just moved here from Pasadena."

"Oh, yeah?"

"Her name is Rowan. She's a year older than me and she's super nice. Aunt Stella took us shopping for swimsuits because Rowan is going to come over the day after tomorrow to hang out and meet some of my other friends."

"That should be fun."

"Aunt Stella thought she should make new friends before school starts."

"I still can't believe you're going to middle school."

"I know, right?"

While Cruz drove faster than Bea necessarily liked, Mari regaled her father all the way to the restaurant with a long story about the classes she was taking and where her locker was and how she hoped it would be close to her new friend Rowan's.

He found a decent parking space outside The Fishwife, Mari's favorite. As usual, when they walked inside, people did a double take as they spotted Cruz Romero. Bea could see the whispered conversations begin.

The townspeople of Cape Sanctuary usually left their hometown boy alone but the tourist season was still in full swing for another month or so and she could sense heads begin to swivel in their direction.

Oh, yeah. Now she remembered why she disliked going out in public with him. Her ex-husband commanded attention wherever he went.

The hostess was leading them out to the patio, at Cruz's request, to the prime seats in the house near the railing that looked over the bay when they passed a familiar figure.

Bea stumbled a little. Seriously? There were at least a dozen nice restaurants in Cape Sanctuary. With all those options, why did Shane have to choose this one?

Mari, of course, lit up when she spotted her buddy. "Hey, Shane!" she exclaimed as they were led past the table where he sat with his very pretty French teacher—who was, in fact, wearing an elaborately twisted silk scarf in a very continental style, as Bea might have predicted.

Shane didn't look nearly as thrilled to see the three of them. He glowered for a moment, which actually made Bea's spirits brighten. Was it possible he wasn't as sanguine about her being with Cruz as he had appeared earlier?

"Hi, Mari, Bea. Cruz."

Cruz put his arms around both her and Mari, clearly staking his territory. "Landry. Fancy meeting you here."

"We're celebrating my birthday again," Mari chirped. "I might even get birthday cake."

"That's what I hear. Happy birthday. Again."

The woman with him was giving Cruz a starstruck look, one Bea had seen countless times before.

She made a slight sound, halfway between a gurgle and a sigh, which compelled Shane to make the introduction.

"Vanessa Martin, this is my, uh, friend and landlady, Beatriz Romero, her daughter, Mari, and her ex-husband, Cruz. Everyone, this is Vanessa. She's a new teacher at the high school, just moved here from Bakersfield."

Bea wanted to dislike the woman but she had such a soft spot for teachers after seeing all the hard work her aunt Stella put in to do her best for her students.

"Hi, Vanessa. Nice to meet you."

"Uh. Thanks." The woman managed to shift her gaze from Cruz long enough to give Bea a tentative smile before she looked back at him with a dazzled expression.

"Mr. Romero," she said breathlessly. "I'm a huge fan. My students turned me on to your music and I just love it so much. I have you in my head all the time when I'm running."

Naturally, she would be a runner, thin and graceful and lovely. Bea was lucky if she could walk down the sidewalk without tripping over a crack.

Cruz gave her his most charming smile. "Is that right? I hope I'm good company."

"The best," she gushed. "You keep me running for miles. My Cruz playlist is my very favorite. If I had you on vinyl, that track would be worn down."

Knowing Cruz, he would have stayed there longer, soaking

in the woman's praise, but the hostess politely cleared her throat and Cruz took the hint.

"It was lovely to meet you, Vanessa Martin," he said with more of his charm, before letting the server lead them the rest of the way to their table.

They were some distance away, much to her relief, and Bea deliberately chose a seat that put her back to Shane and his French teacher.

They were able to order their food without interruption and the rest of the meal passed in relative peace. On the whole, the other diners left them alone to enjoy the patio's lovely ambience and delicious food. Bea didn't have to say much as Mari and Cruz seemed to have plenty to talk about.

She tried not to be too aware of Shane and his date. Okay, she *might* have dropped her napkin a few times as an excuse to turn around.

Right after ordering her favorite dessert here, the chocolate lava cake that always took extra time, Mari excused herself to use the bathroom. When Bea rose to go with her, Mari frowned. "Mom. I'm eleven years old. I'm about to go to middle school. Do you really think I still need a grown-up to take me to the bathroom?"

She sighed and sat back down, knowing she was right. She wasn't happy her daughter was growing up but she was even less thrilled at being alone with Cruz.

"She's a great kid. We did pretty good with that one, didn't we?"

Mari had been a sweet baby who grew up into an adorable toddler and a pretty decent child. Bea thought she'd been a good mother but Mari had made things extremely easy so far.

Every moment of every day, she was grateful for their child.

"She's terrific. The one good thing that came out of our marriage."

"Oh, I wouldn't say that." Cruz picked up her fingers and

played with her rings idly. Though she couldn't see them from her vantage point, she was keenly aware of Shane and his date, some distance behind them.

"Have you thought more about what I said the other night, about giving the two of us another shot?"

Everything inside her seemed to tighten. "Of course I have," she answered quietly. "How could I not think about it?"

"And?"

She slipped her fingers away. "We're different people than we were twelve years ago when we ran away together. I feel like an entire ocean full of water has passed underneath that particular bridge."

He again placed his hand over hers, trapping it against the table and leaving her vaguely claustrophobic.

"Don't you feel like we owe it to our baby girl? She would love to have us back together. You know she would."

Before she could answer, two young women in their early twenties came over. "Sorry to bother you, Cruz, but we just love you and wonder if we could take a selfie with you."

Some celebrities would have told them no, that selfies could wait until this important conversation with his ex-wife was done. Cruz, on the other hand, jumped right up and put on his Sexy Pop Star face.

"You got it, girls," he said. He beamed at them, slinging an arm around one on each side.

"Do you mind?" One of the young women handed her phone to Bea.

She did mind. She minded very much, but since she couldn't very well toss the phone on the table without looking like a bitch, she forced a smile, rose from the table and stepped back to fit all three of them in the frame.

That seemed to start a chain reaction where every other diner on the patio wanted to take a picture with Cruz, and even people from inside the restaurant.

All of them handed their phones to Bea, barely acknowledging her.

Mari came back into the middle of the chaos. Their child rolled her eyes at the people making a fuss over her dad and started working on her chocolate lava cake.

After a few more moments the maître d' finally stepped forward and asked the other diners to return to their meals and allow Mr. Romero's table a little bit of peace to finish their desserts.

She sat back down but had lost her appetite for the fresh fruit tart she usually loved here.

The interruptions provided a stark reminder to Bea of one of the key reasons her marriage hadn't survived after Cruz found sudden fame with his first album.

He was always there for his fans. It was in his nature. He couldn't say no to anyone, no matter the circumstances or the venue. She certainly understood that he was a public person and had to be responsive to those who basically paid his salary, but the result was that she tended to disappear and she hated it. She hated the resentment; she hated the frustration; she hated always knowing she and Marisol would never be first in his world.

"You were gone a long time," she said now to her daughter. "Is everything okay?"

"Yes. I stopped to talk to Shane about our Pinewood Derby car."

"What Pinewood Derby car?" Cruz asked.

Mari immediately looked as if she regretted opening her mouth. Bea didn't blame her. Cruz would posture and strut and claim he could make a far better car than anyone else.

"Oh, nothing. Just a little project we're working on," Mari said.

"For what?"

There was no avoiding it. They would have to tell him. She

and her daughter exchanged looks, Mari's pleading with Bea to help her through the awkwardness.

She finally spoke. "Mari's Girl Scout troop is having a daddy-daughter event the same weekend as the festival. They're having a Pinewood Derby and watching the fireworks together. Mari asked Shane to help her."

"I talked to you about a month ago and you said you would be on tour. Remember? When you said you couldn't come, I asked Shane."

"Plans change. I'll be here the rest of the month, so you can just tell Shane you don't need his help anymore."

"But I already invited him. We already started working on my car." Mari looked distressed. "I can't un-ask him now. That would just be rude."

"I'm sure he would understand. If it's a father-daughter event, your father ought to take you to it, not some jock who moved into your pool house."

Bea narrowed her gaze. "Shane is a well-respected teacher and coach."

"And he's our friend," Mari added.

"And he's our friend," she agreed. She didn't add that Shane was the one there to help Mari with homework or teach her how to make a layup or cheer her on at her soccer games.

Cruz seemed to suddenly realize their discussion was drawing attention from nearby tables. He immediately tempered his stormy expression.

That was another thing she had despised about being married to a celebrity. They could never have any authentic conversation in public without a constant awareness that people were watching them.

They shouldn't be having this discussion now, anyway. She didn't want to ruin Mari's birthday dinner, even if they were celebrating the event three months late.

"We can talk about this later," she said firmly. "Right now let's enjoy our desserts."

Cruz looked as if he wanted to say more but something in her features must have changed his mind. "We have time. The arts festival is still, what, three weeks away? Maybe Mari should build a car with both of us and then decide which one she likes better."

That wasn't an ideal solution, forcing an eleven-year-old girl to choose between her father, whom she loved, and a dear friend whom she had made a previous commitment to.

"We can figure it out," Cruz said amiably. "Meanwhile, I was thinking about going horseback riding tomorrow. If you're free, maybe you both could come with me."

"I can't," she answered with honest regret. She did love horseback riding and knew Cruz kept several excellent horses at Casa Del Mar. "I have to drive up to Trinidad in the morning to take a couple of my pieces to a gallery there. They've almost sold out of their inventory of my work and I promised the owner I would bring more."

She was particularly proud of that, especially the fact that she had achieved it on her own merits, not for being Cruz Romero's ex-wife.

"What about you, pumpkin? Want to go riding with me?"

"Yes," she exclaimed in excitement. "I haven't seen Penelope since the last time you came to town and we went riding. I missed her."

"Great. We'll go bright and early. I can pick you up. Better yet," he said, "how could we convince your mom to let you stay the night at Casa Del Mar?"

She finished as much as she could of her own tart and set her fork down beside her plate. She had planned to take Mari with her to the seaside town north of Cape Sanctuary but didn't have the heart to disappoint her daughter.

"I had the background checks from Peter and everything checks out with your guests. I was going to tell you that at dinner so we could work out a custody schedule while you're in town, but your fan club kind of interrupted things."

"You know how annoying they can be," he said, but she was quite certain he looked smug, rather than annoyed.

She saw Mari wave and turned around to see Shane helping his date out of her chair, their meal apparently finished.

He caught her gaze, and the expression in his blue eyes, complex and unidentifiable, left her restless and achy and ready for her own evening to be done.

Back at her house, after Mari gathered pajamas and clothes she could wear riding the next day, the two of them took off for his house down the road.

Bea watched them go, her mind spinning. Cruz made it clear several times over the course of the evening that he wanted to get back together with her. How could she possibly do it, step back into that world that left her so anxious and uncomfortable? She didn't want to, but would Mari be happier if her mother and father were together so she didn't have to split her attention between them?

She couldn't answer that question tonight but also sensed she wouldn't be able to sleep for some time, so she opted to take Jojo to her studio to get things ready for her trip the next day.

Once at work, surrounded by clay and paints and watercolors she used in her mixed-media canvases, she felt the tension leave her shoulders. Here she felt like herself, as if the rest of the time she was only pretending.

She picked up a new canvas and began an idea that had been kicking around in her head, and before she realized it, an hour had passed and she had done the preliminary outline for a new painting.

"What do you think, Jojo?" she said to Mari's little dog. "Is it working for you?"

The dog cocked his head as if actually studying the painting of Sanctuary Head, where crazy kids dived into the water during high tide.

She decided to celebrate her progress by sitting in the hot tub for a few moments to work out the kinks in her shoulders. She changed quickly into her favorite comfortable one-piece swimming suit, shoved her feet into flip-flops and headed out her master bedroom door to the pool.

A figure was swimming laps there while a big yellow Lab watched from the pool deck and she wondered if this was what had led her outside.

Her mouth went dry and for a moment she stood frozen, not knowing what to do. The coward in her told her to go back inside but she hesitated. It was her house, she reminded herself. Her pool. And Shane was her friend.

She needed to regain that friendship somehow. After a moment, she made her way stealthily behind him. This was the sort of thing they used to do all the time. Tease each other, laugh, dunk each other in the pool. She wanted that back, desperately.

He didn't seem to notice she was there, or Jojo joining up with Sally. Or maybe he did and was simply ignoring her. She pushed away that worry and focused instead on regaining the fun and spontaneity of their prior relationship. Feeling mischievous and playful, she swam quietly behind him, and just before he made the turn, she reached out and grabbed his leg.

Surprising him was a grave mistake. She knew it instantly.

"Hey!" He kicked out, catching her right in the stomach.

Her breath tangled somewhere in her chest and she clutched her stomach as her vision grayed a little.

He looked horrified when he realized what he had done and swam toward her. "I'm so sorry, Bea. Are you okay? I'm an idiot! You startled me and I acted without thinking."

"My fault," she managed to gasp out when she could draw air into her lungs again. "I was…just teasing you. I…thought maybe you…knew I was there."

"I was focused on the workout, I guess. Are you okay?"

"I will be…when my lungs kick in again."

She sucked in a breath and then another until the tightness in her solar plexus eased.

"I really am sorry."

She shook her head. "Don't be. I should know better than to interrupt you when you're in the groove."

She paused, taking another breath, then asked a question she wasn't entirely sure she wanted to know the answer to. "How was your date?"

He treaded water for a moment then flopped onto his back and floated beside her. The night was lush with stars and the quiet murmur of the ocean below them. "It was nice. She seems great."

"Will you see her again?"

"Probably."

If she was a true friend, she would be thrilled he had found someone he liked with potential. She would want him to be happy. He was a good man who deserved someone wonderful.

She didn't want to feel this jealousy that pinched at her like a snotty girl in gym class.

"How about yours?" he asked. "Cruz drew quite a crowd, as usual."

"The food is always good at The Fishwife. You know I love their halibut."

"I'm glad."

They floated for a moment beside each other as the waterfall rippled and the moon crested the mountains east of Cape Sanctuary. She was intensely aware of him beside her, athletic and graceful and gorgeous.

She hadn't realized she'd made a sound until he splashed her a little.

"That was a big sigh. What's wrong?"

She couldn't find the words to tell him about these feelings she was beginning to realize had been growing inside her for a long time. What if he laughed at her? What if he told her he could never consider her anything other than a friend or that kissing her would be like kissing his sister?

Their friendship was too dear to her. She couldn't risk ruining everything.

"Cruz wants to get back together," she finally said, floating a little away from him.

He rose to his feet, the wake washing over her. "Are you going to?"

"I don't know," she answered honestly. "Some part of me thinks of how much easier it would be on Mari if we were back together. No more shared custody, no more having to split her time between us. I'm just not sure I'm ready for all the...stuff that comes with it."

She finally risked a look at him. He looked tough, dangerous, carved from the finest Carrara marble. "What would you suggest I do?"

A muscle tightened in his jaw and he headed for the pool ladder. "I can't make that decision for you, Bea. This one is yours."

She followed after him and reached for her towel. "You're my best friend. I'm asking advice. I'm interested in what you have to say."

He wiped off his face with his towel and lowered it to meet her gaze, his expression unreadable.

"My advice? Don't ask me whether you should get back with your ex. I'm the last person whose opinion you need. I know how much he broke your heart."

"I'm not in love with him anymore. If I went back, it would be strictly for Mari's sake. My heart wouldn't be involved."

"You can tell yourself that story but I doubt you and Cruz would be on the same page. He's probably looking for more."

He was right. Cruz had a pathological need for everyone to

love him. "So you're saying I either have to give everything or nothing."

"I'm saying I'm the wrong person to ask. What do Stella or Daisy say?"

"I haven't told them," she admitted.

"There you go. Start with them."

She could only imagine what they would say. Daisy had married a man decades older than she was, for reasons Bea still didn't understand, and Stella had never dated anyone more than four or five times.

"Sure. Okay. Thanks anyway."

He looked as if he had something else to say but must have changed his mind. He slung his towel over his broad shoulders. "I've got practice early in the morning. I should go."

"Right. Well, thanks for the swim."

She reached up to kiss his cheek, as she had done dozens of times before. Did he have any idea how badly she wanted to slide her mouth to his? To press her body against his?

She didn't do either of those things. She simply stepped away, forced a smile and watched him whistle for his dog then go inside the guesthouse while the air eddied, cool and empty, around her.

Bea tried not to brood the next day as she drove to Trinidad with her pieces, but she had a feeling she wasn't successful.

Even Jojo, whom she had taken along for company, seemed to give her a wide berth. She couldn't blame the dog. She wasn't fit to be around anyone, human or canine.

The drive back down the coast to home cheered her up considerably and she felt better by the time she pulled into her driveway behind another of Cruz's luxury SUVs, this one a white Escalade.

He must have brought Mari home earlier than planned. She let Jojo out of the car, knowing the dog would lead her to Mari.

Sure enough, when she followed the dog, she found her daughter and Cruz kicking around a soccer ball on the grass near the pool.

Cruz stopped what he was doing and gave her what she used to call his smolder look, half-closed bedroom eyes and that secretive smile that drove women wild when he sang.

It used to drive her wild, too. Now it just left her uncomfortable.

"Hi, Mom!" Mari's features were bright and happy, and love for this girl was a thick, heavy ache in Bea's chest. She and Cruz had screwed up so many things but their child was a miracle.

"Hi, baby. How was your day?"

"Super. We had a ton of fun. We went on a ride and then went down to the beach to surf a little."

She shivered. "Crazy people. That water is freezing."

"We had on wet suits. Plus, it's a warm day," Cruz assured her. "We were careful, I promise."

"I believe you," she said softly.

She did. Cruz was always careful about Mari's safety—far more than he was his own.

"Want to join us?" Cruz asked. The eagerness on his features was almost painful to see. "We could use one more out here."

She wanted to soak in her jetted tub with a good romance novel and a glass of wine but she had a feeling that wasn't going to happen.

"Sure. Just let me change."

"You look great, babe. Really great."

She rolled her eyes. She wore four-inch heels and an off-white linen tailored pantsuit with a vibrant turquoise shirt out of what she called her Successful Artist wardrobe.

Sometimes she had to dress the part of a fashionable creative, especially when dealing with gallery owners.

"I'll go change," she said firmly. While the bathtub still beckoned, she changed instead to capris and a T-shirt and pulled her hair up into a quick messy bun then hurried outside to join the soccer fray.

They spent the next hour in the sweet August sunshine, chasing the ball around her lawn and playing with Jojo.

It was almost more relaxing than that bath would have been, much to her surprise.

"That was fun," Cruz said after she went into the house to bring back chilled water bottles for all of them.

He looked gorgeous, relaxed and happy with his dark hair plastered to his head and his T-shirt dampened with sweat.

If his fans could see him now, in this natural element while he played soccer with his daughter, there would be mass hysteria.

They all flopped onto the grass. Jojo crawled onto her lap and she sipped at her water bottle, wondering if there might be a chance they could make things work a second time.

"I have a proposition for you," Cruz said.

Bea frowned. She did *not* want him bringing up his desire to get back together in front of their daughter. That would back her into a corner and leave her in a position to disappoint Mari all over again.

"What sort of proposition?" she asked warily.

"I have to fly down to LA tomorrow. Since I canceled the next few weeks of the tour, I've had a last-minute request from some rich foreign businessman to play at his daughter's sixteenth birthday party. I've been told I can take guests, if I want. I'd like those guests to be the two of you."

"Why would we possibly want to go to a birthday party for someone we don't know?" Bea asked.

He grinned. "Trust me, you'll want to go to this one. It's an after-hours private event at Universal Studios. The park will be closed to everyone but the few hundred guests of this birthday party and any guests I bring along."

The sheer decadence of closing down an entire amusement

park for a private party astonished her, though she knew it shouldn't.

"Wow! Are you serious?" Mari's face lit up. "That would be so awesome! Can we go, Mom? You were saying the other day that we should plan a trip down there to see Hogwarts."

"What about Rowan? I thought she was coming over tomorrow to hang out with you."

"You can invite her, too," Cruz said. "There's plenty of room on the plane."

If they invited Rowan, they would likely have to invite her father, whom Bea had only met once. On the other hand, she could invite Stella along, too, and work on matchmaking.

"I suppose we could do that," she said slowly. "I'll have to talk to Rowan's father. It could be your one big fun event before school starts again."

Mari's face lit up. "Yes. Thank you."

She ran to her father and hugged him tightly. Cruz grinned. Years ago that smile would have sent Bea's insides spinning. Now she felt nothing.

"What time do you want to leave?"

"The party doesn't start until eight and I don't perform until ten. What if we left at two p.m.? That would give us time to fly down and have an early dinner in the city first."

"All right. I'll make some phone calls and see what I can arrange with Stella and Dr. Clayton, Rowan's father."

"Invite Daisy along, too, if you want."

She would extend an invitation but was almost positive her sister would have some excuse for why she couldn't come. Sometimes she felt an almost physical ache, missing the fun, mischievous sister she remembered from her girlhood. Other times she wondered if she had imagined her.

"What about Shane?" Mari asked. "Can he come? He loves roller coasters."

Cruz didn't look thrilled with that idea and Bea quickly

stepped in. "It's a busy time of year for Shane. He probably wouldn't be able to make it anyway."

Mari looked disappointed. "That's too bad. Maybe we can take him next time."

Bea didn't see that happening, ever, especially since Cruz and Shane barely tolerated being in the same room together. She didn't even want to imagine the chaos that might occur on a small private airplane.

1 2

DAISY

"**Y**ou want me to *what?*"

Daisy stared, speechless at her sister's face on her phone screen.

"We're flying to Los Angeles tomorrow afternoon with Cruz and going to Universal Studios, where he's performing at a private event. The park will be closed, just for a small group. No lines, no crowds. Just us and a few hundred strangers celebrating some girl's sixteenth birthday. Doesn't that sound fun?"

It did, actually. But Daisy couldn't possibly drop everything and leave right now.

"This is sort of out of the blue, isn't it?"

"Yes." Bea managed to look both exasperated and amused. "You know how Cruz can be. Apparently, he only took the gig at the last minute, after his schedule opened up from the cancellation of his remaining tour dates. For the record, Stella is coming, too, along with her old boyfriend, the sexy Dr. Clayton, and his daughter."

Daisy made a face at her sister's obstinacy on that particular topic. "We have no proof he was ever a boyfriend."

"He was. Trust me. I know he was the man I saw in that picture she used to keep. This trip will give me the perfect chance to test the waters there and see if there's any chance they could get together after all these years."

She wanted to warn Bea not to meddle again but knew she was wasting her breath.

"You have to come with us. Cruz says there's plenty of room on the plane. Of course there's room. I mean, why would he take a small plane when a big one looks so much more impressive?"

Cruz did love to spend his money but Daisy knew he could certainly afford it. In a case like this, the person throwing the party was probably footing the bill to fly him in, anyway.

"It's going to be fun," Bea pressed. "I know how much you love Harry Potter."

"I do. It's true."

For several years it had seemed as if the books and movies had been one of the few things she and Bea had in common.

"Then come with us! It will be so much fun. Like when we were kids again!"

They had never gone to amusement parks when their mother had been alive, unless you counted the cheesy carnival rides at some of the county fairs where Jewel had tried to sell her artwork.

That sort of thing hadn't been Jewel's scene and she would have hated it. Bea went to Disneyland a few times with her own father. Of course, he never offered to include Daisy in the outings. Why would he?

"I wish I could," she said, somewhat surprised it was true, "but I'm afraid I can't be away that long right now."

Bea frowned. "Don't tell me you have too much work to do.

You're always working. You need to relax once in a while. It will be good for you."

"I can't," she said.

"What's so important that you can't spend an evening with your family, Dais?"

Left with no choice, she scooped up Louie from where he had been chewing one of the toys she bought at the grocery store the other night with Gabriel Ellison.

"This," she answered.

Bea said nothing for a full thirty seconds, until Daisy thought for sure she'd lost the connection. "Oh, my word. He is the *cutest*! When did you get a dog? I can't believe you didn't tell me! You need to bring him over to make friends with Jojo and Sally. They will love him."

"He's not mine," she said quickly, though she was beginning to wish with all her heart he was. "He's a rescue and we're trying to find his owners."

"We?"

"Uh, the person who found him on the cliffside. You don't know anyone who might be missing a little French bulldog, do you?"

Belatedly, it occurred to her she should have asked Bea right away. Her sister and her aunt knew everyone and everything that went on in Cape Sanctuary.

"I haven't heard of anyone but I can ask around. Oh, he's so cute. I can't believe you're fostering a dog. You're the one who's always telling me you don't have time to take care of a pet."

She didn't. But in this case, Louie needed her.

"How did this all come about?" Bea asked.

"It's a long story. I'll tell you when you get back. I don't feel good about leaving him with a stranger right now. He's barely getting used to me, so I'd better not go with you to LA. It sounds fun, though. I'm sure you'll have a great time. Enjoy some frozen Butterbeer for me."

"I will. If you change your mind between now and when we leave tomorrow, just let me know."

Bea hung up a few moments later but Daisy didn't want to move from her spot looking out at the ocean, especially not when she realized Louie had fallen asleep on her lap.

The dog had slept beside her bed since Gabe found him. Every morning he awakened her with a little friendly lick on her cheek that completely stole her heart.

She had it bad for this little creature.

She and Gabe had done their best to find the owner. She had contacted all the vet clinics and shelters in the region and had put notices all over town.

Maybe no one would come forward, but she couldn't imagine there wasn't someone out there missing him. He was the sweetest dog, content to sit at her feet while she worked at her day job and then entertain himself in her studio at night.

She sat for a few more moments, enjoying the calm, and may have drifted off like the dog. The doorbell jolted both of them awake.

"Are you expecting anyone?" she asked Louie.

He hopped down from her lap and raced to the door, plopping expectantly next to it until she headed over and looked through the peephole.

Butterflies suddenly started twirling around inside her stomach when she found Gabe on the other side.

How had she managed to forget how gorgeous he was, how he made everything inside her sigh?

For just a moment she was tempted to ignore the doorbell and pretend she wasn't home but Louie barked a greeting, one of the few times she'd heard him bark at anything.

"Thanks for nothing," she muttered, and unlocked the door.

"Hi," she said, hating her voice for trembling a little.

"Hi. I was out for my walk and figured I would stop by and see how our little guy is doing."

"Louie is good, aren't you, buddy?"

The little dog wagged his tail so hard it made his giant ears quiver.

"You still haven't come up with another name?"

She shrugged. "That's the one he answers to. I don't know if that's really his name but it works. You like it, don't you, Louie?"

The dog barked and licked her hand. Gabe unexpectedly smiled and she ordered herself not to stare.

"Louie it is, I guess," he said.

"Any news on his owners?" she asked, suddenly afraid that was why he had come.

"No. I had a phone call today and one yesterday from people claiming he belonged to them. They couldn't describe him or identify the pattern on his collar, though, so I knew they were just trying to get a free French bulldog."

Gabe had been deliberately vague in his description of the dog to avoid sleazy people coming forward to claim him when Louie didn't belong to them.

"I told you I wanted visitation," he went on. "I came over to see if I could take him for a walk."

"Are you up for that? Did you have to have those stitches repaired?"

"No. I'm fine, as long as I don't overdo. No more cliffside rescues, I guess."

He smiled at her again and Daisy felt her knees go weak.

She was an idiot.

She steeled herself against him. "The leash I bought is in the kitchen. I'll go grab it for you."

"Better yet, why don't you come with us?"

"You want me to go on a walk with you."

"Sure. Why not?"

She did not want to do that. The man was exceedingly dangerous for her peace of mind.

"You can keep me from falling over if I get dizzy," he added, giving her no idea how to refuse.

She could use the exercise, anyway. She had been sitting most of the day, poring over accounts. What would be the harm in going on a walk with him?

"In that case, I'd better go along," she said before she could talk herself out of it. "Cruz would never forgive me if I let you get hurt on my watch."

When he was happy about something, Gabe Ellison's green eyes lit up until they were the color of new leaves unfurling on winter-bare branches.

Not that she noticed or anything.

"Great," he said with another of those dangerous smiles. "Louie and I will just hang out here while we wait."

She hurried to the kitchen and picked up the retractable leash she had bought the night before then returned to her living room.

After she clipped it on, she handed it to Gabe and he walked into the August evening and began heading down the trail beside the road that wound its way along the cliffs, in the opposite direction from Casa Del Mar. The evening was lovely, warm and golden with summer's seductive promise. This was her favorite time of day, about an hour before sunset when the colors were soft and glorious and the air smelled of the sea and sage and pine.

"I'm not sure how far he will be able to go," she warned. "He sleeps a lot and still seems pretty weak from his ordeal."

"We have that in common, then. I feel the same way. We don't have to go far."

Poor man. She could imagine how hard being temporarily sidelined must feel to someone who had led such an active, adventurous life.

"How are you feeling, really?"

He was silent for several more steps, then answered her with what she guessed was more honesty than he gave most people who asked.

"Mostly fine. It hurts, but a little less every day. At this point I'm just frustrated at how weak I still feel. I don't make a very good patient, apparently. Funny, the things you learn about yourself when you need medical treatment."

"This can't be the first serious injury you've ever had. Not when your whole life has been based on risk."

"I suppose I've been lucky up to now. I broke my arm when I was a kid, but I don't remember much about it. We were living in Africa in a little village. The healer for the tribe just washed it in sacred water and then used a couple of sticks for a splint. For a cast, they used leaves and rope."

His life and the experiences he'd had were completely beyond her comprehension. She would not have been able to survive that kind of chaos.

Bad enough that Jewel moved her and Beatriz from hotel to hotel, trailer park to crappy apartment, to homeless shelter. At least they had always had running water, electricity and access to Western medicine—as far as she could remember, anyway.

"You look shocked," he observed.

"A little," she admitted. "It probably seemed perfectly *normal* to you. Growing up in such unique circumstances, I mean."

"I wouldn't say *normal*. And unique is one way of putting it. Others would call it primitive or dangerous or crazy. They did call it that. My mother, for instance. But it was the life I knew, at least from about five or six."

"What about before that?" The question seemed intrusive, and she wanted to immediately call it back, but Gabe didn't seem to mind.

"The first five years were pretty normal, if that is the word you want to use. What most people would consider normal, anyway. We lived outside Wellington, New Zealand. My dad had a job working construction. My mum was a schoolteacher."

New Zealand! That must be his accent, though she didn't think it was a full-on Kiwi, more like an amalgamation of all the places he had lived as a child.

"Like my aunt Stella. She teaches at the middle school."

"It's a worthy profession."

"If you do it right."

"I've heard my mother was good at it—until she decided she wanted something different. She ended up leaving my dad and me for someone she met online."

Daisy frowned. "She left? That's unusual, especially in a woman who must enjoy children or she wouldn't have become a schoolteacher."

She wondered if she had spoken out of turn when his features hardened.

"You would think so, right? But her new Italian boyfriend didn't want children along—especially not a child from her first marriage to another man. Mum decided I was a small sacrifice she was willing to make in exchange for the lifestyle her new husband could provide."

He spoke the words without bitterness but she had to imagine it couldn't be a painless memory. Poor lost little boy. She pictured him, five years old, big, haunted green eyes, trying to understand why his mother didn't want him anymore.

"I'm sorry that happened to you. It must have been terribly difficult."

Walking beside her with his slightly uneven gait, he shrugged. "I still had my father."

Oh, yes. Chet Ellison, who had bequeathed his rugged good looks and chiseled jaw to his son. "I used to watch your father's adventure shows on Saturday afternoons," she admitted. "How did he go from working construction to kayaking down the Amazon?"

He gave a gruff laugh. "You could say being abandoned by my mum did a number on both of us. My father reacted by becoming more headstrong and reckless. He was never happy unless we were off on some new adventure and he never wanted to stay in one place for very long."

"We have that in common," she said quietly. "My...my mother was much the same way."

"Your mother was a reckless adventurer?"

This time she was the one who laughed. "In her own way, I suppose. Life was an adventure to Jewel. She was an artist, one of those daydreaming, head-in-the-clouds types who prefers to dwell in the abstract instead of in hard reality. It's easier sometimes to focus on the brilliant masterpiece you're creating in your head rather than the fact that there's no food in the house for your daughters."

She hadn't meant to say that last part. It sounded entirely too self-pitying. The reality had not been that bad, anyway. Certainly, there had been times they went hungry but she had usually been able to scrounge something for her and Bea at least. She had only had to resort to panhandling a few times to feed her sister.

She didn't like thinking about that time in her life. She still woke up sometimes from nightmares where she was digging in garbage cans to find food.

Things had never been that bleak for them. She had never *actually* scrounged through trash for food, but to a child trying to take care of her younger sister, that desperation had felt very real.

"This is a beautiful view here," he said, pausing when they reached a spot where someone had placed a bench between two giant pines that framed the ocean beyond. "I don't think I would ever get tired of it."

"It is spectacular, isn't it? Why don't we sit and give you and Louie a rest?"

He accepted her suggestion with an alacrity that told her more than she suspected he ever would about how he was really feeling.

They sat together while the wind moaned in the pines and a

songbird trilled from a branch overhead. She looked out to sea. Soon the gray whales would be heading back down to Mexico for the winter. It was a little early in the year to see whale spouts but she never stopped looking.

"So. Tell me how you became Marguerite."

She jolted, taken completely by surprise. She should have known their quiet moment of peace wouldn't last.

"This again? I told you. I'm only her business manager." The words sounded feeble and ineffectual, even to her. Gabe was obviously not convinced, either.

"Here's the thing. I don't believe you. You can feed me that business manager line until you're blue in the face but I still won't bite. I know you're Marguerite, Daisy. You don't have to continue denying it."

"You don't know anything," she snapped, then wanted to groan. Good grief. She sounded like she was eight years old, lashing out at a bully on the playground.

He didn't seem offended. "There are plenty of people who would agree with you on that point. But while there are many things I don't know, I'm right about this, aren't I? In fact, I'm not sure I've ever been more sure of anything in my life."

She didn't know what to say. She wanted to argue but was afraid that would make her sound even more ridiculous.

"I wasn't thinking straight after pushing myself a little too hard while rescuing this guy here," he said, pointing to Louie. "I was in more pain than I wanted to admit, otherwise I wouldn't have believed your protests for a minute. But in retrospect, as I've gone over our interaction in my head, I remembered a few things. You had paint under your fingernails, Daisy. Paint that just happens to be the exact shade of turquoise that Marguerite is known for using often. Why would a business manager have colored paint under her fingernails?"

"I told you, I was cleaning up old paint cans."

"I don't believe you. That's another thing. Daisy. Marguerite. They mean the same thing."

"How do you know that?"

He shrugged. "When you've spent most of your life wandering the globe, you pick up a few things here and there, especially the meaning of words and names. When we lived in Tahiti, I learned French and had a friend named Marguerite. My dad used to call her Daisy."

She gazed out at the ocean, wondering how she could continue the deception. The secret felt so huge, suddenly. She had carried it by herself for so very long. She wanted desperately to tell someone.

The little dog sniffed around a clump of grass and seagulls flew overhead. The moment seemed fraught with significance. No one knew the truth. Why should she tell this man she had only met a few days ago? He had the potential to ruin everything for her.

Somehow, she trusted him. It didn't make sense on any logical level but she did. He had risked his life to save a stranger, her brother-in-law, and risked it again to save a stranded little dog.

Something told her Gabe Ellison was the sort of man she could count on.

She faced him, locking her gaze to his. "You have to swear you won't tell anyone. If word got out, it would ruin everything."

For just an instant shock flared in his gaze, as if he had never really expected her to tell him the truth. He masked it quickly. "I won't say a word. Why would I? So it's true."

"Yes. Ridiculous, isn't it? The most mysterious artist around these days has a secret identity as a boring accountant in a quiet Northern California beach town."

"I wouldn't say *ridiculous*. *Fascinating* is the word that comes to mind. Why the big veil of secrecy?"

How did she answer that without going into the entire story?

She couldn't, she realized. It wasn't enough to tell him she was Marguerite. She had to tell him all of it.

"You have to understand, I never wanted to be an artist. That's why I became a CPA. To me, that world of my childhood represented chaos and uncertainty and I…I hate chaos and uncertainty. I need structure and stability. Order. That's why I love numbers. And, yes, I'm fully aware I probably need therapy."

He smiled a little. "Sounds to me like you understand yourself very well."

She fought the urge to smile back, drawn to this man more than she had been to anyone, ever. *That* scared her far more than telling him about Marguerite.

"I am not the kind of person who is comfortable jumping into the unknown. I always like to know what's going to happen next in my world. I map out driving routes in my head ahead of time to figure out the fastest way. I make a detailed shopping list before I go to the store. I write out my short-term and long-term goals and have a well-structured plan to achieve them."

"Is there something wrong with that?"

She had always felt there was. Stella and Bea were far more spontaneous. They could shift direction on a whim and things seemed to turn out fine. Surprises always left her feeling vaguely queasy.

"I never wanted to be an artist," she repeated. "Don't get me wrong, I love art and have great appreciation for those like my sister who can create something out of nothing but their own imagination and skill, but I never wanted to be among their ranks."

"Yet here you are, one of the most famous artists working today."

"I don't know how things came to this point. When I think about it, I still shake my head and I'm not sure whether to laugh or to cry."

"How did it start?"

He really did seem interested. She told herself it was only because he had a career as a filmmaker, used to finding out people's stories.

She had told him more than anyone else knew. Why not tell him everything?

"My husband was ill the last few years of his life. Longer, actually. Cancer. He was…terminal when I married him."

He looked as shocked as Stella had when Daisy, only twenty-five years old, had told her she was marrying a man more than twice her age who was dying of cancer.

"You must have loved him very much."

"I did," she said softly. She didn't add that their marriage hadn't been a traditional one. James had been her best friend, her mentor, the closest thing she'd ever had to a father figure. Not ever her husband in the true sense of the word.

Gabe didn't need to know those intimate details of her life.

"I'm sorry," he said softly.

Tears welled up in her throat at the sympathy in his voice. Most people, even some here in Cape Sanctuary, thought she had married James because he was a well-respected writer with money and recognition. She hadn't cared about any of that. He had been her friend, someone who truly *saw* her.

"James was a writer and a poet, a quite well-known one."

"James McClure. Of course! I own a few first editions of his books. For me, that's saying something, because I don't keep very many hard copies of books."

She imagined it must be difficult to maintain a library when one lived a transitory life.

"I was his accountant and…caretaker, I guess you could say. I helped him with the gardens and Pear Tree Cottage."

Her friendship with James had grown strong. They had shared a love of opera, of plays, of classic movies, and had bonded over discussions and arguments about books and politics and, yes, art.

"His late wife was an antiques dealer who died years before we met and there was quite a bit of remaining inventory at the house. One afternoon I was helping him sort through some things in the storage building where you found me the other night. We found an old table in there that someone had stripped. James wanted it sent to the junk shop but I loved the lines of it, and the legs were these beautiful carved pedestals. I asked if I could have it, thinking I could paint it and give it to Stella for her house."

The memories of that fateful afternoon came rushing back. She had given it a sea foam–green wash then had followed through on the sea theme by painting a mermaid across the top. James sat watching her without saying a word, his features bright and engaged. The pain, his constant companion, seemed to have left him for those few hours they sat together in the workshop.

"I take it you liked the results."

"I didn't. James did. I thought it looked like something a precocious third-grader would do with markers on the bedroom set her parents bought at JCPenney, but James loved it. He said he had an acquaintance he knew would like it and asked if I would mind if he showed her a picture. By then I knew I could never give it to Stella, so I agreed."

The wind had picked up a little, blowing off the sea. Her hair tangled around her face and she tucked it behind her ear, wondering why she was telling him all of this.

"I take it the friend liked the piece."

"We wouldn't be here, I suppose, if she hadn't. She offered him five figures for it. Five figures! For a piece of scrap furniture I had spent two hours painting, just because it seemed to calm my husband's pain a little."

The memory still made her shake her head. She could vividly recall how stunned she had been when James had called to give her the news. That was two months' salary for her at the accounting firm where she'd been working. She split the commission between the cancer research center where James received treatment and the new charity Stella had recently started to help foster families in the area.

"I thought that would be the end of it. I would be a one-masterpiece artist, kind of like authors who only have one book in them. James wouldn't let that happen. This friend showed her friends the table, and by the time the month was over, I had commissions for two more tables and a chest of drawers."

"And Marguerite was born."

"Yes. I didn't want to use my own name. There are...a number of reasons for that."

"This is the part I don't get. Why not?"

How did she begin to tell him about the complicated reasons for her anonymity, starting with Beatriz? Her sister had been fresh off her divorce and all of Cruz's cheating, her self-esteem raw and broken. Becoming an artist was all Bea had ever wanted to do and Daisy hadn't wanted to sweep in and rub her staggering, wholly undeserved success in her sister's face.

"I have reasons. Let's leave it at that. I've already told you more than anyone else on earth knows. But as you can see, it was really an accident. A mistake, even. I'm not an artist. My sister is. My mother was. I'm just an accountant who happens to be pretty good with a paintbrush."

His rough laugh seemed to slide down her spine. "Marguerite or Daisy. I'm not sure which one is real and which is an illusion."

"I'm Daisy. That's all."

"Whichever one you are, I can't seem to stop thinking about you. And not just about your art."

His words slid through her, seductive and tantalizing. Her? He thought about *her*?

She again didn't know what to say.

"I'm sorry," she finally murmured.

"Are you?"

She was fiercely aware of him, the heat of his shoulder brushing hers, the long, elegant fingers that reached out and brushed an errant strand of her hair back behind her ear.

Her stomach muscles contracted when he touched her skin. "Not really," she whispered.

He gazed at her for a moment, then growled something that was snatched away by the wind an instant before he lowered his mouth to hers.

The taste of his mouth was like the very first sip of the brandy James had loved—rich, heady, intoxicating. Delicious.

Daisy felt instantly light-headed, unable to believe she was really here on a bench overlooking the ocean, kissing the sexy and fascinating Gabriel Ellison.

What was happening here?

She wasn't quite sure. She only knew that the brush of his mouth against hers, tantalizing and soft and incredibly seductive, moved her more than any other kiss of her life.

She wasn't sure she had ever known this sort of sweetness in a kiss.

If she had been on her game—if she hadn't been so very disarmed by this man—she might have been able to brush off the kiss as a random moment of insanity. But all she could think was that it felt...perfect.

She kissed him back. How could she resist? She wrapped her arms around him, careful of his injury, tilted her head just so and savored every second of it.

Oh, she could fall hard for this man.

They might have stayed there until the sun slid below the horizon, if not for Louie. He barked suddenly, startling both of them, almost as if trying to protect her from the consequences of her foolishness, to keep her from making things worse.

Daisy drew away, feeling more flustered than she remembered being in a very long time.

Should she ask him why he kissed her? Was it better to talk it to death or pretend it hadn't happened? She opted for the latter.

"We should, um, get back," she said. "It will be dark soon."

He looked down at her, his breathing fast, and clear attraction in his eyes.

"Yes. You're probably right."

He rose, gripped Louie's leash and turned his back on the glorious sunset to start back toward her house.

She followed, wishing with all her heart that she wasn't so awkward at relationships.

GABE

He didn't know what to think about Daisy/Marguerite.

One moment she was tangled in his arms, kissing him as if she couldn't get enough. The next she was as cool and indifferent as if he'd simply swatted away a fly.

He could tell she was attracted to him. He didn't consider it a sign of a huge ego; it was simple observation. He had seen the way she glanced at his mouth every once in a while, the little shiver she gave when he touched her inadvertently. He was fairly certain she wasn't even aware of doing it but he found it utterly irresistible.

Why, then, had she ended the kiss and returned to this cool formality?

So she didn't want to kiss him. Big deal. He had no reason to be feeling this sense of…letdown.

He hadn't been lying about being fascinated with her. How could he help it? She came across as a stiff, serious, somewhat prickly accountant. She wore plain, drab clothing, almost as if she wanted to disappear.

Yet somewhere inside her was a woman who danced alone to sexy salsa music and hid behind the passion and color and joy of Marguerite.

She was a study in contrasts, which made her infinitely captivating.

He had felt honored that she had told him the truth but Gabe had a rather grim suspicion that he would now have an even harder time shaking this fascination with her. Especially now that he had tasted her mouth, heard the seductive little sounds she made when he kissed her, felt the heat and wonder of those artist's hands against his skin.

If he had his way, his next documentary would be the Marguerite story.

He could see it now, filming her at work while the sun poured in through the skylight of her rustic studio or maybe in the beautiful, wild English cottage–style garden of her house, overlooking the vast Pacific.

He couldn't do it. He wouldn't be filming a moment of her daily life. Daisy was an intensely private person. She obviously had powerful reasons for keeping her identity as Marguerite a secret, even if she hadn't shared those with him.

He had to respect those reasons, even if he didn't understand them.

1 3

STELLA

This had been a crazy idea.

Stella gripped the armrests of her comfortable, oversize chair, hoping against hope that she didn't puke all over this sleek private jet.

She had been feeling good all day long. All week, really. After her initial bout of morning sickness right after her pregnancy had been confirmed, she had felt fantastic. Better than she had in a long time, actually, now that she no longer was anxious about the fertility treatments.

She had carried the secret of her pregnancy close to her heart for days, like a precious little painting only she could see. She didn't want to tell anyone. She wanted to have this time to cherish her secret, her child.

She had been feeling strong and healthy, empowered with the miracle growing inside her.

All that had changed over the past twenty minutes as they

made the short flight from LA back to the small airport outside Cape Sanctuary.

She wasn't sure if it was the six hours they had just spent at an amusement park, the shift in equilibrium she always got when she traveled or the hormones playing havoc with her body.

Either way, slick, greasy nausea seemed to have settled in her stomach and showed no sign of leaving anytime soon.

"How are you holding up?" Ed asked quietly from beside her.

There was something else she couldn't quite believe. She felt like she was the recipient of two amazing events. One was this pregnancy that still didn't feel quite real. The other was the fact that Ed Clayton had returned to her world.

He was the only one besides her OB-GYN who knew her secret. Was that the reason he had been incredibly sweet all afternoon and evening?

She wasn't sure. She only knew he had watched over her with careful concern as they enjoyed the rare outing Cruz had provided them all.

"Can I get you some water or something?" he asked.

She was afraid to answer him for fear that the delicious grilled chicken kebab she had enjoyed in the park would make a disgusting reappearance. Instead, she pointed to her stomach, made a face and said nothing.

"Let me guess," he murmured. "Morning sickness."

"Something like that." Even the small effort of speaking was enough to send the contents of her stomach sloshing around.

She had to get up. Now. Before it was too late.

He must have seen the distress on her features. He quickly rose from his aisle seat to let her out and she hurried to the bathroom in the back of the airplane.

When she came out several moments later, she felt marginally better—though she couldn't recommend kneeling on the floor of a tiny airplane bathroom to anyone.

Ed stood to let her back inside. "Feel better?" he asked.

"A little."

She sat down, still feeling shaky, but was touched beyond words when she found a fresh water bottle in the cup holder. He had fetched that for her, she realized. Something soft and warm and tender seemed to unfurl inside her.

She had been on her own so very long. It was lovely to have someone else on Team Stella, if only for a moment.

Longing, pointed and sharp, jabbed at her. Regret for all she had given up seemed to haunt her. She knew she had made the right choice all those years ago, but sometimes she wondered what would have happened if she hadn't decided she and the girls would only derail his medical career.

They would have been together nearly two decades. They would probably have several children of their own by now and would be a comfortable old married couple, knowing each other inside and out.

She couldn't second-guess her choices. She had done what she thought was best at the time.

"I feel somewhat more human."

"I'll keep my fingers crossed and hope that particular state of being continues through the flight."

"We should be home soon. It's not a long flight."

In the row across from them, she could see Mari and his daughter talking in low tones, their heads close together. As she had expected, the girls seemed to have become instant friends. They had gone on every single ride in the park that had been opened for the private party, many of them multiple times.

"They seem to be getting along," she said, gesturing to the girls.

"They've had a great time. Ro will be talking about this for months. She loved everything about it. Thank you for inviting us."

"You seemed to be enjoying yourself, too. I saw you on a few of those rides."

He smiled. "What can I say? I love roller coasters."

She remembered that. When they were seeing each other, they had hit Knott's Berry Farm a few times and the thrill rides there.

Just a thought of being on a roller coaster right now was enough to make her stomach roil again. She did her best to ignore the nausea.

"It was a lovely evening. I'm so glad you and Rowan could come. It was all Mari's idea."

As she heard her own words, she had to wonder if she was telling him that to make sure he didn't think she had orchestrated the whole thing, that she was somehow desperately trying to reconnect with him.

"She seems like a very sweet girl."

"She is quite remarkable. It can be tough having a celebrity for a father but Mari seems to keep everything in perspective."

"You're very close to the girls, aren't you? Daisy and Beatriz, I mean."

"Yes. We're family. They're like my own daughters. I know that probably doesn't make sense but that's how I feel."

She had sacrificed everything for them. Most of the time she chose not to think about what she had given up to rescue them but sometimes the loss of it hit her hard.

Right now, sitting beside the man she had once loved with all her heart, she was aware as she had never been before that a vein of grief ran through her, deep and well hidden. She had tried to ignore it all these years, had tried to tell herself she had made the right choice to walk away from Ed and allow him his dreams.

What if she had been wrong? What if she had been fooling herself all these years that her decision to cut him loose had been best for everyone?

What if she hadn't been acting out of altruism, some magnanimous desire for him to become a physician without having to be tied down with a ready-made family consisting of two troubled preadolescent girls?

What if she had only been afraid that the one perfect relationship she'd ever known had only been a lie and he would leave her like everyone else she had ever loved, so she had chosen to leave him first?

She closed her eyes, fighting back sudden tears that came out of nowhere. These pregnancy mood swings were killer.

"Mari mentioned you have a foundation that helps foster care families."

She seized on the topic, grateful for the diversion from her entirely too raw self-scrutiny. "Yes. It's called Open Hearts, and the goal is to provide support for foster families. We want to encourage more families to consider opening their homes to the thousands of children who need temporary shelter in California."

"Sounds like a worthy project. Did you start it because of Bea and Daisy?"

"That was a big part of it. There's a huge need for foster families in California. It's at crisis level, actually. More children than ever before need placements at the same time there are decreasing numbers of families willing to step up. I'm hoping to change that trend, at least in our area."

"What sort of activities does Open Hearts sponsor?"

He seemed genuinely interested, and since it was one of her favorite topics, she was happy to reply. It took her mind off her nausea, anyway.

"We sponsor monthly activities, everything from family movie nights at one of the local theaters to respite babysitting for parents to have date nights to a big annual picnic that's coming up in just a few weeks. It's all designed to help families feel like they have a resource in the community."

"You feel strongly about it, don't you?"

"Passionately. There's no way to sugarcoat it. Being in foster care is hard and being a foster parent is hard. We can't solve every problem but we try to make sure both children and foster families know they're supported."

"Good for you. It seems very important to you."

"It is." She paused. "I've been on both sides. A foster child and a foster parent."

"Have you had foster children besides Bea and Daisy?"

She hesitated, not sure how much to tell him. Bea, seated in the row in front of the girls, turned around to do it for her.

"What Stella isn't telling you, Dr. Clayton, is that she has hosted more than twenty foster children since Daisy and me. Including Cruz Romero."

"It's true," the man in question said, giving Stella an affectionate smile. "Only for a few months, after my grandma died. I didn't have anywhere else to go."

"And then you ran away with my niece."

"But you love me anyway," he said with a grin.

"Most of the time."

She did, actually, though she had a hard time forgiving him for breaking Bea's heart.

"Think of all those lives you've changed," Bea said.

Stella felt tears well up and knew she couldn't blame them on pregnancy hormones. Her girls were always great at hitting her in the heart.

"I enjoyed caring for every single one of them," she said. There were a few difficult cases she'd been asked to take on, but for the most part, she felt extraordinarily blessed. Many of them were still in her life, even after they had either returned to their parents or aged out of foster care.

"You're not fostering right now?" Ed asked.

"I'm taking a little break right now," she said softly.

Ed's fingers covered hers on the armrest between them and brushed gently, a quiet signal that he understood why she had opted to focus on something else. That simple gesture brought more of those ridiculous tears welling up in her throat. At this rate, this pregnancy was going to make her leak like a broken irrigation sprinkler.

He was the only one on this airplane who might have some inkling as to why she had stopped when her last foster was able to be reunited with her mother the year before. That was the moment when Stella had decided she wanted to get serious about having a child of her own. She still anticipated she would continue to be involved in the foster care program and provide love in that arena, but she had decided it was time.

"Has Stella told you about the annual Arts and Hearts on the Cape Festival that she organizes?"

Ed raised one eyebrow. "No. I haven't heard about it."

"It's really terrific. All the local businesses get involved up and down the coast. There's an arts festival, of course, and concerts, as well as a 5K run and other events where people get sponsorship. Mari's Girl Scout troop is even doing a Pinewood Derby for sponsorship. It's truly the highlight of the summer. All the money is split among various nonprofits, including Open Hearts."

"I haven't been to that festival in years," Cruz said.

"If you're still in town, you should stop by," Stella said.

"I might," he said. Cruz glanced at Bea, then turned back to Stella. "In fact, I just had a great idea. Why don't I give a benefit concert this year? You've been asking me for years and I've never been able to make it work for my schedule. For once, I'll be here in town. It's the least I can do."

"Are you serious?" Stella asked, stunned. "That would be amazing! I was going to ask you to make an appearance but a concert would be even better."

Cruz had always seemed to avoid coming back to play for the Arts & Hearts event. She had put it down to his desire to leave their small town behind and perhaps some lingering bitterness about the divorce. What had changed his mind?

"The event is only a few weeks away," Bea said. "Does that give you enough time to work out the logistics for a concert?"

"It will be tight, but I think we can manage it." Her mind was already racing, going through all the things she would have to figure out, starting with finding a venue large enough to hold all the fans who would want to come out for it.

"What if we let the foster kids and their families come free but everybody else needs to pay," Cruz suggested.

"I love this idea," she said. "Now I remember why you are one of my favorite people."

He grinned. "You mean it wasn't because I flew you all to Universal Studios for the day?"

"No, but that was fun."

She and Bea talked about logistics a bit more. It would be difficult but not impossible to add a Cruz Romero show to the lineup of events for the festival. She would need to throw an emergency board meeting and talk to the people who had already printed the posters about a new one and try to change her ads on the local radio stations...

The list was endless and suddenly overwhelming. As the plane started to land, Stella leaned back in her chair and closed her eyes.

When she opened them, she saw Ed watching her with concern in his eyes. "Are you sure you're going to be able to handle the details involved in this? It seems like a great deal of work."

She was warmed by his concern but knew she couldn't let herself depend on it too much. "I'll be fine. It's for a good cause. I'll figure out how to make it work."

He lowered his voice so the others couldn't hear. "I'm sure Jo has mentioned to you that you'll want to take things easy, at least these first few months when your body is trying to adjust to growing a new life. I tell all mothers to slow down a little and nap when your body demands it, but that advice is especially relevant to older mothers."

Oh, she really needed him reminding her that she was forty. Again, she wondered where they might have been if she had made different choices nearly two decades ago, but pushed away the regret.

She had done what she thought was best at the time. There was no room in her life to dwell on what might have been.

"I'll be fine," she repeated. She crossed her fingers at her side, hoping she was right.

14

BEA

It was close to midnight when she pulled into her driveway after making the trip from the small Cape Sanctuary airport to her house. She was alone, as Mari had asked if she could sleep over at Cruz's house so they could go horseback riding again the next morning.

While she was happy her daughter was spending more time with her father, Bea had to admit that she would be somewhat relieved when Cruz finally got tired of his R & R and this misguided effort to get back together.

This extended downtime on his part had disrupted their entire schedule. She also worried it gave Mari the skewed idea that life was all about having fun, going horseback riding and playing soccer with her dad and taking wild, extravagant trips by private jet to an amusement park.

Mari had a good head on her shoulders. She knew that. Thus far, her daughter had been great about keeping things in perspective. But she was only eleven and her personality was still developing.

When she called for Jojo inside the house, the dog didn't come running. She walked through, looking for her little dog. Outside she could see the pool lights and opened the curtains to find Shane working at one of the patio tables while Sally and Jojo lay curled up together on their favorite spot, the outdoor rug.

Her heart softened at the sight. Her little dog was going to miss her best friend so much when Sally moved out again.

Not as much as Bea was going to miss the retriever's owner.

The truth was like a fierce, heavy ache in her heart. She was in love with her best friend and had no idea if she could find the courage to try taking things to the next level.

She was tired from the long day and knew she would be wise to simply open the door and call to Jojo and wave good-night to Shane. She couldn't do it.

With butterflies dancing through her, she opened the patio door and walked outside.

He looked up and his smile of welcome seemed to settle every nerve.

"Hi," she said softly. "Thanks for keeping an eye on Jojo." He had a key to the house and often let the dog out when she wasn't home.

"No problem. We enjoyed his company, didn't we, Sal?"

His Labrador lifted her head and almost seemed to nod in agreement.

"The two of them have a funny relationship, don't they?" she said, sliding into the chair next to him.

"They're buds. Nothing wrong with that."

"I always wonder what they're talking about to each other."

"They're dogs. They're probably sharing stories of the bone that got away."

She gestured to his tablet, which looked like a big, complicated game of tic-tac-toe. "You're working late."

"It was nice out here, with that lovely breeze and the water and the full moon. I'm figuring out a couple of new plays we're going to try before our first scrimmage next week."

"Oh, man. I can't believe football season is here already. Where did the summer go?"

"Tell me about it. Fall will be here before we know it."

She wanted to savor August and the last few days Mari would be home from school, but she imagined her daughter would spend most of that time with Cruz.

"Is Mari with her dad?"

"Yes. She wanted to stay over. We were with him all evening, actually."

He set his tablet down. "Oh?"

She found herself strangely reluctant to share the details of the day with him. "It was kind of a crazy night. We went to Universal Studios."

Shane raised an eyebrow. "The one in Hollywood."

"Yes. Orlando would be a little far to fly down and back in a day."

It was no less crazy that they had flown to LA and back, which was usually about an eight-hour drive from here. "Cruz was performing for a private party there and was allowed to take some guests. He wanted Mari to go and she wanted one of her new friends to come. Before we knew it, we were on a plane with Cruz, Stella, Mari, Stella's old boyfriend and his daughter."

"I didn't know Stella *had* an old boyfriend. Sounds like there's a story there."

"I'm so glad you agree with me! Daisy thinks I'm crazy but I know there's something going on between them. He's a doctor going into practice with Jo Chen. Apparently, he's an old friend of Stella's from college."

"And you think they're seeing each other now?"

"I don't know what to think. Daisy tells me I'm imagining

things but I've seen the way she is around him. Tonight, seeing them together, confirmed it."

"Why's that?"

He was such a good listener. That was one of the many things she loved about him. Shane always made her feel like what she had to say *mattered*.

"I watched them all evening at the amusement park and they were so sweet together. He watched over her—not in a creepy, stalky way, just...solicitous. Like whatever he was doing, he had to check to make sure she was okay. And Stella was glowing. I wish you could have seen her."

"She's a great lady. She deserves someone to watch over her."

Bea completely agreed. Her aunt had sacrificed entirely too much in order to care for her and for Daisy. Her entire young adult life had been spent raising two girls who had been too busy being teenagers to show much gratitude.

She, for one, had put Stella through hell. She had started drinking early, used to sneak out of the house to meet up with Cruz and ran with a fast, wild crowd.

She didn't even know why, really. She hadn't even enjoyed the party life but Daisy had been controlled, organized, the ideal student, and Bea had somehow felt obligated to rebel a little against all that perfection.

As a result, she had ended up pregnant at seventeen and had run away with Cruz to LA. For months she hadn't even let Stella know where she was.

It had been childish and irresponsible. When she looked back, she cringed at what she had done to her aunt.

"Do you ever wish you could go back to your teenage self and have a do-over?"

His features looked harsh, though she knew it was only a trick of the moonlight. He was a kind, good man. A hardworking coach, an excellent schoolteacher.

"All the time."

"What would you change, if you could go back?"

He was quiet for a long time, so long she thought he wasn't going to continue. The moment dripped past, like water from a leaky spigot. "I regret not asking you out in high school."

The words shivered between them. She stared at him, not sure how to answer. He had never acted like he *wanted* to ask her out. Why hadn't he?

In an instant, she was sixteen again, best friends with the cute jock who lived by her. All the other girls had crushes on Shane. His locker had been close to hers, as well, she remembered, and girls were forever slipping notes in it.

Shane hardly seemed to notice, focused on school and sports and his family.

He used to tease her every day when they'd bump into each other by their lockers or in the halls or the lunchroom. Coming up with ways to tease him back had become her favorite part of the day.

"What about you?" he asked. "What would you change?"

It was hard to pick, she had so many regrets. But every choice had led her right here. If she hadn't dated Cruz, she wouldn't have Mari and she would never, ever change that.

He was waiting for an answer. She had to say something.

"Too many to count," she finally answered, which was a cop-out. What she wanted to say was that she regretted never telling him that she *wanted* him to ask her out.

I'm in love with you, you big idiot, she wanted to say, but the words caught somewhere between her throat and her mouth and she couldn't get them out.

"So. Cruz. How's that going?"

He asked so casually, she was deeply grateful she hadn't said anything about her feelings.

"It's not. I can't seem to convince him there's no chance for us. We have too much baggage between us. Mountains of it. I don't see how to get past it."

"Are you willing to try?"

"No."

"You say no but you don't sound very decisive. At some point you're going to have to figure out what you want, Bea."

She knew what she wanted. She wanted him. Shane. She just didn't know if she was strong enough to risk losing this friend she could speak with late at night, when the moonlight glimmered on the water and the dogs snored beside them and the night creatures peeped and chirped just beyond the edges of her property.

"What if I want to go back in time so I could start dating the cute football player who used to tease me between classes?"

He gazed at her and again that fine-edged tension tugged between them. "We can't go back."

"No. We can only go forward."

She was tired of being afraid. She was going to just go for it. Just kiss him and see what happened.

All the negative voices in her head told her it was a lousy idea but she didn't care. She had to kiss him. Digging deep for her last ounce of courage, she stood on tiptoe, drew in a breath and brushed her mouth against his.

He didn't move for a moment, muscles taut. She had a horrifying fear that he would push her away, that she had ruined everything. Just as she was about to jerk back and try to make some kind of a joke about it, he made a ragged little sound deep in his throat and returned the kiss with a fierceness that took her breath.

Yes!

Finally!

In her secret dreams she had wondered how his mouth would taste. She had imagined this very moment.

Apparently, her imagination sucked. She hadn't anticipated just how amazing it would be to kiss Shane Landry in the summer moonlight. She hadn't guessed she would be shaky, dizzy, her heart pounding so loudly she was certain he must hear it, or that she would want the moment to go on forever.

This was Shane. Her best friend. She had known him since she was nine years old. It should have felt strange. Instead, it was the most perfect kiss in all the history of kissing.

Bea had heard in songs about kisses where the earth shook, the heavens sang, the entire universe seemed to celebrate. She had always thought that was overblown nonsense. Now she totally got it.

His mouth was warm, firm, focused, and he kissed her as if he had been waiting his whole life for it.

With only their mouths touching, they kissed for a long time. It was tender, sexy, emotional. Achingly sweet.

She didn't want it to end. She wanted to stay in this magical moment, telling him with her kiss everything she didn't have the nerve to say out loud.

No. This wasn't enough. The kiss was amazing but she wanted more. She wanted to feel the heat of his body, the warmth of his arms around her.

She moved closer, reaching her arms up to wrap around his neck. Just before she would have tangled her fingers in his hair, her phone buzzed on the table.

She froze, trying to grab hold of her scrambled thoughts.

She could ignore it. Whoever it was could call back later, when she wasn't in the middle of The Kiss to End All Kisses.

On the other hand, she realized slowly, that was Cruz's ringtone.

And he had their daughter.

Mari would use her own phone to call her if she had a problem, wouldn't she? Unless she couldn't talk, for some ominous reason.

She frowned, hating that she had been yanked out of the mood. But she had to answer.

She wrenched her mouth away from Shane's and fumbled for her phone.

"Hello?" she managed. This had better seriously be good.

"Bea? Did I wake you? Your voice sounds funny."

Maybe because she still couldn't seem to suck enough air into her lungs. "No. I'm up. Just sitting out by the pool."

"Is Shane with you?" Cruz didn't bother to hide the jealous tone in his voice.

She was not in the mood to have this conversation with her ex-husband.

"Yes. He's right here. We were just making out. Would you care to speak with him?"

"Ha ha," Cruz said. He clearly thought she was joking, which she would have found amusing if she wasn't so miserably aware she had made a grave mistake in answering the phone.

Shane stood, his features expressionless in the moonlight.

"I would like to get back to it. What do you want, Cruz?"

"I wanted to talk to you about tomorrow. I forgot I've got an appointment with Daisy again at noon to sign some papers, then Wally and some guys are flying in to work on a couple of new songs. Do you mind if I drop Mari off about 11:30, before I go into town to meet Daisy?"

That was it? He had to call her at midnight to make sure she would be around to handle the parenting responsibilities she usually carried entirely on her own? This could have been handled in a text or an email.

"Yes. That's fine. I'm not going anywhere. I can even come pick her up at Casa Del Mar, if that would help."

"No. I can drop her off. Thanks, Bea."

He paused and lowered his voice into what she knew he thought was Sexy Cruz range. "I had a great time with you tonight, babe. I'm so glad we could share that. You looked great. It was all I could do to keep my hands off you."

She knew Shane couldn't hear the conversation but he could

probably guess at the topic. She was careful not to look at him but could feel tension radiating off him in waves.

"It was a fun night," she said briskly. "Mari and her friend had a wonderful time. I think Stella and Dr. Clayton did, too. Thank you for thinking to invite us along."

"You're welcome. I'm glad they had fun but I did it for you, to show you how perfect we still are together. I need you along with me."

She was not going to have this conversation with him while Shane stood impassively, taking it all in.

"Good night, Cruz," she said firmly. "I'll see you tomorrow when you bring Mari home."

She ended the call before he could continue, wondering what she had to do to get the message across to him that they didn't have a future together.

Bea shoved her phone into her pocket, not sure what to say to Shane, who was watching her out of blue eyes that suddenly seemed remote and cool.

"I'm sorry," she began.

"You'll always answer when he calls, won't you?"

"When he has my daughter, yes."

Shane shook his head. "I get that part. But even if you didn't share a child, Cruz would only have to snap his fingers and you would come running."

His harsh words, especially after the tender kiss they had shared, drew blood, gouging into her skin like sharp claws. "Is that what you think of me? That I'm like Sally or Jojo, trained to heel when he gives the command?"

She was furious at the tears burning behind her eyes and did her best to keep them from falling free.

"I think you've been tangled up over Cruz Romero since you were sixteen years old. Maybe earlier. Even if I had found the nerve to ask you out back then in high school, you never would have gone out with me, no matter what you say now. All you could see back then was Cruz. He's all you've ever been able to see."

She wanted to tell him how very wrong he was, that Cruz was in her past and she was ready to move forward. Before she could choke down the hurt in her throat to get the words out, he picked up his tablet and papers and turned away.

"It's late. I have practice in the morning. Good night, Bea."

He whistled for Sally, who lumbered to her feet and gave Bea and Jojo an almost apologetic look, then followed him to the guesthouse, leaving Bea alone with her dog in the moonlight.

15

DAISY

"Thank you again for agreeing to host the meeting tonight at Pear Tree Cottage."

Though her aunt smiled when she said the words, Daisy did not miss the tight lines around Stella's mouth or the hollows under her eyes. Her aunt did not look well.

Worry weighed down her shoulders. Something was definitely going on with her aunt...and she didn't think Stella was lovesick, despite what Bea continued to insist.

There was more to it. She just didn't know *what*.

She had fretted all day, ever since Stella called her that morning asking if she could host the board meeting for Open Hearts. Her aunt had been evasive, only saying she felt under the weather and would be too busy all day getting her classroom ready for school to start.

There was more to it than that. Daisy just knew it. Yes, she knew she had a particular skill for horribilizing any given situation. Some of that was her personality and some came from the terrible weight of nursing a person she loved who had a terminal illness.

Her experience with James was probably the reason her mind immediately jumped to the assumption that Stella was suffering from some terrible disease. If not cancer, maybe she had multiple sclerosis or lupus or some other life-altering condition.

No. She wouldn't go there unless she had some facts to back up her worry.

Her aunt was still young, barely forty. Stella maintained a healthy diet and exercised regularly. Daisy knew her aunt wasn't invincible but she couldn't believe the woman could be suffering from some ghastly condition without telling her or Bea.

What was going on?

She wanted to take her aunt's hands in hers, sit down beside her on the sofa and interrogate her until Stella shared the truth. Now wasn't the time, when the ten board members for Stella's Open Hearts foundation would be arriving at any moment.

She forced herself to smile. "I'm happy to do it. I'm only sorry you weren't feeling up to it."

"I'll be fine. I'm only tired and a little, um, queasy. It must have been something I ate. Will you excuse me for a minute?" Stella hurried to the bathroom without waiting for Daisy to answer.

Daisy stood uncertainly outside the bathroom, listening to the unmistakable sound of retching from within.

Stella should have just rescheduled the meeting when she was feeling better.

She wanted to storm in and tell her aunt that but the doorbell rang with the first arrivals to the meeting.

Louie hurried to the door first and gave one well-behaved bark. With a look back at the closed bathroom door, Daisy sighed and went to answer the doorbell.

When this meeting was over, she intended to force the truth out of her aunt.

The members of the Open Hearts board were all prompt, and several had ridden together to her house. Within ten minutes everyone was there, mingling in her kitchen and snacking on the vegetable plate and cookies from the Sweet Spot bakery in town.

"Where's Stella?" Bea asked a few moments after she arrived.

Daisy frowned. She didn't need someone *else* to worry about. Bea looked her usual self, wearing a perfectly fashionable tunic and leggings with her hair curled and wild over her shoulders and chunky charm bracelets on each wrist, but she had dark smudges under her eyes.

"In the bathroom," she said in an undertone. "She said she doesn't feel well."

Worry clouded her sister's eyes. "Should we cancel the meeting?"

"Let's give her a minute."

"You know, she spent a lot of time in the bathroom when we were on our little adventure to Southern California the other day. She said she thought she was a little bit motion sick."

"Do you think that's all it is?"

"What else could it be?" Bea asked.

Before Daisy could go into the whole grim litany of possibilities, Stella came into the kitchen with a bright smile for the other members of the committee.

"Hello, everyone!" Stella said. "Thank you so much for coming. I see Daisy has fed you all. That's the important thing. We have a lot on our agenda with the picnic this week and the festival a few weeks after that, plus our exciting new headliner concert. Shall we get started?"

If Stella wasn't feeling well, Daisy had to admire her strength. It wasn't easy to be bright and bubbly when a person felt terrible. She had watched the heartbreaking efforts of James as he tried to keep up a positive attitude in those last months of his life, until the strain became too great for him.

Determined to ask her aunt later, Daisy turned her attention to the board meeting. She took her job as controller and treasurer of Open Hearts very seriously. The work they did here was important, providing support and help to foster families.

At last count Stella's contacts at the state child welfare agency estimated an additional five hundred children had been placed in foster homes because of Open Hearts instead of being housed in temporary shelters.

She found fierce satisfaction in that, for purely personal reasons. She didn't like thinking about her own experience in foster care or the scars that time had undoubtedly left on her psyche. She had been powerless and afraid then but she wasn't now. She had skills and connections and wasn't afraid to use them to help children who often felt as if they had no one else on their side.

They were about halfway through Stella's agenda when Daisy's doorbell rang again.

Bea looked around the living room at the eight women and two men. "Are we expecting anyone else?"

Stella shook her head. "Everyone's here who said they could make it. Maybe Carol was able to find someone else to babysit her grandchildren or maybe her daughter didn't need her after all."

Daisy rose and went to the door. Everyone had a clear view and she could feel the attention on her. When she opened it and discovered Gabriel Ellison on the other side, Daisy could swear she felt an electric current rush around the room, at least among the women.

She couldn't blame them. He looked gorgeous, with that dark, wavy hair, piercing green eyes and sexy stubble.

Louie rushed to Gabe immediately and started dancing around as if he hadn't seen him in days, instead of the day before when his rescuer had come to walk him.

Gabe came every day around this time. She had been so worried about Stella all day, she had totally forgotten to give him a call and tell him she would be occupied today.

"Is this a bad time?"

Yes. The worst. She could see the curious looks being sent her way from every direction.

"No. It's fine. My aunt runs a charity to encourage foster families. I think I may have mentioned it to you. We have a couple of events coming up, so we're working out last-minute details."

"I'm sorry to interrupt. We can skip the walk today."

Louie heard the magic *W* word and that only made him more excited. How could she disappoint the dog by depriving him of his favorite part of the day?

"No. It's fine. Go ahead."

Gabe knew right where to find Louie's leash, hanging next to the door. He couldn't have made it more clear this wasn't his first time here if he'd walked into the kitchen and helped himself to a glass of water.

She didn't dare look at Bea or Stella, knowing their speculative looks would be the hardest to avoid.

Gabe clipped the leash on the dog then gave a collective smile and wave to the room. "Sorry again to interrupt. You're doing good work here."

"Thanks."

As soon as she closed the door behind the two of them, Daisy returned to her spot and picked up her pen. "Okay. Where were we?"

"Oh, no, you don't," Bea said, eyes wide. "Do you know who that was?"

"Yes."

"I don't, but I'd like to." Stella's best friend, Cleo Tenaglia, grinned and Daisy could feel herself flush.

"That's Gabriel Ellison!" Stella said.

"The documentary guy?" John Pearsey, the retired elementary school principal, looked stunned.

"That's the one," Bea said. "He's staying with Cruz right now."

"Oh! Is he the one who saved Cruz's life? You never told me that was Gabe Ellison!"

"I used to love watching his dad's adventures." Gibb Lyman, the other man on their committee, looked nostalgic. "Man, that guy knew how to live!"

"Wow! I wonder if we could talk him into filming some kind of promotional spot for us," Nancy, John's wife, suggested.

"That's a terrific idea," Stella exclaimed. "He would do a marvelous job!"

"Daisy should ask him," her friend Paula suggested. "They're obviously friends."

Paula looked a little put out that Daisy hadn't told her she knew Gabe. How was she supposed to have done that? Just drop into casual conversation the fact that a gorgeous man knew all her secrets and had kissed her until she couldn't see straight, then acted like nothing happened?

"He's staying at Casa Del Mar while he recovers from his injuries. It doesn't really seem appropriate to enlist him to make a promotional video while he's on a medical break."

"It doesn't hurt to ask," Cleo said.

She was quickly losing control of the conversation. "That's not really why we're here today, right? We still have a lot to do. Can we get back to the agenda?"

"You're right," Stella said. "I know you all have other things to do today. Let's hurry through the rest of the agenda so you can be on your way."

Daisy breathed a sigh of relief as her aunt turned the discussion back to the picnic the following weekend and the fundraising events planned during the festival.

Gabe still had not returned an hour later, by the time they

wrapped up the meeting. Daisy suspected a few of the others, like Paula and Cleo specifically, were lingering in hopes of seeing him again.

She really hoped he was okay. The man was still recovering from his injuries. He had no business traipsing around all hours of the day and night with a mischievous little dog who had an unfortunate tendency to fall down cliffs.

Finally, she was able to push the last board members out the door, until only Stella and Bea remained.

"That was a good meeting," Stella said. "Thank you for keeping us on track."

She wanted to think her aunt looked better. Still, Daisy couldn't ignore the pinched lines around Stella's mouth or the fatigue in her eyes.

She needed to get to the bottom of things.

"Stella. Honey. What's going on? Are you sure you're feeling all right?"

Stella's eyes widened. "Why do you ask?"

"Because you threw up in my bathroom before the meeting."

"And you spent a lot of time in the bathroom when we went to LA," Bea added.

Stella busied herself organizing the papers in front of her. "I am just fine. Stop worrying about me."

Daisy met her sister's gaze and saw her own worry reflected back at her. Bea went to Stella and put her arms around their aunt.

"It's our job to worry about you, honey. You spent years worrying about us. Now it's our turn. If something's going on, you need to tell us."

Daisy thought for a moment her aunt would reveal whatever was happening in her world. She opened her mouth and Daisy could see the uncertainty in her eyes.

Stella quickly blinked it away. "Nothing is going on. You two are the biggest worrywarts. I promise, I'm fine. Now, Daisy.

Tell us about this handsome man who shows up to walk that cute dog I had no idea you even had until I showed up here this afternoon. What's the story there?"

Stella was obviously trying to distract them. Daisy didn't want to let her, but Bea was so easily distracted, she let Stella lead her in a whole new direction.

"Yeah, Dais. What's the story? I had no idea you even knew Gabriel Ellison."

If Stella was going to continue keeping things back, why did Daisy have to be honest? She didn't want to talk about her personal business but she had a feeling neither her sister nor her aunt would be content until she gave them some kind of answer.

"It's a very long story. Last week Gabe rescued Louie—that's the name of the little French bulldog—and came here looking for his owner. I ended up offering to keep him here. The dog, I mean. Not Gabe. He's still staying with Cruz."

She was rambling, something she never did. As soon as she realized it, she clamped her lips shut.

"So Gabriel Ellison rescued a stray, you agreed to keep the dog here and now a legendary documentary filmmaker just casually drops by to take the dog for walks?"

She didn't like thinking of him as a legendary filmmaker. He was only...Gabe, who had somehow become her friend when she wasn't looking.

"That's about it," she said.

Stella still looked confused and Daisy couldn't blame her. She still wasn't sure how it had all come about.

"It's only temporary. I'm sure we'll find his family soon."

"Are you going to be able to give him back when that happens?" Bea asked.

"Sure. Why wouldn't I?"

"I know I would have a hard time with it. He's just so cute. It's hard to give up something you've handed your heart to."

"I'm sure it will be fine," she said.

Bea didn't look convinced. Daisy could guess what her sister was thinking:

Brisk, no-nonsense Daisy. She never lets anything or anyone too close.

If Bea only knew. The truth was oceans away from that image she projected, so far that it would be laughable, if it didn't make her want to cry.

GABE

Apparently, her meeting was over.

Gabe stood on Daisy McClure's front step, gazing out at the nearly empty driveway. What had looked like a parking lot when he stopped by earlier now only contained two vehicles, a late-model SUV and an older Volvo.

The dog bounded up the steps with more energy than he had demonstrated all evening, when he had plodded along reluctantly the whole walk.

"You are a rascal dog," Gabe said to the little Frenchie. Louie gave him a sideways look, apparently not disagreeing.

After he rang the doorbell, it took a moment before Daisy opened it. Her hair was pulled up in that tight updo style she seemed to favor, but stray tendrils had slipped free, framing her face.

He had a vivid memory of their kiss, her arms around him, her mouth warm and yielding.

He wanted to take a picture. Stills, not video. He would frame her here in this beautiful garden around her house, with sunlight filtering through the trees and kissing her skin.

He didn't expect he would be able to capture her particular mystique, but he would certainly love to try.

She had that funny look in her eyes again when she looked at him, the one that made him wonder if she was thinking about their kiss, too.

Daisy scooped up the dog. "How was your long walk, Louie? Are you completely worn out?"

"I didn't mean to be gone so long. Sorry about that. We headed back to Casa Del Mar for what I thought would be a quick stop but I got distracted with a phone call from one of my producers discussing the press tour for the last film we made."

"I was hoping I wouldn't have to launch another rescue effort and come looking for you two."

He rather liked the idea of her searching for him. "Sorry to make you worry. I should have skipped the walk so I didn't have to interrupt your meeting earlier."

She shrugged. "It's fine. We were able to get back on track eventually."

There were two other women inside. He recognized one as Bea Romero, Cruz's ex-wife. He had met her briefly after he showed up at Casa Del Mar with Cruz. She had been effusive in her gratitude. Though they had just met, she had hugged him tightly, thanking him for saving Cruz's life. Several examples of her artwork were displayed at the house and there was that photograph outside his room of Daisy, her sister, her niece and her aunt.

"Hello again."

She waved with a friendly smile.

The other woman made a small noise that finally drew Daisy's attention. "I'm sorry. This is my aunt Stella."

The woman couldn't be more than a decade older than Daisy. She was pretty in an elfin, winsome sort of way, though she had circles under her eyes and an air of fatigue. He wondered if she'd had a recent health crisis.

"Stella, this is Gabriel Ellison."

She had a warm smile, despite the other signs of illness. "Gabriel. How wonderful to meet you."

"Gabe. Please."

"Gabe. I very much enjoy your documentaries." A little furrow appeared over her eyebrows. "*Enjoyable* isn't exactly the right word, I suppose. *Compelling* fits better. Once I start one, I can't stop watching and I always learn something, whether I want to or not."

"Thank you." He still found it surprising when people knew of his work. Most of the time, he felt like he worked in obscurity.

"Are you working on anything now?" Daisy's aunt asked in what sounded like a deceptively innocent voice.

"Stella." Daisy said her aunt's name like a warning.

"What? I was just asking."

"I'm actually considering a couple of projects. I'm suddenly interested in the artist Marguerite."

It was a calculated risk and not very nice of him. He saw panic flicker momentarily in Daisy's eyes and tension steal over her features but no hint of reaction other than polite interest in the expression of her aunt or sister. As he suspected, they didn't know Daisy's secret identity.

"Oh, that would be fascinating. I would love to find out who it is. My theory is Marguerite is a man," Bea said. "An old guy."

"Really?" Stella looked disbelieving. "I can't believe that, with her sensitivity and elegance. It's definitely a woman. Do you have any leads into who it might be?"

Daisy looked trapped, suddenly, like a tiny mouse cornered against a kitchen baseboard by a giant wielding a broom and a dustpan.

Regret swamped him. He had vowed to keep her secret and the first thing he did was bring it up with her family members. He was about to change the subject but she beat him to it.

"My aunt and sister were actually wondering if you might be interested in filming a short commercial promo for the fundraiser we're doing at the end of the month," she blurted out. "We are hoping to generate more interest and awareness in Open Hearts throughout Northern California, both from potential donors and from the population we're trying to serve."

The moment she said the words, he could tell she didn't want to, especially when Bea and Stella both looked at her in shock and surprise.

No doubt she was only using the topic as a diversion, to keep her aunt and her sister from finding out the truth about Marguerite.

Again, he had to wonder why she was guarding that secret like it was a stolen masterpiece.

What was she so afraid of? They seemed like very nice people. Did Daisy really think they would shun her for finding incredible success as an artist?

He felt guilty enough about bringing up the topic she so desperately wanted to avoid that he was compelled to make amends. "Sounds intriguing, especially as the foster care crisis is a cause close to my heart. I might be interested."

He saw the three women exchange glances. "Really?" Stella asked, eyes wide.

It wasn't usually the sort of thing he did, but he might be willing to make an exception in this case, especially if it would help further his own cause, finding out more about the intriguing Daisy McClure. "Sure. I would love to help out. I would have to set one condition, though."

Again, the women exchanged glances. "What would that be?" Daisy asked, a subtle thread of apprehension twining through her voice.

She thought he was going to blurt out her secret. He probably deserved her suspicion, considering he had brought up the topic in the first place, but it still hurt a little that she didn't trust him to protect her.

"None of my regular crew is around, so I'm going to need an assistant. Daisy, how about it?"

She looked shocked. "I don't know anything about making a documentary."

"But you know about Open Hearts."

"The money side of things. That's it. Nobody wants to see that kind of boring information."

Stella frowned. "Why do you always underestimate your contribution? We would truly be lost without you keeping us on track."

"Stella would be the best one to help you," Daisy insisted. "She's the founder and organizer of the charity and does most of the nitty-gritty work."

"The very reason I can't have her working as my assistant on a promotional shoot," Gabe said. "She'll be one of the sources. No. It definitely has to be you."

She glared at him, her usual calm reserve nowhere in evidence. He had to admit, he loved breaking through her composed veneer and drawing a reaction out of her.

"You have to help him, Daisy," her sister urged. "This is an opportunity we can't turn down. Think of how wonderful it would be if we had a promotional spot created by none other than Gabe Ellison himself. The publicity alone surrounding the promotion would be fantastic. You can't say no."

Daisy frowned at all of them but especially at him. "What if I don't have time right now?"

Bea scoffed. "You're always saying how busy you are. I don't get why. You should have more time than any of us! You work a job with regular hours that you can walk away from at the end of the day, you don't have kids and you don't have a husband or an ex-husband to deal with."

"Bea." Her aunt's voice was full of censure.

"Well, she doesn't. Daisy uses her packed schedule as an excuse for everything. She never has time for lunch, she's busy in the evenings when we want to go to dinner, and heaven forbid we want to do something on a weekend. I'm so over it. This is a big deal. *Gabriel Ellison* agreeing to produce a promotional shot for us is a big deal."

"I know that," Daisy said stiffly.

"Then maybe you could adjust your important schedule a little just this once."

Ouch. He didn't realize he was poking at old scabs. As he watched, Daisy seemed to curl into herself, like her namesake flower trying to protect itself from harsh conditions.

Stella stepped in to smooth the waters. "You don't have to if you really don't have the time," she said, gripping Daisy's hands in hers. "But it would be wonderful if you could make it work."

Daisy drew in a deep breath, looked at her aunt and her sister, then faced him with her shoulders tight.

"I'm happy to help you," she said, though her body language conveyed exactly the opposite.

"Daisy, I'm sorry," Bea began.

She ignored her sister. "What do you need me to do?"

He didn't want to be the cause of discord between them. He almost told her to forget it, that he would call his actual assistant and see if Gina could come out for a few days to help him.

"We won't have much time, maybe a one-minute spot that local television stations can air as part of their public service announcements, right?"

"Exactly," Stella said.

"I suppose my first step will be to find out everything I can about what you do. Can you send me all the background information you have?"

"We have a press packet, as well as the website that I maintain in my copious spare time," Daisy said.

Her younger sister winced a little but said nothing.

"Sounds like a good place to start. If you could send me that, I'll do some digging on my own and come up with some ideas."

"Thank you so much," Stella said. "This is so exciting! I'm thrilled you're even considering it."

"I'm happy to do it. This recovery has been making me a little bit crazy. This will give me something worthwhile to focus on. Apparently, I'm not very good at doing nothing. But don't worry. We'll come up with something great."

At least now he would have more than just the dog tying him to Daisy. Maybe while they were working on the promotional spot for Open Hearts, he might be able to convince her to let him do a longer piece on Marguerite.

It was worth a try, anyway.

16

BEATRIZ

Bea knew she owed her sister a big apology. She had picked up the phone half a dozen times since the day before, when she had been rude to Daisy about her busy schedule. Each time she set it down again, not knowing how to find the right words.

Daisy was so private, so contained. Sometimes it drove her crazy.

She loved her sister deeply and admired her for many things. In reality, Daisy had been more of a mother to Bea than even Stella had been, always watching out for her, taking care of her, giving her advice. She remembered plenty of times when they were small when Daisy was the only solid thing she had to hang on to.

That was probably why it hurt so much when Daisy shut her out of her life. Her sister kept her emotions so carefully controlled. Sometimes she would give anything to have Daisy yell at her or get angry at a driver who cut her off in traffic or cry when she was having a bad day.

Some part of her also wished she could be more like Daisy, at least in that respect. Bea's emotions always seemed close to the surface, ready to bubble over into laughter, sadness or snippiness, as she had demonstrated the day before.

She needed to talk to Daisy before things got even more awkward between them. She reached for her phone to call, just as the timer went off on the oven. Later, she promised herself. She would call later to clear the air.

She opened the oven to check on the chocolate chip cookies currently sending out their delicious aroma through her kitchen.

Shane had texted her an hour ago, asking if he could bring his team over to watch some highlight films in her screening room since the team couldn't cram into the living space of the guesthouse.

Of course she had agreed, despite the awkwardness that still lingered between her and Shane.

Who *hadn't* she pissed off this week? she wondered.

At least she would have cookies for the team. She was one of the unofficial team moms and took her responsibilities seriously.

She was scooping the cookies from the tray to the cooling rack when the doorbell rang. "Coming," she called, then wiped her hands on a dish towel and hurried to the front door.

She expected to find members of the Cape Sanctuary high school football team. Instead, only her ex-husband stood on the porch, carrying a guitar case.

Of all the lousy timing. Why did he have to come *tonight*, when Shane would be there shortly with his team?

She had gone over her conversation with Shane hundreds of times since the night they kissed and still didn't think she was wrong to take Cruz's phone call, especially when her child was involved.

If Shane couldn't see that, the problem was *his*, not hers. That didn't mean she needed Cruz to be hanging out in her house right now, the first time she had really seen Shane since that night.

"Cruz! I wasn't expecting you. I'm afraid Mari is spending the night with Aunt Stella. They're going to dinner and a movie later tonight."

"I'm not here to see Mari. I'm here to see you."

She could feel her stomach muscles tense. There went all the calm she had tried to attain through yoga that morning.

Why couldn't he get the message that she didn't want to reconcile with him?

The timer went off with the next batch of cookies before she could answer. She looked back at the kitchen and Cruz gestured with the hand not holding the guitar.

"Go ahead. Take care of that. Whatever you're cooking smells delicious."

Without waiting for an invitation, he walked inside, closing the door behind him. With a sigh, she headed back to the kitchen, aware of him following close behind.

"I'm making cookies for the high school football team. They're coming over in a moment to watch films."

"Don't let me stop you. I don't want to be in the way but I need your input for a song I'm working on. You were always so good at helping me get unstuck."

That was an approach he hadn't yet tried, enlisting her help with songwriting. "I'm kind of in the middle of something."

"This won't take long, I swear." She wasn't at all surprised when Cruz followed her and snatched up one of the cookies from the previous batch off the cooling rack.

"Mmm. Delicious. I always loved your chocolate chip cookies."

She had never been much of a cook but liked to bake treats once in a while for parties and gatherings. Chocolate chip cookies became her specialty. She could make them without a recipe and used to bake a batch every time he had a gig for him to take and share with the band.

She had tried hard to be a perfect wife. Maybe too hard.

He ate it in two bites and reached for another. "They are as delicious as I remember," he said around a mouthful. "You could seriously go into business baking and selling these, babe."

"I have a career, remember?"

"I'm just saying, if you get tired of the art thing, this would be a good fallback."

The *art thing* was her passion and her soul. It wasn't a career; it was who she was. She would have liked to think that a musician, a fellow artist, would recognize that.

She would like to think a lot of things about Cruz Romero but reality had taught her not to be surprised by anything.

"The team is going to be here within the next half hour. I can give you that much time but that's it. What do you need?"

He sat on one of the bar stools and watched while she spooned cookie dough onto a cookie sheet lined with parchment paper for the next batch.

"I've hit a wall. To be honest, I'm stuck. I haven't been this stuck in a long time."

She knew that feeling well in her art. The hardest part for her was facing a blank canvas and trying to grab hold of only one of the thousands of ideas tumbling through her head.

"Why do you think you're having trouble?"

"I've been messed up since that idiot came at me with a knife. Every time I pick up my guitar to work on a song, I keep going over and over in my head that moment when I thought I was a goner."

Compassion replaced some of her annoyance. He could have died. She didn't like thinking about how close he'd come. It was only natural for an experience like that to mess with his head.

"Maybe you should give yourself a little more time. There's

no rush to come up with a new album, is there? Your last one only came out four months ago."

"You know how it is. I always want to be working on the fresh stuff."

Yes. She did know how it was, especially with Cruz. The grass was always greener for him, in many other arenas of his life besides his songwriting.

"I don't know how you think I can help you."

"You were always so good at talking me over the hump when I was stuck. Remember how hard you worked with me on 'Baby Don't Go'?"

That had been early in her marriage, when he had listened to her opinions. It had also been one of his biggest hits. Not that she was petty about it or anything.

"Let's hear what you have so far."

Cruz played a few bars. The song was a ballad, lyrical and sweet, about love and pain and loss. It hit a little too close to home for her.

"Sing it again," she said.

He did and she thought again how evocative his voice had always been. He could wring emotions out of a marble statue.

He was a good songwriter but had a few consistent weaknesses.

She came around and looked at the scribbled music he'd set on the kitchen breakfast bar.

"I think you need a different bridge here," she said, pointing to the sheet music. "What if you went…" She sang a couple of lines a little differently, changing a couple of words to tweak the emphasis.

His eyes immediately lit up.

"You mean like this?" He followed her example, adding his own unique style and flavor. She could sense the magic in the song. This one was going to be another hit; she could tell right away.

"Yes. And instead of going down in the last bar of the chorus, what if the notes went up? It puts more of a positive spin on it."

He tested it out and she knew even before she saw his sudden grin that she was right.

"That is actually perfect," he exclaimed. "Just what I needed. How do you always get to the heart of things so quickly?"

She would be lying if she said she wasn't flattered by his approval. Once, it had been the most important thing in her world.

"I don't know," she admitted. "It's only your songs. I doubt I could help anyone else. I guess I know your voice so well, I know what works for you and what doesn't."

"I have missed this. I can't tell you how much. We always made a great team when it came to the music."

Too bad life had been far more than just making music. Too bad they'd had to deal with her immaturity and his infidelities and substance abuse.

"That's exactly what I needed. I'm going to give you credit on the song."

"That's silly. I helped you for ten minutes. I don't exactly deserve cowriter status."

He grinned. "You do if I say you do. Seriously, thanks, babe."

He reached in to kiss her before she could move away. She turned her head, and at that moment, of course, Shane walked in.

He stood in the doorway, gazing at the scene with an expression she couldn't read. She immediately stepped away from Cruz then hated herself for feeling flustered. Damn it. She hadn't done anything wrong.

Anyway, if Shane wanted more from her than friendship, why hadn't he done something about it before now?

"Hi," she said, trying for a cheerful tone. "Is the rest of the team with you?"

He inclined his head behind him, where several burly young men came in behind him.

"Hey, Ms. R.," said Travis Taylor. He was one of her favorites, the starting quarterback for the year who was only a junior.

"Hi, Travis. Hey, everybody."

In moments her kitchen was filled with teenage football players, a good twenty-five of them. They were larger than the average high school student, but still so young it made her heart ache. What did life have in store for these boys? She hoped the world would be kind to them.

She hadn't enjoyed her high school years and had dropped out of high school midway through her senior year to run away to LA with Cruz. Stella had *not* been happy about it, which she understood through an entirely different lens now.

She'd gone back to finish her GED during those early years of their marriage and had even earned an associate's degree later. Still, sometimes she regretted not taking the traditional route.

"Cookies!" one of the football players exclaimed.

"Can we have one, Ms. Romero?" Tony Feola eyed the entire tray with a ravenous eye.

"Guys. You can at least say hello to Bea first before you start pigging out on the snacks she didn't have to make," Shane said sternly. He was very good at making sure his team was courteous. As a coach, Shane didn't tolerate disrespect or slovenly behavior. His players were expected to live up to a high standard and set an example to all other students at Cape Sanctuary High, not just athletes.

A chorus of hellos greeted her at that, which made her smile. She gave a general wave. "Hey, everyone. You can have a couple of cookies each. There should be enough. I made popcorn also. It's already waiting in the viewing room."

"You're the best, Ms. R.," Travis said with his charming smile.

She really enjoyed being part of the football team, even on the periphery. Since Shane had come back to Cape Sanctuary to teach, she had attended every home game and many of the away ones. It was the sort of thing a wife or girlfriend would do, if Shane had one. Since he didn't, she loved filling in.

"Thanks, guys. Go ahead and help yourself."

"Take a couple of cookies, then head to the media room so the rest of our teammates can grab theirs," Shane ordered.

As they moved around him to reach for the cookies on the kitchen island, they finally caught sight of Cruz. The mood in the room immediately changed. Though they weren't exactly slouching, the boys seemed to straighten to attention, clearly knowing his identity.

Cruz Romero was a small-town boy from Cape Sanctuary who made good. Everybody knew him. She wanted to think the team liked her for herself, because she was kind to them and supported them, but she had a sneaking suspicion some of her popularity among the players had more to do with her ex-husband.

The whispers started first from the front line of players, then seemed to grow louder.

"Cruz! How are you, man?" The first boy to break the awed silence was Carlos Ayala, who had been one of Aunt Stella's foster children, until he had been adopted by a neighbor. Because Cruz had *also* been one of Stella's foster kids, Carlos considered them as good as family, which she thought terribly sweet.

Cruz slapped his back. "Hey, Carlos. How's it going, man?"

"I'm good. I'm good."

Carlos stepped up to introduce the rest of the team members and they all seemed predictably awestruck to be hanging out in the same kitchen as their local celebrity. Several asked for selfies with him and Cruz was, also predictably, happy to oblige.

She shifted, wishing she had been able to push him out of her house before the team arrived. Shane didn't say anything, but she could tell he wasn't thrilled at having his team meeting commandeered.

After about fifteen minutes he seemed to run out of patience. "We should probably get cracking if we want to get through the films. Practice comes early in the morning and you boys need your sleep."

"Yeah, guys. Let's go."

Travis, a natural leader, led the team down the hallway to her home theater, which was a sheer luxury she enjoyed very much, with several rows of sofas and the giant-screen TV. Bea sometimes had movie nights with her girlfriends and Mari loved having her friends over and binge-watching their favorite TV shows.

"Sorry about them," Shane said stiffly after the boys tromped out. "They're good kids, but can lose their heads around celebrities."

"Not a problem at all. I'm used to it."

"No doubt." Shane gave a smile that didn't quite reach his eyes. He didn't look at her as he spoke and she fought the urge to explain the kiss wasn't what he thought.

She didn't owe him any explanations. Not when he had been so cold since their own kiss.

"I can bring more cookies in when this next batch comes out of the oven."

He finally met her gaze. "Thanks, but you really don't have to. I didn't mean for you to go to so much trouble."

She gave a determined smile. "I know I didn't have to do it but I wanted to."

He looked at her for a long moment with that unreadable expression in his eyes again. "Thank you," he said before heading to the media room with his team.

"It's nice of you to help Shane's team out," Cruz said.

"They're nice young men," she said. "Many of them come from tough situations. He's been a great role model to them. He cares very much for them. All of them, even the boys who don't have much athletic skill at all. It's about the team to him and helping each one find his own strengths."

"I can see that," he said, surprising her a little. "I imagine he's a good coach."

"He is," she said. *And I'm in love with him, so you're going to have to get used to that.*

"Well, you've got your hands full. I'd better get out of your hair. Thanks again for all your help with the song. It works much better now. I'll let you know if I need something else."

Cruz seemed a little subdued and she wondered what she had said but didn't have time to worry about it as the timer went off on the next batch of cookies.

After delivering the plate to the media room, where everyone was engrossed in watching footage of the team they were playing for their opener in a few weeks, Bea retreated to her studio to take care of some paperwork and do some planning for her next gallery show at a studio in Carmel in a few months.

An hour later, when she heard cars leaving out front, she headed back to the media room to find it empty except for Shane, who was picking up disposable cups and popcorn bags.

"You don't have to do that. I can clean up."

He rolled his eyes at her. "My team. My mess."

My house. My guests, she wanted to say in reply, but knew she wouldn't win the argument. "Fine. I'll help you."

She headed back into the kitchen for a garbage bag and her vacuum then returned to the media room. "How were the films?" she asked.

"Good. It wasn't really about the films. I just need my team to come together. We've been struggling with that a little bit this year. We've got a couple of stubborn rich kids who think they're too good to play with the dairy farm dudes."

The demographics of Cape Sanctuary were a mixed bag and that could cause occasional social discord. Because it was a coastal community, it brought in wealthy people who wanted seaside homes, but the area had been founded by farmers and ranchers. A few miles inland was all agriculture. She remembered those cliques herself from high school. The farm kids would hang out in the parking lots in their pickup trucks and John Deere hats while the surfer dudes would mock them in their clothes from Roxy and Aeropostale.

"I'm sure you'll bring them together."

"I'm trying."

He grabbed the vacuum from her so he could clean up the loose kernels.

"I'm coming to the game this weekend," she told him when he turned off the vacuum cleaner. "Is there anything I can bring? Gatorade? Orange slices? More chocolate chip cookies?"

"I think we're good," he said as he wound the cord. "The booster club has really stepped it up this year. Hopefully, we won't have to lean on you as much as we had to last year."

"I didn't mind," she told him. "I love the guys on your team."

"And they love you—though maybe not as much as they love your husband."

"Ex-husband," she said firmly.

"Not if he can help it, right? He wants you back."

"What he wants doesn't really matter, does it? It's what I want that's important."

A muscle flexed in his jaw. "I'm not sure you know what you want."

"I'm sure I know what I *don't* want. Another man telling me what I should or shouldn't feel."

"Is that what you think I'm doing?"

She sighed, afraid again to ruin their friendship by bringing up her new feelings for him.

On the other hand, their friendship was already cracking apart because of the effort it was taking her *not* to tell him.

She had to find the courage to tell him. She was tired of being timid. He might reject her, yes, but she wouldn't know unless she told him.

"Shane, you're my best friend. You have been for years and I'm so grateful for that, but I...I don't want to be your friend anymore."

Hurt glimmered in his eyes. "Fair enough. I get it."

"I don't think you do."

She stepped forward. "I want to be more than friends. I've wanted that for a while now. Am I wrong or do you…do you want that, too?"

He gazed down at her. "What about Cruz?"

"He has nothing to do with this. With us."

"That's where you're wrong, Bea. He has always been there, between us. An hour ago you were kissing him."

"He was kissing *me*. There's a big difference."

"Have you told him that you're not getting back with him? Just came out and said it?"

"I've tried. You know how he is. He hears what he wants to hear."

"You asked my opinion. Here it is. If you have any feelings left for Cruz, I think you owe it to your child to try. You came from a screwed-up home life and I did, too, always split between the people we loved. Divorce is tough on kids, no matter how amicable it is. I love that kid and want the best for her. If there is any chance a reconciliation with Cruz is better for her, I can't stand in the way."

She didn't know what to think. Yes, what he said was rational, but every part of her cried out in protest. "You sound like you've given the matter some thought."

He gave her a look filled with raw emotion. "Of course I have. I care about you, Bea. You're my oldest and dearest friend. I'll always be grateful for what we shared but lately…lately I've come to accept it's not enough for me anymore."

She felt the first struggling seedlings of hope. "Then we're on the same page. It's not enough for me, either. That kiss the other night made it clear, I think, that we both want to take the next step in our relationship."

"And what? You juggle me and Cruz until you decide what's best for Mari? No. I can't do that. I'm at a place in my life where

I'm ready to find someone and settle down. Losing my dad this year was a wake-up call. My life is finite. I want to fill what's left of it with kids of my own and a woman who is completely free to love me. I don't think I can find what I need while I'm living in your guesthouse."

Those tendrils of hope withered and died at the finality in his voice. "Your house isn't ready yet. You can wait until it's done, can't you?"

"No. I think it's better if I move out sooner. My new assistant coach, Marcus, just leased a house on the other side of town with a fenced backyard for Sal. He's offered to let me crash there for another few weeks."

"What's wrong with the guesthouse?"

"Nothing is wrong with it. I've enjoyed being close, hanging out with Mar and with you. But by staying here with you, I think I'm making it harder for you to figure out what you really want."

"I know what I want. I want *you*, Shane. I've loved you as a friend since I was a girl and now I'm coming to see there's more to it. If you…if you feel the same, I'm not sure where the problem is."

A muscle flexed in his jaw. "Cruz. I hate that he hurt you again and again and yet he'll always have a part of your heart that I can't touch."

"We share a child. At this point that's the full extent of our relationship."

"If that was all, you would tell him it's time for him to move on, too, that you're never getting back together with him. You haven't done that, though, which makes me think some part of you is still wondering if it's possible for a reconciliation."

"What do you want me to do? Take out a newspaper ad?" She fought the urge to dump the can full of garbage over the stubborn man's head.

"No. I only want you to be clear about what you want and I

don't think that can happen while I'm here. I'll move my things over to Marcus's place this weekend."

He didn't give her a chance to argue, just picked up the bag of trash and walked out, leaving her angry and hurt and fearful that she had just lost her best friend.

17

STELLA

Inviting her niece to spend the night at this particular stage of her pregnancy may not have been Stella's greatest idea.

"Are you sure you're okay?" The worry in Mari's voice coming from outside the bathroom door broke her heart.

"I'm fine, honey," she lied, just as what was left of her stomach lining insisted on coming back out.

"I don't think you're fine at all," Mari said. "You've been puking for like twenty minutes straight."

Oh, she hated this stupid morning sickness! Whoever named it that was obviously a man who didn't understand it could hit at any moment. She had been nauseated on and off for days now and had spent entirely too much time bent over a commode.

"Just give me a minute," she managed. "It's probably something I ate."

"That's what you said when we went to Universal," Mari said. "You must be eating some bad stuff."

She was going to have to tell someone. She had carried this alone for too long. She had done her best to keep her pregnancy a secret but her severe morning sickness was interfering in her life.

"Give me a few more minutes then I'll drive you back home."

She threw up one last time and was wiping her mouth and brushing her teeth—grateful she had taken to keeping dental hygiene supplies in every bathroom—when she heard the doorbell ring.

Oh, great. She was *not* in the mood for company right now.

"Whoever that is, tell them I'm not home," she said weakly. She didn't think Mari was still outside the bathroom door but it was worth a try.

She opened the door, only to find Ed Clayton walking toward her with a very worried-looking Mari.

"It's too late for that," he said.

Of all the people she did not want seeing her like this, Ed was right at the top of the list. She knew she looked like death warmed over, with messy hair, pale skin, deep hollows under her eyes. It was the very reason she had been avoiding everyone as much as possible.

"Oh, Stell. How long has this been going on?"

She wanted so desperately to fall into his arms and weep. "It feels like decades," she admitted. "I'm pretty sure it's only been a few weeks. The past five or six days have been the worst. I thought today was better but it hit me hard about an hour ago."

If she hadn't already made plans several weeks earlier to take Mari to the movie premiere of one of her favorite continuing sagas, she never would have invited her to spend the night.

"How did you know I was sick?" she asked.

"Me," Mari said, chin jutted in defiance. "I texted Rowan and told her to tell her dad that you fainted after dinner and that you've been throwing up ever since you woke up. I know you must be really, really sick. Are you dying, Aunt Stella?"

"No. No, honey." She closed her eyes, trying to find the energy to explain in a way Mari could understand.

"You did the right thing, calling for help," Ed told her great-niece. "Stella is not dying. I suspect your aunt is dehydrated. She's going to have to go to the ER for some IV fluids."

"Can't you do that?" Stella asked him hopefully. She didn't want the fuss and bother of going into the hospital, where everyone would have to find out about her pregnancy.

"You don't want me giving you an IV, I promise. The ER nurses are much better at that than I could ever be. Has Jo given you a prescription for anti-nausea medicine? There are certain things you can take that are completely safe for you and the..." He glanced over at Mari and Rowan, who had followed her father into the house.

"For everyone," he amended quickly, avoiding mention of the word *baby* that seemed to hover over them. She was grateful for his discretion.

"Come on," he said. "Let's get you to the ER."

She didn't want to go but knew he was right. She hadn't kept anything down, even water, in days. She and her baby needed fluids. School was starting soon and she would need all her strength to take on a new year and new students.

"What about Mari and Rowan?"

"I already texted my mom," Mari said. "She's coming to pick me up. If it's okay with my mom and with Dr. Clayton, Rowan can hang out at my house while he takes you to the hospital."

She was going to have to tell both Bea and Daisy. It was past time. She should have done it earlier. She should have told them after the Open Hearts board meeting. Keeping the secret had been selfish, her wish to keep the knowledge of her child growing inside her close to her heart a little longer.

"I need to call her," Stella said. "I need to call Beatriz and Daisy both."

"I don't think you're going to have to do that," Ed predicted.

She wasn't sure how he knew, but he was right. A moment later the door burst open and Bea rushed through. She looked distraught, almost haggard. Was that only from worry about her? Stella couldn't be sure.

"What is going on, Aunt Stella?" she demanded. "Mari texted me that you've been sick all evening and that you even passed out for a minute."

Mari was a little snitch. But Stella couldn't blame her.

"It's nothing. Ed thinks I need to go to the ER for some fluids. After that I'll be as good as new."

"This stomach bug has lasted for weeks. Are you sure it's not something more? You said you were feeling better or I never would have sent Mari to stay over."

Daisy burst through the door before Stella could answer.

"You told Daisy?" Stella asked. She wasn't happy about it, but at least the two were talking. She had worried after the board meeting and Bea's unkind words that a rift might grow.

"Somebody had to. This has gone on long enough," Daisy said in her best Daisy-stern voice. "You need to tell us what is going on. I don't want to hear about the flu. I don't want to hear about food poisoning. Tell us the truth."

Almost against her will, Stella looked at Ed for strength. He placed a reassuring hand on her shoulder and she felt the heat of it soak through her entire battered body.

Oh, how grateful she was for him. What would she do without him back in her life?

"I'll tell you," she finally said.

"Why don't we let Stella sit down first?" Ed suggested.

They moved into her living room, with the stained-glass windows and the gorgeous woodwork she had so painstakingly restored. She loved this room. Would her baby love it? She would definitely have to do some babyproofing before she delivered.

"Mari, Rowan. Why don't you go pack up Mari's things and take them out to my car?" Bea suggested.

The girls looked disappointed at not being privy to the big reveal but she had a feeling Bea would tell her daughter anyway and Mari, in turn, would tell her friend.

It didn't matter. The whole world could know now.

"I'm not sick," she began.

Daisy raised an eyebrow. "Huh. You're certainly giving a pretty good imitation of someone who's gravely ill."

"I don't have influenza or food poisoning, at any rate."

This was harder than she'd expected. What would Daisy and Bea think of her? Would they think she was too old to be embarking on this journey on her own?

"The truth is, I have bad morning sickness."

For about thirty seconds, nothing but silence met her announcement. She saw the shock in both Bea's and Daisy's expressions.

Daisy was the first to speak. "You're...you're pregnant?"

"Pregnant!" Bea turned to Ed, much to Stella's mortification. "Are you the father?"

"No!" she said sharply. "I hadn't spoken to Ed in years when I got pregnant. He has nothing to do with this."

Why did his jaw tighten when she said that? What had she said to annoy him? She couldn't worry about that now; she had to explain to her nieces.

"The baby is mine. I got pregnant through a sperm donor and artificial insemination. It's something I've been wanting for a long time, a decision I thought long and hard about. I'm having a baby."

"Wow. That's a big step. I can't believe you didn't discuss it with us," Daisy said.

"What wonderful news!" Bea exclaimed. "I'm so happy for you!" She jumped up and hugged Stella. After a moment Daisy did the same, though she still looked worried.

"I loved the chance I had to raise you both, as well as all

the foster children who have come through those doors, but I wanted a child of my own. Someone who...wouldn't leave."

She hadn't meant to say that last bit. It slipped out before she could clamp her lips down and hold it back. Ed's jaw tightened again and she could see he had plenty of things he wanted to say to her.

He hadn't left. *She* had left *him*.

She knew exactly what was running through his mind and she had no defense against the truth.

"I think it's terrific," Bea said stoutly. "You're a wonderful, nurturing woman with so much love to give. I'm thrilled for you."

"If this is what you truly want, I'm happy for you, too," Daisy said. Despite her words, Daisy still looked stunned and worried.

Stella could relate. She hadn't yet found her happy place with the whole idea yet, either.

"Thank you, my darling girls." She hugged them both, then had to sit down, afraid she would pass out again.

"She's dehydrated because she hasn't been keeping anything down in days," Ed said. "Right now the important thing is to get her to the ER for IV fluids as soon as possible."

"I'll take you," Daisy said promptly.

She dearly loved her niece, but right now, for a hundred different reasons, she wanted Ed.

"I would rather have Dr. Clayton, honey."

She didn't want to look at him to see his reaction, though she sensed his surprise.

"Do you mind?" she asked.

"As long as Bea is okay with Rowan hanging out with Mari for a while."

"Of course I don't mind. She can stay over and you can get her in the morning."

"Dr. Clayton is right. The important thing now is for you to take care of yourself," Daisy said.

"You and the baby," Bea added.

"I'm trying."

She was grateful beyond words for these girls who had added so much joy and laughter and life to her world. Yes, she had sacrificed a great deal to take care of them. At the time she felt as if she had no choice. They had been so very needy, lost and alone, separated by the foster care system.

She wasn't sure exactly what had happened to them in the year they were in the system, before she found out Jewel had died. What little she did know broke her heart. Daisy, at least, had suffered things she didn't want to think about. Her oldest niece had gone from a bright, happy, passionately loyal girl to a child who had been withdrawn, silent, careful not to show any emotion.

It still hurt her heart when she thought about it.

She couldn't regret any of her choices—even giving up Ed, though she had ached for him for nearly two decades.

She didn't know what it meant that he had come back into her life at this stage. She didn't have any expectations that they could pick up where they had left off in their relationship. He had made that clear enough.

Since he had come to Cape Sanctuary, Ed had been friendly enough to her, but he seemed very much like Daisy. He seemed to hold all his emotions back behind a barrier she could not breach.

He was here now. He was willing to help her at the hospital, concerned over her welfare and that of her unborn baby.

For now, that would have to be enough.

18

DAISY

Daisy closed the door after Stella and Dr. Clayton, still try-ing to process the shock of the past few minutes.

Pregnant. Stella!

Sometimes she forgot her aunt was still a relatively young woman, barely forty. Stella had tried so hard to be an authority figure with her and Bea when they first came to live with her that Daisy had gotten into the habit of thinking of her as older than her years.

What she never forgot was how very much she and Bea owed their aunt. She had brought her nieces here to begin rebuilding their lives and now she was going to have a baby here.

"Stella's having a baby. Can you believe it?" Bea's chandelier earrings danced as she shook her head.

"No. For weeks I've been coming up with all kinds of hor-rible scenarios for why she's been so ill. I wouldn't have guessed she was pregnant in a million years."

"It's a relief, though, right?"

"Certainly beats a lot of the alternatives," Daisy said.

"Why has she kept it a big secret, do you think?" Bea asked. She sounded a little put out, which mirrored many of the thoughts running through Daisy's head. Stella had obviously been working toward becoming pregnant for some time. Why wouldn't she have wanted to share this journey with Bea and Daisy?

"Maybe she wasn't sure it would work out. She's an older mother, after all."

Stella was only a decade older than Daisy. Her own biological clock ticked louder with every passing year, something she was finding harder and harder to ignore.

"So what do we do now?"

As always, Bea looked to her to lead the way. It had been that way when they were two girls living in a chaotic world, basically raising themselves. She was the older sister and it had always been her responsibility to watch out for her younger sister.

"We're family. We support each other, no matter what."

To her shock, tears gathered in Bea's eyes. "I'm sorry, okay? I'm sorry I was a bitch to you after the Open Hearts meeting. I…I've been under some stress lately and I took it out on you and I'm sorry. I shouldn't have said those things about you not being busy. I tried to call you a hundred times today to tell you how bad I felt and I was too stubborn to do it."

Daisy's heart melted and she hugged Bea. She might not always understand her sister's vivacity and her spontaneity but she loved her. Beatriz would always be her baby sister.

"I love you," Bea said. "I don't say it enough, but I do."

Something else was going on here, Daisy suspected. Her sister wasn't crying only because of their spat the day before, which was relatively minor compared to some of the fights they used to get into as teenagers.

"It's okay. I know. I…love you, too."

Bea rested her head for a moment on Daisy's shoulder and she patted her wild tangle of curls, her throat aching with emotions while her sister cried.

After a few minutes Bea pulled away and grabbed a tissue off a side table. "I'm sorry. It's been a rough evening for me. I was so scared about Stella when Mari texted me."

That wasn't everything, she suspected. "What else is going on?"

"I... Nothing." Bea gave a smile that was obviously fake. "I'm just worried about her. I hope she knows what she's getting into. Being a single mother is not an easy road, even when you have a great support system. It still comes down to you being wholly responsible for the life of someone else."

Daisy blinked at the stark honesty in her sister's words. She was a little ashamed at her own insensitivity. She had always thought Bea had things together.

Some corner of her heart had always resented her sister a little. Everyone had always taken care of her, starting with Daisy when they were kids. From Daisy's perspective, her sister hadn't had to struggle much. At least not financially. Maybe in the early days of her marriage, she and Cruz had eaten plenty of macaroni and cheese, but Cruz's career had hit fast and hard. He made pots of money—which she knew full well as one of his financial managers—and he shared generously with his ex-wife and child.

She wasn't shallow enough to think money solved every problem. She'd seen too much of life to believe that. But considering so much of her childhood had revolved around her struggle to make sure her baby sister had food and shelter, financial security equated to peace of mind to her.

A person could have more than enough money and still be faced with hardships. Bea had been divorced young from a husband who could never be faithful. And obviously, she struggled more than Daisy understood with being a single mother.

"Stella has a wonderful example in her own family of how to be a single parent with grace and grit," she said softly.

Bea's eyes filled up again. "Thank you."

"And anyway, she won't be alone. We'll be here to help her."

"You're absolutely right. Also, did you see the way Dr. Clayton was looking at her? Tell me I'm crazy now. The man clearly has feelings for Aunt Stella. Wouldn't it be wonderful if they could get together again, after all these years, especially with a baby in the picture?"

Was Ed truly Stella's lost love? Was he the reason she had never married, even after Daisy and Bea had moved out?

Had she been carrying a torch all these years for the handsome doctor, transferring her need to love and be loved to taking in strays?

It was strange enough thinking about Stella having a baby. Having a baby *and* a new romantic interest at the same time might blow Daisy's mind.

"Let's focus on one thing at a time, should we? You need to get Mari and Rowan home. I'll wait here to make sure Stella is settled when she gets back."

Bea smiled, looking a little less lost. "You're right. You're always right."

Daisy only wished that were true.

She was still trying to process the stunning events of the past few hours when she finally drove from Three Oaks to Pear Tree Cottage after Stella returned from the hospital and was settled in her bed with plenty of fluids, her TV remote and her cell phone.

Daisy had wanted to spend the night but Stella had insisted she would be fine and felt a million times better after the IV fluids.

She had looked better. Not 100 percent, perhaps, but happier, certainly. And Dr. Clayton had been adorably attentive, making sure she had his number programmed into her phone and had everything she needed. He said he would stay until she was asleep, since his daughter was spending the night with Mari.

Was there something between them? She was beginning to suspect Bea was right. Stella certainly seemed to rely on the man.

What had broken them up in the first place?

She knew Stella had just graduated from UCLA when she was able to finally get custody of her and Bea. If they'd known each other in college, was it possible Stella had broken things off with him because of *them*?

It would be just like Stella to sacrifice her own chance at happiness for her nieces.

If that was the case, maybe Bea was right. Maybe they did need to step in and try to push the two of them back together.

She was trying to figure out ways to do that when she pulled into her driveway, feeling the sense of homecoming she always did here at Pear Tree Cottage.

She loved this house, not only because it provided financial stability, but also because for the first time in her life she had something of her own.

The moment she opened the door, Louie came running out to greet her, his stump tail wagging and his grumpy little face looking so adorable she had to scoop him up.

"How's my good boy? Did you miss me?"

The little Frenchie licked her face, which she took to mean, *Absolutely and I'm so glad you're finally home.*

She had a million things to do. Quarterly taxes, several investment reports, not to mention half a dozen new commissions for Marguerite to finish. Right now she wanted to do none of those things.

"Let's go for a walk," she said to the dog, who yelped in excitement and wriggled around in her arms.

She found his leash, hooked it to his collar, grabbed a flashlight and the container of pepper spray she carried when she walked—a girl couldn't be too careful, after all—and the two of them headed out the door.

The night was glorious, with a full moon hanging over the ocean and a glitter of stars overhead. The ocean below pounded against the rocks in the soothing rhythm that always seemed to provide such peace to her soul.

She and Louie walked the path beside the road that followed the cliffs. He sniffed at every blade of grass and every small crack in the sidewalk while she ambled along, enjoying the wind in her face and the smell of the sea.

She loved it here. Cape Sanctuary was home to her, a beautiful and welcome haven after her first chaotic decade on the planet. Her aunt had made it a stable and supportive place to grow up.

She was so grateful to Stella. *Gratitude* seemed a completely inadequate word. The debt she owed her aunt was impossibly vast. She could never hope to repay it. She would, however, do her best to support Stella and her unborn baby in whatever way necessary.

Bea would do the same, she knew. They would both help Stella raise her child.

She and Louie were about halfway between Pear Tree Cottage and Casa Del Mar when she spied a dark figure crouched over something at an odd angle. Louie spotted the figure at the same time and started barking—not his stranger-danger bark but his friendly, I-missed-you yip.

The dog's eagerness immediately gave away the identity of the person. Her heartbeat seemed to accelerate as she recognized the figure now and realized the strange stance came from bending over a tripod.

Oh, she really hoped Gabe didn't think she had come looking for him.

In the moonlight, she could see him watching their approach with a smile. "Hello. Beautiful night for a walk, isn't it?"

"That moon is stunning," she answered. The moon was passing right over the bridge that crossed the Sanctuary River where it fed into the sea north of town.

"I couldn't resist trying to shoot the reflection on the water. What brings you out?"

"I needed some air. It's been a long day."

"Pull up a bench and tell me about it," he said, gesturing next to him to one of the many observation spots thoughtfully placed along this beautiful stretch of coastline.

She wanted to talk to him. The memory of that kiss had been haunting her for days. She hadn't slept well since that night and would awaken feeling the emptiness of her bed for the first time in her life.

The air smelled of sage and sea as she sat on a boulder next to him and pulled the dog into her lap. For several minutes she was content to watch him working, framing the moon and the bridge and shooting the long exposure with a remote.

"My aunt is having a baby," she finally said.

He looked over, distracted from the shot. "That's terrific. Congratulations. You're happy for her, aren't you?"

Happy? She wasn't sure she was quite there yet. "Stella is an amazing woman who has sacrificed so much for others. If she wants this child, I want it for her."

Was she being a pessimist for the vague unease that had been bothering her since she found out about Stella's pregnancy?

"You seem conflicted."

She sent him a swift look. How could he be so perceptive? "Not conflicted, exactly. Only worried. She's forty years old. A great deal could go wrong."

"True enough. But think of all the things that could go right."

She wanted to be the sort of person who could focus on all the possibilities in a given situation instead of the potential pitfalls.

"You're right. You're exactly right. That's where I need to put my attention. Stella wants a baby and I want her to be happy."

They were quiet for a few moments, the only sound the click

of his shutter, the wind in the treetops and the waves pounding the shore far below them.

"You and your husband didn't have children. Was that because of his illness?"

His unexpected question came out of nowhere, nearly knocking her off the boulder. "That is an unbelievably personal question."

And intrusive, she wanted to tell him, but she was too busy trying to add salve to the wound his words opened up in her heart.

"I know. Do you have an unbelievably personal answer you care to share? You don't have to if you don't want to."

She didn't. Her first instinct was to snap at him that her marriage was none of his business. Her second was to cry.

She drew in a breath and finally decided on a carefully worded answer.

"Children were...never in the cards for us. I knew that going into the marriage."

"I'm sorry. It was a rude question. That's what comes from being raised in the jungle."

From what she understood of his upbringing, Gabe had largely raised himself. His father had abdicated all responsibility for his child, much the same way Jewel had done for her and Bea.

He said nothing more and they sat in silence for long moments while the night seemed to settle around them. Suddenly, contrarily, she wanted to tell him the truth. All of it, things not even Stella or Bea knew. He already knew about Marguerite. He might as well know the rest of her secrets.

"My marriage was never a...conventional one. More of convenience, I guess you could say. James and I were friends. Dear friends."

"There are worse reasons to marry someone."

"Yes." She looked out to the vast darkness of the sea. "I told you James was ill when I married him. Dying. His wife had died three years before we married and he was terribly lonely. Ill and lonely. I couldn't bear the idea of him living here by himself in his last months."

"So you married him."

She sighed. "I didn't want to. I offered to stay without marrying him but James insisted that was the only way."

He had been so traditional in some ways. "Frances was the love of his life. He told me once he felt as if his heart had been cremated and scattered in the ocean along with her and he had been a shell ever since."

She had wondered what it would be like to have that kind of passion for someone, to give your heart so fully. It had seemed a completely foreign concept to someone as careful and guarded as her.

"James and I were friends and it was a mutually beneficial partnership. He needed my help and I…I guess I needed to be needed."

He shifted from his camera to study her and she was grateful for the darkness so he couldn't see her blush at all those words probably revealed about her.

"He didn't have a good relationship with his family," she went on quickly. "He had a brother and sister-in-law he loathed, Realtors in Eureka. They were his last living heirs and were desperate to get their hands on Pear Tree Cottage. James wanted to prevent them from buying the house and tearing it down for development. He felt like the best way to prevent that was to leave it to someone he trusted."

"You."

"Yes. I didn't want it. I told him he should leave it to his favorite charity but he said houses were meant to be lived in. He was afraid if he left it to any organization, they would only turn around and sell it to developers. The house has a rich history of artists and writers. He wanted someone he cared about to live in it and preserve the legacy of the house and of his career."

"You agreed."

She remembered the arguments she and James had about it. Gradually, he had worn down her resistance and she had agreed to be the executor of his literary trust as well as his house. All the proceeds from that trust went to those charities he had supported, mostly environmental and social equity groups.

The house was hers, though. She hated that there were probably some people—his family among them—who thought she was a gold digger who had only married a lonely, dying man for his house and the cachet of being married to a respected author.

They were so wrong. Their relationship had been so much more than that.

"He was only supposed to live another six months after we got married, but we were fortunate enough to have two great years together. He finished a book and a collection of short stories in that time and considered them his finest work. If I hadn't been here, I'm not sure he would have made it even another month. He was…a very dear friend."

"You still miss him."

"Every day."

"I'm sorry for your loss," he said softly. His words were genuine and made tears burn behind her eyes.

Families came in different shapes and sizes. Hers hadn't been a conventional marriage but she had come out of it a much better person. She would never regret those years she had cared for James.

After a few moments more, he began disassembling his camera setup and returning the lens and camera body to his bag.

"Did you get some nice shots?"

"Hard to tell. I won't really know until I get home and look at them on my computer, where I can do some initial editing."

"I hope so." She set Louie down on the ground and rose from her bench. "Thank you for letting me watch you in action. It's very interesting to see how you frame the image."

"You're welcome. I enjoyed the company."

"So did I," she said softly. It was the truth. She liked Gabe Ellison, entirely too much.

"Have a good evening," she said, then turned to walk toward her house. To her surprise, he turned and walked along beside her, in the opposite direction of Casa Del Mar.

She paused and gave him a look. "You know Cruz's house is that way, right?"

"I do know, thanks. I'm actually quite good at navigating. I guess that comes from living most of your life out of a duffel bag. I'll walk you home. I want to be sure you make it safely."

She gripped Louie's leash, shocked and a little flustered. Most people assumed she could take care of herself. She *could* take care of herself. She had that pepper spray, after all, which she had found the very night he showed up in her studio.

"It's not necessary, but I would enjoy the company."

If he sensed how difficult that admission was for her to make, he didn't say anything, only walked along beside her as they continued down the road, back to the house that had become her refuge.

1 9

GABE

What was it about this woman who fascinated him so much? Gabe walked along beside Daisy while the moonlight lit up the path, and the night became alive with the sounds of all the creatures who only ventured out after dark.

She reminded him of those creatures a little. He sensed she was conflicted by her need to stay hidden, safe in her little burrow, even as some part of her yearned to be out exploring the world or soaring through the night.

He was fiercely attracted to her. He still didn't quite understand why. She was complex, layered, with a depth he found undeniably intriguing.

Beyond that, he felt *calm* when he was with her. It was an odd thing to crave but he felt at peace in her company. He was gradually coming to realize it was something he'd been seeking for a long time.

"I suppose we should be making some plans for the promotional video or shooting."

She sighed. "You can't let my aunt and my sister guilt you into doing this. It was kind of you to agree but I know it's not your usual thing."

"I want to do it. I'm bored here and need something to occupy my time."

"Why did you come here? To Casa Del Mar, I mean. I can't imagine it's the most relaxing place to recover from your injuries. Don't get me wrong, I love Cruz, but he's not the easiest person to hang out with. I swear, his mind goes a million miles a minute."

He actually liked Cruz more than he'd expected. The guy bordered on a narcissist, but Gabe had met many people in the public arena who were the same.

"I don't know that he gave me much choice, to be honest. My doctor said I couldn't be alone right after the surgery and needed to be surrounded by people. He also didn't want me checking into a hotel, so Cruz insisted on bringing me here."

"Don't you have a home somewhere, with friends or neighbors who could have kept an eye on you?"

"I've spent most of my adult life on the go, traveling around to other countries while I'm filming. I have an apartment in Manhattan Beach, close to LAX, that I pay the lease on for a home base, but I'm hardly ever there. I actually have to keep the address in a memo on my phone because I keep forgetting it. I don't really know any of my neighbors."

Did that make him sound pathetic? Probably. He wasn't. He had good friends all over the world. Give him a country and he could name a close connection there. Unfortunately, his doctor hadn't wanted him to fly overseas because of potential complications.

He could have stayed with someone else in the States—several friends had offered—but with Cruz insisting he come here to Casa Del Mar, Gabe hadn't had the energy to argue at the time.

"Do you enjoy all that traveling?"

He shrugged. "A nomadic life is the only kind I've ever known. I've never stayed in one place even for a full year."

It was another example of how very different they were. Daisy was all about home and family and making a place in her community. None of that had ever meant much to Gabe. His dad taught him the world was his neighborhood and he had taken the lesson to heart.

"Do you ever wish your life had been a little more...traditional? That you had been given the chance as a child to put down roots somewhere?"

"Not really. If my life experiences had been different, I wouldn't have turned into the person I am. And I kind of like that person. I'm a pretty decent sort, believe it or not."

"I wish I shared your attitude."

He couldn't see her features well in the moonlight but thought he heard envy in her voice.

"You don't think I'm a decent sort?"

She laughed a little. "I didn't mean that. You know I didn't."

He wasn't sure, actually. He didn't know what she thought of him and was a little afraid to ask.

"I guess I was thinking of myself. I hated being on the go all the time, maybe because we were always only a step or two ahead of CPS or the bank repo people or angry landlords looking for back rent. I hated it. I wanted to, just once, finish a school year in the same place where I started."

She had told him her childhood was chaotic but he hadn't realized the extent of it.

"I suppose it's no wonder you paint furniture, then. What is more permanent than a massive dining table?"

"Right? Especially when it's decorated with bunnies and chipmunks."

He had to smile at her self-deprecating tone. Yeah, he was completely intrigued with Daisy McClure. The things she had confided in him that evening only seemed to intensify his fascination.

Before he realized it, they reached her charming little house, with its wild garden, unique angles, spectacular views.

He didn't want the evening to end. He wanted to stand here with the sweet sea breeze and talk to her for hours.

"What happened to your mom?"

She looked surprised by the question. "Why do you ask?"

"I just wondered how you came to be living here with Stella."

"She died when I was ten and Bea was eight."

He listened for pain in her voice but heard only a matter-of-fact tone that he sensed hid oceans of emotion.

"Oh, Daisy. That must have been tough. I'm sorry."

She shrugged. "She overdosed. It was only a matter of time. She lived a crazy life and felt as if she could only truly be creative when she was high. Unfortunately, she was beautiful and fun and found a steady stream of men willing to provide that high. And if she got tired of one, she would move on and find another one."

Dragging her daughters along with her. Daisy must have hated that.

"Stella and Jewel had lost touch by then and Stella didn't know she'd died. We were kids and didn't know how to reach her to tell her, so we ended up in foster care for a while, until one day just before she was about to graduate, Stella bumped into Bea's father by chance, who told her about Jewel. She dropped everything and came to find us."

She clearly loved her aunt. He could hear it in her voice. "How long were you in foster care?"

"A year." Her voice was clipped. "A year too long. We were separated, in different placements. Bea was with a pretty decent family. I was put in a group home."

He knew instinctively it was not a good situation, simply by the sudden remoteness of her voice.

Sympathy for two lost little girls was heavy in his heart.

"I'm sorry," he said. "That must have been tough, all the way around."

She sighed. "Now I know why your documentaries are so insightful and gripping. You get people to tell you things they never had any intention of talking about with anyone."

He had always been a good listener, a skill he probably picked up during his own chaotic childhood.

"Everybody needs a superpower."

Her rough laugh seemed to slide beneath his skin, seductive and tantalizing.

She was most definitely like those nocturnal creatures, hidden from view. He liked the idea that he was the only one to see through her camouflage, that no one else could truly see her.

He liked *her*, entirely too much.

"I very much want to kiss you right now," he said. The words came out of nowhere, as if they were something he hadn't realized he had been holding tight inside him.

She stared at him, eyes wide in the darkness. "Do you?"

He took a step closer, and to his vast relief, she didn't back away. "Yes. Would you mind?"

He expected her to say no but, as usual, she surprised him. "I don't think I would."

He had time for only a fierce moment of triumph before he leaned down and brushed his lips against hers.

Her mouth was warm and soft and tasted as he remembered, sweet and delicious.

She wrapped her arms around him, holding on as if he was the only secure thing in her world. It made him tighten his arms in return, wanting to watch over her and make sure she never had another moment of worry or strain.

He had never felt like this for a woman, this sense that he

wanted to stay here with her, in this moment forever. That alone should have sent up alarm bells. Gabe wasn't the staying kind of man. He couldn't be. He had worlds to explore, stories to tell.

None of that mattered right now, when he had this fascinating woman in his arms, who could be prim and proper but kissed him like she had been waiting her whole life for this moment.

"You are a contradiction, Marguerite."

It was exactly the wrong thing to say. He knew it as soon as the words were out. She stiffened in his arms, sliding her mouth from his. Her eyes were dazed, aroused, for only a moment. Then he watched all her defenses click back into place like some high-tech suit of armor.

She slipped away, gripping Louie's leash, ready to escape. "I'm not Marguerite. I told you, she's an illusion. I'm Daisy. CPA and businesswoman."

"Perhaps you're both."

She shook her head. "Don't make the mistake of thinking you can turn me into something I'm not, Gabe. I'm practical, organized, boring to a fault. That's all."

Did she really believe that about herself? He wanted to argue but she didn't give him a chance.

"Thank you for walking me home. It's been a long day and I need to check on my aunt again."

She unlocked her door and hurried into the house, leaving him frustrated and cold and aching for something he suddenly realized he wanted more than anything else in the world.

20

BEATRIZ

"I miss Shane. Why did he have to move out?"

The question from Mari came out of nowhere, hitting her right in the solar plexus. She looked down at her daughter, sitting in the bleachers beside her as they waited for the Cape Sanctuary High School football game to begin.

"We talked about this, honey. He had his reasons."

She couldn't explain any of them to her eleven-year-old daughter, especially when she didn't really understand them herself.

"It's not fair. He's supposed to help me finish my car for the Pinewood Derby. How am I supposed to do it without him?"

Oh, no. She had completely forgotten that. "I thought your dad was going to help you make one. At least you could have a backup."

Mari frowned. "He said he wanted to, but every time I tell him we need to get started, he's busy with something else."

That didn't surprise her at all. "I'm sure he'll get to it," she said.

"But school starts next week and I won't have as much time, with homework and stuff."

She was only too aware. This home football game on the Friday before the actual start of school was the kickoff to the new academic year. She was always a little melancholy when the summer ended and they returned to regular life.

"You have this weekend and Shane will still be in and out. You can ask him if he's still going to be able to go with you and help you with a car."

"I guess." She still didn't look happy about it. Bea didn't know what to tell her. She wasn't exactly thrilled about Shane moving out, either. All her worst fears were coming true. She had worried that telling him of her feelings, making a move, would jeopardize the close friendship they'd had for years. She should have just listened to her gut and buried how she felt about him. She would rather have *some* of Shane than none of him.

She was lost in those grim thoughts when she heard a commotion and looked over to see her ex-husband making his way toward them.

"Cruz!" she exclaimed as he slid into the seat on the bleachers next to her. "I didn't expect you to be here."

All around them, she could see high school students whispering among themselves and pointing. The man certainly knew how to make an entrance.

"It's my alma mater. Why wouldn't I be here?"

As if he cared about high school football. Or high school at all. Cruz had barely graduated. He had certainly never been very interested in athletics, in any form.

"Hi, Daddy." Mari beamed at him, showing none of the resentment over the broken Pinewood Derby promises. One of the joys of being a single mother—Bea got the fun of trying to comfort her child through all those disappointments while Cruz only got the best of their daughter.

"Hi, pumpkin." He smiled right back and Bea tried to swallow her annoyance.

Cruz loved Mari and wanted to spend time with her, which was a good thing and more than Bea's own father had ever wanted.

She tried to turn her attention to the game and not spend too much of it staring at Shane's back as he walked back and forth on the sidelines.

It was quickly obvious that the smaller Cape Sanctuary team was no match for the football players put up by the larger school. They were scrappy, certainly, but the other school had bigger, obviously more experienced, players. By halftime, Cape Sanctuary was behind two touchdowns.

Last year Stella had come with her to all the home games. Even Daisy had come to a few, when she could tear herself away from her paperwork and her numbers. It had become something of a tradition among the three of them, something she had come to cherish. They would eat popcorn and talk to neighbors and cheer on their local boys.

But when she stopped to check on Stella earlier in the day to remind her this was the opening game, her aunt had said she wasn't quite up for it and probably should stay home to rest.

Bea couldn't blame her, especially not with school starting the next week. While the ER visit and the subsequent anti-nausea medication she had been prescribed seemed to have helped with the effects of her acute morning sickness, it was obvious Stella was struggling with her energy level.

She was still worried about her aunt, though Stella seemed to be slowly regaining her strength. Bea could only hope Stella knew what she was doing and would be able to handle the responsibility of having an infant along with teaching full-time.

Daisy had turned down her invitation, too, citing work obligations.

She missed both of them, especially since that meant Cruz thought he could have her whole attention.

He was very solicitous. She would give him that. When she shivered, he took off his own jacket and put it on her shoulders.

He slid down a little so she could see the action better. He offered to get drinks or popcorn refills.

While the halftime entertainment was going on, she finally excused herself to go to the restroom and headed down the bleacher steps.

What was she going to do about him? The man was driving her crazy.

After she fixed the lipstick she had chewed off watching the first half, she returned to the field in time to see the Cape Sanctuary team returning, followed by their handsome coach.

The lights gleamed in his blond hair and he looked so tough and gorgeous as he followed his boys that everything inside her sighed.

As she watched, the lovely new French teacher, Vanessa Martin, wearing a Cape Sanctuary High hoodie, hurried to the sidelines and handed him a water bottle. He smiled down at the woman and Bea stopped in her tracks, her heart pounding and her chest achy.

She had waited too long to let him know how she felt. It was obvious that Shane was moving toward a relationship with the teacher. Bea hated this jealousy inside her. It made her feel small and selfish and insecure. She ought to be happy for her friend, that he had found someone who interested him.

Perhaps Vanessa Martin was the reason he had moved out of her house and he had only used Cruz as an excuse. Maybe it was too awkward to be dating someone else seriously now that Shane knew Bea's feelings for him went beyond friendship.

She should never have told him. She should have kept things casual and fun between them. Maybe then she wouldn't be feeling as if somebody had just ripped out her heart and kicked it through the goalposts.

In the end Shane's team pulled out an amazing victory, coming from three touchdowns behind to move the ball fast in the last quarter and win by a thirty-yard field goal.

Beatriz screamed so loud, she lost her voice, and she left Mari with her father so she could rush the field along with the rest of the fans in the stands, to hug the football players she considered her boys.

She hugged everyone in sight, and before she quite realized it, the crowd pushed her toward Shane and he was in front of her.

"Congratulations!" She had to yell to be heard above the sound of the crowd.

"Thanks!" he shouted back. His voice sounded hoarse. She hoped wherever he was living, he could get some tea with honey in it when he went home.

She was just about to hug him when the French teacher stepped forward and wrapped her arms around him.

He gave Bea a quick look she couldn't read, then returned the embrace of the pretty new teacher. She was obviously angling for a kiss, lifting her mouth up to his, but Shane only pecked her cheek and released her.

Bea forced a smile, waved at both of them, then turned away to hug Tony Feola's mother.

She needed to figure out a way to get over him. If she didn't, if she couldn't manage to put away her growing feelings and regain a little perspective, she was afraid she would lose a cherished friendship.

If it wasn't already too late.

21

STELLA

Usually the Open Hearts annual picnic was the highlight of her year, but right now Stella wanted to curl up on the grass under a tree at Driftwood Park and take a long, glorious nap.

She had never expected being pregnant to make her feel like she was eighty years old.

The anti-nausea medication she had been given for morning sickness was doing an excellent job of keeping her from feeling sick every moment of the day, but a side effect was sheer exhaustion. Considering she was basically a senior-citizen mother at forty and was still in the first trimester of the pregnancy, where fatigue was a common thing anyway, she hoped it was normal that she wanted to spend all day in bed.

She couldn't, of course. She had people who counted on her, so she would persevere.

She couldn't wait until she started having energy again. As soon as she had the thought, she pushed it away. She had made a vow to herself that she wouldn't wish away any part of the pregnancy, good or bad. More than likely, this would be her only chance to give birth and she wanted to savor every moment of it—even the fatigue that left her feeling like a piece of seaweed that had been dashed against the rocks for a few weeks.

Clipboard in hand, Daisy approached where Stella was sitting on a lawn chair she'd brought along. "The caterers say everything is ready."

"That's good. As soon as a few more families show up, we can start."

Stella tried not to feel guilty about having the event catered this year. Usually, they grilled brats and burgers and spent several days ahead of the picnic making salads and slicing fruit. After a surprise donation to the foundation a few days after Stella's trip to the ER earmarked specifically for the picnic food, Daisy had wisely suggested they cater it this year.

Daisy had done all the work, arranging for one of Stella's favorite restaurants, a local Mexican café, to provide all the fixings for street tacos, *elote*—Mexican grilled corn—and various salads.

It all smelled delicious and Stella was grateful her appetite was beginning to return a little.

Around her, she could see families from throughout the region arriving and greeting each other with hugs and exclamations of delight. This picnic was more like a family reunion, a beloved tradition among foster families in the area and among children who had "graduated" from foster care and were now young adults. Some even brought their own families now.

"It will be perfect. Thank you, darling," Stella said to her niece. "Weren't we fortunate to get that last-minute donation? It was almost as if someone knew I would be too tired to handle the food preparation this year."

"It's like a picnic miracle," Daisy said, her voice so bland, Stella couldn't tell if she was being sarcastic.

She didn't care; she was just so grateful to Daisy for stepping up and handling the last-minute details. The cute little dog Daisy was fostering was attached by his leash to Stella's chair so he didn't run away. He sat up on his hind legs and Daisy reached down to pet his head with an affectionate look.

The dog had been good for her, Stella thought. Daisy needed something to remind her life was more than to-do lists. She adored Daisy but worried her niece hid so much of herself behind her need for order and control.

Mari and Ed's daughter, Rowan, who had become fast friends since their trip to Universal Studios, came over to her, arm in arm.

"Our game is all ready, Aunt Stella," Mari said.

"Which one are you doing, again?"

Every year they hosted a mini carnival for the kids, which was always a highlight.

"We're doing the fishing game."

"And we have tons of prizes for the kids."

"That will be so wonderful."

"Is there something else we can do to help?" Mari asked Daisy.

"You can check to be sure there are enough paper products near the food table. If you want to set out more plates, they're under the table."

"Okay."

The girls ran off, chattering with each other. Rowan was a sweet girl and Stella was grateful she and Mari had hit it off so well. It would make things much easier for Rowan to have a friend at school.

"Is Gabe coming?" she asked Daisy.

A strange expression crossed the other woman's features. Something secretive and feminine. Stella was interested to see color seep across Daisy's normally composed features. "He said he was. He's planning to videotape the picnic and the games, as well as talk to some of the families. I'll make sure we have releases from everyone."

"Oh, lovely. He seems like a very nice man."

"Yes," Daisy said. "He does."

She still didn't quite understand how Daisy had become friendly with him but she wasn't going to look a gift horse in the mouth.

"And didn't Bea do a good job with the decorations?"

The large covered picnic area at the park had been transformed into a carnival tent, with red and white streamers billowing down from a center spot in the ceiling and strings of lights completing the effect.

"She's amazing," Daisy said. Stella gave her a careful look, wondering if the two had managed to make up after their little argument the other day at the board meeting.

A few more families started to arrive and Stella was busy talking to a friend from farther north in the state who had adopted two of her foster children when she sensed, rather than saw, Ed's arrival.

She had been wondering if he would make it as he'd said he would but had felt weird asking Rowan.

He went straight to his daughter at their swimming pool fishing pond. Rowan hugged him and spoke animatedly, pointing to the pool and obviously explaining how it worked as if people hadn't been doing fishing ponds at kids' carnivals since carnivals were a thing.

Sunlight picked up golden highlights in his brown hair as he listened carefully to his daughter, asking questions and having her demonstrate how a child would throw the pole over the curtain and come back with a prize attached to it by Mari and Rowan on the other side.

They were so close, it warmed her heart. He was a wonderful father to Rowan—just as he would have been a wonderful father to Daisy and Bea, if Stella had given him the chance.

Everything inside her seemed to soften. Oh, how she had missed him over the years. She thought she was doing so well, going on to have a good life without him. Since he had been back in Cape Sanctuary, she realized how she was fooling herself. He had slipped past her defenses somehow and become once more vital to her existence.

He and Rowan stopped by almost every day after school, bringing dinner most nights but sometimes just coming to hang out and make sure she was all right.

She tried so very hard not to need him but it was becoming more impossible by the day.

She was more in love with him today than she had been when she was twenty-one and thought her heart would break apart at having to walk away from him.

How would her life have been different if she had made other choices back then?

She couldn't think that way. She had done what she thought was right at the time. How could he have handled being an instant father to two needy preadolescents while going to medical school at the same time? He had spent his own childhood raising his siblings while his single mother worked multiple jobs and she knew she couldn't have burdened him with her nieces.

After he left Rowan to help another child at the fishing pond, he looked around the busy park until his gaze landed on her. Was she imagining the way his eyes lit up? Her heart seemed to pound faster as he made a beeline to her.

"Hi," he said with a bright smile.

"Hi," she said, wondering where this sudden shyness came from.

He leaned in to kiss her cheek and she wanted to inhale the scent of him into her being, cedar and musk in some sort of citrusy base.

"Sorry I'm late. I got held up at the hospital. One of my patients had twins."

"Are they all right?" She would have asked that question

anyway, but it seemed more significant than ever, now that she was pregnant.

"Everyone's doing fine. Except the dad, anyway, who passed out right around the time the second twin was making an appearance."

This made her smile, even as she was aware of a little pang in her heart that her child wouldn't have a father who would pass out during its birth and she wouldn't have a partner to share all her joys and fears with.

She had made the choice to go through this alone. It wasn't as if she hadn't dated at all since Ed. She had, though at first she'd been too busy figuring out how to be a mom to the girls that she hadn't had time to think about a social life. In the years since, she'd gone on plenty of dates and been serious enough to think about marriage to two men.

Both had been good men, decent and kind, but neither had been able to touch the place in her heart that had always belonged to her first and dearest love.

She sighed now, pushing away the past she couldn't change.

"Where do you need me?" he asked.

She had a hundred different answers to that but forced a smile. "Daisy knows better than I do this year. She's kind of taken over running things."

"Good. You're doing exactly what you need to be doing. I'll find her."

"Ed, thank you for making the effort to come and help. It means a great deal."

"Are you kidding? Rowan's been talking about nothing else for days. She would never let us miss it."

He was here for his daughter, Stella reminded herself. Not for the pregnant, slightly queasy, exhausted forty-year-old woman who had walked away from him.

When she had a little more energy, Stella did her best to circulate among the families in attendance.

Everyone seemed to be having a great time. This was a vital part of their mission at Open Hearts, to bring together families in the same circumstances who were struggling through similar things.

Several of the children she had fostered were here, too. Not children anymore, she corrected herself. Though she fought through exhaustion, she had a wonderful time catching up with people.

She was watching the softball game that usually pitted current and former foster children against parents when Gabe Ellison sat down beside her with his camera.

"Since you're the founder and organizer of Open Hearts, I would love to speak with you for the promotional spot."

She still couldn't believe an Academy Award–nominated documentary filmmaker was making a commercial for her organization. The thought of it left her slightly breathless.

"Certainly," she said, though she knew she probably didn't look much better than she felt. "Do you want to do it right here?"

He looked around. "Why don't we find a corner that's a little quieter?"

He led the way to a quiet bench in the sunshine on the edge of the park, with a lovely view of the Pacific.

He stood some distance from her with a camera on a tripod. "Why don't you start by telling me your name, your occupation and why you started Open Hearts?"

It was painfully difficult to talk about her reasons, some of which were too personal for her to ever reveal in such a public arena.

She rubbed her hands on her jeans, then folded them together in her lap.

"My name is Stella Davenport," she began, "and I am a middle school English teacher. I started Open Hearts more than a decade ago because, as a foster parent myself, I saw a powerful need to encourage and support foster families."

She went on to outline the group's mission and some of the successes she felt most strongly about.

Gabe was a wonderful interviewer, with insightful questions and considerate directions to her about how to come across best on screen.

What was his relationship with Daisy? She wanted to ask but didn't think her niece would appreciate it. *Something* was there or Daisy—normally so cool and contained—wouldn't get so flustered when his name was mentioned.

She hoped there *was* something between them. Daisy needed someone exactly like Gabe Ellison, someone a little wild around the edges, with a reckless heart that would remind Daisy she wasn't a middle-aged society matron. She was still a young woman with so much love to give.

"Those are some perfect sound bites," he said after their short interview. "I can definitely work with what you've given me."

"Phew," she said. "It's tough work, being interviewed."

He smiled. "You're doing the tough work here. It sounds like your festival next week is a huge deal."

She was overwhelmed just thinking about it. "It is, but everyone in town pitches in to make it a success. We raise fully a third of our operating costs through our various events during the festival. I'm happy to say many of the other local charities benefit, as well, through booths at the fair and sponsored events."

"Where does the rest of your operating budget originate?"

"We have donors from across the country. It's quite remarkable. Just this week I had an anonymous donation from someone, earmarked for exactly this picnic, so we could cater it instead of cook the food ourselves, as we usually do."

He looked intrigued. "Is that right?"

"Yes. I would love to know who that donor is. Whenever we have need of extra funds for a grant or for some special event, somehow our guardian angel finds out and the funds come in shortly after."

"Isn't that fortuitous?" he said in a curiously flat voice.

"Yes. Very. At one point I thought it might be Bea. Cruz is very generous with his child support, and she makes a good living with her art, but she swears up and down it's not her."

"Interesting."

She shrugged. "We'll probably never know, unless the person wants to come forward. I wish they would. I'd love to be able to thank them in person. I'm overwhelmed at the generosity in the world. That's one thing I've learned from Open Hearts. People are generally good and want to help. Have you seen that in other places as you've traveled throughout the world?"

"Yes," he said, with an odd look she didn't understand. "Some of the most generous people are those who have little themselves."

22

GABE

G abe had a fairly concrete idea of the identity of the mysterious Open Hearts benefactor.

How convenient, that whenever Stella's organization had a
need, someone stepped up, instinctively knowing how to help.

Someone with inside information about the group's finances
would be in the perfect position to step in when the need
arose. Someone like, oh, the treasurer and controller of the
organization…who also happened to be a brilliant artist, with
a worldwide following.

He shouldn't be surprised that Daisy was generous with her
money, donating to Open Hearts when necessary. She might
give the appearance of a stiff, somewhat stuffy accountant, but
there was so much more to the woman.

He wanted to say something. The words hovered on his tongue,
but he swallowed them back. None of Daisy's many secrets were
his to reveal. If she wanted her aunt to know about her secret

identity and about the donations he was certain she was making, Daisy could tell Stella herself.

Was it any wonder he was utterly fascinated with her, though?

He looked through the crowd and spotted Daisy sitting in the stands and watching the softball game. Bea was right in the middle of the action, laughing as she took a wild swing and missed the pitch completely, but Daisy seemed content to sit on the sidelines.

Why? Why not be right there with her sister, hitting grounders past the shortstop then running with crazy abandon to first base?

He found it astonishing that a woman who could paint with her passion and emotion could be so reserved in the rest of her life.

His Marguerite.

The thought came out of nowhere and he was glad he was holding on to his camera so he didn't drop it into the grass.

Where did that come from? She was not his anything! Sure, they had kissed a few times. Sure, she fascinated him more than any woman in a long time—maybe ever.

That didn't make her his. She was quite plain about that.

He had to stop thinking about her and focus on the interview so he could let Stella return to the party. He shifted his gaze back to the woman and found Daisy's aunt watching him with a curious expression. Had she noticed where he was looking? Her next words seemed to confirm it.

"I worry about Daisy," she said quietly.

To his embarrassment, Gabe felt his face heat. When was the last time he'd blushed? He couldn't remember. He had to hope she didn't notice.

He studied Stella, who looked much younger than forty with her stylish glasses and trendy haircut. She certainly looked too young to have raised her nieces when she wasn't much older than they had been. The concern in her expression instantly set him on edge.

"Why? Is she all right?"

Stella looked over at the baseball field and Daisy. "You're not taping now, right?"

"No." To prove it, he turned the whole thing off and put the cap on the lens. It was the small, lightweight film camera he favored for location and action shots. "We're done, as far as I am concerned. Now, tell me why you're worried about Daisy."

She narrowed her gaze at him. "Am I wrong to think you... care about my niece?"

Was she asking his intentions? He could feel himself flush again, not sure quite how to respond. He finally settled on the truth. "Yes, I care about your niece. She's a remarkable woman."

Stella smiled a little, though the worry didn't leave her eyes. "I think so, too. It's hard for some people to see past the walls she likes to put up."

"They're not just walls. They're walls covered in razor blades and concertina wire and guarded by wolverines with machine guns."

She laughed softly then grew serious again. "If you want the full, honest truth, Daisy is the reason I started Open Hearts."

"She is?"

She chewed her bottom lip a little as if not sure whether she should expand on that startling statement. "She wouldn't be happy with me for telling you this," she finally said, "but I trust you, Gabriel. I can't explain it, but I do. I hope that trust isn't misplaced."

He sat beside her on the bench, not sure he wanted to know what she was about to tell him. Daisy McClure had already crept her way beneath his defenses. He didn't need more reasons to be drawn to her.

"Daisy and Bea were in foster care for a year before I could arrange to take legal custody after my sister died."

"Daisy told me that."

Stella's eyes widened. "She told you she was in foster care?"

"Yes. She said you didn't know about your sister's death until months later and then it took you time to make the legal arrangements to take custody."

"I can't believe she told you that. She *never* talks about it."

He was honored that she had confided in him, though he still wasn't sure why she had.

"What else did she tell you?"

"That she and Bea were separated."

"Yes. I can't imagine how hard that would have been on two girls who had never spent a night apart. Bea landed in a fairly good foster home, fortunately. Daisy, though..." She hesitated, her features troubled. "Daisy was put in a group home because that's all that was available for her and she was...not treated well there."

He closed his eyes, not wanting to hear this. Damn, he didn't want to hear it. Children deserved love and care, to feel safe and protected. He wanted to tell Stella to stop but knew he couldn't do that. She wanted to tell him, for reasons he didn't fully understand, and some part of him felt like he needed to know.

"She was...abused by one of the older boys in the group home. He was seventeen and she was eleven."

His swearing was fierce and raw and vicious.

"Exactly. I don't know how far things went, but any amount is too much for a vulnerable child. She didn't tell me for years. She held it all inside. When I finally did get custody, she was so withdrawn, so...independent. She never let anyone close, even Bea, who once had been her best friend. I think she somehow internalized it was her fault, as so many victims of sexual assault do. She finally trusted me enough to tell me a few years after we came here to Cape Sanctuary, and I made her get counseling. We... I wanted to press charges but the boy was out of the system by then and had died in a gang-related fight."

Good. Gabe didn't consider himself a violent man but he hoped it had been a long, lingering, painful death.

His heart ached for Daisy. He could picture her all too clearly, young and lonely with those big hazel eyes, thrust into a situation beyond her control.

"I'm afraid I waited too long to get her help. By then she was this self-contained person who worked hard not to depend on anyone else. When she was younger, she was sweet and loving, with such a generous heart, who took care of her mother and her sister. She was different when I took custody of her. Still loving, still sweet, but so very determined not to need anyone."

His heart felt scoured by the revelation, and it was all he could do not to go to Daisy right now and pull her into his arms.

"Because of what happened to my beloved niece, I needed to do everything possible to make sure no other child suffered as she did," Stella said fiercely. "I had to. It's hard enough for any child to be forced into the system by circumstances out of his or her control. No child should be mistreated or abused in the very situation that is supposed to be helping them. I can't change what happened to Daisy, but through Open Hearts, I can do all I can to protect other children."

Stella was a remarkable woman and he sensed she had been largely responsible for raising her nieces to become remarkable women in their own rights.

"Thank you," he said sincerely. "For rescuing her in the first place but also for trusting me enough to tell me."

"I think she likes you, Gabe. And I think you scare her."

"I would never hurt her," he protested.

She smiled a little. "I sense that or I wouldn't have told you what I just did. She's not fragile. I hope I didn't give you that impression."

"I know."

"Daisy is an amazing woman who deserves to be happy with a man who can shatter her defenses to find the woman inside."

Gabe instinctively wanted to protest that he wasn't that man. He couldn't be. While he might have feelings for Daisy that seemed to be growing stronger with each day he stayed in Cape Sanctuary, he could never act on them. He wasn't the man for her—Gabe was a rambler who never stayed in one place for longer than a few weeks. He had spent his entire life on the go and didn't see how that could change.

Before he could come up with an answer, a little girl of about five with dark curls and big eyes wandered over to them and climbed onto Stella's lap.

"Stel," she said.

"Hi, Elisa, honey. Where's your mom?"

A woman came over looking frazzled. "Sorry for the interruption. She got away from me."

"No problem," Stella said. "I understand you have exciting news."

"Yes! The best! We're adopting Elisa and her younger brother."

The two women became engrossed in conversation, leaving Gabe to gather up his equipment and try to process what he had just learned about Daisy.

He was still absorbed in what Stella had told him as he finished shooting footage for the Open Hearts promotional spot.

Usually, large public gatherings always left Gabe slightly edgy, not sure where he fit in. Whether it was a tribal dance in New Guinea or a pickup soccer game in South Africa or a mad horse race among the people of Mongolia, he always felt a little on the fringes, compelled to document instead of participate.

Oddly, he had felt none of that during the Open Hearts picnic. He felt...connected to the people here. Everyone had been very warm and accepting of him. Even after he put his camera gear away, he didn't want to leave.

The party went on until twilight, until shadows began to lengthen and the sun began to steal across the horizon and the children began to fall asleep on their foster parents' laps or any other convenient spot.

Daisy was holding a little girl who was probably about four, with dark hair and long, long eyelashes. The girl was asleep, her cheek nestled against Daisy's chest, and Gabe felt something stir inside him, something primitive and raw.

He was messed up over her, more than he'd ever been for another woman. There was a very good chance he was falling hard for her.

A few moments later the little dark-haired girl was scooped up by her foster father. She nestled against his shoulder, and again Gabe felt something stir inside him, almost...envy.

He had always thought children weren't in the cards for him, assuming he would probably be a terrible father. He hadn't exactly had the best parental examples in his life, with a mother who hadn't wanted him and a father who hadn't known what to do with him.

Suddenly, he started to wonder. As he saw all these people who had opened their hearts and their homes to children in need, he wondered if he could handle what they were doing: be vulnerable enough to love somebody he knew would likely be taken away at some point.

Daisy rose and started clearing up discarded cups, plates, napkins. He joined her, dragging over a garbage can to make her job a little easier.

She looked startled at first, then grateful. "You've done more than enough, Gabe. I saw you put your camera away quite a while go. You really don't have to stay to clean up."

"I don't mind. The only other thing on my agenda is walking our dog."

He hadn't meant to use the plural possessive, but it somehow seemed to fit. He had come to adore little Louie, as he sensed she did, as well.

"I'm not sure he's going to need any more exercise. He's been chasing after kids all day."

"True enough."

Louie had once more proved how lovable he was by playing happily with any child who paid attention to him. Right now Louie was plopped on the grass, cuddled with another little black dog he had learned belonged to Bea and her cute daughter, Mari.

Daisy gave him a hard look. "I'm not sure you need more exercise, either. You're still recovering and you probably over-did things today. If you're not careful, you're going to end up back in the hospital."

Her concern warmed him more than it should. It was addictive, actually, probably because he wasn't used to people worrying about him.

He'd been on his own so long, it seemed strange to be the recipient of others' concern. First Cruz, now Daisy. Where Cruz's concern made him feel a little suffocated, with Daisy, he wanted to savor every bit of it.

"I'm doing fine. I'm actually feeling better than I have since the attack. The doctors told me it would be two weeks before I would start feeling human. It's been three, and I'm finally starting to get there."

"I'm so glad."

He did not want to talk about his injury or the recovery that was taking longer than he'd expected.

"You'll be happy to know I got some great video of the picnic today. Several of the parents were willing to talk to me and I was able to interview them about the value they find from Open Hearts. Plus, I had a chance for a long talk with Stella."

He didn't want to think about everything Stella had told him. It made his heart ache every time he did. He couldn't seem to stop imagining a little girl with Daisy's eyes, lost and afraid and in a situation she couldn't control.

"She's wonderful, isn't she?"

"Yes. And I think she did a pretty good job of raising two wonderful nieces."

Her features warmed at that, her eyes going soft and tender for just an instant before she blinked the emotion away and became brisk once more. "Well, Bea, at least."

"Both of you," he said firmly. "You organized this whole picnic, didn't you?"

"Somebody had to. Stella wasn't up to it. She's still not feeling herself with the pregnancy."

"I have a question for you."

"What?" she asked, her features suddenly wary.

"Your aunt was telling me that Open Hearts has quite a mysterious yet insightful benefactor. She said whenever the foundation needs extra funds for something, the money mysteriously appears out of nowhere."

Though the light was fading at the park, he could see a hint of nerves flash across her expression. "We have been amazingly lucky, haven't we?"

"Luck is one way to put it."

She frowned. "What are you implying?"

"I'm not implying anything. I have a strong suspicion that there is no such thing as a coincidence. At least not in this case. I think the mysterious benefactor might have something to do with Cape Sanctuary's other puzzle. A certain intriguing and elusive artist."

She blushed a little in the twilight, confirming his suspicion. "I don't know what you're talking about," she said stiffly.

"I think you do, Marguerite," he whispered.

She looked around as if to make sure nobody had overheard. He noticed she especially looked in the direction of her aunt and sister. As he suspected, they were the two she most worried would find out her secret.

"You have a big mouth," she snapped.

He really shouldn't tease her but he couldn't seem to help it.

"There's no one else around. Everyone is too busy loading up their vehicles. Unless Louie decides to spill your secrets, they're still safe with me."

His words didn't appear to mollify her. "You said you wouldn't say a word. I should never have told you."

She looked genuinely panicked and he was immediately filled with guilt.

"I'm sorry."

He *had* promised her and he intended to keep that vow. "But tell me I'm wrong. Does Marguerite channel a large portion of her income into Open Hearts?"

"If she does, so what? It's her income—her completely *unexpected* income. She can do what she wants with it."

His chest seemed tight suddenly, a tenderness he didn't know what to do with seeping through him.

He thought of everything she had been through, how it must have shaped her, the demons she may still wrestle. She could have become bitter and angry. A victim. Instead, she insisted on giving back, channeling her past into creating works of whimsy and light that gave joy to others.

He wanted to pull her close again but knew she wouldn't welcome that here, surrounded by friends and family.

"I think Marguerite is pretty amazing. And you are, too," he said quietly.

She gazed at him, eyes wide. He saw her usual defenses there but something beneath them, a softness and a vulnerability that reached right in and grabbed at his heart.

A few weeks ago he would have said Daisy McClure was the exact opposite of his type, but the more he came to know her—the more he began to wriggle out her secrets—the more he wanted to know.

She fascinated him on every single level. He loved her laugh, husky and slow and filled with hidden passion. He loved her smile, reserved at times, secretive at others, but occasionally open and warm and enough to knock him to his knees.

He was falling hard for her and suspected that if he wasn't careful, he was going to come away from this visit in Cape Sanctuary with more scars than he had received from taking a hunting knife to the gut.

2 3

DAISY

"How do you think the filming went? Did you get enough for a thirty-second spot?"

"More than enough. I could fill at least an hour, maybe more. If I had more time, I would. I actually was thinking I'll take what I shot today, all the footage I can't use for the promotional spot, and do a longer video for you to have on your website."

"You would really do that?"

He looked slightly annoyed at the doubt in her voice. "Sure I would. It's a great cause. You're all doing good work here. I'm glad to do anything I can to help."

She wanted to hug him but was afraid she wouldn't want to stop. "Thank you. That would be wonderful. Stella will be thrilled."

"What about you?" he asked, his eyes glittering.

"Yes. I'm thrilled, too. I would love to see our work expand beyond Northern California. The foster crisis hits the entire country right now. If you can help us get the message out about what we do, that would be terrific."

With a start, she suddenly realized that she had failed miserably in her assignment. "You asked me to be your assistant, didn't you? I'm afraid I really didn't help you very much."

"It's fine. You were busy. There is work to be done, though. Tomorrow I'll be going through what I filmed today and beginning the editing process. I could use help with that. What's your schedule like?"

The next day was Sunday and she had planned to spend the entire day in her studio. She almost told him as much, but swallowed down the words. She had promised to help him, and Daisy was a woman who took her promises very seriously.

She would simply have to work extra hours during the weekday evenings for the next few weeks to finish her commission projects.

"Tomorrow works for me. Do you have editing equipment?"

"These days I can do most of what I need on my laptop, especially for a spot that will only be a minute long."

"Great. I'm all yours, then."

His gaze sharpened and she wished she had chosen her words more carefully. "We can work on the editing all day, if you need to," she corrected quickly. "Do you want me to come to Casa Del Mar?"

"If you think we can find a quiet place there."

Doubtful. Cruz's place was a party every minute, filled with people and commotion and music, offering no chance to find a quiet spot to work.

"Never mind. Let's do it at Pear Tree Cottage, where we won't be disturbed. Will that work?"

"Sounds like a plan. Does two work for you?"

That would at least give her the morning to work on some of her own projects. Marguerite had a big commission due for a credenza from a Seattle designer.

"Sounds good. I'll see you tomorrow afternoon."

Anticipation curled through her, sweet and heady. She tried to ignore it, fully aware it would be a struggle to keep her attention focused on the video, given her fascination with the man, but she would do her best.

After Gabe loaded his things into an SUV she recognized as one of Cruz's and drove away, Daisy turned her attention to finishing the cleanup at the park.

Most of the mess had already been taken care of by the caterers and the foster care families, but Stella was helping Bea take down the decorations inside the armory. Her aunt looked pale in the twilight, her features pinched and her eyes sunken. So far this pregnancy was not turning into the happy event she was certain Stella had expected.

School would be starting soon and Daisy wasn't at all sure whether Stella would be able to find the strength to make it through six class periods full of thirty students each.

She headed in her aunt's direction, about to tell Stella to go home and let her and Bea finish cleaning up, when Dr. Clayton beat her to it.

Daisy watched him go to her aunt, place a hand on her shoulder and point to Stella's old Volvo. She was too far away to hear what he said but she could still tell Stella did not like his words. She shook her head and pointed to the park and the few items remaining from their picnic.

Ed pointed more forcefully and Stella stubbornly shook her head. Daisy decided it was time to intervene. She adored her aunt but sometimes the woman could be as obstinate as a mule with a toothache.

She approached them and gave a supportive smile to the doctor. "You need to go home," she said firmly to Stella.

"Thank you," Ed said. "Exactly what I was just saying."

He seemed like a sweet man. She really hoped Stella could find room in her heart and her life for him.

"I'm fine," her aunt answered sharply. "Everyone needs to stop worrying about me. I'm having a baby. It's not like I have cancer or something."

Beside her, Daisy was aware of Ed stiffening and saw Stella's features soften. "I'm sorry. I wasn't thinking about your wife. That was cruel," her aunt said.

So Ed had a wife who died of cancer. Poor man.

"You're having a baby," the doctor said, "which means you have somebody else to worry about, not just yourself and what you want."

"I know that."

"Do you? I had hoped that the past two decades might have made you a little less certain that your way is the only way and that you and you alone know what's best for the whole damn world. Apparently, I was wrong."

He stalked away, leaving a stunned silence behind him.

"Wow," Daisy said after a moment. "That came out of nowhere."

"Not really." Stella looked as if she wanted to cry but was courageously holding it back. "It's been twenty years overdue."

"I'm sorry," she said awkwardly, not sure what to say.

"So am I, my dear," Stella said. "More sorry than I can say."

"Go home." Daisy used the gentlest tone she could manage. "We don't have much left to clean up. Bea and I can handle it and I'm certain you would feel better if you went home and rested. More important, you would make *us* feel better, knowing you're taking care of yourself and the baby."

Stella seemed to take that to heart, finally. "Yes. You're right. I know you are. I should rest."

"Good night, Aunt Stella. It was a great picnic."

"Because of you this year."

Stella gave her one last hug, then made her way to her vehicle.

Daisy watched until she slid behind the wheel then backed out of the parking lot before she turned back to the picnic cleanup.

24

STELLA

E d's words, harsh and condemning, rang in her ears the entire time she drove home.

*I had hoped that the past two decades might have made you a little
less certain that your way is the only way and that you and you alone
know what's best for the whole damn world.*

Was that what he thought of her? That she always had to have
things her way? That she was rigid and unbending and couldn't
compromise?

Was he right?

She didn't want to think so. The truth was, she didn't want
to think at all. Right now she wanted to step into a hot shower
for about three hours and then collapse into her bed for another
twelve.

When she walked into Three Oaks, the house seemed to echo
with emptiness. She missed having kids around. This house
was made for children and teenagers, leaving their mess, ex-

perimenting in the kitchen, doing homework at the big table in the dining room.

Soon, at least, she would have a baby's laughter to fill the house. She could take comfort from that. A baby, then a toddler, then a preschooler and a school-age child. She couldn't wait for all the wonderful stages of life she would experience with her baby.

She was just filling the cat's water bowl when she heard a car in the driveway. She assumed it was her friend Cleo or one of the girls needing to drop something off, until she heard a knock.

Daisy or Bea wouldn't knock. This had been their childhood home. She had always told them to walk right in.

When she pulled the curtain aside on the long window beside the front door, her heart started to pound when she discovered Ed standing on the porch.

Some part of her wanted to let the curtain fall and ignore his knock. She wanted to hide away in her bed with the comforter over her head but that would be childish, the sort of thing a woman of twenty-one would do.

The sort of thing she *had* done at twenty-one.

These days they called the way she had treated Ed *ghosting*. She hadn't really broken up with him; she had simply...walked away. She stopped taking his calls or emails and basically ignored him.

Every time she tried to call him to say she couldn't see him anymore, she had chickened out, certain she would lose her will and would end up begging him to forgive her and take her back.

Finally, after a month of her ignoring him, he had called, leaving a terse message that he was making the eight-hour drive from LA all the way up to Cape Sanctuary in order to force her to talk to him.

In response, she had found the strength to call him back. She had been abrupt and dismissive to him and had told him not to bother making the drive. She was moving on with her life, she told him, and she suggested he do the same. What they had was a foolish college fling and she had zero interest in rekindling it.

Even now the memory of that lie filled her with shame.

Was it any wonder he couldn't truly forgive her? Nearly twenty years had passed and the pain of that last phone call was still as fresh as if it had happened the day before.

She was older now, more mature. She couldn't walk away from this confrontation that had been building since he came to Cape Sanctuary.

Slowly, she opened the door. As always, her breath seemed to catch in her chest at the sight of him.

He was far more handsome than he'd been all those years ago, his face shaped and sculpted by all the experiences of life.

Once, she had loved him with every inch of her young heart. She still did.

It was a startling revelation. So startling it stopped her in her tracks.

She was still in love with Ed Clayton.

"Come in." She managed to find the words through her shock.

He walked inside and stood in her entryway.

"I owe you an apology," he said stiffly.

Tears welled up at his words. "You don't. Oh, Ed. You don't."

"Yes, I do. I was unnecessarily cruel to you tonight. I'm very sorry."

"You said nothing that wasn't true. I'm the one who is sorry. I'm sorry for being obstinate today when you were only looking out for my welfare and my baby's, and I'm sorry, more than I can ever say, for my stubbornness nineteen years ago."

Tears began to trickle down her face, tears of loneliness and sorrow for all the days and nights and weeks she had spent alone. She still wasn't sure she could have made any other choice, but she couldn't help wondering how her life might have been different, if she had.

She wasn't quite sure how it happened, but one moment she

was silently weeping for the pain she had caused them both, and the next she was in his arms.

He pulled her against him and she settled there as if she had never left. She was safe here. Safe and warm and cherished.

Always watching out for her, he led her to the sofa and they sat together there, in this room she and the girls had so carefully restored.

He didn't let go, simply pulled her into his arms so she was cradled there, with her head resting against his chest.

She was so tired. She wanted to close her eyes and sleep in the security she found here for at least a month or two.

"Where's Rowan?" she asked.

"Home. I told her I needed to run an errand. I was going to call our neighbor in the condo next door to sit with her but Rowan reminded me that she's twelve, we have a security system and she is more than capable of being home by herself for an hour or so, especially when I'm only a phone call away."

"She's a great girl. You must be so proud of her."

"She is pretty terrific," he said. "I think she knew I was coming over here to apologize. She likes you, by the way. She has told me as much."

"I like her, too," she said softly. "Your wife must have been very special to produce such a kind child."

"She was," he said gruffly. She felt no pain or jealousy that he had loved someone else, only sadness that Holly would never have the chance to see her daughter grow up.

She wanted to stay here in his arms but knew she wasn't done trying to make amends. She had so many things inside her, things she had been holding back since he came to Cape Sanctuary.

"I'm the one who owes you an apology, Ed. Everything you said tonight was true. I made choices twenty years ago, thinking I knew what was best for you. For everyone. I shouldn't have done that. I should have been strong enough to let you make that choice."

"You pushed me away because of the girls, didn't you?"

She didn't like remembering those months as she had fought for custody of them, having to prove she was stable enough emotionally and financially to provide for them. She had been afraid she would lose them into the system forever.

"It seemed for the best at the time, but I wasn't really thinking straight. They were lost. Bea was wild and undisciplined, thinking she could do whatever she wanted because she'd never had a mother figure to tell her otherwise. Daisy..."

She swallowed, thinking about all her older niece had endured.

"Daisy needed so much attention and love. You were deep into medical school and I knew how hard you had fought to get there. I knew I couldn't ask you to give up your dream. I also knew I couldn't manage a long-distance relationship while trying to give the girls what they needed. I didn't know how to handle everything. Something had to go."

"You chose me, unilaterally, without giving me the chance to have any say in the decision. Despite everything we were to each other."

"Yes. It was wrong and I'm more sorry than I can ever say."

He exhaled and it was as if he released all the pain and sadness on his breath. "It's done. We can't change the past. I'm not sure I would if I could. I grieved for you and our love for a long time, wondering what I had done wrong and how I could have lost the best thing that had ever happened to me."

More tears trickled down and she wiped at them with her sleeve.

He held her closer. "Then one day I woke up and I decided I had to move on. I started dating again, met Holly, and two years later we were married. If not for everything that happened, I wouldn't have Rowan. I hated losing you but I wouldn't trade Ro for anything."

He was a wonderful father to his daughter, just as he would have been a wonderful father to her nieces.

"I'm sorry I hurt you. I grieved, too. I'm not sure I ever stopped grieving."

"Why didn't you ever marry?"

She sighed. "I came close, twice. Both of them were good, honorable men. But neither was you, the love of my heart."

His eyes gleamed with emotion and he angled his head to brush his mouth against hers.

His kiss was everything she remembered from all those years ago, heat and tenderness and joy. How was it possible for years to have passed, a lifetime for each of them, yet they could still fit together like two pieces of a puzzle?

After a long moment he lifted his head. "Do you think, after all this time, we could try again?"

She felt tears burn again. At this rate she was going to be dehydrated, from the crying alone.

"Is that what you want?"

"Something led Rowan and me here to Cape Sanctuary. I thought I was coming here for a fresh start. Now I wonder if everything was simply leading me back to you."

He kissed her again, until she felt all those years melt away. One thing still niggled at the back of her mind, a huge part of her life.

"What about the baby?" she asked.

His smile was as sweet as it was reassuring. "I never expected to have any more children. Holly had to have a hysterectomy because of complications after Rowan, and I was fine with one. I think we should take things slowly, of course. Get to know the people we've grown into over the years. But if things go forward with us, as I fully expect them to, I would love the idea of helping you raise your child."

More tears, only this time she was laughing and crying at the same time and so very grateful to God or fate or kismet or whomever had decided, after all these years, to once more merge their separate paths into one.

2 5

BEATRIZ

Oh, how she wished every Sunday afternoon could be like this one.

The day after the picnic Bea sat on a huge pillow on her pool deck with a wide kaleidoscope of color spread out in front of her, glittering and bright.

She was trying something new, a mosaic made out of glass crushed from trash she'd found the last time Open Hearts did their annual beach cleanup at Breakers Beach a few months earlier. She still didn't have a clear vision but thought she would try a mermaid, with swirls of blue waves for hair and an iridescent green fin.

Working on a new project always excited her, especially trying a medium outside her usual comfort zone.

When people asked her to describe her art, Bea struggled to come up with the right words. She considered herself an explorer, someone constantly trying to find new ways to get her message across. She loved what she created, especially when all the pieces came together.

This one was working beautifully. She could already tell it would be better than she had hoped. It might even be something she decided to keep and hang here instead of putting up for sale at one of the galleries that displayed her work.

The art wasn't what was making her so happy, though she found her usual joy in the act of creation. It was the activity going on at the table next to her. For the past two hours, Shane and Mari had been busy working on Mari's car for the Pinewood Derby.

It was truly destined to be epic. The car was painted in rainbow colors, glossy and bright under the August California sun. Now the two of them were trying to decide if they should attach Skittles candy to the car for decoration and for weight.

This was the first time Shane had spent any length of time here since moving out. He seemed relaxed and happy, teasing Mari and even smiling at Bea once in a while. It almost felt like old times, before the awkwardness of the past few weeks.

She had missed this friendship. She had missed *him*. Shane was an integral part of their lives. How could she convince him that both she and Mari needed him to stick around?

She had to just tell him she was in love with him. No more dancing around the subject. She had to sit him down, hold his hands in hers, gaze into his blue eyes and tell him she knew what she wanted, and it was a future with the football coach and biology teacher at Cape Sanctuary High.

She had to find the courage somehow. She had been so afraid of losing this friendship she treasured. Wasn't she already losing it by not being honest with him?

As she worked with the cut pieces of glass, arranging the shattered pieces into something bright and beautiful, she thought about how life was like art in many ways. Broken pieces could be formed and shaped into something better.

"This is looking so good," Mari exclaimed. "I bet I'm going to win."

"It's not necessarily about winning. It's about knowing you tried your best."

"Is that something they teach you in Football Coach 101?" Bea teased.

He smiled. "Something like that. Along with, There's No *I* in Team and Keep Your Eye on the Ball."

They ultimately decided against the Skittles for now, though Shane told Mari they could add them later if they decided the car needed them.

When they were starting to clean up, Bea knew she had to act. She couldn't say anything to him with Mari there, but if she extended the evening, perhaps she could keep him there after Mari's bedtime to talk.

Did she have the nerve?

She had to find it. She had spent enough of her life living with regrets. She couldn't regret not taking the chance to tell him of her feelings.

"Shane, do you have dinner plans?" she blurted out. "I made pizza dough earlier. There's plenty, if you want to stay."

She didn't have many culinary skills, but she made a mean pizza. After she and Cruz moved to West Hollywood, one of her several part-time jobs had been at a neighborhood pizza place. The owner, Mr. D'Angelo, had been kind to her, showing her how to prep the dough, flip it, spread it into a circle and even how to shake it off the pizza peel into the wood-fired oven.

She had hated leaving after she found a much more lucrative job waitressing at a fancy sit-down restaurant, where she could make more in tips on one busy Friday night than she could in a week of working afternoons at D'Angelo's.

"I do love your pizza," Shane said, "but I'm afraid I can't tonight."

"Why not?" Mari pouted.

"I have plans already. Sorry."

"Is it a date?" Mari teased.

"None of your business, Sunshine," he said, though he looked uncomfortable at the question, which Bea took as confirmation.

He had a date. He was leaving her and Mari to go out with someone else.

Was it with the French teacher? The woman was obviously interested in him. That had been clear enough at the football game when she had seen them together.

Shane must feel the same.

He had someone else. She had waited too long to act.

The knowledge took all the joy out of her afternoon. She looked down at her mosaic, at all the broken shards of glass that now only looked like a hodgepodge of mismatched trash.

"What time do you want to go next week?" Mari asked him as Shane was preparing to take off.

"Your invitation said dinner is at seven. I'll pick you up about six thirty." He paused. "Are you sure you don't want to go with your dad, since he's in town? The other girls will have their fathers."

Mari shook her head. "I already gave you the invitation. It would be rude."

"I would certainly understand, Sunshine. It won't hurt my feelings."

She shook her head again. "I want you to be my date. Unless you don't want to come with me."

"That's not it. You're my favorite eleven-year-old in the whole world. You know that. But I don't want you to miss a chance to hang out with your dad."

"I've been with him like every day since he's been here. I already told him I was going with you. He knows."

"In that case, I'll see you Saturday night, for sure."

"Bye, Shane. Thanks for helping me with the car."

"You bet." He hugged Mari and then turned to Bea. Suddenly, the ease of the day seemed to have dissolved into awkwardness. After a moment he hugged her, too, and it was all Bea could do not to hang on tight.

"I'll see you later, too," he said.

"Bye. Have fun on your date."

He gave her a searching look, nodded and let himself out.

She hadn't said anything about her feelings. What would be the point? She had waited entirely too long to come to her senses. Now that she knew exactly what she wanted, it was too late. He was dating someone else.

If he married the French teacher and they settled here in Cape Sanctuary, what would she do? Somehow she would have to find a way to be happy for him, for the sake of the friendship she had cherished for most of her life.

2 6

DAISY

She wasn't sure when she had enjoyed a Sunday afternoon more.

Usually, she spent the day with Stella or Bea or alone in her studio. She enjoyed both of those options, but there was something magical about this particular Sunday. Daisy sat in her most comfortable chair in her small living room with Louie on her lap and a book open in front of her.

Gabe sat on the sofa with his laptop propped in front of him. He had been editing for the past two hours, with an intense, single-minded focus she found fascinating.

For the most part he was silent, headphones clamped over his ears as he watched and listened to the footage he had shot at the picnic.

Every once in a while, he let out a sound that made her smile and made Louie jump in his sleep. Despite her best efforts at interpretation, she couldn't tell whether his random sounds were frustration or triumph.

She wanted to help. She had *tried* to help when he first came over to her house. They had watched about an hour of footage together, interviews and candid shots of families together at the picnic. It quickly became apparent that Gabe was used to working alone and really didn't need any help.

He knew exactly what he was doing and she figured out early on that she was only messing with his process.

Eventually, she had slipped to her bedroom and found the mystery novel she was reading on her bedside table. Gabe had been so engrossed in the project, she wasn't sure he even noticed she had moved to the other chair and was no longer sitting beside him.

She wasn't making much progress on her book, since watching him work was far more engrossing than her novel. He worked the laptop like it was a Stradivarius and he was a virtuoso.

Gradually, his frenzied movements began to slow and finally stop. He winced a little and stretched his back. She could only imagine he hurt, being in one position for so long. She should have insisted he get up and move around before now.

"Is it really seven o'clock or is my computer time wrong?"

"It's seven," she answered. He had arrived at two and hadn't left the sofa since he started. "You've been hard at it for hours."

He made a face. "Sorry. I tend to get wrapped up in a project and lose track of space and time. And company."

Daisy saw no reason to be offended by that. She did the same when she was hard at work in the studio.

"I actually didn't mind. Louie and I had a nice visit and I've enjoyed reading and watching you."

She wished she hadn't added that last part, especially when he gave her an interested look. She quickly changed the subject.

"Are you close to being done?"

"Maybe another hour. Maybe less."

"Are you hungry? Do you want to take a break to eat some-thing?"

He blinked, a frown furrowing his brow. "Yeah. Actually, I am hungry. Do you want to go somewhere?"

He needed a keeper, someone to make sure he took care of his temporal needs. She should have done a better job of that, as his official assistant on the project.

"I have things to make sandwiches, if you'd like to eat out on the patio."

"That sounds great. I can help."

"No need. Everything's already in the refrigerator. It will only take a minute to put it together. Why don't you take Louie out and I'll bring the food in a moment?"

He rose slowly, wincing again, and she resolved to make him at least take some pain reliever.

It only took her a moment to throw together chicken salad sandwiches on the fresh ciabatta rolls she had purchased earlier that morning. She added cut vegetables from her refrigerator, some of the gourmet cheese James had introduced her to and a couple of fresh early-crop apples and headed out to the patio to join him.

When she walked out she found him standing on the edge of the low stone fence that enclosed her patio, gazing down the steep cliff toward the water.

From here she had a view for miles up and down the coast in both directions.

Louie barked when she came out, which made Gabe turn. He shook his head. "This view. It's spectacular!"

She had to smile. It did take the breath away. From the front her house looked like a quaint little cottage surrounded by flowers and trees and strange little whimsical statues. Back here the cliff sloped away into nothing. The terrace went straight to the edge. If not for that low fence, she would worry about stumbling over the side to the water hundreds of feet below.

She didn't like heights in general but she forgot that fear here, with the sheer magnificence of the view.

"It takes my breath away every time I walk outside."

"Why do you ever go inside?"

She smiled a little and set the tray out on the wrought iron table. She brought along a lighter and spent a few moments igniting the citronella torches around the edges of the terrace that helped keep away any mosquitoes.

It was entirely too romantic a scene, she realized too late as she watched Gabe pour wine into the two glasses she'd brought out. Would he think she intended that? She should never have suggested they come out here.

"I think I would become a hermit if I lived here," he said as he sipped at the wine.

"It is hard to leave sometimes," she admitted.

"This house suits you."

"Why do you say that?"

"It appears to be one way from one vantage point. Nice enough. Pretty, even. When you take the time to explore a little deeper, though, you discover something completely unexpected. Something so extraordinary it takes your breath away."

Heat seemed to flash through her, fierce and wild. She didn't know what to say. No one had ever said anything like that to her before, looked at her that way. No one had ever bothered to see beyond the surface except James, a man whose heart wasn't free for him to give.

She wanted to soak in the wonder of the moment. When he left Cape Sanctuary and moved on to other projects and places, she would remember that once Gabe Ellison had stood on her terrace and said words to her that seemed to reach right into her heart.

"That...is a lovely thing to say."

"I mean every word," he murmured. And then, as she had been hoping, he leaned down and brushed his mouth over hers.

Now the evening truly was perfect.

She wrapped her arms around him, loving the heat of him and the way his mouth danced over hers as if he couldn't get enough.

It seemed inevitable, as if it had been foreordained eons ago that they would be here at this moment, with the sweet smell of the flowers in her garden drifting around them and the spectacular setting laid out ahead of them.

She was falling in love with him.

She had always assumed she was immune to that particular emotion. She had dated before she married James, in college and after, and had never even been close. Here she was, though, head over heels with Gabe Ellison—a man she knew would be leaving Cape Sanctuary as soon as he could arrange it.

She had always been so careful, so determined to protect herself. Yet now she was destined to wind up with a broken heart. She saw no possible way to avoid it.

She wasn't going to worry about that right now. For this moment they were here and he was in her arms. She was determined to savor each taste, each touch, each moment with him while she had the chance.

2 7

GABE

He hadn't been lying. This house mirrored her perfectly. It was charming, whimsical, overflowing with surprises.

Daisy was the most intriguing woman he had ever met. She was a puzzle he had a feeling he would never grow bored trying to solve. He missed her when he wasn't with her and couldn't wait for the moment when he would see her again.

He wanted to know everything about her, and every new discovery made him more intrigued. He was attracted to her, wildly attracted, but it was the astonishing tenderness that surprised him most. She put on a front as a tough, pragmatic accountant, but her heart was as soft and vulnerable as a hatchling turtle.

He didn't know how long they stood there on her spectacular terrace, entwined together. As far as he was concerned, not long enough. She was the one who finally slid her mouth away from his.

"If we don't eat those sandwiches, I suspect Louie will do it for us."

Louie, he noticed through the haze of desire, was sitting up and looking at the table and the dinner she had prepared with an avaricious eye. He sighed, not wanting the moment to end.

"You're probably right. He's a rascal, that one."

The dog gave an innocent *who-me?* sort of look that fooled neither of them as he and Daisy sat down.

"Do you ever paint out here? I would think you would find it very creatively stimulating."

"I would. But there are also bugs and dirt and leaves and that ever-present wind. I can't imagine spending days trying to paint a whole piece of furniture in precisely the perfect way and then having to redo a section because a spider wandered over it and got stuck in the wet paint."

He could understand that.

While they ate, they spoke of the projects she was working on and he shared details about the previous film he had just finished.

"Can I ask you a question?" he asked when the meal was almost done.

She looked nervous momentarily but covered it with her usual dry tone. "It seems to me you have done nothing but ask me questions since you brought Louie here that first night."

"It's a hazard of my job, I'm afraid. I like knowing about things and people."

"I suppose that's what makes you so good at your job."

He wasn't sure about that, though he was enjoying doing the promotional video for Open Hearts.

That wasn't the source of his curiosity about Daisy, however.

"I'm wondering why you continue to keep your identity a secret from your family. Bea and Stella are both lovely. Do you really think they would be upset to discover the niece and sister they love is Marguerite?"

She reached for her wineglass. "I told you. I have my reasons."

He should leave it at that. Her tight tone told him this wasn't a subject she wanted to discuss. He couldn't seem to help himself. Hazard of the job, again.

"What are you afraid of, Daisy? That they will finally see inside to the real you?"

She set down her wineglass so hard it sloshed a little. "My reasons are my own."

"In other words, none of my business."

"You said that. I didn't."

He was annoyed with her suddenly. Annoyed with her prickliness on the subject, annoyed with her secrets, annoyed in a weird way on Marguerite's behalf, that Daisy was so ashamed of her. "You're a gifted artist. Don't you think they deserve to know that someone they care about is so beloved around the world?"

"Drop it, Gabe."

"Why?"

"I told you I don't want them to know and that's the end of it. I don't want *anyone* knowing. I hate that *you* know."

Her words, as fierce and passionate as her kiss had been a moment before, cut him to the bone.

"I wish I had never said anything to you," she went on, her voice almost bitter. "I should have simply continued denying it. You had no proof of anything."

"Wow. That's harsh. You don't trust me to keep your secret?"

She rose and started clearing away the few dishes, though he saw she had hardly eaten anything. "I don't even know you. Not really. Why should I trust you?"

How could she say that? He was beginning to think she knew him better than anyone on earth.

"Because we're friends. Because of this…thing between us."

"There is nothing between us but a few kisses. They're not real."

He had literally taken a knife to the gut a few weeks ago that hadn't hurt as much.

"They felt pretty real to me just now. I'm attracted to you and it's fairly obvious you feel the same way."

He wanted to leave it at that but knew he couldn't. Not when there was so much more to his feelings.

He gripped her hands. "I'm not simply attracted to you. That wouldn't keep me up at night, thinking about you and aching for you. The truth is, I'm beginning to have feelings for you."

She lifted her gaze to his and for an instant he was almost certain he saw a shocked sort of joy there in those lovely hazel depths before she quickly veiled her expression and slid her hands away.

"You don't have to lie to me, Gabe."

He blinked. This was the first time in his life he had ever told a woman he was falling in love with her. Of all the ways he might have expected her to respond, outright disbelief wasn't on the list.

"Where's the lie? You think I don't have feelings for you?"

Her mouth tightened. "I think you want to be the one who reveals to the world the truth about Marguerite. I think your intentions are good but I think you'll do anything to convince me to trust you. Even lie about this."

That ache in his gut seemed to twist harder. Where the hell did that come from?

"What have I done to give you such a poor opinion of me?"

"Nothing. I don't blame you. It's only natural. You're a storyteller. It's who you are. You're a storyteller and I'm a possible source."

"That's not all you are."

"Tell me you don't want to be the one who reveals the truth about Marguerite to the world."

He could lie to her but knew that would only make matters worse. "I would. I think your story would fascinate the world, Daisy. But that's not the reason I'm here."

"No. You're here because my aunt and my sister wanted you to film a promotional spot for Open Hearts."

273

I'm here because I'm in love with you, you stubborn woman.

He wanted to say the words and everything else that had been building inside him during his time in Cape Sanctuary. "You're wrong," he said quietly. "But I have a feeling I would be wasting my breath to try defending myself."

He didn't know how to convince her she could trust him. Her life experiences had taught her to rely only on herself, which filled him with sorrow. His had the opposite effect. He had learned that a person's life was only enriched by making connections with others. That was the core message in every one of his documentaries.

Wasn't that the entire message of Open Hearts? Children in foster care needed strong, loving families willing to welcome a child going through a hard time.

Daisy was determined not to let *anyone* in. She was closing herself off to so many of life's joys.

There was no point in arguing with her. Gabe knew when a battle was lost before it even began.

"If that's how you feel, I guess that's it. There's nothing for me to say."

"Gabe."

He didn't want to hear more. He was already hurting enough. "Thanks for dinner but I'm going to take off. I'm almost done and think I can finish what's left back at Casa Del Mar."

She looked briefly miserable. Good. He wanted her to suffer a little.

"I understand."

"I have to make a trip out of town tomorrow," he said on the spur of the moment. He would find somewhere to go. "I probably won't be around for a few days to walk Louie."

"We'll be fine," she said.

That was the very problem. She had convinced herself that she would only be fine on her own, needing no one, trusting no one, taking no chances that she might be hurt.

He had no idea how to convince her how very wrong she was. The best moments in life contained some risk. They were about reaching outside your safety net and embracing opportunities and people and emotions.

He was afraid Daisy Davenport McClure would never be able to learn that lesson.

2 8

STELLA

If she could keep feeling as good as she had the past few days, she just might make it through this first trimester.

Stella slid into her Volvo in the school parking lot, glad to be going home at the end of the day.

She was tired, but that wasn't anything unusual. Most teachers she knew ended up almost catatonic after they went home at night during that difficult first week of trying to learn all those new faces and names and establish a new routine for the year.

She hadn't been sick in days, had been almost back to normal since the picnic the previous weekend. Except for a nagging backache and a little crampiness, she felt great.

Some of that was this newfound happiness with Ed, she knew. They had spent time together every night, along with Rowan. They fixed dinner together and laughed together and delighted in learning more about the people they had each grown into over the years.

One thing hadn't changed. Ed made her happy. Adding his delightful daughter into the mix only seemed to add to her joy.

The world seemed wonderful right now, bright and full of possibilities. She pressed a hand to her abdomen, to the child she couldn't yet feel moving.

"He's pretty amazing, little one," she said. "I think you're going to love him, too."

She looked around to make sure none of the other teachers caught her talking to herself. When she saw the coast was clear, she started her Volvo. She was about to back out of her parking space when her phone rang.

Thinking it might be Ed calling to change their dinner plans that night, she turned off her ignition and reached for her phone.

It wasn't Ed but a number she didn't recognize. She almost ignored it. Since she had her phone out anyway, she answered.

"Hi, Stella. This is Gabe Ellison."

"Oh. Gabe. Hello!"

If she could reach through the phone lines to hug a man, she would. "I'm so glad you called. I was going to grab your number from Daisy as soon as I got home so I could call you and thank you."

"You got the clip I sent you, then?"

"Yes. I watched it after school and cried for ten minutes straight. Happy tears, I promise. It's fantastic. Absolutely perfect. People are going to love it. I can't thank you enough."

"I'm so glad you enjoyed it. I was happy with the way it turned out, too."

"I can't wait to show it to everyone. Have you sent it to Daisy?"

"I haven't. I wanted you to be the first one to see it."

"Maybe I'll have a viewing party."

"That's actually the other reason I called. I want to let you know, a friend of mine is the station manager at one of the regional network affiliates. I sent it over to him and he called me right back and wants to run it during the evening news tonight. They had a cancellation for another ad and he said the Open Hearts spot would be the perfect fill-in."

"Wow! Tonight? That's tremendous!"

"Yes. Probably about halfway through the newscast. I thought you might want to know. Hopefully, it will generate interest in the Arts and Hearts on the Cape Festival this weekend. I added a tie-in to that with a link to the website for more information and also did a second one without it so the TV stations can run the ad later without that time element."

"Thank you!"

"I've got contacts at the other networks and I'm speaking with them, too. We'll see if we can get a buzz going."

"Oh, Gabe. Thank you so much! I don't know how we can ever repay you."

"No need. It's a worthy cause and I'm honored to be part of it in this small way. While filming the picnic, it was obvious you're making a real impact in people's lives."

"Thank you." She couldn't resist adding a sly little matchmaking effort, maybe because she was so deliriously happy. "You said you didn't send Daisy the clip but have you told her about tonight, that it's airing during the news? I'm sure she's absolutely thrilled."

"I haven't spoken with her since Sunday," he said, his voice curiously tight. "I'll let you be the bearer of good news."

That didn't sound promising. She frowned. Had something happened between them? She had been so certain after Saturday that the two of them were developing feelings for each other. Gabe had always kept an eye on Daisy, no matter where she had been at the park, and Daisy blushed every time Gabe was close, something Stella had never seen her do. She never would have confided in the man about Daisy's past if she hadn't seen he had feelings for her niece.

If she knew her niece, she suspected Daisy had done her best to push the man away. Her heart ached, wishing she knew how to talk some sense into her.

"I'll tell her. We would love to have you join us for the viewing party." Maybe she could do something to mend whatever rift Daisy had created.

"I would enjoy that," Gabe said, "but I'm afraid I'm out of town right now."

Too bad. "Well, let me know when you're back so I can at least have a party for you after the fact. First, you saved Cruz's life. Now this. We're deeply in your debt, Gabe Ellison. Don't think I'll forget."

After they said their goodbyes, they hung up, and Stella quickly typed in a text and sent it out to Daisy and Bea, Ed, Shane, Cruz and the Open Hearts board members, letting them know about the broadcast that night and that she was hosting a last-minute viewing party to watch it.

She would send an email to the broader Open Hearts population as soon as she was home to let them know. Too bad she couldn't have everyone over.

Want to do it at my place? Bea texted privately.

It made more sense, especially with the beautiful home theater Bea had. She texted her agreement in response and also told Bea she would provide refreshments. After sending one *more* text to the group about the change in venue, she started her car and headed out of the parking lot.

On the way home, her back was aching more, but she ignored it as she bought a couple of veggie trays and a giant bag of the delicious movie popcorn they popped right in the store.

Yes, she was probably going overboard for a one-minute public service announcement, but she didn't care. This was a big deal and she wanted to celebrate. It wasn't every day that an Oscar-nominated documentary filmmaker considered the cause closest to her heart important enough that he would agree to make a promotional spot for it…and then go out of his way to make sure the spot was viewed by as many people as possible.

When she pulled up to Bea's lovely home a short time later, she found several cars already in the driveway, including a flashy red sports car that no doubt belonged to Cruz.

She climbed out of her vehicle and felt a sharp twinge in her abdomen. She frowned. Oh, she hoped she didn't start feeling queasy again. The pain didn't quite feel like the nausea that had tormented her the past few weeks.

Pregnancy at forty definitely wasn't for the faint of heart.

"This is so exciting," Bea exclaimed as she answered the door. "Have you seen the spot?"

"It's wonderful. Gabe did a marvelous job. I can't wait for you all to see it."

Bea took the groceries from her and carried them into the media room, where she already had a snack table set out with some of her famous chocolate chip cookies and some chips and salsa.

Ed arrived as she was carrying in napkins and paper plates. He gave her a secret smile and she wanted to run into his arms and kiss him, but she hadn't told the girls they were back together yet. She wasn't really keeping it a secret but wanted the chance to tell both of them at the same time, and Daisy hadn't arrived yet.

Only Paula Bullen and the Lymans from the board were able to make it.

Shane showed up just a moment before Daisy. "Sorry I'm late. Practice just ended," he said.

"You made it in time. It hasn't started yet," Bea said. A strangely tight note in her voice had Stella looking closer. Was *everyone* fighting? Bea and Shane were usually laughing and joking with each other but now they looked as awkward together as her seventh-graders at their first dance.

"It should be on in a moment," Stella said. "I don't know exactly where in the newscast our bit will run, so we should probably watch all of it."

"Should we take our seats?" Daisy suggested.

"Yes, everyone," Bea said. "There's plenty of seating for everyone."

The way things turned out, Stella was sandwiched between Rowan and Ed. Not a bad place to be.

"Are you feeling okay?" Ed asked her quietly. "You look a little pale."

The concern in his voice made tears rise in her throat, for reasons she couldn't have explained. She wasn't sure why he even wanted to be with her, since she had felt like an invalid since the moment he came back to Cape Sanctuary.

"Yes," she lied. In reality, her backache had intensified and so had the abdominal cramps. Maybe the salad she'd taken for lunch had been off.

"It's too bad Gabe couldn't be here with us to watch this big moment," Bea said. "It's all because of him. Cruz, why didn't you bring him?"

"He's not at my place right now," Cruz said. "He drove down to the Bay Area. Said he had a doctor appointment and also some business meetings."

"Is he coming back?" Daisy asked, looking miserable.

"He said he was. I don't know, though. He took everything he brought with him."

"I hope he does come back," Bea said. "He seems very nice. Don't you think so, Daisy?"

Apparently, Bea had noticed the heat simmering between them. She frowned at the girl for goading her older sister. Daisy, if possible, looked even more miserable. "Yes. Very nice," she said stiffly.

They didn't have time to talk more because the news flashed to a commercial and suddenly there was Cape Sanctuary filling the screen.

"Turn it up," Shane said.

Bea fumbled with the remote and everyone went quiet as they watched the spot that showed several families playing together, laughing together, enjoying the end-of-summer picnic while statistics about the grim foster care situation flashed across the screen. The increasing numbers of children who needed placements and the decreasing numbers of families stepping up to provide them. Finally, Stella came on screen talking about Open Hearts and their goal and mission.

The bit ended with more shots of the families together—a father watching the baseball game while cradling a sleeping toddler, a mother leaning down to push a joy-filled child on the swings, a couple of teenage girls, arm in arm as they laughed in the sunlight.

It was emotional and compelling and so much better than it had looked on her small computer screen at school.

"He is so good," Bea breathed.

"Get ready for the donations to start pouring in," Daisy said. Her tone might be prosaic but Stella saw rare emotions brimming in her eyes.

"You looked great, Aunt Stella," Mari said. "I couldn't even tell that you were sick that day."

"She's right. Great job." Ed's smile was filled with pride and love, and she wanted to soak it in.

"Thank you, everyone. Not just for coming to watch and support us but for everything you have done over the past five years since we started Open Hearts. I don't know what I would have done without you all."

The tears that always seemed close to the surface right now started to spill over and she knew she had to get away to compose herself. As she rose, the ache in her back and the hard, painful cramps stole her breath.

"There are refreshments. Enjoy. Excuse me, won't you?"

She hurried from the room. Just as she reached the hallway,

the ache turned into a stabbing pain and she felt a warm gush between her legs.

Please no. Please no. Please no.

The words bubbled out of her, a mantra, a prayer, a plea, as she stumbled to the guest bathroom next to the media room.

She couldn't lose this baby. Not after she had tried so very hard to get pregnant.

She couldn't. She couldn't. She couldn't.

"Stella?" Ed's voice sounded outside the bathroom door five minutes later.

She should probably open it, but she couldn't make herself move. She couldn't answer. Could barely even breathe. She was frozen. Numb. Everything inside her ached.

"Stella," he called with more urgency in his voice.

She was going to have to say something, do something, or he was going to break down the door. Bea wouldn't like that sort of damage to her lovely guest bathroom.

She was fairly certain she would never be able to walk into this bathroom again. Maybe not even the whole house.

"Are you okay?"

She was not okay. She wasn't going to be okay ever again. She sobbed, a harsh, guttural sound that seemed to well up somewhere deep inside her. All her dreams, all her hopes, everything she had worked and fought and prayed for over the past year was gone in a moment.

She didn't have absolute proof she had lost the baby, only a large amount of blood, but somehow she knew.

She could hear a flurry of sound outside the door but she couldn't seem to summon the energy to care. Her grief was too huge, too overwhelming.

Bea and Daisy both came through the door a moment later. She wasn't sure how they did it. Bea must know the secret to unlocking it. This was her house, after all. Bea, in particular, had never been good at accepting locked doors or cabinets or drawers.

"Aunt Stella? Are you all right?" Daisy was the first to speak, her voice hesitant. "Dr. Clayton said he knocked and you wouldn't answer. He's... We're all worried about you."

She couldn't answer them. If she spoke, she would start sobbing, and once she started, she wasn't sure she would be able to stop.

"Is it...is it the baby?" Bea asked.

She nodded slightly, the tiny movement followed by a sob she couldn't contain.

At the sound, Ed pushed his way in, past the girls. "You're bleeding. Oh, babe."

He wrapped his arms around her and the grim finality in his voice confirmed just what she suspected. He was an OB-GYN. He would know the signs of a miscarriage better than anyone else.

"I think I'm losing the baby."

She couldn't hold back the sobs then, wrenching, heartbroken sobs that came from the very depths of her soul.

29

DAISY

She wasn't sure she had ever been so very heartsick.

After spending the evening in the waiting room of Ed and Jo Chen's offices until after midnight, where the doctors had confirmed there was no longer a heartbeat and Stella had indeed lost the baby, Ed had taken Stella home and Daisy had run home only long enough to grab Louie and take him back to Three Oaks.

She and the dog had slept curled up together on the sofa outside Stella's bedroom. She was unwilling to leave her aunt alone. She had wanted to sleep on the floor beside her bed, as she and Bea had done in those first days and weeks after Stella had found them and adopted them, but her aunt wouldn't hear of it.

Stella was in a strange place, a place where Daisy wasn't sure she would be able to reach her.

After that first initial burst of despair, her aunt had been brisk and almost detached as Ed ushered her out to his car and drove her to the clinic, where Dr. Chen met them. She hadn't wanted them back in the exam room with her. Ed could stay, Stella said.

Apparently, the two of them were a thing now. Under other circumstances, Bea would be happy to know her suspicions were confirmed, though Daisy had a feeling none of them would be able to find much to be happy about for a while.

Stella had wanted this baby so much. If ever there was a woman who deserved her wish of having a healthy child, Daisy would put her aunt at the top of the list.

It broke her heart that Stella had to go through losing this child, after she'd tried hard to become pregnant.

She opened her aunt's door carefully without knocking. It was almost noon but every time she had peeked in previously, Stella had been sound asleep... Or at least pretending to be. Now, in the small sliver of light filtering in through the closed blinds, she could see her aunt's eyes were open. She was lying in her bed, gazing at nothing.

"Is there anything I can get you?" Daisy asked carefully. "Some toast or a banana or something?"

"No. I'm all right. You really don't need to stay with me."

"I'm here, along with Louie. I've got a briefcase full of work and my laptop. We are here for the duration."

"The duration of what?" Stella's voice was hard, flat. Daisy didn't have an answer for her. How could she say *until your heart begins to heal*? For all she knew, Stella's heart would never heal.

She left for a moment and returned with a tray. "I've brought you some juice and crackers. They're your favorite kind, the buttery ones."

"No, thank you."

"You have to drink something, at least. Dr. Clayton says you need a lot of fluids."

"I don't need fluids. I don't need anything."

Daisy didn't know how to respond to this shadowy, withdrawn version of her aunt, who was usually so energetic and vibrant.

This listless, broken woman was completely out of her experience.

"You're being irrational," she said, trying for a stern voice when all she wanted to do was gather her aunt in her arms and weep with her. "You know you need fluids to live. Come on, Stella. Drink some juice."

After a moment her aunt reached for the juice glass and sipped it with an air of almost defiance before she set it down on the tray. "There. I drank. You can report back to Dr. Clayton that I did what I was told, like a good girl. I'm tired now. I need to rest."

She'd been sleeping all morning—or at least pretending to. Daisy didn't know what else to do but leave her to it.

She was doing a load of Stella's laundry when Bea showed up. "How is she?"

"Shattered," Daisy said. "She's heartbroken and a little numb, I think. She's slept most of the morning.

She didn't know what to do for her aunt and she hated this helpless feeling, knowing someone she loved was hurting over something Daisy was unable to fix.

Bea's eyes were red-rimmed and sad. "Poor thing. Has Ed been by today?"

Daisy nodded. "He stopped first thing before going into the clinic. She was asleep and wouldn't open her eyes, even when he came into her room."

She had a feeling Stella had known he was there but she hadn't acknowledged him. Was it because she didn't want to share her grief with him?

"I'm here now," Bea said. "I can be here all day, until Mari gets home, if you would like to trade off. I'm sure you have things to do in the office."

Only a few hundred of them, but right now her aunt needed her.

"I'll stay. It might comfort her to have both of us here."

She wasn't sure if it did or not, since Stella barely reacted to either of them. She and Bea sat outside their aunt's room, mostly in silence. Bea brought a sketchbook and set of charcoals and was drawing various things around the room. Daisy's fingers itched to do the same but she tried to focus on work until lunchtime, when she and Bea worked together to make grilled cheese sandwiches and tomato soup, the comfort food of their childhood.

"Why do you think she wants to have a baby so much?" Daisy asked while she ladled soup into three bowls. "It's not as if she doesn't have children in her life already. She has fostered dozens of kids in need, plus she teaches school all day. Two hundred different kids every semester. I would think she'd have her fill."

Bea gave her a somewhat pitying look. "It's not the same as when you hold your own baby in your arms. You'll do anything for them. Fight any battle, slay any dragons, vanquish any monsters."

"Get back together with your ex-husband because you think it might be in your child's best interest?"

Bea stared. "You don't know what you're talking about. I haven't done that."

"You're considering it, though, aren't you?"

"I... No."

Bea's hesitation was its own answer. She really hoped her sister wasn't that foolish. Cruz Romero had been a terrible husband, and Daisy knew the years since the divorce wouldn't have changed that.

"Don't do it, BeaBea," she said softly. The childhood nickname made her sister blink.

"We're not talking about me," she said stiffly. "We're talking about Stella. Do you think she'll try again?"

Daisy had been wondering that very thing all morning. Now she shook her head. "I think she had poured everything into this pregnancy. I'm not sure she'll want to open herself up to that kind of pain again."

"She has to be devastated," Bea said softly.

Louie, who had been sweet as could be all day, started whining suddenly. "He needs to go out. We both could use some air. Do you mind if I take him for a walk?"

"Good idea. You really don't have to stay. I'm not going anywhere, except to go pick up Mari after school."

"We'll walk around the neighborhood a little bit. If she wakes up, try to get her to eat and push fluids. Dr. Clayton said she needs plenty."

Bea nodded and returned to her sketchbook. Daisy hooked the leash on Louie and the two of them headed outside.

Stella's house was a few blocks from the ocean and her steps inevitably led to the beach. It was an incongruously beautiful day for all the personal sorrow consuming her family, with high, patchy clouds drifting across the cornflower-blue sky. She could not replicate that exact color in her artwork, no matter how hard she tried. Nothing was ever quite like the pure beauty of a sunny California afternoon.

Louie was happy to be out of the house and toddled along, sniffing at every rock or piece of driftwood along the beach.

She loved this little dog. In a few short weeks he had become so much a part of her life, she couldn't remember a time before him.

She felt the same way about Gabe.

Had he left town permanently? She couldn't blame him. She had been so cruel to him the last time she saw him, out on her terrace. She cringed when she thought of how self-protective and suspicious she had been.

She hated that about herself. She wanted to be generous and open and loving, like Bea, but she didn't know how to start.

After half an hour Louie started acting tired, so she headed back toward Three Oaks. They had just turned onto Stella's street when her phone rang.

She looked at the caller ID and her heart started racing. Gabe. Almost as if he knew she had been thinking about him.

"Hi," she answered, somewhat breathlessly. "I thought you were out of town."

"I'm coming back early." There was a note in his voice, something strange and ominous. "I have…news."

Something in his tone filled her with dread and she suddenly didn't want to hear what he had to say. She wanted to hang up the phone without even saying goodbye.

What more could go wrong in this horrible week?

She wasn't sure she could take any more stress right now. But she had learned a long time ago from hard experience that she couldn't bury her head in the sand simply because she didn't want to hear bad news. It always found you anyway. Far better to be prepared when it did.

"What is it?"

"I think I'd better come tell you in person. Are you at home? I can come by. I'm driving now and should be there in a few hours."

"I'm at Stella's. She lost the baby last night."

There was a long pause and then Gabe swore. "I'm sorry. So sorry. How is she?"

"Heartbroken. Probably about what you would expect. She wanted the baby very much."

"I'm so very sorry," he said again. "It's a bad time for this. I wish my news could wait but I'm afraid it can't. Should I come there?"

Daisy felt so wrung out, she wasn't sure she could face seeing him today, especially not after the way things had ended between them.

"Stella isn't really in the mood for visitors. She doesn't want anyone here, not even Bea or me, but we're sticking around anyway. Whatever you have to tell me, you should probably just do it over the phone."

He was silent for a long time, so long she almost thought she had lost the connection until she heard his sigh. "It's about Louie. Or I guess I should call him Blue. That's his real name, which he must have thought sounded close enough to Louie. I got a call an hour ago from his family. The Johnsons. Joe and Emily. They've been looking for him and want to come pick him up tomorrow."

She sat down on the steps of Stella's porch, shock and dismay crashing over her. Louie came over to her and licked her hand and she felt as if tiny cracks were spreading across her heart.

"Now? After all this time? It's been *weeks*!"

"Yes. They live in Redding. How Louie or Blue ended up all the way out here, I have no idea. The owners apparently have been in Europe on an extended trip for the past six weeks and he's been in the care of a house sitter, who dropped the ball. He ran away and she never told the family until they returned from their trip."

She couldn't believe it. It was impossible! She pulled the little dog into her lap and clutched him close, wishing she could tuck him under her shirt and hide him away.

"How can you know for sure Louie is the dog they lost? They could just be saying that, like the other people who have called. It makes no sense that he could get from Redding to here on his own."

"I had my own doubts that it was the same dog but they emailed me pictures, a whole album of them, with a dog who looks exactly like him. Same color fur, same white patch on his chest, same little nick out of his ear, which they told me came when he was attacked by a much larger dog while he was trying to protect their daughter when he was just a puppy."

Of course he would do that. Because Louie was the most amazing dog in the world.

"It can't be him." She wanted to cry. It was ridiculous, she knew. Stella had lost a *baby*, and here Daisy was, wanting to weep over a dog she had only been fostering for a few weeks.

"The house sitter says he ran away three weeks ago. I wonder if someone picked him up, intending to keep or resell him, since French bulldogs can be valuable, and he somehow escaped from them and ended up on that cliffside. It doesn't really matter how he got here. The point is, this is his family and they have been distraught that he's gone."

How could they be distraught? They left him for six weeks with a stranger! Louie wriggled to get down. She let him but held tight to his leash. She didn't want him to get away.

"They've been searching for him since they returned and found him missing. They called every shelter within a hundred miles and finally reached the one we called in Weaverville."

They couldn't have him. They hadn't taken the right care of him, hadn't found a responsible person to watch over him. As far as Daisy was concerned, they had relinquished all rights to care for him. She wanted to say so. The words crowded in her throat, tumbling over themselves to come out.

She couldn't. She looked at the little dog, happily sniffing the flowers in Stella's garden. Her heart ached. She couldn't do it. How could she just turn him over to strangers? He had become so dear to her over the past few weeks.

"When...?" She had to clear her throat before she could go on. "When are they coming?"

"They wanted to come right away, tonight, but I held them off a little bit. I told them I was out of town and tomorrow would be better. They want to come around noon."

She felt as if somebody had wrapped Louie's leash around her neck and was cutting off her air supply.

After the silence dragged on, Gabe finally spoke. "I'm so sorry, Daisy. After we put up the signs and contacted shelters but still didn't hear from anyone the first several days, I was convinced he was a stray. This isn't what I wanted to have happen. I know you've come to care about him. I have, too."

She had to pull it together. She couldn't let Gabe see how devastated she was. "If Louie…if Blue is their dog, they must be missing him terribly." She was relieved to hear her voice only shake a little. "He's probably m-missed them, too."

"They were over the moon when I sent them pictures I had. Their little girl has been crying herself to sleep every night since they returned to find him missing."

Her throat tightened. So much for her plans to pack Louie into her car and head to Mexico, where no one could find them. He had a little girl who loved him. How could she get in the way of that?

"You said noon tomorrow?"

"Yes. Are you spending the night with Stella?"

"Yes, but she has an appointment in the morning. Ed Clayton insisted on taking her. I'll be home."

"I'll let the Johnsons know your address. Can I come by and take him for one last walk around ten?"

He cared about the dog, too. She couldn't forget that. "Yes. That's fine."

"It will be hard to say goodbye," he said.

"Yes." It never got easier, she had found.

After they ended the call, Daisy sat on Stella's porch steps, feeling as if her bones had turned to stone.

Louie, adorable as he was, seemed to sense something was wrong. He gave a concerned bark, licked her arm, then sat down on her foot. Tears trickled out as she scooped him up again and buried her cheek against his fur, missing him already.

30

GABE

He hated goodbyes—hated them so much, he usually preferred to keep them out of his vocabulary and use a completely different word. Aloha. Adieu. Anything else that didn't seem so…final.

He had said plenty of goodbyes in his life, starting with his mother when he had been too small to really understand she was leaving.

He hadn't had the chance to say goodbye to his father, either. Chet had died in a free-climbing accident in South Africa, taken far too early. While he had been filming a segment for his adventure show there, he had made the critical mistake of deciding to climb on his own that morning, no cameras, so nobody really knew what had happened.

Gabe had been fifteen, still sleeping at base camp when Chet had left. When his father didn't return, he went looking for him and found his crumpled body at the base of the steep face.

When he thought about it, he was still angry with his father for being so foolhardy and, as usual, not sparing a moment's thought for his son or the possibility that he might die and Gabe might be the one to find his body.

This wasn't anything like that. He was losing a dog that hadn't ever really even been his. Like so many other things in life, Louie had been temporary. If he could manage to keep that in mind, he might survive the next few hours.

Louie's owners were so very happy to have their dog back. They couldn't wait to see him and wanted to come first thing that morning. It had been all he could do to convince them to wait a few hours.

He pulled up to Daisy's house, with its wild garden and honey-colored brick and the secret terrace that offered fabulous views.

How was she really doing with all this? When he had told her at first the day before, she had seemed stunned, but by the end of the call, she had been her normal composed self.

It was an act. Or at least he was almost positive. He just didn't know how to pierce through her hard skin to the real emotions seething beneath.

He knocked on the door, trying not to remember the tenderness seeping through him when he had kissed her the last time he had seen her.

It seemed a lifetime ago, though it had been less than a week.

When she opened the door, looking lovely but restrained, all his own tangled emotions seemed to chase each other around in his chest, especially when Louie came trotting over to greet him. He reached down and petted the dog, wishing he could pick him up and make a run for it before the Johnsons arrived.

"Gabriel. Hi. Come in. How was your trip?"

He walked inside, wanting to break her polite facade into tiny little pieces.

"The trip was fine. I met with the liver doc, who said I'm healing well. Better than expected."

"That's great."

"How's Stella?"

That did seem to create a crack in her composure. For just an instant, emotions flitted across her features. She shook her head. "Not good. She is deep in grief. She's pushing everyone away."

"I can't begin to imagine how difficult it must be for her."

"It is. She wanted the baby so much. I don't know how she'll make it through."

"I'm sure it's been tough on all of you. You and Stella and Bea are very close. You all must be suffering."

She didn't answer, only looked down at the ground for a moment. When she met his gaze again, her features were composed but her eyes looked haunted. "We barely had time to get used to the idea of Stella having a baby. It's just so very sad."

He wanted to hug her, wrap his arms around her and provide what little comfort he could, but the tension between them held him back.

"Anyway, we're trying to be there for her. It's all we can do right now." She glanced down at Louie, who had planted his haunches on Gabe's shoe. "I have all Louie's things gathered up, waiting for his family to come back. Did you want to take him for one last walk?"

The words wrenched at his heart. He didn't want to take the dog for one last walk; he wanted to take him for hundreds more. "A walk would be good. Would you...care to join us?"

For an instant he thought she would agree to come with him but she shook her head. "He and I have already been out for a long walk as soon as we came back from Stella's this morning. I don't really have time for a second walk. You go ahead and take him."

He knew her excuse was just that. An excuse. She didn't want to be alone with him. He didn't need her to spell it out.

"His leash is there by the door," Daisy said.

He nodded and reached for it, feeling defeated and more depressed than he'd been since receiving the call the day before from the Johnsons.

Louie danced around in excitement as Gabe put the leash on and walked outside with him.

He took the dog farther than he had before, past the spot where he had rescued him along the path that ran atop the cliffs. The Pacific gleamed in the late-morning sunshine and gulls wheeled overhead, and he even spied a couple of osprey nests, high in the cliffs.

The Johnsons weren't supposed to arrive until noon. It was only half past eleven when he made his way back along Seaview Drive to Pear Tree Cottage, but he immediately spied another car already there, a late-model Mercedes SUV.

The Johnsons had sounded very kind on the phone and truly distressed at losing what was apparently a beloved family pet, but he disliked the entire family sight unseen, as unreasonable as that was.

His legs felt as if they weighed a ton each and his stupid wound burned as he reluctantly walked the remaining hundred feet to her house.

Daisy opened the door before he even reached the bottom step.

"Here you are. Finally," she said, making him wonder just how long the Johnsons had been there. Daisy would have hated trying to make conversation with strangers who were only there to take something she loved.

Inside he spotted a well-dressed couple on the sofa, along with a girl of about seven, who sat on the edge of her seat.

The moment he and Louie walked into the house, the dog immediately began barking, tugging at the leash. The girl jumped down and raced to him.

"Blue! It's you! I knew it! Hi, boy. Did you miss me? Did you?"

The dog licked the girl, sniffing and dancing with his butt wriggling a million miles a minute.

The little girl was laughing and crying at the same time, hugging him close. Her parents joined her, both beaming broadly.

"There's our boy. There's our good boy," the girl's father said, his voice gruff, and Gabe's resentment slid away. This was obviously the dog's forever family. It was clear in all of their reactions, sheer joy at being reunited.

"Where did you say you found him?" Joe Johnson asked. He wondered if he was imagining the suspicion in the man's voice. Did they think he or Daisy had kidnapped him? Why would they go to the trouble of contacting shelters if they had?

"Right down the road," he answered. "I can show you if you'd like. I was taking a walk one night and heard a whimper. He had fallen down an embankment about twenty feet below the road."

"What Gabe is not telling you is that he risked his life to rescue Louie, er, Blue, just days after a severe liver injury and major surgery."

Her quick defense of him took him by surprise and warmed him. He didn't have time to savor it, though.

"We cannot tell you how very grateful we are. Blue is a vital part of our family," Emily said. "We've been absolutely sick for three days, since we returned from Italy and found out he was gone."

"I hope you fired your house sitter for not telling you."

"Unfortunately, it's my younger sister," Joe said. "I can't fire her from being my sister, but she'll certainly never stay in our house again."

The dog seemed to be racing from person to person in his little pack, as if making sure each was all right. Daisy, he noted, stood apart, watching the scene with the detachment he knew she used as protection.

"He's a great dog," Gabe said. "I can see why you're upset at losing him."

Beside him he thought Daisy may have made a small sound

of distress, but when he shifted his gaze, she was looking at the family with the same pleasant, almost blank, smile.

"We are so very grateful to both of you, for finding him and for taking care of him these past few weeks," Joe said. "We'd like to give you a reward."

"No," Daisy said, the word sharp as a scalpel. She glanced at him, swallowed and moderated her tone. "Not necessary. We... I'm just happy he's found you both again. All dogs deserve to have a loving family."

The family argued for a few moments but Daisy stood firm. She helped them load up the things she had purchased for him then gave the dog a hug. Louie nuzzled against her as if he knew he was saying goodbye and wanted to memorize the scent of her, and Gabe had to swallow a thick ball in his throat.

Moments later the family drove away with Louie on the little girl's lap in the back seat, his face pressed against the window until they were out of sight.

Daisy stood in her driveway watching after them, her hands curled slightly at her sides.

"Daisy. I'm so very sorry."

She looked up as if she'd forgotten he was there. "Why are you sorry? Louie is right where he should be, with the family that loves him. I still can't think of him as Blue."

Her calm tone somehow was the last straw. He was being strangled by sadness, yet she stood here acting as if nothing had happened.

"You don't have to pretend you're okay with this. It's just the two of us now. You can yell or cry or whatever you need to do."

"Why would I do that?"

"Because you're not a freaking robot. Because I can tell that you're as upset as I am. He was a great dog and we both came to care for him. It's okay to be sad about that."

She looked away. "I don't have time to be sad. I have too much to do today. And I have to get back to Aunt Stella."

"Daisy." He needed a reaction from her. Anything! "Let go."

She folded her arms across her chest. "What do you want me to say, Gabe? Yes, I cared about the dog. But he wasn't mine to care about and I can accept that. I don't see the point in wailing and carrying on."

"A woman who paints with such charm and joy can't possibly be this cold."

If he hadn't been watching so closely, he might have missed her flinch. She masked her reaction quickly and offered a cool smile. "Maybe I've just learned how to control my emotions."

"There's a difference between controlling emotions and shoving them down so far inside you, you don't know how to find them when you need them."

"I feel things. I feel them deeply. But what's the point of being a drama queen about things?"

"I am in love with you, Daisy McClure. Does that merit any kind of response?"

3 1

DAISY

Through her grief and her sadness, she heard his words as if from a long distance away. He had said something similar the last time they spoke but she hadn't believed him. Now she was torn between joy and fear.

She wanted to wrap her arms around him and hold on tight, let him comfort and soothe this vast ache in her chest.

He was leaving, just like Louie. She knew Gabe would be gone again on his next project. Then where would she be? More heartbroken than she was right now.

"I'm in love with you," he went on, "but if you want the truth, I feel like I'm in love with two different women. There's Marguerite, the passionate, creative, wild-hearted artist. Then there's Daisy, the woman who can lose a creature she has loved for weeks without showing any sign that it hurts."

His words were proof that he couldn't be in love with her. How could he think she wasn't impacted by the loss of Louie, when every muscle and joint ached like she had the worst case of flu ever?

Gabe had visited the dog like some kind of noncustodial parent. Like Cruz did with Mari, for brief, fun little encounters. *Daisy* had been the one caring for the dog twenty-four hours a day. The one who had bathed him and fed him and sat with him at her feet while she worked.

She had given her heart to the little dog, and she was not someone who could give her heart easily.

"Just because I don't show every emotion doesn't mean I don't have them."

"Do you? Because I'm beginning to wonder."

"What do you want me to do? Scream? Tear out my hair? Flop down on the ground and pound my fists?"

"Anything would be better than this cold...nothing. What are you so afraid of? That people will judge you poorly for being human, like the rest of us?"

She lifted her chin. "I'm not afraid of anything."

He gave her a pitying look. "Oh, Daisy. You can't believe that. You're in hiding. Not just from me, but from everyone. From the world. You won't even tell your sister and your aunt—the two people you claim to love the most—that you are a brilliant artist who has achieved amazing commercial and critical success."

"I told you. There are reasons for keeping it a secret."

"The biggest reason is your fear. You're afraid to show people who you are inside. You're afraid they'll reject you if they know your psyche is as messy and wild and unrestrained as everyone else's."

She dug her fingernails into her skin. "You don't know what you're talking about."

He looked sad suddenly. Sad and defeated, an expression she had never seen on his features before. "Maybe I don't. Maybe I'm crazy. I would like you to trust me enough by now to show me what's really in your heart. I believe there's more of Marguerite than Daisy inside you—the passion and energy and joy she is able to show to the world. I'm in love with you. All of you. The messy parts, the secret parts, the emotional parts you want to hide away. I'm in love with the careful Daisy, the woman who is so organized and efficient at everything she does. But you are more than that. It's obvious you don't return my feelings or you would be willing to share your fears and your joys and your sadness with me."

"I...care about you," she said. She wanted to tell him that what she felt was so much more, but she couldn't form the words.

"Obviously not enough."

He gave her one last, sorrowful look before he turned around and walked to his vehicle, climbed in and closed the door behind him with a decisive click.

And then he was gone, too.

His words echoed through the garden long after he drove away. They were like acid on her soul, etching deeper into all the grooves created by the chaos of her childhood. She couldn't be that woman he wanted her to be. She had worked too hard, too long, to become as she was.

Daisy was strong. She wore her control and reserve like armor against the world that could wound so sharply.

Yes, she had been afraid. Of *everything*. Of the dark, of sleeping in their car, of not having enough to feed her sister. She had been afraid of moving into a new apartment and of her mother getting another boyfriend who wanted her to sit on his lap a little too long and of not being able to protect Bea from the same kind of attention.

Marguerite, on the other hand. She was a piece of work. She was flighty and fickle, more interested in flowers and bunnies, pretty colors and elegant lines, than in creating a safe, secure future for herself.

She didn't miss the irony, fully aware that the whimsy she embraced as Marguerite had been the very thing to provide more security and safety than Daisy's accounting degree or wealthy clients or carefully tended portfolio ever would.

She sat on the carved bench in her garden, half waiting for a little dog to come scampering over to sit on her feet.

Whoever would have guessed that a heart could break into so many pieces?

Louie was gone. The sweet, uncomplicated, adoring little creature who had wriggled his way into her heart.

And he had taken Gabe with him.

The sobs came then, noisy and harsh. She buried her face in her hands and cried until she was utterly drained from it.

For Stella's poor little baby, for Louie, gone forever, and for Gabe. The man she only now realized she loved with every ounce of her heart.

When the tears began to slow, she scrubbed at her face and inhaled a long, cleansing breath.

Gabe was right about one thing. She was tired of secrets. She needed to tell the truth, to stop hiding and let Marguerite come out into the light.

The first step in the process, she knew, was to tell Stella and Bea. Not this moment, when Stella was grieving, but soon.

She had to reveal the truth. No matter how difficult.

3 2

STELLA

At some point she was probably going to have to get out of bed.

She didn't want to. She wanted to stay right here, tucked under the crazy quilt she and the girls had made during one particularly rainy January when she had been trying to teach them how to sew.

She remembered that time with such longing, sitting by the woodstove and going over the stitches with them. They had found peace inside this house, the three of them together.

She wanted to go back, to the time when she had known her role. She had been filled with purpose, to raise the girls and provide the secure and loving home for them that she and Jewel never had as children.

She had been good at it, she wanted to think. She had taken two broken, scared and—whether they wanted to admit it or not—*angry* girls and helped them begin to heal.

Because she thought she had been good at it, she decided to foster another child when Cruz had needed a place to stay. And then Bea got pregnant and ran off with Cruz to LA.

For a while, she had considered that a failure but had decided to try again.

She had been good at providing a warm home to children in need. At least she wanted to think so. She was fairly certain the foster children she had housed here at Three Oaks would agree. She had showered them with kindness and love, had provided a sounding board, had helped set them on a better course.

Hadn't she been a good person? Hadn't she sacrificed enough? She always recycled; she was kind to the elderly; she paid her taxes on time. She had tried to live a good life. Apparently, that wasn't enough to ensure she would receive the one thing she wanted more than anything else.

Life, unfortunately, didn't work that way. She didn't believe there was some cosmic ledger where good people only ever received good things in return.

If only that was true.

While she stayed here in her bed, she could keep the vast ocean of grief at bay.

Her heart felt as fragile as a thin, ancient glass wind chime, as if the slightest breeze would send it tinkling against her lungs and shatter it completely.

It was raining today, which seemed only fitting. She rolled over and watched Mother Nature's tears streak down the window.

Eventually, she had to go back to work. It had been a week since she lost the baby and she knew she couldn't continue with substitutes handling her classes. A few more days. She would go back on Monday.

She also still had the Arts & Hearts on the Cape Festival to get through. The very idea of it filled her with dread, having to smile and pretend her heart wasn't broken.

She still had a few more days before the festival kicked off with Cruz's concert. A few more days where she could lie in bed and gaze at the rain and try not to feel.

She was doing exactly that a few moments later when her cell phone rang.

She wanted to ignore it but her phone was set so that only those she had designated as emergency contacts could get through, which meant this was either Bea, Daisy or Mari.

She hadn't put Ed as an emergency contact. His pity was harder to endure than anyone's.

She had to at least look to see who was calling. With a sigh, she picked up her phone. Daisy, the caller ID read.

She placed the phone back on the bedside table and rolled over. Daisy could leave a message. It wouldn't be an emergency. Daisy never had emergencies. Her life was too carefully orchestrated for that.

The phone went to voice mail but started ringing again a moment later. With a sigh, Stella picked it up again. Daisy was persistent. She knew Stella was here, probably knew she was in exactly this spot, blankets tugged up to her chin, and would keep calling until she answered. And if she didn't answer, Daisy would stop by the house to see what was going on.

"Hello?" Her voice sounded raspy, raw, as if she hadn't exercised her vocal cords in weeks.

She hadn't spoken much since her baby and her dreams died, but one would think all the tears she had cried would leave it well lubricated.

"Aunt Stella. How are you this morning, my dear?"

An unusually stupid question, coming from Daisy. How did she *think* Stella was?

"Fine," she lied mechanically. "How are you?"

"I'm bringing lunch today," Daisy said without answering her question. "I would like to ask Bea to join us. I need to talk to you both. Would 12:30 work for you?"

Stella looked at the clock. It was almost noon now. How long would it take her to shower away the grime and grit that had accumulated over the past several days?

"Today is not good for me," she said.

No day would be good again, she was very much afraid.

"I know, honey." Daisy's voice was gentle. "Can we come anyway? You need to eat and I want to check on you. Plus, I have something to tell you. It's kind of important."

She was going to have to shower eventually. It might as well be today.

"I suppose. You said Bea is coming, too?"

"I haven't asked her yet, but I'm sure she will if she can arrange it. We'll see you in half an hour."

She ended the call and set the phone back on the bedside table. It took every bit of strength she had not to pull the blankets over her head.

When had the world become so gray and ugly?

A week ago she might have been curious about Daisy's news. Her older niece was not the sort to call out of the blue to share things with Stella or Bea.

More than likely, it had something to do with the fund-raiser auction that was part of the Arts & Hearts celebration. Maybe Open Hearts had received another big donation from their mysterious benefactor.

She wanted to care. She *did* care, somewhere deep inside. Right now, though, it was hard to focus on other things when the world seemed so relentlessly bleak.

3 3

BEATRIZ

She wasn't sure if she was more frustrated with Daisy right now or with Cruz.

Both were on her list. Maybe the two of them had conspired to drive her crazy on a day when she still had three pieces she was trying to finish for the art auction, opening in only two days.

First, Daisy had called her to a family meeting she insisted was important, as if Bea had nothing to do but come when she snapped her fingers.

Then, as she was driving to Stella's house, Cruz had called and showed no sign of wanting to hang up, despite her broad hints.

"You're coming to my concert tomorrow night, right?"

Bea tightened her grip on the steering wheel to keep from tearing out a few hanks of hair. Cruz had called her four—repeat *four*—times that morning, using various excuses. The same question had come up each time, however.

"Of course we'll be there. You know Mari wouldn't miss any chance to see her dad perform."

"You wouldn't, either, right?"

"Sure. I'm looking forward to it."

They had been through the same conversation already that day. Did he even hear her?

She didn't think so. No matter how many times she told him she wasn't about to get back together, Cruz heard what he wanted to hear. She had no idea how to convince him.

He didn't listen to her. Nobody did.

She was the problem. Nobody believed she meant what she said. Okay, maybe she'd been a little fickle and flighty when she was a teenager. Maybe she had been focused on the wrong things, like partying and listening to loud music and wearing cool clothes.

She was a mother now with a daughter on her way to being a teenager herself. Did no one think she could grow and change over the years?

Shane certainly didn't. He thought she still wanted Cruz, despite all the times she had told him otherwise.

She sighed as she pulled up in front of Three Oaks and parked behind Daisy's old BMW.

Daisy didn't listen to her, either. Bea had tried to tell her sister she didn't have time for lunch today but Daisy had begged her to come. Something in her sister's tone had told her this was important to Daisy. Her projects could wait.

"I have to go," she told Cruz now as she grabbed her slouchy bag and climbed out of her car.

"Where are you? Want to meet for lunch?"

"I can't. I have plans."

"With Shane?"

She fought the urge to bang her head against the car door a few times. Shane was hardly speaking to her, but Cruz didn't need to know that.

"Shane teaches school, remember? He can't just drop every-thing and go on lunch dates. I'm at Stella's."

To give Cruz credit, he quickly lost his jealous tone and his voice became much more concerned. "Give her a hug for me, would you?"

"Yes. I'll do that."

"And tell her she's not that old. She can probably try again. Those fertility clinics can do great things."

Something told Bea that wouldn't be the most comforting thing she could say to Stella. Her aunt was grieving the specific child she lost, not only the pregnancy in general.

"Thanks, Cruz. I'll see you later," she said firmly.

When was he leaving town? Surely, he had recording con-tracts or show dates to meet. Whenever it was, she was sorry to realize she couldn't wait.

"I really do have to run. I'm here at Three Oaks and it looks like Daisy is already here. I don't want to keep her waiting. You know how busy she always is, making money for you."

"She's good at that," Cruz said. "All right. Bye, babe. I'll call you later."

She really didn't want him to, with her full to-do list. With any luck, he would get busy with something else and forget.

"All right. See you."

She hung up, feeling the familiar frustration she always did when she talked to Cruz. This alone should have convinced her that they could never have a chance for the joyous reunion he wanted. The constant phone calls and texts she had found sweet when she was sixteen and seventeen were not nearly as attractive now that she was almost thirty and needed a man who could survive a few days without her.

Three Oaks was locked when she tried the doorknob but she had her own key. Plus, she knew where Stella kept her extra. She unlocked the door in just a moment and slipped inside to the cool, lofty house that had been so important to her childhood.

The house had been a tumbledown wreck when Stella bought it, barely inhabitable. It had taken them years of elbow grease but now the place was a showpiece, tastefully and lovingly restored.

She had loved living here with Stella.

Where would she and Daisy have ended up if not for their aunt? Stella had rescued them, just as she had rescued all the other foster children she took in after her job with them was done.

"Daisy?" she called.

"In here," her sister replied from the kitchen. She followed the sound and found Daisy there, setting take-out bags from The Ocean Club on the table.

"Sorry I'm a little late. I was on the phone with Cruz and I couldn't quite get him to hang up."

"Is he still trying to push for reconciliation?" Daisy asked.

She really didn't want to talk about her romantic failures with her sister right now. "He is. I'm standing my ground. We are not getting back together."

"Cruz wants to get back together?" Stella stood in the doorway, pale and fragile-looking.

"Yes. But it's not happening. I had solid reasons for divorcing the man and little has changed."

Stella came farther into the room. "I think that's a good decision, my dear."

She stared. "You do?"

Stella adored Cruz. Sometimes Bea thought her aunt loved him even more than she loved *her*.

"You're not in love with him anymore. You're in love with Shane."

Bea just about spilled the teakettle. "What makes you say that?"

"It's obvious when a person sees you together. It's about time you figured it out. And he's in love with you, too."

She did *not* want to talk about this. Not when Stella was so very wrong.

"I didn't come here to talk about Shane. Daisy called a family meeting. What's so important?"

"Why don't we eat first?" Daisy suggested. She lifted a shaking hand to shove back a couple of strands of hair that had fallen from her ruthless updo.

She looked nervous. Now, that was strange. Bea never saw Daisy flustered.

Stella said little. She picked at her food, mostly moving things around on her plate, lifting her fork to her mouth and setting it down again without taking a bite. Did she think they wouldn't notice?

"Eat," Bea said sternly.

Stella pushed away her plate. "I'm not hungry. I really feel like I need to lie down again."

The miscarriage had been more than a week ago. She knew physically her aunt was probably healing. Emotionally? That was another story.

"What's this about? Why did you need to call a family meeting?"

Daisy started fiddling with her napkin. Like Stella, she had eaten little. Only a few bites were gone from her plate. Apparently, Bea was the only one in the family with an appetite today.

"I have to tell you something. Something I should have told you both a long time ago."

Secrets from her staid, boring sister? Bea could hardly believe it. "Don't tell me. You're going to marry Gabe Ellison and run off to Papua New Guinea with him."

She had only been teasing and had never expected the wild, raw emotion that flashed across her sister's features. Daisy looked... destroyed.

"No. That's not it. Not at all," she said quickly.

She was so shocked at that reaction, she had to quickly make another joke. "You've lost all our money and we're going to have to start busking in the streets."

"Bea, stop teasing your sister," Stella said sharply.

Stella so rarely spoke in that tone that both Bea and Daisy looked at her in surprise. Their aunt certainly had plenty of cause to discipline them after she took custody, but she had usually done it with kindness and patience, as she did the students in her classroom.

"I'm sorry. I'll stop. What do you need to tell us?"

"I wish this were about running off with someone or...or even losing your money."

Now Bea was becoming concerned. Whatever it was, this was serious. Daisy wasn't sick, was she? No. She couldn't bear that. Her sister could be as frustrating as Cruz in her way but Bea loved her.

She reached a hand out and covered Daisy's fingers with hers. "I'm sorry," she said again. "You know we're here for you, whatever it is, right? The Davenport girls stick together, no matter what."

If she thought her words might comfort her sister, she was wrong. If anything, Daisy looked more distressed. "I should have told you. It was wrong to keep it a secret. I don't...I don't even know why I did."

"You're beginning to scare me," Stella said with a frown.

If nothing else, whatever Daisy's big secret was, it was yanking Stella out of the despair she had slipped into after losing her baby. Nothing was guaranteed to distract Stella from her own pain than someone else needing her.

"Are you sick, honey? Are you...dying?"

"No!" Daisy looked genuinely shocked by the suggestion. "It's nothing like that. It's just..." Her voice broke off. "Oh, this is so much harder than I thought it would be."

"Just tell us. Rip off the old Band-Aid. That's what Stella used to say whenever we were fighting about something as kids."

Daisy released a deep breath. "It...it might be easier if I show you."

She left the room and returned a moment later with one of Stella's prized possessions, a small, intricately painted side table that usually held pride of place in the front room. Daisy had given the original work of art to her aunt a few years earlier and Stella liked to show it off to everyone, telling them her niece discovered Marguerite before Marguerite was a thing.

"Be careful with that," Stella said. "That's priceless to me. You shouldn't be hauling it around like it's something you bought at a yard sale."

Daisy looked at the table and then back at the two of them. "Don't worry. If something happened to it, I could always paint you another one."

Bea laughed. She couldn't help herself. "Sure. No problem. Can you pull off a Picasso, too? Is that your big secret? Are you an art forger?"

Daisy curled her hands together and looked down at the table. "No. But I am Marguerite."

This time Bea's laughter was even louder but it quickly trailed off when she realized no one else in the room appeared amused.

Stella was staring at Daisy, eyes wide as if she'd never seen her before. Daisy was looking at both of them like a dog that had been kicked repeatedly and expected every encounter to result in another boot to the side.

"Marguerite," Stella breathed. While her eyes still looked haunted, there was dawning wonder in them. "You are Marguerite. Are you serious?"

Daisy nodded tightly. "It all started as a lark. Something I could do for James as he was dying. He loved to watch me paint and it seemed a small gift I could give him."

Bea felt as if the world had twisted around like something out of an M. C. Escher work, where nothing was as it seemed and reality was another trick.

Filtering through her initial shock was a vast, deep sense of betrayal. She didn't want to believe it.

315

"You can't be Marguerite," she said flatly. "She's an artist and you've always looked down on artists."

Daisy looked genuinely shocked at that. "I have not. Why would you say that?"

"Oh, so it's not all artists. Only me."

"I never looked down on you. I think what you create is wonderful."

Bea scoffed. "How many times when we were girls and I would tell you I wanted to be an artist when I grew up did you tell me that I needed to come up with a backup plan? That few artists ever made an actual living out of what they created?"

"Is that wrong? You're in the artistic community. You know how hard it can be. You and I *lived* it with Jewel. Remember what it was like, how we always had to scramble to pay rent or buy food. Jewel refused to get another job, no matter how bad things got, certain it was beneath her and that her next commission would make everything right again."

She always found it disconcerting that she and Daisy remembered their childhood so differently.

Bea remembered Jewel as crazy and funny and creative. She had always smelled good, like flowers and paints and gesso, and she had marvelously fun ideas, like painting their bedroom, rented or not, to resemble the inside of a fairy cottage.

Whenever Jewel had been there, the world had seemed brighter and more colorful, like she carried the sun with her.

Yes, she had been an irresponsible mother. Yes, she'd had a substance abuse problem and moved from man to man, but Bea had still adored her. She had seemed *magical*.

Daisy had always seemed too old, even when she was a girl, to see the magic.

That was why she couldn't be Marguerite. It was impossible.

"I didn't want that for you," her sister said now. "That… insecurity. I only thought you should have something else in the wings. A teaching degree like Stella or something else you could fall back on. You're doing well now, but think of how much sweat and toil and hard work it took to get where you are."

"You are really Marguerite," Stella said. "I can't believe it!"

Bea looked from Stella back to Daisy and realized it wasn't a joke. Her sister was serious.

All this time she had felt the weight of Daisy's disapproval on her for being misguided enough to actually believe she had the talent to make it as a professional artist.

While she had been living under that weight, trying so desperately to impress her older sister, Daisy had somehow become one of the most sought-after artists in the country without anybody noticing.

"How have you managed to keep it secret all this time?" Stella asked.

"More important, why are you telling us now?"

Bea had never considered herself the envious type. She usually had the philosophy that a rising tide lifted all ships. Another artist's success didn't take away from her own. People could appreciate a Monet and a Picasso and a Rembrandt, each very different but brilliant just the same.

Yet, if this was true, if Daisy was indeed Marguerite, she didn't know how she could be anything *but* envious.

Eventually, she might be thrilled to be connected to such a success, but right now she couldn't get past the betrayal.

"I'm sorry I didn't tell you. At first, it was something only for James and me to share. After he died, painting became my solace and seemed too personal to share with anyone. By then Marguerite became kind of a big deal and I was...well, I was worried you would both be angry with me for not telling you."

With good reason, Bea thought. She was furious and hurt and betrayed and, yes, more than a little jealous.

"Someone told me recently that I...that I need to figure out who I really am. That I won't be truly happy until I can reconcile Marguerite's world with Daisy's. That starts with telling the two of you the truth. And then, I suppose, going public to the world."

Daisy gave a tremulous smile, looking so uncharacteristically insecure that it made Bea take a breath and try to contain her wild jumble of emotions.

Her sister always seemed completely in control of every situation. Was it possible that was all an act and this insecure, tentative, uncertain woman was the real Daisy?

"I just can't believe it," Stella said again.

"I want to go public and I was thinking...I was thinking the Arts and Hearts auction this weekend would be a good time to do it. I have several pieces I was going to donate as Marguerite. How would you feel if I donate them as Marguerite but also put my real name there, as well?"

"Can you imagine the publicity? Yes! What an amazing idea. Oh, Daisy. This is wonderful. Maybe you could collaborate at some point with your sister."

"I would love that," Daisy said, giving Bea a look of apology that soothed her soul a little more. "I was thinking...maybe we could eventually open a gallery together."

"What a lovely idea," Stella said. She sat back, shaking her head. "I still can't believe it."

"I'm sorry I didn't tell you before."

"Well, you've told us now. Thank you. But I have to tell you, all this excitement has exhausted me. I feel like I need to lie down."

"Of course. I'll leave the leftovers in the refrigerator for you," Daisy said.

Stella nodded, hugged both of them, then made her way to her bedroom, leaving the two of them alone in the kitchen.

3 4

DAISY

She couldn't tell what Bea was thinking. Her sister, usually so free with her emotions, had become like a carved block of alabaster as she helped Daisy clean up the take-out bags.

"Aren't you going to say anything?" she finally demanded when the silence dragged way to the other side of awkward levels.

Had she ruined her relationship with Bea permanently? She had been terrified about this very thing. If she was honest with herself, that was the main reason she had kept Marguerite a secret all these years.

She had told Gabe she wasn't afraid of anything. What a joke. He was so very right. She was afraid of *everything*.

"What do you want me to say, Daisy? Or do you prefer to be called Marguerite now?"

She made a face. Sarcasm was better than no response, right?

"Call me whatever you want. I'm sure you can think of some choice names."

Bea plopped onto the kitchen chair. "I can't believe you kept something so huge from me."

The accusatory tone stung but was nothing less than she deserved. "I know. It was wrong. I'm sorry."

"Didn't you trust me to keep your identity a secret?"

"It had nothing to do with not trusting you. Not at all!"

"What, then? Did you think I couldn't handle the fact that my sister is more talented artistically than I am?"

The hurt in Bea's voice was the final proof of how badly she had mishandled the entire situation. It would have been far easier if she had come clean from the beginning instead of hiding her success and having to backpedal now.

"No. Oh, honey, no. I'm not! Gabe once told me I'm nothing but a glorified folk artist."

"Gabe knows you're Marguerite."

Her heart twisted whenever she thought about Gabe and their painful last parting. Had he left Cape Sanctuary? She hadn't seen him since that night, nearly a week earlier. It had taken her that long to find the courage for this meeting, which shamed her more than she wanted to admit.

"Gabe came to Pear Tree Cottage one night when I had been painting. I had forgotten to lock the door of my storehouse I use for my studio. He picked up certain clues and put everything together."

"That old place on your property? That's where you paint? I thought it was just an oversize garden shed!"

"Yes. It's not a bad space. It's got skylights and I can pull the curtains open to have a beautiful view down the coast. You should come check it out."

When Bea made no response, Daisy sighed. Her sister, usually so out there with her emotions, seemed as closed up as a can of new paint.

"Are you angry?"

"Yes. But I'm more hurt than angry."

"You have a right to be."

"Tell me the truth. Did you keep the truth from me because you thought I couldn't handle the fact that my sister is more talented artistically than I am?"

"Okay, first of all, Marguerite is not more talented than you are."

"*You* are Marguerite. Stop referring to her in the third person."

Gabe had said the same thing. She somehow considered her artwork separate from her real self. She had to find a way to reconcile the two. She was a financial planner and an accountant. And she was an artist whose work people seemed to love, for reasons she still didn't entirely understand.

"Okay. I am not more talented than you. We work in different mediums. That's all. You can't compare them. It's like asking which makes a better long-term investment strategy, real estate or government bonds or mutual funds."

She could see she was losing her sister. "It just so happens that Marguerite...that *I* have found success in my particular medium, success I never expected and, frankly, never really wanted."

Bea scoffed at that. "Oh, please. If you didn't enjoy it, you would have stopped after James died. You must love it."

Bea's words made her catch her breath as if she'd just caught a cold water balloon in the chest. Her sister was right. She could have stopped painting at any point.

She had told herself she was only doing it because she liked the freedom her success gave her, the chance it offered her to secretly donate the proceeds from her artwork to organizations like Open Hearts and the local coast preservation society, but it had all been a lie.

She loved baring her heart and her soul in her work, and she loved the idea that she was making other people happy with what she created.

"You're right," she whispered. "You're absolutely right. I love it. All this time I thought I was only doing it for the money, but it's so much more."

Bea's rigid features seemed to soften a little. "Creativity does that. It's a fire inside you that has to come out."

Yes. Bea understood the heart of it.

Perhaps the two of them were far more alike than they were different.

On impulse, she reached over and took Bea's hand in hers, thinking of the times she had held her sister's hand to walk across the street when they were little or in the back seat of the car as they drove to a new town or as they stood beside their mother's grave.

"You're also right. Part of the reason I didn't tell you I was Marguerite was because I didn't want to hurt you by throwing her...er, *my* success in your face. That was completely not fair to you and I'm sorry. I think I must have been reverting back to when we were kids, when I had to protect you and take care of you. It was a role I took very seriously."

"No kidding," Bea said. Her tone was tart but not bitter, a big and wonderful difference.

Daisy smiled a little, the first she had let herself smile in days. Probably since losing Louie and Gabe in one fell swoop.

"Well, someone had to take care of you. We both knew it wouldn't be Jewel, since she wasn't capable of even caring for herself." She squeezed Bea's fingers. "For the record, I have nothing but admiration for you. You are a wonderful mother. Mari is a good, kind person because of the way you're raising her."

"Only partly because of the way I'm raising her. She came that way."

"Maybe, but you're helping to keep her amazing. You've created a beautiful life for yourself and your daughter here. I respect and admire that, Bea. Believe me."

"It's a good life," Bea said. "Not perfect, but happy."

"That's the best kind," Daisy said. "Do you think that there's a chance you might be able to ever forgive me for not telling you the truth?"

"Eventually. Maybe around the time Mari goes to college."

"I've got time," Daisy said softly, feeling better than she had all week. "I'll wait."

3 5

STELLA

Stella felt as if all the joy and color had been sucked from the world and she hated it.

Even heading with Bea, Mari, Rowan and Ed to Cruz's concert for the opening event of the Arts & Hearts on the Cape Festival wasn't enough to shake her out of the deep place she had sunk into.

"I can't wait to see Cruz Romero in concert. This has to be the best night of my life." Rowan was practically whirling in circles with glee. Her joy made Stella feel about a thousand years old.

"Thank you so much for inviting us," the girl said, beaming at her. "I don't know how I'll ever repay you."

Stella managed to summon a smile for her and even found a little one for her father. She was glad Rowan and Ed were able to come with her to the concert as their special guests. She only wished Ed would stop studying her with that concerned expression that made her feel like bursting into tears whenever she caught it.

Things were awkward between them, something she should have expected. Since losing the baby, she had done everything possible to avoid him. She wasn't strong enough to bear the weight of his sympathy. It would crush her, and it was all she could do to remain in one piece right now.

Why would he want anything to do with her? She was a complete mess and she couldn't anticipate that changing. A month from now, two months, six months, her baby would still be gone.

"It should be a fun concert," Bea said. "Cruz always manages to put on a good show."

Stella was still shocked that Cruz would volunteer to give a concert here. He had always supported Open Hearts in the background but preferred to downplay his own time in foster care.

Ed was driving. Bea would leave her car at Stella's house to avoid the hassle of parking and traffic.

After some last-minute scrambling, since Cruz's offer to play had only been a few weeks earlier, they had finally obtained permission to have the concert at the baseball arena at Driftwood Park. It was close enough to walk from her house, but not with lawn chairs and blankets and snacks.

"Are you guys ready for this?" Ed asked.

No. She wanted to usher them all out of her house and climb back into her bed.

She knew she couldn't legitimately get away with that, especially considering the entire concert was to benefit her own charitable organization.

She nodded and everybody piled into Ed's SUV, Bea in the back with the girls, leaving Stella to sit up front with Ed.

"I'm so excited, I feel like I'm going to explode," Rowan said.

"Not in my car, please," Ed said, which made Mari giggle. "Wait until we get out, where it would be easier to clean up."

"You're so gross, Dad," Rowan said, but she gave her father

an exasperated smile. As soon as he backed out of the driveway, the girls immediately started singing in the back seat.

It was a good thing Mari was a fan of her father's music. It must be a surreal experience for her, now that her friends were discovering Cruz, too.

"How are you?" Ed asked in a low voice as he drove toward the park.

"Fine," she answered tersely.

"You don't sound fine. How are you really?"

Bea was texting something and the girls were busy chattering away in the back seat about the merchandise they wanted to buy at the concert, paying them no mind.

Stella would much rather be talking about merchandise than thinking about the sorrow that seemed to have seeped into her bones.

She shrugged. "I've been better."

Whenever she thought of those magical few days they had before she lost the baby, she wanted to cry all over again. She wanted that joy back, that feeling that the world was filled with possibility.

She wasn't sure she knew how to find her way back from this sorrow. She could barely get up in the morning.

"You're in a unique position, bearing the grief alone. I always tell my patients who go through pregnancy loss that it's important they don't close themselves up inside their pain. Have you talked to anyone about what you're feeling?"

"You're not my doctor, Ed." Embarrassment sharpened her voice. "Nor are you my therapist."

He gave her a long look. "No. But I am someone who cares about you. You shut me out twenty years ago. I won't let you shut me out again. Like it or not, I'm in your life now and you'd better get used to it. I'm not going anywhere."

Before she could come up with a response to that firm declaration, they arrived at the concert venue and, after Bea showed a VIP pass to the parking attendants, they were ushered to a close parking lot.

She was still trying to figure out how to tell Ed he would be better putting his energy and time into a woman whose heart hadn't been shattered as they found their seats inside the small stadium where a stage had been set up in center field.

Daisy had come separately as she had other details to work out for the concert ahead of time. She had really shouldered the bulk of responsibility for the arts festival booths, which opened the next morning first thing.

Every time she thought about her niece, she was shocked all over again at her revelations of the day before. Marguerite! Stella still had no idea how Daisy had managed to keep it a secret for so long.

What talented family members she had. She still considered Cruz one of hers. He was Mari's father, after all. The dear man had agreed to waive all fees and to pay for his sound and lighting systems and crews to be brought into town out of his own pocket, which was extraordinarily generous of him.

Her board had really come through to pull this off in such a short window of time, especially when she had been curled up in her bed, wanting to disappear.

By the time they arrived, the venue was filling up. She knew they had sold out.

Somehow, she wasn't sure how, Stella managed to hold it together through the opening act, a local band of high school students, two of whom she knew had been in foster care.

She clapped and rose to her feet along with everyone else when they finished and then a few moments later, when Cruz came out to wild applause.

Instead of focusing on her grief, she forced herself to focus on the excitement of everyone around her as he started performing. Cape Sanctuary and the surrounding communities certainly loved their hometown boy.

After three or four songs, Cruz stopped and gripped the stand microphone.

"Tonight, as you all know, this concert is a benefit for a cause important to me. Open Hearts supports foster families throughout Northern California, families who are helping kids in need."

His face took on that soulful look that drove fans wild. "A lot of my fans don't know this but there was a dark time in my life when I was one of those kids in need. A wonderful, caring neighbor took me in. Those of you from Cape Sanctuary know her well because she's been helping troubled kids for years. This next song is dedicated to Stella Davenport, one of my personal heroes."

Her face went hot and everyone looked over at her as Cruz picked up an acoustic guitar and started singing "Ripples," one of his early hits, a ballad about courage and change and how small acts of kindness can change the world. It was always an emotional song, and as she looked around, she saw she wasn't the only one sniffling.

His band segued into another of his hits, this one with a sexy salsa beat that always made the crowd dance. As the fans rose to their feet and started swaying, Stella suddenly felt trapped, claustrophobic.

Her pain suddenly seemed too big for her to keep contained.

She had to get out of here, to a place where she could breathe again.

"Excuse me. I need...some water," she said to Ed.

She made her way to the aisle and rushed off the field.

"Let me stamp your hand so you can come back," a ticket agent said. She blindly thrust her hand out, but it was shaking so much it was tough for the woman to stamp it.

Without a clear destination, only needing to be away from the cloying press of people, she headed to the edge of the park, where Driftwood Park turned into Driftwood Beach.

It was quieter here, with only a few people walking by or trying to hang out and listen to the band without paying for tickets.

She plopped down onto the sand, letting the soothing music of the waves wash over her.

She had only been there for a moment when someone joined her. Somehow, she knew without looking away from the vast expanse of sea whom she would find.

"When you said you needed water," Ed said, "I assumed you meant a drink. Not the whole ocean."

"I think it was my spirit that was thirsty."

He was such a good man. A good man who deserved more than she could offer right now. Still, she didn't push him away when he sat beside her and pulled her into his arms.

The sense of safety and warmth and peace was overwhelming. She wanted to close her eyes and simply rest here, with the Pacific murmuring its soft song.

"Stella. Don't shut me out this time."

She sighed. She didn't have the strength to push him away. Not when she knew now how very much she needed him.

Ed Clayton soothed her soul even more than the ocean waves.

"Why did you walk away twenty years ago?"

"You know why. I had to focus on the girls. You didn't need a ready-made family when you were still in medical school."

"Did it ever occur to you that sometimes you don't always know what's best?"

"All the time."

"We loved each other. We could have figured out a way to make it work somehow. You don't have to carry everything alone. Then or now."

Tears began to trickle down and she sniffled. She had caused so much pain for both of them, thinking her way was the only way.

"I love you, Stella Davenport. In good times and bad."

She didn't deserve him. But, oh, how she wanted another chance.

"I know you're grieving your baby. Take as long as you need. Just don't shut me out, okay? Not like you did then."

"I don't know how to navigate this," she whispered.

"Like anything hard in life. You breathe through it for one minute at a time. That becomes ten minutes, then twenty, then an hour. And before you know it, you've made it through another day, then a week, then a month. And if you're lucky, very lucky, you have someone there to hold your hand and help you through."

"You're right. That's the only way."

He entwined his fingers with hers. His skin was warm and she thought of how many lives he had brought into the world with those hands.

"The difference this time is that I want to be standing by your side, Stella. I'm not going anywhere."

She rested her head on his chest and he wrapped both arms around her, resting his chin on her head, both of them looking out at the last dying rays of the sun.

"I wanted to be a mother. But as I listened to Cruz tonight, I understood in a way I never have before that there are many pathways to being a mother. I was a mother to Bea and Daisy, to Cruz, to the other young people I have cared for in my home and taught at school over the past twenty years. I don't need to have a baby to nurture children."

"It just so happens that I have a daughter who could greatly benefit from some of that nurturing," he said. "And if you decide down the line you want to try again for a baby, the traditional way this time, it's possible I might know somebody who would be more than happy to help you out with that."

She smiled, her first genuine smile in what felt like a lifetime. "I believe I would enjoy that very much, Dr. Clayton."

He laughed softly and a breeze caught it. She kissed him as

the waves brushed against the shore and the stars began to pop out, one by one.

As their mouths met, familiar yet new, she felt that breeze carry some of her sadness out to sea.

3 6

BEATRIZ

She always enjoyed watching Cruz perform.

Her ex-husband came alive on stage. He was not only musically gifted but also energetic and athletic and engaging, with the stage presence that had turned him into a star.

No matter what song he performed, people couldn't look away.

Women old enough to be Cruz's grandmother were actually weeping at times as he sang. His fan base wasn't strictly female, though. Guys admired his guitar work and the whole persona of Cruz Romero.

It seemed strange when she tried to articulate it to herself, but she was proud of him. Cruz had followed his dream of making music and turned it into something bigger than either of them could have dreamed, back in the days when they had existed on ramen noodle soup and peanut butter and jelly sandwiches.

How many hours had she spent at his side, listening to him

try out the lyrics to a new song? Or trailed across the country after him as he played in small clubs and tried to convince somebody, anybody, to listen to his demos?

Those had been wonderful, heady times and she would always be grateful for them.

But she also remembered the heartbreak the first time she found out he slept with a groupie while he was out on tour. Then another. Then another.

She had fallen out of love with him somewhere along their journey, maybe the fifth or sixth time she caught him cheating on her.

That didn't mean she couldn't appreciate his talent and the way he had the crowd at the ballpark totally engrossed in the show.

Except, maybe, her. She kept looking over to where Shane sat, on the other side of the stage and four or five rows back. He was with his new assistant coach Marcus Robinson, who had also come from playing professional football, and a couple of their players.

She told herself she was only looking back to check on Stella after she left, but she knew that was a lie. Anyway, Dr. Clayton had immediately risen to follow Stella, asking Bea if she would mind keeping an eye on Rowan for him.

Once when she looked back, she was almost positive she saw Shane looking in her direction, but he shifted his attention back to the stage quickly.

He wasn't with his French teacher tonight. Bea didn't know what to think about that.

She tried to shift back to the concert as Cruz ended a long up-tempo song that had most of the crowd dancing and reached for the microphone again.

"I want to thank everybody for showing up tonight. This has been amazing. There's nothing like a summer evening in Northern California and what a beautiful venue, here in my hometown of Cape Sanctuary."

The crowd went crazy, cheering loudly both for Cruz and for hometown glory.

"I have two people especially to thank for tonight. If not for one of these people, I wouldn't be standing here. I wouldn't be standing anywhere." Cruz grinned and the crowd laughed along with him.

"I want to introduce you all to my special guest, Gabriel Ellison."

Beside her, she heard a gasp from Daisy, who straightened to attention to watch a moment later when a surprised-looking Gabe came out from behind the stage and mounted the steps to join Cruz.

Bea didn't know what was going on but she was more interested in Daisy's reaction than whatever Cruz had planned. Her sister couldn't seem to take her gaze away from Gabe, her expression a raw mixture of emotions that totally shocked Bea. Pain and longing and something else she couldn't read.

Her sister was in love with him! Talk about secrets! Forget about Marguerite—now, *this* was something worth talking about. Her careful, introspective, sometimes boring sister was in love with an adventurous filmmaker who had probably not spent more than a month in one place in his life!

She suddenly remembered Daisy saying Gabe had been the one to tell her she needed to let her family know about Marguerite.

Something was definitely going on between the two of them. She had *known* there must be more to the story when the two of them had ended up sharing responsibility for that sweet little dog.

Daisy was in love with Gabe Ellison, but judging by the misery on her features, the relationship wasn't going well.

How could Bea fix that?

She couldn't, at least not right this moment, so she shifted her attention back to Cruz, realizing he was telling the crowd about how he had met Gabe.

"Some of you know that I was attacked almost a month ago at a concert very much like this one, on a beautiful summer evening. If not for the bravery of one man, that would have been the night the music died, for me, at least. Gabe Ellison stepped in front of a knife for me. We were all but strangers, yet he was willing to risk his life to protect me. This man right here is the very definition of a hero."

The crowd went crazy at that, roaring and clapping. Daisy, Bea noticed, clapped harder than anyone.

As soon as they quieted, Cruz went on, "Gabe, from the very bottom of my heart, thank you. In your honor, I am donating one hundred thousand dollars to the Open Hearts foundation."

Again, the crowd went crazy. Gabe looked shocked, especially when a couple of scantily dressed girls came out carrying one of those giant cardboard checks, written to Open Hearts.

Oh, Stella would love this, but she wasn't back yet. At least there were a couple thousand people with their phones out, videoing the moment.

"There is one more person I need to thank tonight. I would like to get her up on stage, too, if I could. Everybody give a hand for my beautiful wife, Beatriz Romero."

Everything inside her froze. He couldn't have called her out, had he?

She shook her head vigorously but the crowd around them, all people she knew from town, urged her to go up on stage. She was seriously going to kill the man, the first chance she had.

"Come on up here, babe," he said again.

"Go on, Mom," Mari said, eyes wide with shock.

She did not know what to do, but with everyone in the crowd watching—with their *daughter* watching—she was pretty sure she didn't have much of a choice.

Daisy gave her a sympathetic look as she rose on knees that suddenly shook and made her way to the steps to the side of the stage. The security team made way for her, and as she started to go up, her gaze seemed to instinctively find Shane, who stood a half head taller than just about anybody else there, big and blond and gorgeous.

With the glare of the spotlights burning on her, she couldn't see his expression. She didn't need to. She knew he would be frowning.

As soon as she was on stage, Cruz wrapped his arms around her in a tight hug that again made the crowd go nuts.

"What the hell are you doing?" she whispered to Cruz, hoping his mic didn't pick up the words.

"What I should have done a long time ago," he said.

Suddenly, before she realized what was happening, he started to go down on one knee. Oh, no. He wanted to propose again. She could not let that happen but how on earth was she going to stop it?

In a panic, she looked again toward Shane, wishing he could come rescue her, but she couldn't see him. She had to do this herself.

On instinct, she snatched the microphone out of Cruz's hand and headed to the other side of the stage, hoping with all her heart that he hadn't made it all the way down to the stage yet.

"Have you all had a fantastic time tonight? Give it up for our hometown hero, Cruz Romero."

The crowd cheered like crazy. She was aware of him coming to take the microphone from her but she wasn't going to surrender it that easily. Sure, he had a headset mic, but he couldn't talk over her.

"If we all ask Cruz really nicely, maybe he will sing the song everybody wants to hear, his first Grammy-winning single, 'Life Rolls On.' What do you say? Can we persuade him?"

The noise level was off the charts. Cruz didn't look happy with her but she didn't care. She had told him over and over she was not getting back together with him. It was unfair of him to try pressuring her into it, in front of two thousand of her closest friends.

As she might have predicted, Cruz couldn't resist giving the crowd what it wanted.

"I was saving that one for an encore, but since you asked, we can do it now."

His backup band hit the first chords and Cruz started to sing. While he was busy catering to his fans, she slipped back down the steps, into the crowd.

"That was so awesome!" Rowan Clayton looked absolutely thrilled that someone she knew had been on stage with Cruz Romero, which Bea found hilarious considering Mari, Cruz's daughter, was quickly becoming Rowan's best friend.

"Was it?" She looked for Shane but she couldn't see him. She needed to talk to him. To explain once and for all that she wasn't getting back together with Cruz.

"Nice save," Daisy said.

She smiled a little just as Stella and Ed came back to join them.

"What did we miss?" Stella asked.

"We'll tell you later," Daisy yelled over the music. "But Open Hearts is going to be able to expand its operations, maybe all the way down to the Bay Area."

Bea didn't know what had happened between Stella and Dr. Clayton, but she thought there was a different light about Stella. She still seemed sad, which was totally understandable, but there was also something almost *hopeful* in her expression.

She was also holding hands with Ed and didn't seem to want to let go. She and Daisy both noticed at the same moment and exchanged a smile.

Good for Stella. She deserved a great guy like Ed Clayton, who clearly adored her.

Bea deserved a great guy, too.

The knowledge hit her like the stage set falling on her.

If she wanted a good man like Shane, she had to be willing to fight for him, no matter what.

With new drive, she listened to the few remaining songs in Cruz's repertoire. He didn't sing the new one he had been working on, the one he'd asked her help on. She could only be glad for that.

"Can we go backstage and see Dad?" Mari asked when the lights came up and the exhilarated crowd started to disperse.

The last place Bea wanted to go was backstage to face the ex-husband she had just brushed off in front of all of his adoring fans, but she couldn't figure out a way to avoid it.

"For a moment. I imagine he'll be busy talking to fans."

"I just want to tell him what a good job he did," Mari said. "And Ro wants a picture with him."

After making sure it was all right with Dr. Clayton, she led Rowan and Mari to the area that had been roped off for post-concert mingling among the musicians, the crew and their special guests.

Security instantly let them through with her all-access pass.

As she might have expected, Cruz was surrounded by fans. He spotted them after just a moment, though, and made his way toward them. He hugged Mari and went to hug Bea but she managed to avoid it by reaching down to adjust her sandal.

"Great show, Dad," Mari said.

"Thanks, Mar. We had some technical difficulties but the fans still seemed to like it."

"You remember my friend Rowan, right? She came to Universal with us."

"Sure I do."

Cruz aimed his thousand-watt smile at the girl, who flushed.

"Can we have a selfie with you?"

"Sure. How about one with all of us?"

Bea couldn't avoid it as he put his arm around her and had

someone from his crew take a picture of the four of them together.

She was giving her best fake smile to the camera when she
spotted a tall blond man coming through the crowd.

Shane! He approached, along with a couple of his players and
Marcus.

The group came over to greet Cruz, who made a big deal
about shaking hands with the athletes and the other coach.

Somehow, she ended up right next to Shane.

"I didn't expect to see you back here," she said.

He didn't look thrilled to be there.

"Cruz specifically asked to meet a couple of our players and
Marcus. He said he used to watch him when he played for the
Patriots."

"I see."

She had missed him. She wanted to stand and drink in the
sight of him and especially the way everything inside her seemed
to sigh and relax around him.

"Hey, Sunshine," he said to Mari.

She beamed at him. "Hey, Shane. I can't wait for tomorrow.
It's going to be so fun."

Cruz looked up from talking to the other coach. "What's
tomorrow?"

Mari looked uncomfortable. "It's the Pinewood Derby, remember? You should see the car Shane and I made. It's so cool!"

Cruz looked from Shane to Mari. "I can't believe I forgot to
tell you, in all the last-minute craziness before the concert. I had
one of my guys make us a car to race. It's fantastic and looks just
like my Lamborghini. We are going to kick butt."

Bea suddenly wondered if the reason Cruz invited Shane and
his athletes backstage had anything to do with her. Had he expected her to accept his proposal onstage and wanted the chance
to rub Shane's face in it?

She really hoped that wasn't the case but suddenly wouldn't put it past Cruz. His ego was huge these days.

"What time is this thing tomorrow, again?" Cruz asked.

Mari sighed. "I'm not going with you, Dad. I told you that."

Cruz looked around at the athletes and others nearby, none of whom were really paying much attention to the conversation. "We can talk about this later."

"No, Dad. We did talk about it. I invited Shane before you came back to town, when you told me you weren't going to be here. I made a promise to him and promises are important."

Shane smiled down at her, and Bea's heart threatened to burst with pride.

"Shane is my friend," Mari went on. "We spent a lot of time building our car. It would be rude of me to ditch him and take you with a car that I didn't even build, someone else did. That's not the way it works. Maybe next year you can come with me, if you can arrange your schedule."

Bea wanted to cry. Her daughter had more courage than she did. Mari had no problem calling out her dad for his bad behavior and sense of entitlement. If Mari had that kind of strength, didn't Bea need to demonstrate the same?

Cruz didn't look nearly as proud. He looked furious. In response, he threw his arm around Bea, as if staking a claim wherever he could find it.

"Fine. Have your fun tomorrow. Especially because you and I will be seeing a lot more of each other, when your mom and I get back together."

Bea froze. He hadn't just said that, had he? Okay. It was on now. He couldn't just make that kind of declaration in front of their daughter and Shane and everyone else here.

Bea let out a deep breath. She wasn't a slow learner. She could take a lesson from her daughter.

She did not want to do this in a public venue. It was the reason she had cut things off on stage, because she hadn't wanted to embarrass him in front of his fans. But Cruz was the one who started this. If it took a public declaration for her to get the point across, that's what she would do.

"Cruz," she snapped, wriggling out from under his arm. "For the last time, we are not getting back together. Ever."

He looked around at the people who were now starting to pay them attention. "You're just saying that. You'll come around, babe."

"I will *not* come around. Look, I'll always be grateful for the years we had together but I'm not interested in repeating them. I know you had your grand epiphany when you almost died, but I've had an epiphany, too. You want to know what mine told me? That I'm in love with Shane Landry and I have been for a long time."

Rowan and Mari gasped and looked enthralled at the drama. Bea wanted to die, but she had to go through with it. It had to be said.

She couldn't look at Shane and wanted to slink away into the crowd, but now at least he knew.

She could see the hurt in Cruz's eyes and regretted again that she hadn't been able to convince him any other way. She didn't want to be cruel. They did share a child, and would for the rest of their lives.

She took Cruz's hands in hers, gentling her tone. "You know some part of me loves you, but you have to see that those last years we had together were miserable. I was no longer the person you needed and we both knew that. But come on. You're Cruz Romero. Half the women in the world are in love with you. You'll find someone who can make you far happier than I ever could."

Cruz looked around, obviously trying to figure out how to save face. "Yeah. There are a hundred women here tonight who could do that."

Who could screw him, anyway, and make him happy for the

moment. Bea had to hope he eventually figured out that wasn't the answer.

As if they had been cued to approach at exactly that moment, two beautiful blonde college-age young women came over, giggling and laughing, asking Cruz if they could have their picture taken with them.

He gave Bea a defiant look. "Sure, girls. Let's go somewhere a little quieter to do it."

"Bye, Dad," Mari said.

He had the grace to at least look back and give their daughter a hug. "Love you, pumpkin," he said before he let the coeds drag him away.

"Let's go," Bea said to Rowan and Mari, not ready to face Shane.

His hand on her arm stopped her from escaping and she finally lifted her gaze to his. His blue eyes glittered in the artificial lights, with an intent, fierce expression that took her breath away.

She sighed. "I didn't want you to hear that, but I guess I'm glad you did. Was that clear enough for you?"

He grinned. "Yeah. Pretty clear."

"We can talk about this later," she said.

"Now is as good a time as any."

She didn't know where to start. "I...know you've been dating Vanessa. I don't want to get in the way of that. But I had to be honest with Cruz, to convince him to get this crazy idea of a reconciliation out of his head."

He nodded slowly. "I see that. For the record, I am no longer dating Vanessa."

Relief and happiness flooded her. "Oh? Why is that?"

"I wanted to make it work with her but realized after only a few dates that it wasn't fair to lead her on when my heart belonged to someone else." He paused and clasped her hands tightly. "When my heart has always belonged to someone else."

"Oh," she whispered. It was all she could manage. In front of everyone, he lowered his mouth and kissed her softly, tenderly, so sweetly, she felt a deep ache of love for him.

Okay. They could stay right here doing this until the crews packed up all the lights and the speakers and they were the only ones left in the entire field.

As soon as she had the thought, she remembered her child— oh no, her daughter! She pulled out of his embrace and saw Mari and Rowan beaming at them.

"About time," Mari said.

Bea blushed at the realization that this probably wasn't the most appropriate place and time, backstage after her ex-husband's concert.

"I need to get the girls back to Stella and Dr. Clayton."

"Yes. Let's do that," Shane said. After he checked to be sure his players all had rides home, he walked with her out of the roped-off area and back to the chairs where Stella and Ed were waiting, still holding hands.

Daisy had disappeared, Bea noticed through the haze of happiness that seemed to surround her.

Had she gone home? If she had, it hadn't been with Gabe. She had noticed him still backstage, talking to a couple of members of Cruz's entourage.

As they walked, she was aware of Shane's athletic grace beside her. Oh, how she had missed him.

"Are you girls ready to go?" Ed asked, reminding Bea that Mari was spending the night at Rowan's.

"Yep. We're going to stay up all night," Rowan said.

"Not *all* night," Shane protested. "You'll be too tired for the race tomorrow."

"Some of the night, then," Mari amended.

"All right. Let's go. Stella needs to rest."

Stella looked between her and Shane, and Bea wondered what her aunt could see. "Bea, are you coming with us or do you have another ride?"

"She has a ride," Shane said immediately.

Her stomach muscles seemed to flutter as if she'd been working on the ab machine for a few hours. "I'm good. I'll see you first thing tomorrow at the pancake breakfast," she told her aunt.

After they left she and Shane walked in silence to his SUV, emotions swirling between them. She had a million things she wanted to say, but he didn't give her the chance. The moment they reached his vehicle, he wrapped her in his arms and kissed her fiercely.

She threw her arms around him and held on tightly, joy bursting through her in wild, colorful streaks.

"If you haven't figured it out yet, I'm in love with you, too," he murmured, a long time later. "I have been since we were kids, but you only ever saw Cruz."

She hadn't. She had always seen Shane, too, but Cruz had been flashier, louder.

"I'm sorry I wasted so much time figuring out what was real."

"You didn't. Everything that has come before has led us to this moment. And I wouldn't change this moment for anything."

He kissed her again, with all the heat and passion and magic that had been seething between them for years, and she knew this was exactly where she belonged.

3 7

GABE

He had no idea why he was still in Cape Sanctuary.

He needed to take off. Right now he didn't even have a host. Cruz had left that morning, just twelve hours after his triumphant concert. He had told Gabe he was flying to Mexico for a couple of days with some new friends.

By *new friends*, Gabe assumed he meant the two blonde women who had climbed into the helicopter with him.

Cruz had told him to stay at Casa Del Mar as long as he needed for his recovery, that his permanent staff still would be there to meet his every need. Gabe had politely thanked him for hosting him but told him he needed to be on his way. Now that he was well on the road to recovery, he itched to get back to work.

He had been prepared to leave right after Cruz did, until he received a phone call from Stella Davenport, thanking him profusely for the donation.

"It wasn't me," he had explained to Stella. "I didn't know anything about it until Cruz handed me the giant check. Good luck carrying that into your bank, by the way."

She had laughed and he was heartened to hear she sounded a little less fragile than the last time he spoke with her. "Fortunately, Cruz's people gave me a regular-size one last night, which will be much easier to fit into a deposit envelope."

"Good to hear."

She had paused. "I suppose now that Cruz is leaving, you'll be taking off, too."

"That's the plan." He had surprisingly mixed feelings about it.

He liked Cape Sanctuary. The town was on the touristy side but the residents had still managed to retain a small-town vibe. Everyone here had been kind and welcoming to him—with the exception of one particular secretive artist.

And he had fallen in love here.

He sighed, missing Daisy with a physical ache he tried to tell himself was just his knife wound making itself known.

"You could stick around a little longer. At least stop into the Arts and Hearts on the Cape Festival today. Now that you're such a huge donor, you ought to know some of the other things we do to raise awareness for Open Hearts."

He *had* been wanting to get a little more footage, in case he decided to film a longer promotional video for Stella to put up on her website.

What did he have to rush off to, anyway? He was still working out details for his next project.

And he needed to talk to Daisy.

He hadn't spoken with her since he stormed away from Pear Tree Cottage. He had seen her the night before at the concert and had looked for her when the music ended, but she disappeared as soon as the crowd started to disperse.

The words he had said to her that last day haunted him. He owed her an apology for kicking her when she was down. She had been grieving the loss of Louie in her own way. He could see that now. She might not have been sobbing about it, but the pain had been there. He had been too overwhelmed with his own to look for the clues that she wasn't as controlled as she had let on. The slight trembling of her hands, the tightness of her mouth, the sorrow she hid behind polite control.

She had been sad over losing the dog she cared about and he had basically piled on, accusing her of not responding the way he thought she should.

He was ashamed of himself. Somehow, he had to find a way to make it right.

That was the real reason he was here, he acknowledged to himself, and the reason he had agreed to come back for the concert the night before when Cruz had insisted.

He had to find Daisy and he suspected the best place to do that was the Arts & Hearts Festival.

He walked through the crowd with his camera ready, talking to artists here and there, soaking up the atmosphere. After about an hour of wandering through the booths and stopping to listen to some of the musical offerings, Gabe started to hear buzz about something going on in the huge white tent that housed the silent art auction.

A sort of heightened excitement seemed to sweep through the crowd, sending his instincts into alert status. Maybe a guest artist had appeared or something. But would that have people hurrying into the tent? ·

He was debating whether to follow the festival-goers or use this opportunity to get something from one of the food trucks when he bumped into Beatriz Romero.

Her pretty features lit up when she spotted him. "Gabe! How are you? I'm sorry I didn't get the chance to speak with you last night."

"There was a lot going on, what with the giant check and all."

She made a face. "Cruz likes the grand gesture." Her smile dimmed a little. "How is he? We sort of had...words last night."

That explained a great deal. Cruz had rushed out of town like he was being chased by ghosts. "He took off for some resort in Mexico this morning."

He decided not to mention the two young women who had been all over him. Apparently, he didn't need to.

"Let me guess. He had female company."

Gabe shifted. He really didn't want to answer that.

Bea laughed at his discomfort. "I'm sorry. You don't have to tell me. If he did, I have to admit, I would be a little relieved. That would tell me his pride wasn't damaged beyond repair. So are you sticking around without him?"

"Not for long. It feels too weird to stay at Casa Del Mar by myself. I'll probably head down to the Bay Area after I leave here, to stay with some friends. Stella asked me to shoot a little more footage for Open Hearts, and then I'll be taking off."

He had to find Daisy first. After that he didn't know what he would do.

Bea gave him an intense look. "Have you gone into the auction tent yet?"

He looked over again as more people hurried in. Everyone seemed in a big rush. "Seems pretty packed. I figured I would wait until the crowd dies down a little."

"That may not happen for a while. I think you're going to want to make a stop in there." She sent him a sidelong look. "In fact, let's go now."

Daisy's sister grabbed his arm and steered him toward the tent. "Get your camera out," she ordered.

Were all the women in the Davenport family this bossy? He turned on his camera and filmed some of the crowd as they went inside. It took his eyes a moment to adjust. When they did, he saw that everyone seemed interested in something at the far end of the tent.

He heard the word *Marguerite*, which instantly caught his attention.

What had Daisy done?

"What are they looking at?" he asked Bea.

She gave him a mischievous look. "Let's go see."

Whatever it was, he was sure if Marguerite was involved, it would be remarkable. He was filled with a funny sort of pride and wished everyone could know how wonderful she was.

After making her way through the crowd with a determination he figured was another Davenport family trait, Bea dragged him to the piece that seemed to be generating the most attention.

It was indeed a Marguerite, an armoire, large and curvy and beautifully, intricately painted.

"Wow," he said, camera rolling. "You've got an original Marguerite in here."

"There are actually three. The others are a little smaller."

He saw them now, a graceful table similar to the one at Casa Del Mar and a little wooden jewelry box, each with her distinctive, charming style.

Oh, Daisy.

"Those should fetch a pretty penny for Open Hearts in the auction."

"You have no idea," she said.

It was all he could do to not tell her right that moment that her sister was the one responsible for the largesse that would soon be coming the foundation's way.

"We should take a closer look. Come on."

She dragged him up to the armoire, which was roped off to keep it safe from grabby hands. There was a sign on it, he saw now.

Find Your Heart. Original by Marguerite. AKA, Daisy Davenport McClure.

He stared, as shocked as if the whole thing had fallen on his head. "What!"

"Why, would you look at that!" Bea exclaimed. When he looked closer, he saw that she wasn't at all surprised, only amused. "And all this time, I thought Marguerite was some old guy in a nursing home."

"You knew! How long have you known?"

This was why the auction tent was buzzing, he realized. Why people were clustered around the Marguerites. They were buzzing about the identification underneath it and the knowledge that the famous artist was the very unlikely Daisy McClure, who had been hiding in their midst like a proverbial fox in the henhouse.

Bea chuckled. "Not long. Only a few days, actually. Daisy called a family meeting to tell us. Apparently, *someone* told her that we needed to know the truth, after all this time."

She did it. He couldn't believe it!

He closed his eyes, his love for her as big and intricate and beautiful as that armoire.

"Thank you, by the way," she murmured.

"For what?"

"I put the pieces together. Daisy told me you knew. And she also said someone told her it was past time she shared her identity with her family. Since you're the only one who knew, as far as I can tell, I am guessing you are the one who persuaded her to tell Stella and me."

"I figured the people she loves best ought to be fully aware of how amazing she is," he said gruffly.

"Oh, I like you, Mr. Ellison," Bea said, giving his arm a little hug. "And you're right. She is quite remarkable. She could have had a press conference or appeared on a local news show but it was her idea to go public here, where she could make the most impact for Open Hearts."

He decided since Bea knew this much, she ought to know the rest. "You do know she is the mysterious benefactor who is always making a donation to Open Hearts right when the foundation most needs it, don't you?"

Bea blinked. "I do now. Funny. That doesn't surprise me at all."

His love for Daisy seemed to grow with every passing second, expanding to fill the large tent. He had to see her. He had to apologize for his words and he had to tell her how very amazing she was.

"I don't suppose you have any idea where I might find Daisy, would you?"

She gave him a careful gaze, protective of her sister, he could tell. "Not for certain, but I have an idea. Stella and I wanted her to stick around here in the tent, but after the first hour of people mobbing her once the news became public, she freaked out a little and said she had to go for a while. She plans to be back tonight when the auction ends, to meet the winning bidders. If I had to say she was anywhere, I would guess she's gone home. Back to Pear Tree Cottage."

"I have to go," he said, already heading for the exit.

Her laughter followed him. "I was hoping you'd say that."

3 8

DAISY

It was fairly depressing to discover her courage had its limits. She had managed to find the strength to put her actual name on her artwork. She even managed to hang around for a while and speak with the public as people started to find out.

But all those questions, all those stares and whispers, had become more than she could bear. Yes, it had been gratifying to hear how people loved her work, but it had also been terrifying.

She had finally escaped, though she knew she should be helping Stella and the rest of the committee with the inevitable headaches that came from throwing a huge festival like Arts & Hearts on the Cape. She only needed an hour or two to regain a little equilibrium then she would return.

She had retreated to her terrace, to the spectacular coast view of sea and mountains and sky that inevitably calmed her spirit. A glass of iced tea and a magazine that had come in the mail that morning were on the table beside her. She hadn't opened the magazine yet. She needed to simply *be* for a few more moments.

With her eyes closed, she was doing some deep breathing when she gradually became aware she wasn't alone.

Her eyelids flew open and she jerked her head around to see the man who hadn't left her mind in weeks walking toward her around the side of the house. So much for calming breaths. Her entire body went on alert, her pulse pounding and her heartbeat kicking wildly.

She rose. "Gabe! Cruz told me he was taking off this morning. I assumed you would have gone, too."

He didn't answer at first, only continued walking toward her with that intense, almost fierce look in his eyes.

She suddenly remembered the first time she had seen him, in the toothpaste aisle of the grocery store in town a lifetime ago. He had looked at her in much the same way as if he wanted to burn her image into his mind forever.

Then, as now, that look made everything inside her shiver.

"I didn't leave."

"I...see that."

"Instead, I went to the Arts and Hearts Festival, where your sister dragged me into the auction tent."

"Did she?"

Her hands were shaking. She told herself it was because she wanted to strangle Bea. She loved her sister but Beatriz Romero needed to stop matchmaking. She was wading into things she knew nothing about.

Gabe stepped forward and picked up one of those trembling hands and did something that completely stole her breath. He raised her fingers up and pressed his mouth to the back of her hand, then did the same to the other hand. No one had ever done anything so impossibly, heartbreakingly sweet to her before.

"You did it! Marguerite went public."

She was lost. Completely in love with him.

"It was time. A wise person I knew told me it was time I stopped hiding."

"Sounds like a smart-ass know-it-all."

"He's okay."

She wanted to slide her arms around his waist and hold on tight but a kernel of fear, small and ugly, held her back. Oh, for crying out loud. She had just faced her biggest fear, going public with her art. She could certainly admit the truth to Gabe. She smiled a little, suddenly completely at peace. These wild, wondrous feelings between them were nothing to fear. They were real and right and perfect.

"Actually," she said softly, "he's better than okay. He happens to be the man I am in love with."

A fierce light leaped into his gaze, making their green depths glitter in the sunlight, brighter than the ocean. "Well, then. He's a lucky guy."

She couldn't resist. "Why do you insist on speaking of yourself in the third person?"

He laughed, the sound rippling out across her terrace. "I would very much like to kiss you right now, Marguerite slash Daisy slash the woman who owns my heart."

"What's stopping you?"

"Nothing. Absolutely nothing." He reached for her and kissed her, his mouth warm and sweet on hers. She wanted to cry at the sheer perfection of the moment, here in the sunshine in a place she loved, perched on a cliff overlooking the ocean.

After a long moment he lifted his head. "I love you, in case you didn't pick that up yet."

She smiled and kissed him back, all her doubts and insecurities floating away. She still didn't quite understand how it had happened, what he saw in her, but she wasn't going to question the gift.

"I might start believing it, after I've heard it a few hundred more times."

He smiled against her mouth. "I'd better get started, then. I love you, Daisy. I love your smile and your kindness and the way you watch over your family. I love your earlobes and your organizational skills and the way you dance to music when you think no one is looking."

"My earlobes?"

He sucked softly on one. "You have very sexy earlobes."

Her insides trembled. "If you say so."

He laughed at her tone. "Trust me."

She did. She trusted him and she loved him. He had seen her when no one else did, the heart of her. The messy, emotional, wild part of her she was slowly beginning to embrace. They still had things to work through. His job, for instance. He would need to travel. That was unavoidable for a man so gifted at documenting the world, but she could provide a warm, happy place for him to come home to here at Pear Tree Cottage where he was deeply loved.

She might even think about getting a dog.

She kissed him, joy, pure and bright and lovely, singing through her like the murmur of the sea.

EPILOGUE

DAISY

The babies were coming.

Daisy rushed into the hospital, Gabe at her side. They hurried up to the second floor, straight to the labor and delivery unit.

Bea was in the waiting room, Shane holding her hand and Mari reading a book next to him.

"There you are!" her sister exclaimed, jumping up. "Finally."

"My fault." Gabe gave her a hug before reaching out to shake Shane's hand. The two men had become good friends over the past year, since the summer that had changed everything. "Daisy was picking me up at the airport when you called and my flight was late."

So much for the passionate reunion with him she had been fantasizing about since he left town three weeks earlier. She had barely had time to kiss him and hold him for a wonderful fleeting moment before Bea's frantic call had them rushing back to Cape Sanctuary.

There would be time, she told herself. One delicious thing she had discovered about being with a man who traveled often: during the times he was home with her, they never wasted a moment.

"How is she?" Daisy demanded.

"Stella is fine," Bea said. "Ed, however, is a mess."

She grinned. "You're kidding. The OB-GYN is freaking out about his wife being in labor?"

"Right?" Bea grinned back. "I've never seen him so pale and he can't seem to let go of her hand."

"Have you been in to see her yet?"

"Yes. We just came out a moment ago. She was having a pretty bad contraction and Shane was getting a little weak-kneed."

"Was not," he protested.

"Was, too." Bea grinned and kissed him to take the sting out of her words.

If he was weak-kneed at *Stella's* contractions, Daisy couldn't wait to see how Shane reacted when Bea had a baby. They hadn't announced it yet but she had a strong suspicion it wouldn't be long. Maybe they were waiting until the twins were born.

The two of them were so perfect together, Daisy couldn't believe it had taken them both so long to figure it out. Shane clearly adored Bea and treated her exactly as she wanted a man to care for her younger sister. He was sweet, caring and supportive.

No one had been surprised when they married only a few months after Stella and Ed.

Even Cruz seemed happy these days. He was seriously dating a woman he had met the summer before when he went to Mexico after his concert for the Arts & Hearts on the Cape Festival. Nora was a marine biologist, smart and funny and sassy. Daisy liked her very much. More important, Bea did, as well, especially since Mari and Rowan both wanted to follow in Nora's career footsteps.

"I'm going in," Daisy said.

"I'll go with you," Bea said. "They recommend only a couple of visitors at a time. Why don't you guys wait out here? Do you mind, Gabe?"

"Not at all."

Shane stretched his legs out in the waiting area, all too happy to comply with that, and Gabe took the other sofa.

The labor and delivery room was state-of-the-art, warm and comfortable. Stella sat in a recliner playing cards with Rowan while Ed stood protectively next to her, the dear man.

Their aunt's face lit up when she spotted them. Stella reached out a hand. "There are my girls."

Daisy kissed the top of her head, then hugged Ed and Rowan in turn. She loved these two so much, not only because they were terrific people but especially for the light and happiness they had brought into Stella's world.

"How are you doing?" Daisy asked.

"Great. It won't be long now," Stella said. Her features tightened for just a moment, clearly in the grip of a contraction.

This pregnancy had been unexpected but no less joyful. Only a few months after losing her first pregnancy, Stella had discovered she was expecting again, this time without means of artificial insemination or any help from fertility treatments. She and Ed had already been talking about marriage. The pregnancy had accelerated the whole process and they had a beautiful wedding at the little chapel in town where Stella worshipped.

Daisy had sobbed like a baby watching Stella walk down the aisle toward the man who had loved her for decades.

Only a few weeks after their honeymoon, Stella had discovered she was not only pregnant but also expecting twins, reinforcing Daisy's belief in the old adage about being careful what you wished for.

Throughout the pregnancy, Stella had glowed. This one was uneventful, almost too easy, which was a relief.

Ed had still been a nervous wreck throughout.

"Can we get you anything?" Bea asked. "Ice chips? Chewing gum? Anything?"

"I'm absolutely fine. This might take some time. You know you girls don't have to stay here through the whole labor and delivery."

"Are you kidding?" Daisy exclaimed. "You're stuck with us. We're not going anywhere."

"These are our babies, too," Bea said.

"The good news is, there will be two little ones to cuddle afterward," Daisy said. "That means I get to hold one and the rest of you can fight over the other."

Ed smiled, looking moderately calmer. "By the way, we love the new cribs from Marguerite."

"They are absolutely stunning," Stella said. "We have the most gorgeous nursery in the world. Thank you, my dear."

"And when the babies outgrow them, we can always sell them to cover their college tuitions," Ed teased.

"We are not selling them," Stella said firmly. "I have a feeling Bea might be needing at least one of them sooner, rather than later. And who knows? Daisy might want one, too, down the line."

"She could always paint two more," Rowan pointed out with irrefutable logic.

The idea of a baby wasn't as astonishing or terrifying as it might once have been. Not yet, but someday soon. She and Gabe were engaged, planning a wedding at Pear Tree Cottage in April, one of the most beautiful months there.

"Is everything ready for the festival?" Stella asked. "I'm sorry about the timing of this."

"Don't worry about anything," Bea said. "Daisy and I have the whole thing under control."

Had it really been a year since the last festival? This had been a year of change, of growth. Marriages, second chances, love. Soon two new lives would join their family.

She and Bea visited for a few more moments, mostly to distract Stella from the pain and make sure she knew they were there for moral support.

"You don't have to leave," Stella said when Daisy saw she was having another hard contraction and nudged Bea that it was time to go.

"We won't stay in the delivery room," Daisy said. "This is a special moment for you two and Rowan to share, but we'll be out in the waiting room when you need us."

Stella didn't answer, breathing through the pain, but Ed nodded, gave them a distracted hug, then turned back to his wife.

After they walked out, Daisy stood in the doorway of the waiting room, her heart catching at the sight of Gabe asleep in one of the chairs. He had been traveling for hours, just to make it back to her.

The moment she sat down beside him, his eyes opened and a lump rose in her throat at the sheer love in them.

Only an hour later Rowan rushed in. "They're here! A boy and a girl! The girl came first. She has a *ton* of hair. The boy came like two minutes later. He's smaller but cried harder. They're both *so* cute."

"How's Stella?" Shane asked.

"She's great. She said she's ready for everyone to go back. She wants her whole family around her."

They rose together, all the people Daisy loved best in the world. This time the emotions in her heart spilled over and she grabbed a tissue out of a box on one of the side tables. Gabe pulled her close, his arms warm and familiar.

As she sank into them, she couldn't believe she had ever been so determined not to need him or anyone. He had told her once that life was enriched by forging connections with people, letting them into her heart.

Because of these people, hers was more beautiful, more colorful, more *perfect*, than anything Marguerite could ever dream of painting.

★ ★ ★ ★ ★